Original Skin

ALSO BY DAVID MARK
FROM CLIPPER LARGE PRINT

The Dark Winter

Original Skin

David Mark

W F HOWES LTD

This large print edition published in 2013 by
W F Howes Ltd
Unit 4, Rearsby Business Park, Gaddesby Lane,
Rearsby, Leicester LE7 4YH

1 3 5 7 9 10 8 6 4 2

First published in the United Kingdom in 2013
by Quercus

Copyright © David Mark, 2013

The right of David Mark to be identified as
the author of this work has been asserted by him
in accordance with the Copyright, Designs and
Patents Act, 1988.

A CIP catalogue record for this book is available
from the British Library

ISBN 978 1 47123 228 2

Typeset by Palimpsest Book Production Limited,
Falkirk, Stirlingshire
Printed and bound in Great Britain
by MPG Books Ltd, Bodmin, Cornwall

MIX
Paper from
responsible sources
FSC
www.fsc.org   FSC® C018575

For Nikki – like everything else.

But I say, anyone who even looks at a woman with lust in his eye has already committed adultery with her in his heart. So if your eye – even if it is your good eye – causes you to lust, gouge it out and throw it away. It is better for you to lose one part of your body than for your whole body to be thrown into hell.

Matthew 5:28–30

Nymphomaniac: a woman as obsessed with sex as an average man.

Mignon McLaughlin,
The Neurotic's Notebook, 1960

PROLOGUE

Should have Hoovered, he thinks, picking a piece of fluff from his tongue. *Should have made it pretty.*

He feels a pressure in his lower back.

Should have had a piss too.

He pushes himself up, raising his body from the floor, a mermaid ascending in a crash of spray, and attempts to brush the crumbs and cat hairs from his shiny chest.

All this bloody oil, he thinks. *So slippy. So slick. Going to be like wrestling a dolphin . . .*

The alarm on his phone bleeps. It is gone ten. His visitor is later than he had intended to allow.

Big girl's blouse, he calls himself, and then, in his father's voice: 'Fucking poof.'

The boy has been here some time. He is feeling uncomfortable. The wrong kind of dirty. Desire is starting to fade.

He wonders if there is a word to describe this opposite of ardour: the dissipation of lust; the moment when passion loosens its noose.

He is beginning to feel a little silly. A little undignified.

He tries to think of a better way to describe the sensation. He likes words. Likes to be thought of as articulate. Uses the apostrophe in the right place when promising to fulfil any lover's desire. Takes an effort with his poetry.

Shabby.

He is suddenly aware of the shabbiness of this picture. Here, in his cheap, first-floor flat, naked on his cheap carpet, shooing away his cat when she appears at his bedroom door and fixes him with an expression of sneering superiority.

'Five more minutes,' he says again, and wonders if this will be another let-down. Whether he will have wasted time and expectation on another coward.

His back and shoulders are beginning to burn in the glare of the three-bar heater. It's an odd feeling. The rest of him is shivering and goose-pimpled. He turns himself over, suppressing a giggle as he thinks of himself as a chicken on a rotisserie.

'Spit-roasted,' he says to himself and laughs into his bare arm.

His face is now in the glare. It's too hot. He turns back again, concerned that he will look red and sweaty. He raises a hand to pick more crumbs and fluff from his face.

The lad is in his mid-twenties, tall and thin. His face, beginning to carry the imprint of the dusty carpet that covers the entirety of his one-bedroomed flat, is split by fleshy lips and a too-large nose. He is not attractive, but there are benefits to his company.

'I'm accommodating,' he says into the carpet, his mouth and forearm making a pocket of cigarette breath, and wriggles, willing himself back into character.

He is naked. Starfished, face-down on the floor of his living room. There is not much room for his gangly frame. He has had to push back the charity-shop two-seater sofa and throw the old takeaway pizza boxes into his bedroom to be able to suitably accommodate his visitor.

'Five more minutes,' he says again, reluctant to accept that tonight's fantasy will remain just that.

He reaches out for his mobile phone, tucked inside one of his battered white trainers. No new messages.

He reads the recent ones.

Oh yes.

Feels the excitement build afresh. Has to reposition himself to accommodate the growing hardness between his legs.

Begins to feel the hunger. A languid luxury easing itself into his movements.

Time to walk like a panther, He giggles.

Hard as nails. Pretty as a picture.

You should charge, boy. You're a fucking treat.

Like a fleetingly sober drunk gulping whisky, the returning rush of sexuality alters his perceptions. He begins to feel better about the picture he presents. Remembers kind words and grateful embraces. Preens a little as he imagines the picture he presents to the open door. He knows his back and buttocks to be a breathtaking display; the ink that crawls up to his shoulders worth the agony that he screamed into the tattooist's table.

He will make his visitor happy.

There is a sudden creak on the stairs.

He smiles, and his breath comes out in a tremble. *Here we go.*

He arches his back. Presents himself for inspection. Raises his face to ensure the belt, coiled snake-like, is where he left it.

'Is this what you wanted?' he asks, throaty and sensual.

There is silence for a moment. The floorboards creak.

Then he feels the familiar weight on his back. The sensation of being pinned beneath another human being. The excitement of welcome helplessness that comes with giving yourself to another.

In the periphery of his vision, the belt is scooped up in a gloved hand. He closes his eyes, eager to play.

'Am I your fantasy?' he asks again.

The reply, when it finally comes, is hissed into his ear: a tumbled rush of excited words.

'To die for.'

There is a sudden, biting, flesh-ripping sensation, as though his Adam's apple is being forced up into his skull.

'Her name!'

Spittle hisses from between his ghoulishly parted lips, frothing on his chin, into the dust and crumbs. His eyes bubbling, popping, like microwaved soup . . .

In an instant, his faculties are at once dulled and frenzied, his thoughts twisted and squeezed.

Too tight, too hard, too much; fantasy becoming fear.

The words again . . .

'Your friend. Pink blossoms. The laughing girl.'

There is only confusion and hurt, a sensation of becoming somehow less; of reducing, melting, puddling into nothing . . .

'The girl. Laughing at me . . .'

Darkness closes in as his oily fingers and skinny legs drum on the dusty floor.

An instant of clarity. A sudden heartbeat of understanding. What this is for. Why he is dying. Why the life is leaving his body and the poetry leaving his soul. What they want. What he must do . . .

The voice again, wet in his ear.

Anger. Venom.

'The one who looked and laughed . . .'

A knee now, hard in his spine; his back arching, teeth bringing blood to his thin lips, blood thundering in his ears . . .

He wants to plead. Wants to beg for his life. Wants this to stop. Wants to live. To write and create. To fuck and dance.

'Name. Her fucking name.'

He knows now. Knows these will be his last

words. Knows that all the warnings were for nothing. He's going to die, and his final act in this life will be one of betrayal.

The cord loosens for the slightest of moments. The strong hands readjust their grip.

The boy takes a gulp of air. Tries to swallow it. Manages only to hiss, before the cord cuts back under his jawbone and an explosion of sweet-smelling blood flowers and flows from his eyes.

'Suzie . . .'

Her name at once an act of treachery and a dying invocation.

CHAPTER 1

'They weren't here when I went to bed at midnight. Bold as brass when I got up at six a.m.' The man waves an arm, despairingly. 'I mean, when did they turn up?'

Detective Constable Helen Tremberg shrugs her shoulders. 'Between midnight and six, I'm guessing.'

'But they made no noise! And now listen! It's bedlam. How did they not wake anybody up?'

Tremberg has nothing to offer. 'Perhaps they're ninjas.'

The man fixes her with a look. He's in his late thirties and dressed for an office job. He has greying black hair and utterly style-free glasses. Something about his manner suggests to Tremberg that he is on a low-risk pension plan, and has a tendency to examine the contents of his handkerchief after blowing his nose. She fancies that after his second glass of wine, his sentences begin to start with the words 'I'm not a racist, but . . .'

He saw the travellers from his bathroom window as he was brushing his teeth. Saw, in his words, 'the sheer pandemonium' and rang 999. He was not the first person on the leafy street overlooking the football field to do so, but he is the only one who has decided to get in Tremberg's face about the situation.

Until half an hour ago Tremberg had been looking forward to today. She has been pretty much desk-bound since her return to work, unable to take part in even vaguely interesting operations until she completed her chats with the force psychologist and had her doctor sign the last of the seemingly endless forms promising that the slash wound to her hand has left no permanent damage. Tonight, all being well, she's allowed back to the sharp end of policing, watching her boss, Trish Pharaoh, slap cuffs on the wrists of a gangland soldier and closing down a drugs operation. She wants to be involved. Needs it. Has to show willing and prove she hasn't lost her bottle. Wants to demonstrate to anybody who doubts it that nearly getting her throat cut by a serial killer has been laughed off and dealt with 'old school' – voided from her system with vodka and a good cry.

'When will they be gone?' the man is asking her. 'What are you going to do? This is a nice neighbourhood. We pay our taxes. I've nothing against them, but there are places. There are sites! What are you going to do?'

Tremberg doesn't offer an answer. She has none. She does not want to talk to this man. She wants to get to work. She doesn't want to be leaning against the goalposts of the playing fields that stitch the affluent villages of Anlaby and Willerby together. She feels like a goalkeeper watching a match take place at the opposite end of the pitch.

'Should have stayed in the car,' she says to herself and looks past the man to where the caravans are parked up, not far from the halfway line of the adjacent rugby pitch. Drinks in the pandemonium.

Six caravans, four off-road cars, a Mercedes and three horseboxes, at least two generators and, as far as she can see, a portable toilet. They are arranged in a loose semi-circle around three floral-print sofas and a sun-lounger on which a rapidly multiplying number of traveller women and children are sitting drinking tea, talking to uniformed officers, and occasionally shouting at the schoolchildren and bored motorists who have got out of their motionless cars to watch the commotion through the park railings.

Like most of East Yorkshire, Tremberg is stuck here. Her car is a few streets back, snarled up in the bi-monthly gridlock caused by a local transport infrastructure with the breaking strain of a KitKat.

Bored, with nothing to do but look at the dark, gloomy sky through the dusty glass of her Citroën, she had switched on the radio in the hope of finding something soothing. She was two minutes into 'California Dreamin'', and idly wondering why it appeared to be the only song owned by Radio Humberside, when the traffic report cut in. Half a dozen horses loose on Anlaby Road, and travel-lers causing uproar on the playing fields by the

9

embankment. She'd had little option but to get out of the car and see if she could lend a hand.

'Are you going to shoot the horses?'

Tremberg gives the man her attention. 'Pardon?'

'The police! Will you shoot the horses?'

'Not personally,' says Tremberg, close to losing her patience. 'The Animal Control Unit is on its way. They're stuck in traffic too. We're doing our best. I could go get one of the bastards in a head-lock if you keep hold of its legs . . .'

Ken Cullen, the thin, bearded, uniformed inspector currently in charge of trying to bring some degree of order to the scene, overhears the dangerous note in the detective's voice and hurries over.

'I'm sorry, sir, we're doing everything we can. If you could just return home for the moment and allow us to deal with this . . .'

Tremberg turns away as somebody better equipped to tolerate wankers sends the busybody on his way. The inspector fixes her with a bright smile as he spins back to her.

'Bet you wish you'd never stopped to help, eh?'

'Nothing better to do, Ken. Stuck here with every bugger else. Thought I'd see if I could assist, but this really isn't my cup of tea.'

'Dunno, Helen. You've got the physique for crowd control!'

Tremberg shares a laugh with her old uniformed sergeant recently risen to inspector, who has moved, like her, across the water from Grimsby.

10

'I was pleased to hear you're on the mend,' he says and means it. 'All better now?'

Tremberg flicks a V-sign at him. 'Lost none of my dexterity,' she says, smiling.

Cullen gives her a quick once-over. Takes in the thin sports cagoule she wears over sensible pinstriped trouser suit and white blouse. Her hair is cut in a neat bob and she wears no make-up or jewellery. He knows from quiz nights and leaving dos that she scrubs up well and has extraordinary legs when she hitches her skirt up, but Tremberg is deliberately sexless when on duty. Many other female detectives have adopted her approach, appalled by any suggestion they have used their femininity to gain favour, but in so doing have opened themselves up to suggestions of lesbianism. Tremberg frequently wishes she could possess the carefree, fuck-you attitude of Trish Pharaoh, who wears what she wants and doesn't give a damn whether people think she is after dicks or dykes.

For a while the pair of them grumble about the local council closing off the rat runs and giving commuters nowhere to go if the main arteries in and out of town are snarled up. They agree that the local authority is staffed with do-gooders and morons and that the new chair of the Police Authority will no doubt balls it up even more.

Their pleasantly English moan is turning towards the grey skies and the cost of petrol when a young WPC approaches. She looks harassed and wind-blown in her muddy yellow waterproof.

11

'We've got all but one of them, sir,' she says, in a voice that suggests she has struggled to avoid using a more vulgar term. 'Sergeant Parker and Dan managed to box them in. They're in the car park in the Beech Tree. Can't get out. Another bloke with a Land Rover blocked the gap. The owners are trying to get them roped now. It's chaos, sir. Poor Mickey's ripped his trousers trying to pull one back by the hair. The mane. Whatever. Half of Anlaby's covered in horse shit. And the bloody pikey kids aren't helping, singing bloody "Rawhide" . . .'

Tremberg has had to hide her face as she pictures the local bobbies desperately trying to round up the escaped animals, clapping and hollering and trying to stop the nags from eating the herbaceous borders of anybody important.

'And the last one?' asks Cullen, pulling on his peaked cap.

'It's a real nasty shit. Pikey said it was a stallion who smelled a mare in season. Put a dent in half a dozen cars so far. Seems to particularly hate Audis.'

'And the animal team?'

The WPC snorts, herself momentarily horse-like. 'Having a very helpful meeting in the back of their unit. Lots of flicking through guidelines and phoning vets. I'm not expecting much in the way of action. I'm backing the big fella.'

This last she says with a genuine smile.

'Big fella?'

12

She turns herself to Tremberg. Smiles in a way that the detective is starting to recognise. 'Scottish bloke from your unit. The one who . . .'

'McAvoy?' Tremberg's eyebrows shoot up and she looks around as if he may be watching.

'Yeah. One of the lads gave him a ring. Said he knew about animals. Farmer's boy, or something, isn't he? Just turned up a minute ago. Don't know where he parked his car but I think he ran here.'

'And what's he doing?'

The officer takes off her hat and gives an appreciative little shake of her head.

'About to start playing tug-of-war with a horse.'

Detective Sergeant Aector McAvoy spent his first months in plain clothes taking the title literally. He all but camouflaged himself in khaki-coloured trousers, hiking boots and cheap, mushroom-hued shirts; tearing them fresh from polythene packets every Monday. The disguise never worked. At 6 foot 5 inches, and with red hair, freckles and Highlander moustache, he is always the most noticeable man in the room.

It was his young wife, Roisin, who put a stop to his attempts to blend in. She told him that, as a good-looking big bastard, he owed it to himself not to dress like 'a fecking bible-selling eejit'. Roisin has a way with words.

Despite his objections, he had let her style him like a child playing with a dolly. Under her guidance, and blushing at every alteration to his

13

wardrobe, McAvoy had become known within the force as much for his smart suits and cashmere coat, for his leather satchel and cufflinks, as for his detective skills and scars.

Now, flat on his back, staring up at the swollen clouds, with mud and stallion spit on his lapels and horse shit streaking one leg of his dark blue suit, he wishes he were back in khaki.

McAvoy tries to ignore the cheers of the onlookers and climbs back to his feet.

'Right, you bugger . . .'

He had been on his way to the Police Authority meeting when the call came through. One of the constables tasked with corralling the escaped animals had lost his temper after being dragged into the side of a bottle-bin by one of the mares, and had decided it was time for some specialist help. The officer had only worked with McAvoy once, up on the Orchard Park estate. They had been tasked with guarding the door to a crime scene until the forensics van turned up and had not been made welcome by the locals. He and McAvoy had tolerated the abuse and even the first few bottles and cans, but when the snarling Staffordshire terrier had been let loose with instructions to see them off, it had been McAvoy who stood his ground while the junior officer tried to persuade a brick wall to absorb him. The giant Scotsman had dropped to his knees and met the dog face on, turning his head and opening his eyes wide, showing his wide, flat palms to the creature

14

and flattening himself to the cracked pavement, submissive and unthreatening. The dog had stopped as if running into glass, and was on its back having its tummy tickled by McAvoy's great rough hands by the time backup appeared and the crowd were chased away. The young PC had taken McAvoy's number, having the foresight to realize that such a man was worth knowing. Today he had figured the big man was worth a call.

McAvoy, who would have agreed to a head-butting contest with an escaped antelope if it meant taking his mind off the impending Police Authority meeting, had been only too glad to dump his car and sprint to the scene.

He limbers up. Stretches his arms and cracks his neck from side to side. There are a few hoots from the watching motorists, and from the corner of his eye McAvoy is appalled to see that many of those watching are recording the footage on their camera-phones.

'Just shoot it,' comes a voice from somewhere in the hubbub. It is a suggestion met with murmurs of approval by some.

'Can't you tranquillise it?'

'I've got a tenner on the big man!'

McAvoy tries to ignore the voices, but the laughter and groans that rang out when he was knocked flat by the charging stallion have turned his cheeks the colour of crushed cranberries.

'You shoot that horse I'll fecking have your eyes.'

The voice, its accent unmistakable, causes a

momentary silence and McAvoy turns. The man who has spoken stands to his left, leaning against the bonnet of a blue Volvo. The car's owner has adopted the peculiarly English expedient of pretending he cannot see the large, daunting traveller who is pressing his buttocks into the hood of his car.

The gypsy is squat and balding, with a round face and shiny cheeks. Despite the cold and gathering clouds, his arms are bare. His flabby gut and torso are not flattered by the white sleeveless T-shirt or too-blue jeans.

'Yours?' asks McAvoy, with a nod towards the horse.

The man answers with a shrug, but the length of rope in his hand suggests he had been about to try and reclaim his property before he saw McAvoy take the burden upon himself.

'In season?'

The man nods again. 'Horny as a Cornishman, first day out the mine.'

'Bloody hell.'

He'd nearly had him moments ago. The stallion had only been a few feet away, tearing some daffodils from a grass verge of one of the side streets leading off the busy thoroughfare. McAvoy's soft voice and gentle movements had allowed him closer to the animal than anybody else had managed since this unexpected carnival began, but as the beast swished its head back and forth, one of the passers-by had loudly shouted encouragement, and the burst of noise had spooked it, sending McAvoy, and his expensive clothes, into the dirt.

'Got a name?'

'Me or the horse, sir, me or the horse?'

'The horse.'

'Fecked if I know. Try Buttercup.'

Slowly, taking care to keep his feet steady on the tarmac, McAvoy moves towards where the animal now stands. Wild-eyed, muddy and sweat-streaked, it has moved into the garden of one of the nice detached properties set back from the road. Its occupants are staring out of the large double-glazed front windows. With no car in the driveway and the horse showing no apparent interest in their magnolia trees, they are enjoying the show.

'Easy, fella,' breathes McAvoy, as he spreads his arms and moves towards the open driveway. 'Trust me.'

He knows what will happen if he fails. Vets will try and get near with a tranquilliser. They will fail, going in mob-handed and merely scaring the animal. Then some well-intentioned farmer will turn up with a tame horse in the hope of attracting the stallion to within range. The stallion will get over-excited. Damage cars. Damage itself. Eventually, a marksman will be called and the horse will be hit with as many bullets as it takes to get the city moving again. McAvoy doesn't want that to happen. The call from the young PC had informed him that the horse had escaped from

17

land where travellers had set up home. In his experience, travellers love their animals, and this one, though grey and with shaggy forelocks that put him in mind of tasselled boots, looks like it has been looked after as well as worked hard.

'Easy, boy. Easy.'

McAvoy closes the gap. Raises his hand, palm out, and whispers, soft hushes and gentle songs, in the animal's ear. It whinnies. Begins to pull away. McAvoy tilts his head. Exudes both the size and the gentleness that so define him; locks brown eyes with the confused, frightened animal . . .

The horse barely shies as he slips the rope around its neck. He carries on singing. Whispering. Crooning the only traveller song he can remember and wishing he had the same soft voice that his bride uses when she softly hums it into his neck.

This time the cheer from the crowd has little effect on the horse. It allows itself to be led out of the driveway: its unshod hooves making a pleasing clip-clop on the pavement.

McAvoy looks up and sees smiling faces. His cheeks burn and he struggles to keep his face impassive as the motorists give him a little round of applause, delighted to know they will soon be in fifth gear and hurrying towards jobs they hate, to tell the story of this morning's fun and games.

'Good job, sir. Good job.'

The traveller has detached himself from the crowd. Unasked, he crosses to the far side of the animal and gently takes it by the ear, leaning in to nuzzle the animal's neck and call it a 'great eejit'.

McAvoy enjoys the display of affection. The man knows animals. Loves horses. Can't be bad.

Together, they wind their way through the cars and towards the playing fields. Three uniformed officers are leaning, exhausted, against the bonnets of two parked patrol cars. They look ragged and worn out. They nod their thanks as McAvoy passes by. The young constable who called him raises a fist of triumph and leans in to say something to a colleague. There is a burst of laughter and, instinctively, McAvoy presumes himself to have been the butt of the joke.

'We'll tie 'em up, sir,' says the traveller. 'We thought the fence went right round. Gave me a fright when I saw them gone, so it did.'

McAvoy getting his breath back, looks over the horse's wiry mane at the man. 'It's not a halting site, sir. It's a football pitch. You know you can't camp here.'

'Ah, would yer not show a little leeway?' the traveller asks, fixing bright blue eyes on McAvoy and suddenly exuding a twinkly, impish charm. 'We've had a bit of a barney, me and one of the families up there. Not welcome. Just a night or two, put it to bed, make friends again.'

McAvoy isn't really listening. This isn't his call. He's just going with it for now. He was asked to round up an escaped horse and has done so. The excitement is over. Now he has to try and make himself presentable enough for a meeting with the new-look Humberside Police Authority, and try to explain to the new chairman why his unit should be preserved, and exactly why the violent crime statistics are on the rise. It is a prospect that has kept him awake as efficiently as his three-month-old daughter, and its sudden re-emergence at the forefront of his mind brings a wave of nausea to his stomach.

A gust of wind brings with it the scent of frying bacon and hand-rolled cigarettes. His raises his head, eager for a breath of cleansing fresh air. Opens his eyes. Stares into a sky the colour of a black eye, rain just seconds away.

They approach the semi-circle of mobile homes. There is a whoop that McAvoy traces to one of the women sitting on the sofas outside the nearest caravan. She is in her forties, with curly blonde-brown hair, and is wearing a white jogging suit two sizes too small.

'Ah, yer a good lad,' she shouts, as they get nearer. She puts down her mug of tea and levers her small, curvy frame off the sofa. 'Knew it was all reet, didn't I?'

She shouts this last at the two teenage girls who sit on the opposite sofa, both in pink nighties under grey hooded tops. One is perhaps a year older than the other, but both have sleek black hair cut in the same side parting, and wear an equal amount of hooped gold at their throats and earlobes.

McAvoy hands the rope to the man, who gives a genuine bow of thanks. 'You're a good man, sir. A good man. Scotsman, ye'll be, yes?'

McAvoy nods. 'Western Highlands.'

'No kilt?' he asks, with a grin.

'I get enough funny looks.'

The traveller laughs louder than the joke deserves. Claps McAvoy on his broad forearm. 'By Christ, but you're a big one.'

McAvoy's blush threatens to return to his cheeks, so he just gives a nod. Returns to business. 'Keep him tied up. Buttercup. It's not fair.'

'Aye, sir. Aye.'

McAvoy looks around him. At sofas, the generators and toilets. At the faces emerging from behind spotless net curtains at the windows of the caravans, as interested in what is happening on their doorsteps as the faces behind the glass in the four-bedroom detached properties that ring the fields.

He can't help but picture his wife. She lived like this when they first met. Wasn't much older than the girls on the sofa; her eyes just as distrustful, her world just as small . . .

'McAvoy!'

He turns to see Helen Tremberg and Inspector Ken Cullen walking swiftly across from the adjacent football pitch. He gives a wave, not quite sure whether he is to be treated as hero or interfering fool.

'McAvoy, is it? Is that what she said?'

There is something in the way the old traveller repeats his name. Something that tells McAvoy he is known.

He gets no chance to press the man. The clouds that have been slung low, like damp laundry, finally split. Rain thunders down. Tremberg, not given to squealing, emits a shriek and stops short, pulling up the hood of her jacket. The travellers emit a cacophony of swearing and McAvoy's new friend barks orders in an accent so thick it could be a different language. Half a dozen young men appear from inside caravans, and the sofas are quickly dragged under tarpaulins and windows pulled fast shut.

'Christ,' says Tremberg, pulling her hood up and beginning a swift retreat to her vehicle. 'They really are ninjas!'

McAvoy doesn't follow her. He's standing, arms wide, letting the downpour soak him to the skin. He knows that he will be tried and tested at this morning's meeting. Knows it will be a painful experience. And knows too that he will make life slightly easier for himself if he turns up merely damp, rather than covered in manure.

CHAPTER 2

9.31 a.m. High Street, Old Town.
Blades of rain, scything down from a pewter sky.

A narrow row of handsome old mercantile palaces. Of insurance brokers and solicitors, art galleries and museums.

Detective Sergeant Aector McAvoy, running through the rain – committee papers clutched inside his sodden jacket, droplets splashing from his lips and nose.

Up the steps, feet slipping on the mosaic which serves as welcome mat to the Police Authority headquarters, a rose picked out in red and white tiles, beneath an archway of expensive wood and glass.

He flashes his warrant card at the security guard on the desk, and then bounds up the stairs three at a time.

Assistant Chief Constable Everett is waiting outside the meeting room. He is immaculately turned out, his blue uniform crisp and freshly laundered.

'Good lord, Sergeant!'

Everett looks aghast at the sight before him. Aector McAvoy has come to serve as his pet symbol of the modern face of Humberside Police. Educated, polite, supremely computer literate and respectful of every new guideline dreamed up by the powers that be, he has served the assistant chief at endless committee meetings and public engagements.

'Look at the state of you! I needed you at your best, man!'

Strictly speaking, there is no need for a detective sergeant to ever appear before the police authority, but ACC Everett is expecting difficult questions from the authority's new chairman, and has managed to ensure that McAvoy is there to answer them. He is pinning his hopes on McAvoy absorbing the worst of the barrage.

'I'm sorry sir,' gasps McAvoy, trying to catch his breath. 'There was a horse . . .'

Everett, a thin-faced and ratty-looking man who managed to rise to the second-top job in the force without appearing to be any good at anything, grabs McAvoy's coat and forcibly strips it off his shoulders. Before he can protest, Everett is pulling out a comb from his back pocket, and reaching up to comb his junior officer's hair.

McAvoy backs off. Takes the comb.

'Thank you, sir.'

He does what he can. Slicks back his hair and wipes the moisture from his moustache with finger and thumb. Catches his breath. Fastens his suit jacket and secures his tie inside it. Wrings out his turn-ups, and straightens the creases with his palm.

Follows Everett into the meeting room.

Over a dozen men and women sit around a number of tables arranged in a vague U-shape. The surfaces are covered in jugs of water and empty glasses, notepads and official-looking papers. At the back of the room, a large pink and blue painting of a Manhattan skyline covers one wall. It was a gift to the Authority from a previous chairman, and nobody has been impolite enough to take the monstrosity down.

'Bloody hell, Everett, are you making your officers swim here?'

The booming Yorkshire voice emanates from the large, bearded man at the head of the table.

Everett gives a false little laugh as he and McAvoy take a seat the nearest empty desk. 'Sorry, Mr Chairman, Sergeant McAvoy was called away to deal with an important development in the case you have shown such an interest in.'

Tressider waves his hand, dismissively. He looks at McAvoy.

'Important development, eh? You sure you weren't helping a bunch of gypsies round up their horses?'

McAvoy colours instantly. Can feel steam rising from his damp hair.

'Oh bugger, can't say gypsies, can I?' Tressider turns to the secretary, busy jotting down the minutes of the meeting. 'Scribble that out, would you, love?'

The other members of the authority exchange glances, but nobody says a word. Tressider dominates the room. He has a remarkable presence, and enough personality to dominate any environment, even without the benefits of his broad frame and deep Yorkshire accent.

He's a man on the up is Peter Tressider. One to watch, with coat-tails worth riding.

Now in his mid-fifties, he was already famous as a businessman before taking his first steps into public office on the Conservative ticket a couple of decades back. His family runs a timberyard, distribution company and a couple of property agencies, as well as investing heavily in various safe-bet start-up companies. He was elected on to East Riding Council in 1997, and was moved up to the authority's cabinet soon after, holding high-profile positions on committees responsible for crime prevention, education and social inclusion.

Tressider was popular in the press from the off, making headlines for his plain speaking, his witty comebacks and his anti-bullshit stance. He was censored several times for swearing during committees, and revelled in the public perception of him as a proper Yorkshireman who says what he likes, and likes what he bloody well says.

He was elected to the Humberside Police Authority a couple of years back, and set about making it his own. The role suited him. In 2005 Tressider was among the councillors who refused to enforce the Home Secretary's order that the then Chief Constable be suspended after Humberside Police's record-keeping was found to be dangerously flawed. He gained favour in many quarters for telling the politician to 'keep his nose out' of local affairs. Always good for a soundbite, the local papers are having a ball imagining the fun he will have if he is chosen by the Conservatives to stand as an MP at the next general election.

'Anyway, glad you could make it, Sergeant. We have things to discuss.'

Tressider pulls his papers towards him and peers at an agenda item. Then he raises his eyes and examines McAvoy more closely. 'The *Yorkshire Post* says you're the face of sexy policing.'

There is a titter from the other committee members, who all turn their attention to McAvoy.

'I'm sorry, Mr Chairman?'

'Here,' he says, and locates a photocopied piece of paper among the documents on his desk.

McAvoy recognises the piece. Feels his heart sink.

Tressider clears his throat, theatrically.

'Some might say they represent the "sexy" side of detective work. They are the men and women who delve into the very heart of the most high-profile murder cases, using skills and expertise that will eventually jail killers and make the streets a safer place.'

Tressider looks up. Smiles.

Continues: 'It is a role that spawns images of fictional detectives like Morse, Rebus and Thorne.'

Moves his finger along the page before him, enunciating every word.

'But in a humble room next to the canteen at Courtland Road Police Station on Hull's Orchard Park yesterday, the scene was a far cry from a TV detective show.

'The *Yorkshire Post* had been invited to meet a team formed last year with a Home Office grant, which is helping to change the way major incidents are investigated, both locally and nationally. They are the Serious and Organised Crime Unit – the force's murder squad. The team at Courtland Road represents one strand of a hundred-strong pool of civilian and police officers on both banks of the River Humber, which investigates all suspicious deaths and other serious crimes. Many of the civilians are themselves retired police officers, who sift through the mountains of information that pour into the Major Incident Room. They are using decades of experience that the force is reluctant to lose through retirement.'

Tressider stops. Gives McAvoy a grin.

Reads on.

'Detective Superintendent Patricia Pharaoh, senior investigating officer, said, "We're trying something a little different and the assessment so far is that it's working. The volume of documents alone requires such careful and meticulous flow to the right people and our processes are very rigid. It's hard to quantify the successes in the past few months but we know this squad is making a difference. We hope that, even in the face of budget constraints, people realise how important this unit is."'

There is muttering from some of the other committee members.

'Nicely done,' says Tressider with a nod. 'There's more, by the way. Shall I?'

McAvoy says nothing. Wonders if he will get the blame for the newspaper article as well as everything else.

Tressider continues. 'Even though the force now uses the Holmes computer system, much of an investigation is still paper-based. The Serious and Organised Crime Unit receives all the information. Every item goes to a receiver, who reads it and decides how it will be dealt with. The indexers then put the information into the system before it is read by a dedicated document reader. This person rereads every document that comes in and decides on any other work that needs to be done. The action manager then allocates work to action teams based on whether the work is high, medium or low in conjunction with policy. This all then comes back to the office manager, who gives the final signature on all actions and is responsible for the major incident room running as it should.'

Tressider stops. Raises his head and gives a mock yawn. 'I, for one, was bloody enthralled.'

McAvoy looks up, changes his mind, and turns

his attention to ensuring his cuffs are the right length. The material squelches between his fingers.

'Sexy, Sergeant?' Tressider gives him a mock once-over. 'I'm not sure I can judge. You might be the wife's type!'

He turns to his vice-chair: a grey-haired and nervous woman in a twinset and pearls. 'What you reckon, Noreen? Sexy policing?'

The lady gives an embarrassed giggle, which seems to somehow disappoint Tressider. It's clear how the big man became chairman with such ease. Clear, too, what an asset he will be to his Party if they give him the nod and jockey him to Westminster the way so many are predicting.

'Good publicity, anyway,' says Tressider, picking at his teeth with a large finger. 'We'll be looking at your unit in time, Sergeant. Looking at budget usage across the board. But I don't mind headlines like these. Don't mind at all.'

McAvoy looks at his papers. Tries to unfold them and finds they are too soggy to come apart. 'The reporter made the request for access through the official channels,' he says. 'I was just there on the day . . .'

Tressider waves him into silence with his paw of a right hand. Sits forward in his chair.

'To business,' he says, and there is a general murmur from the assembled committee members.

They represent the great, the good, and the interfering bastards from the local community. The authority consists of seventeen members.

Half are elected councillors from the area's four councils, and the others are independents. They are the top bosses. The men and women who make the big decisions and appoint the top brass. And there's not a copper among them.

'Detective Sergeant McAvoy is here to address your particular questions about the increase in violent crime, Mr Chairman.'

Tressider fixes Everett with a withering look. 'I believe it was your presence I requested about that, Everett.'

Everett squirms. 'McAvoy is a key member of the team currently investigating that particular issue, and . . .'

Tressider nods. Turns his attention to McAvoy.

'Vietnamese, I'm told,' he says brusquely. 'Always been a bugger for the cannabis, ain't they? But it seems to be getting nasty. Stop me if I'm wrong.'

McAvoy takes a breath. Wonders where to start.

For the past five years the local cannabis market has been run by Vietnamese gangs, setting up farms in disused warehouses and abandoned buildings, quietly cultivating their crop and then selling on through a network of dealers. Things ran smoothly. The people who got hurt had usually rocked the boat, and Humberside Police paid little attention to the cultivation of a drug they expected to be legalised within the next parliamentary term.

Then a year or so back the Drugs Squad began to hear rumours that, on this coast at least, the Vietnamese were being outmuscled and outgunned.

31

Somebody else was moving in and their methods of persuasion were not pretty.

A few months ago two Asian men were found unconscious on the shingle at Hessle Foreshore. Their faces showed marks of sustained beating, but it was the injuries to the rest of the two men's bodies that caused the paramedics to gasp.

Naked, foetal, their hands had been nailed to their knees.

Strips of flesh on their torsos and backs had been melted to the colour and consistency of burned jam.

There was every indication that a nail gun had been used to drive in their restraints, and a heated paint-stripping tool used to inflict the damage.

The men were alive purely because the message their attackers wished to send was made more potent by their mutilation.

Neither spoke a word of English, but their eyes told a story in a universal language.

A couple of months later a terraced house in the west of the city was burned to the ground – the occupants still inside. The smell that billowed out from the smashed windows put fire-fighters and officers in mind of a community barbecue. Half of the neighbourhood got high on the fumes as a massive amount of fresh-picked cannabis went up in smoke. It could not quite mask the reek of burning flesh.

Despite the protestations of Detective Superintendent Adrian Russell on the Drugs Squad, a decision was taken to make the investigation into the assaults the priority, and Trish Pharaoh was given command.

Nobody has any doubts that the victims were involved in cannabis production. Their clothes had shown traces of marijuana, of fertiliser – even the brand of sparkling mineral water known among the experts to produce a flowering harvest.

She got little from the witnesses at first, but by pulling in a few favours and suggesting she could assist with their pleas to be allowed to stay in the United Kingdom rather than be returned to Vietnam, she managed to get descriptions of the men who had hurt them. They spoke of big white men. Men who had been giving them orders ever since they smashed down the door to one of their marijuana farms and pressed a mobile phone to their foreman's ear. Their gang leader was relinquishing authority for their operation. The crop, and the workers, were now somebody else's property. They were to cooperate. Work hard. Their families would be taken care of.

The men's transgression was never truly explained. They upset somebody. Did something wrong. Said the wrong thing, perhaps. Made a call they should not have made. They fell foul of their new bosses. And they paid the price.

Little was yet known about these new players on the drugs scene, but the next set of crime statistics was an embarrassment to the top brass. The number of incidents of cannabis possession was up 17 per cent in twelve months. More than that, violent crime was on the rise. It wasn't the street dealers who were taking the beatings. It was the people with back-room growing operations. People who grew enough to supply themselves and their friends. They were the ones being beaten down in the street. Beaten beyond recognition. Rendered too afraid or too unintelligible to talk.

Tressider is sufficiently concerned to demand answers. And Everett has none to give.

Stammering at first, and then warming to his theme, McAvoy outlines the situation as best he can. Tells the committee that it is not merely a matter of insufficient resources. It is a case that the new drugs operation is, in no uncertain terms, 'very, very good'.

'Bloody cannabis,' says Tressider. 'Should just legalise it. Get it over with. Going to happen, isn't it? Backwards and forwards this country. Can't have a fag in a pub but you can drink a litre of supermarket cider for £2.50! And all this nail-gun business! By Christ but that's vicious.'

'We've tried to find examples of similar techniques used nationally, but we're having no success, sir. These people seem to have appeared out of nowhere. They took over, and now they're having their way . . .'

'But cannabis? Why not cocaine? Ecstasy? Heroin even?'

McAvoy feels a vibration in his pocket, and

discreetly retrieves his mobile phone. He has to fight to keep the smile from his face.

'We've made a significant breakthrough, sir,' he says firmly. 'An informant of Detective Superintendent Pharaoh has supplied us with the location of the current bulk of the cannabis operation. We're hopeful a raid will be imminent, and that the perpetrators of the foreshore attacks will be present.'

Tressider holds McAvoy's gaze for a fraction of a second longer than he is comfortable with. He is not sure what the chairman is thinking, nor whether he is about to be praised or bawled out.

'It's a relief to find some bugger who knows what he's doing,' says Tressider at length. 'Sounds like you've got a busy day ahead of you. We won't detain you further.'

McAvoy begins to stand.

'Actually, a piss would be nice. Shall we call a break?'

Amid mutterings of both consternation and agreement, the committee members stand. McAvoy gathers his things.

'A shambles,' says Everett under his breath. 'Bloody shambles.'

McAvoy presumes the remark to be directed at himself. Chooses not to hear it.

Squeezing through the throng of bodies and careful not to touch anybody with his damp clothes, he makes his way out of the room and down the stairs. He can feel a fizz of excitement building inside him. Pharaoh has made progress. Leanne has an address. And within the hour they could have everything they need to kick in some doors and slap on handcuffs.

He emerges back onto the High Street to find that the rain has paused for breath. The cold wind grabs his soaking clothes and instantly brings goose pimples to his skin. He shivers. Looks at his watch and tries to decide what to do for the next hour. He has some time to kill before meeting Pharaoh five minutes' walk away in one of the quieter pockets of the city centre, and were he to drive back to the office he would only have to turn round and come back again. He looks around.

Next door to the police authority stands the Hull and East Riding Museum. He has been here plenty of times with Roisin and Fin, but Lilah is probably still too young to appreciate the giant woolly mammoth that stands in the entrance, or the siege gun commissioned by Henry VIII, which was dug up by archaeologists excavating the city walls and placed on display alongside other exhibits from the city's colourful past.

His feet take him past the entrance and down to the water's edge. The River Hull gives the city its name, and scythes into the city centre then onwards into the dark, muddy waters of the Humber. He stares down at the dirty water. At the feet of thick mud, which sit like so much chocolate mousse against the brick and timber walls of the footpath upon which he now stands.

To his left is the *Arctic Corsair*, an old-fashioned sidewinder trawler transformed into a floating museum by well-meaning types keen to ensure that everybody gets a chance to experience the hell of life on board a distant-water fishing vessel.

Idle, directionless, he walks along the towpath by the river. Looks up at the busy dual carriageway overhead. Past the flyover, to where the curious, curving pyramid structure of the city's aquarium sits, incongruously modern and shiny, on the muddy spit of land called Sammy's Point.

The rain begins to fall again. He wonders for a time whether he should huddle under the bridge until he dries out. Perhaps phone Roisin, or call Helen Tremberg to see if anything has occurred that requires his attention.

Realising he has thought himself into inertia, he retreats from the renewed downpour and leans against one of the concrete columns that support the flyover. Closes his eyes. Wonders for a time whether he should have responded to ACC Everett's muttered criticisms, or whether he was right to keep his mouth shut.

He looks back the way he has come. Back at the city where he has spent most of his career so far. Where he has risked his life, and captured men and women who have claimed the lives of others. It is a city he cannot love, and yet he feels an affection for it. A closeness. Feels a bond with this city at the end of the motorway, which grew to prosperity on the back of an industry which killed its men, only to slump into listlessness and decay when it disappeared.

At the back of the Police Authority building he can make out the shapes of two stick men. Two silhouettes, picked out against the white paint of the *Corsair* and the grey of the sky.

He wonders if they are committee members. Whether they are councillors having a shifty smoke, or laughing at the great, hulking sergeant who had turned up damp, but still somehow seemed to persuade Tressider that the sun shone out of his arse.

McAvoy begins walking back. He makes no attempt to protect himself from the rain. He is too soaked to see the point.

Lost in thoughts, adrift in a not-unpleasant daydream, he does not see the two figures depart. He finds himself back at the riverside quicker than he had expected. Gives a last look at the water. Indulges himself in a smile as he looks at the wheels of the supermarket trolley sticking out of the mudbank. The bottles and mattress springs that litter its surface. The mobile phone, sitting on the thick and cloying surface like a tooth left in the frosting of a chocolate cake . . .

He moves to the water's edge. Crouches down.

The mud stops perhaps ten feet below him. Slopes down to water six feet below that.

From this angle, the phone looks relatively new. He wonders if it has slipped from somebody's pocket. Whether it has been kicked accidentally over the side, amid the chaos and frenzy of the rain.

McAvoy screws up his eyes. He's surprised the phone hasn't yet slipped beneath the surface. Whether it is his duty as a policeman to try and recover such obviously valuable property.

Leading down from the footpath, nailed into the river wall, is a metal ladder; its surface slick and grimy, mud-soaked and treacherous.

Is it worth it, Aector? Seriously?

He looks at his watch.

It could belong to one of the committee members. Could be important.

Screws up his eyes.

You could fix it, if it's broken. Would be a challenge for you.

Lifts one gigantic leg over the side.

Just see if you can reach it . . .

Begins to climb down.

CHAPTER 3

10.46 a.m. Eighty miles west.

A light drizzle falling softly on grey, uneven pavements, on plywood shopfronts and untaxed cars.

'Shit-tard bollocking fuckcunts!'

Harry Tattershall is a magnificent and venomous swearer: doing things with words that other people would require a snooker ball and a football sock to achieve. Were he able to do the same with the non-vernacular, he would be Poet Laureate.

'Twat-box cock cunt!'

He picks up the bundle of dropped keys from the damp, dirty kerb. Bangs his head on the wing mirror of his old-style Saab as he rights himself.

'Fucking wank-titting monkey pisser!'

He rubs a hand over his forehead and pushes the raindrops back through his thick, grey hair, then takes off his cola-bottle glasses and smears the moisture and fingerprints into a new pattern, before replacing them on his broken nose. He shivers, wishing he'd thought to pull on more than jogging pants and lumberjack shirt before slamming the door closed at his housing association

40

flat. He is a short, fleshy-limbed man in his late fifties, who does not enjoy the cigarette that is habitually hanging from his lower lip. He just keeps it there to light the next one.

Harry exults in his job title of general manager of the private members' club, but on days like these he can't help but feel like little more than the caretaker. Were it in his power to appoint somebody to the role of watchman he would do so in a flash, but the owners grumble if he so much as changes to fresh from long-life milk, and in his words are 'tighter than a ladybird's chuff'.

The blue light is flashing on the burglar alarm, but there is no sound. They disabled the bell months ago to keep the neighbours sweet. This is not a nice spot, a mile to the east of central Huddersfield, on the corner of a run-down row of pizza shops and budget-hairdressing salons. Despite the less than beautiful location, the club has still faced plenty of problems from protesters and busybodies. Its licence is dependent on the council not having a good reason to shut them down, so keeping the locals happy is paramount.

Harry scrabbles through the many keys on his chain and finds the big one that opens the closed front door. He does not even think to try the handle. He has no doubt the alarm has gone off for no good reason: the same way it always seems to when he gets himself settled in front of a new blue movie with a pot of tea and a packet of HobNobs.

The big blue-painted door swings open and he

stands for a second in the draughty, unpainted, breeze-blocked cubicle where, on week nights from seven p.m., consenting adults stand in their lace and PVC finery, sliding a £10 note and their membership card through a hatch in the interior door, and waiting to be let in for an evening of no-strings coupling, tripling, and on one memorable occasion, human-centipeding.

He unlocks the inner door and steps into the dark of the downstairs bar. It's red-painted, with brass wall lamps, and silhouettes of naked women stencilled artistically around the room. The floor is black lacquer and the booths and bar stools are covered in imitation crushed velvet that, as Harry knows too well, does not wipe 100 per cent clean.

With quick, practised steps, he crosses to the bar and switches on the downstairs lights. It takes a moment for the bulbs to kick in and there is a brief flickering before the room is illuminated.

At once Harry knows something is wrong. The computer behind the bar is whirring. It's an old machine and the internal fan is dust-clogged, so it habitually makes a noise like a helicopter in distress. The motor is spinning now. The monitor may be switched off, but recent use of the computer itself is betrayed by a green light winking beneath the bar.

Harry switches the monitor back on. Wiggles the mouse. Screws up his eyes as the database of members' names and addresses gradually comes into focus on the screen.

'Fuckbollocking titshits.'

He says this under his breath, resignedly, already knowing that his day has just been ruined. They've had break-ins before, of course. He's turned up at work to find an entire week's worth of booze nabbed from the storeroom, and the fancy leopard-print throw from the circular bed in the viewing room had only lasted a week before it found its way into the depth of a voluminous handbag. But this is the first time the computer has been targeted. He doubts very much any intruder would have deemed the machine itself worth the bother of carrying, but there are bits and pieces stored on its hard drive that he knows, with sudden crystal-clear hindsight, he should have protected better.

'Shit.'

He surprises himself with the simplicity of the statement. Pulls up a stool and begins tapping at the keyboard. He would never call himself a computer expert but he knows how to build a database and surf for porn. He also knows how to transfer footage from the CCTV camera in the swing room to his own personal file.

Harry spins away from the keyboard, grabs a half-pint glass from beneath the bar and holds it to the vodka optic, gathering up a healthy double measure. He opens the beer fridge and removes a bottle of Holsten. Takes a swig of vodka, then dilutes the burn with the lager. He's not worried yet, but his mind is racing. He wonders if he will be blamed. How they got in. How they got out . . .

It occurs to Harry that he has not yet checked the rest of the building. There is another bar downstairs, with a dance floor, pole and large flat-screen TV where they show pornos to get clients in the mood. Upstairs there are five private bedrooms with doors that lock, and three where the policy is very much open door.

In the old-school boozer where Harry used to work, there was always a rounders bat next to the till. He wishes he were there now. But there hasn't been any trouble in the two years he has run the place. The members are like-minded and friendly. They know the rules and play the game. They take no for an answer and leave when asked. Harry likes working here. With two students running the bar and a bouncer on the door for three hours on Friday and Saturday nights, the place works like a dream. At the last count they had over 1,000 members, and there can be upwards of fifty people who make this their regular Friday night outing, turning their backs on regular haunts for an evening where they can be who the fuck they like in the company of people who don't judge, and are grateful for the attention.

Harry's mind whirs with the same grinding difficulty as the computer fan. He tries to imagine who would break in, and why they would go straight to the machine. He has had plenty of time to get to know the clientele over the past couple of years, lounging at the end of the bar with a mug of coffee, nodding appreciatively at the lads and ladies in their eclectic wardrobes. He could write a book on the sights he has seen. The people. The pervs. The giant, hairy Asian man in the dog collar and leotard. The big one in the gold mask who made a noise like a heifer in distress when he reached orgasm. The woman in her seventies who had to be helped out of the love swing when her hip came out. The fat lass in the pirate costume who cried rape when one of the four men she was fucking tried to put it in her arse . . .

He taps the keyboard again, unsure what to do. Wonders about the potential consequences of inaction. Suppose he confronts a burglar? Suppose they have seen the footage on his private files. He can't afford to be blackmailed. Would simply have to admit culpability to the bosses and look for another job. He doubts there would be charges. But who would target him? He shakes his head and downs his vodka. Perhaps somebody is looking for information. Perhaps a member wants to find out more about somebody who caught their eye or pissed them off. Perhaps they want to delete their own information. He knows from experience that members are notoriously shy about giving real names and real addresses, so doubts anybody would think it worth their while to even try and get a name or phone number for another member.

His train of thought is derailed by an unmistakable creak from upstairs.

He closes his eyes, takes a breath, then picks up the nearly empty bottle of Holsten and upends it;

a dribble of beer running over the blurry blue ink of his tattooed forearm.

He pulls open the door to the stairway and peers into the gloom. The cord-carpeted stairs disappear into darkness halfway up, and there is nothing appealing about climbing them. Harry pauses, already half decided.

There is another creak.

'Fuck.'

He puts his foot on the bottom stair. Puts a hand on the banister and pulls himself up, trying to stand on the corners of each step so as not to make a sound.

As he reaches the top step, the last dribble of beer runs over his wrist. The sudden coldness makes him jump and he lets out a small exclamation, which he follows with a curse.

Harry knows he has given himself away. Whoever is waiting in the dark can fuck-buggering stay there.

He turns. Begins to creep back down the stairs.

This time the sound is unmistakable. Running feet. Sudden movement. Coming closer.

Harry looks up.

Crack.

Opens his mouth to let rip with a stream of invective, but finds himself wordless. His tongue has been crushed to pulp between his back teeth; a reflex reaction to the hammer blow that has struck him just above the left temple.

Movement. Bone-jarring impact. Thuds and cracks.

Harry finds himself upside down. Right way up

again. Feels his old limbs twisted into unnatural directions as they jar with the brick and stair.

Darkness.

Now red clouds.

A sensation of friction at his back and pressure at his wrists.

Now he is looking at the artexed ceiling from an angle he has never seen it before. Now there is dusty, cheap carpet by his face. How did that happen? Why am I at the bottom of the stairs?

He blinks. The effort pains him. It seems to awaken other sense.

Agony grabs him. Twists him in its fist.

He looks up. Sees a face. Halfway familiar; attractive and cold.

A voice. Soft, in his ear.

'Her real name. It's not here. Just "Blossoms". I already know that.'

The voice sounds as if it is underwater. Harry hears an echo. Feels dampness on his skin.

'I never really thought it would be here. I knew you wouldn't check. Just a name and a number. And the number isn't real.'

Harry wants to speak. Wants to ask for help. An ambulance.

Harry manages a croak.

'I'm sorry. I'm getting desperate. I had to try. I don't even know if it's her. He said Suzie, but he could have lied . . .'

He croaks again. Tastes blood. Blood and vodka.

'It keeps getting worse. It could have been simple. Now look where we are. There will be more, I know it. I've just made it worse. He'll be so angry . . .'

Harry knows what he wants to say. Can feel the words lining up in his mind. Wants to say that, whatever this is about, he will never speak of it. Wants to say that he can feel himself dying and cannot stand it. Wants to know where his glasses are, and whether they can be fixed.

'I thought your neck was broken. I think it is. I don't know. I could have walked away if your neck was broken. Now it has to be an accident.'

Harry tries to move. Realises he cannot feel his limbs. That it only hurts on one side of his body. On the other, he can feel nothing.

'I'm so sorry.'

He lies broken. His limbs broken branches, his back shattered glass. He is on his back, wedged in the doorway. His positioning tells the story of his death. Of a man who slipped climbing the stairs, and who could not put out the flames . . .

His neck is twisted gruesomely to the left, so Harry does not see the cigarette butt that a gloved hand grinds into vodka-soaked T-shirt. Cannot move his arms to flick it away. Can only watch, eyeballs climbing out of his skull, as it begins to smoulder.

He sees his killer walking to the back door, the

same hammer in hand that was used to force the lock and crack his skull.

Pain, now. Heat. Smoke and flame.

He gulps, hard trying to clear his mouth; to speak.

Swallows clotting blood. Begins to choke.

Coughs and pukes, choking on blood and sick, as the flames take hold of his ragged clothes and spread to the floor.

He is dead before he has to endure the stench of his own cooking skin.

CHAPTER 4

Suzie's posture implies prayer. She is bent forward, elbows on her knees, palms clasped fast, both thumbs pressed hard enough into her forehead to make grooves. Her lips move soundlessly, as though begging forgiveness or benefaction.

Her thoughts are far from divine.

She is lost in memory. Consumed by a recollection that has surfaced, unbidden.

For a moment, she is entering the red room, with its glitter ball and its velvet sheets. She is gazing upon naked forms. Is recoiling, spluttering in nervous laughter, drunk and giddy enough to change the mood. She is staring into a mask; leering and lascivious, incongruous atop a fleshy body that makes no concealment of its desire.

She is controlling herself, now. Saying yes. Letting go. Feeling a warm, familiar hand in her own. Accepting permission like a blessing.

She is on her back, weight upon her. Light making shadows of a grunting, thrusting face, given over to pleasure that could just as well be pain . . .

She shakes it away. Forces the memory back. Pushes her features into a smile. Hides it. Hides her feelings, even from herself . . .

Suzie is twenty-six years old. Petite. A little fleshier than she would like to be around the middle. Kooky, her bosses call her, when clients remark on her multi-coloured nails and chunky, home-made jewellery. Today she's dressed in a short black skirt over footless leggings, a long-sleeved white top and flip-flops. The fleecy Disney scarf around her neck covers the top end of a tattoo that her bosses at the law firm have deemed unsuitable for exposure. Her elbow-length lace gloves were considered more off-putting than the butterflies they obscured when she had tried to show willing and cover up the ink on her wrists, so she has taken to wearing fluorescent towelling sweat-bands. She expects to be asked to remove them as soon as one of the senior partners plucks up the courage. Her shoulder-length hair is dyed a colour somewhere between copper and autumn, and today is held back from an unremarkable but pretty face by a pink band. Tiny hummingbirds dangle from the lobes of her multi-pierced ears.

She is fun to look at.

She makes people smile.

The bells of St Mary's Church inform her it's one p.m., although she does not need their help. She has always just reached this stage in her lunch when the hour chimes. She fears she's becoming a creature of habit.

51

Suzie wonders why there are not more people here. It's a pretty spot, and she finds herself surprised on a daily basis to have it to herself. She's five minutes from work and a stone's throw from the relative bustle of the Old Town end of the city centre, but in the three months she has been eating her packed lunch here she's only had to share this lovely little courtyard garden a handful of times.

She's in the only green square to be found in the Museums Quarter; hidden away at the centre of this pocket of gorgeous old buildings and cobbled streets, constructed two centuries before in the angle between the Rivers Hull and Humber. Here, between Wilberforce House and the Streetlife Museum, she has found a place of near sanctuary. Here, protected by red brick and sloping archways, she feels delightfully invisible, set back under the protective branches of a tree she has come to think of as her own.

The spitting rain picks up its pace. The larger drops make a pleasing noise on the tree's burgundy leaves. She spots one leaf bulging under the weight of collected droplets and reaches out with her left leg so that, when it spills the cold water, it will trickle onto her bare toes. The sensation, when it comes, is exhilarating.

Suzie takes the iPhone from the pocket of her bag. It was an extravagant purchase, forcing her to live for a month on sausage rolls and biscuits from the office tin as a consequence of using her food budget for its acquisition.

She logs on to Facebook. Two pokes from old schoolfriends and a new post from her mum.

A song thrush has fluttered damply down to the nearest flowerbed. Suzie looks on the bench for a crumb to give it. She finds one in her scarf and chucks it to the bird, who ignores it and flies away.

'Marmite. Either love it or hate it . . .' she says under her breath.

She opens her email account. Ignores the messages from the various websites that send her discount codes for music downloads and vouchers for chain restaurants.

'What we got . . .?'

Two messages.

She finds herself smiling. A tickle of excitement flits between her stomach and chest.

'Still going strong . . .'

He sent one mid-morning, and another five minutes before she came out for lunch. A query about whether she touched herself when she woke up, and a one-line missive informing her that he is 'so damn hard' at the thought of her.

'Sweet,' says Suzie, hitting 'reply'.

She got talking to 'Dom' last night: half-heartedly at first, distracted by the vampire movie she was watching on the laptop, then later with an enjoyable intensity.

His advert on the website had been straight to the point. 'Dominant male seeks under-30 playmate. Must be up for anything. Are you game? Put your body in my control. Be my ragdoll.' He had put a little 'x' at the end of the posting. She had liked that.

'Hey there,' she'd said in reply. 'Saw your ad. Think we could have fun. Am twenty six and Ok looking. Have played this game before. Love to be dominated and test myself to the limit. Am I your sort of girl?'

Dom had replied within a minute. Told her he was 'aching' to know more. Said he 'yearned' for the taste of her. Was 'consumed by a need to lick the tears from her face'. His words had a lyrical quality that Suzie approved of. Suzie likes words. Completed a year of an English literature degree before her fiancé's job moved them to Hull and they had decided that his new, bumper wages made her continuing on the course a waste of both of their time. When they split up, not long after, she took solace in few things, but words were among them. She enrolled herself on a creative writing course. Met the skinny, giggly, lovingly absurd little peacock who would become her best friend.

Suzie enjoyed last night's chat with Dom. He seemed genuine. She has been playing these games for a couple of years now and knows that, nine times out of ten, the blokes begging her to fulfil their every fantasy when they're texting each other's brains out will chicken out before meeting up. She has had text-sex with countless online finds, but only a handful have had the bottle to say hello in the flesh, and fewer still been able to deliver on their promises.

'I want you to make me cry.'

Suzie presses 'send'. Waits a minute. Hopes for an immediate response.

This is the thrill of it. For her, it is not the sex itself. It is the game of it all. The naughtiness. The apprehension and excitement that make her shiver and wriggle as she checks her screen time and again, waiting for a new message like a wartime bride awaiting a love letter.

Are you a big brave girl? You want to show me what you've got?

Suzie grins as she reads the message and takes another sip of her juice before replying. She had half expected last night's flurry of messages to be a one-off. She is used to the swift curtailment of her cyber-sex: all too often the result of a spouse coming home early or knocking on the bathroom door.

'I am yours to command.'

She stares at the screen for a moment, and when no answer is immediately forthcoming, she opens up one of the Internet pages stored in her Favourites section. She looks at the latest tattoo designs and wonders whether she would suit the small posy of dandelion seeds highlighted as the 'tattoo of the day'. She isn't sure. Her tattoos are all designs she has created herself, though it is the lilies and pink cherry blossoms that wind from the backs of her thighs to the nape of her neck of which she is most proud. She and her friend had gone on the same day: he to be adorned with peacock feathers, she to become a Chinese garden. The results were stunning. The tattooist couldn't stop smiling. Took their pictures from every angle and asked if they would mind him using the images in his promotional material. They had preened and agreed, loving their own prettiness.

Want to see what you can do.

The message flashes up in the corner of the screen. She wrinkles her nose in disappointment. She has a limited amount of time. Wants him to send something not just suggestive, but filthy and obscene.

'Anything.'

The memory of the day of blissful agony in the tattoo parlour brings her down. Such thoughts always do. It is six months since she lost her best friend. Half a year since the boy with whom she giggled and cried and gossiped and played, wrapped a cord around his neck and hanged himself in the kitchen of the flat she had one day planned to share.

What you doing tonight?

Simon used to keep her safe. They played these games together. Best friends. True friends. Him keeping her safe from herself, and providing a reassuring closeness as she indulged in the liaisons that helped her feel alive. Her giving him reasons to feel loved and needed; an escape from the dark thoughts that made him seek out punishment and abuse, threatening to pull him under . . .

You promise you've got tattoos?

Suzie sighs, excitement dissipating. 'Pink blossoms all over my back. Butterflies on my wrists. A zip on the back of my thigh. All begging for your tongue to trace.'

There is no reply. Suzie wonders if this is where it will end. She will not be disappointed. This is the game.

Her phone beeps.

Tonight. Want to see your blossoms. Want to see you get nasty.

Suzie gives a little grin, crossing and uncrossing her legs as she allows herself to imagine that this one may actually happen.

She has no time to reply before the phone beeps again.

Come alone.

Half a mile away, raining twice as hard . . .

Trish Pharaoh looks her sergeant up and down.

Then back up and further up. She places her takeaway cup of coffee between her knees. Reaches forward. Takes his tie in both hands, and wrings it out as if she is throttling an eel.

'Road-testing a new anti-perspirant?' she asks sweetly. 'It's not working.'

McAvoy presses his lips together. Smiles a little, unsure what facial expression to pull, and eventually lets his features settle into a mask of embarrassed gormlessness. It is a countenance he has grown used to wearing in his boss's company.

Pharaoh lets go of his tie and shakes the water off her hand. Wraps both palms around the polystyrene cup. Points at the rain, which billows wave-like across the deserted square. 'You did this,' she says accusingly.

McAvoy sniffs. 'It's coming in off the sea . . .' he begins defensively.

'Hush now.'

She turns away from him. Sips her coffee.

'I didn't get you one,' she says, gesturing at her drink without any hint of apology. 'Figured you would file a report about attempted bribery or sexual harassment.'

McAvoy nods solemnly.

'Oh bloody hell, Hector, you are as much fun as paper cuts.'

McAvoy apologises. Hangs his head.

They are standing under the awnings of a jewellery shop in Trinity Square. The grey slabs of the piazza have been washed then varnished by the downpour, and the great wooden doors of the city's biggest church, a hundred yards from where they stand, have been soaked to a rich chocolate brown. McAvoy gives the church only the briefest of glances. He cuts this thought dead, before he begins to question how much rain it would take to wash away the blood that was spilled within Holy Trinity's embrace just a few months ago . . .

'Were they bastards?' asks Pharaoh, finishing her drink, and pausing for a moment until the bells of St Mary's, half a mile away, finish chiming the hour. 'The Authority? This new bloke as much of a bully as they say he is?'

McAvoy still hasn't made up his mind. 'He's in your face,' he says, thoughtfully. 'Big man. Big personality. Very well informed.'

Pharaoh looks at him, expecting more.

'He's clued up on what we're up to. The unit. Seems to read the reports and retain the info.'

'That's the last thing we need,' says Pharaoh, throwing her cup in one of the bins that dot the square.

'He wants real progress on the drugs, Guv. Wants arrests. Busts. A bit of action is what he said.'

Pharaoh rolls her eyes. 'He wants to be an MP, Hector. He wants some good publicity so he can bugger off to Westminster.'

McAvoy says nothing. He puts his hands in his pockets. Feels the outline of the mud-caked phone. Presses his fingers over the keypad. Pictures himself sitting at the kitchen table at home, delicately taking the machine to pieces with fragile tools held in too-large hands. Wonders again what possessed him to pick it up, and whether he has any damn right to root around inside.

'Wish I'd brought a brolly,' muses Pharaoh, watching the rain as it scythes down into the square. She looks at McAvoy. 'We wouldn't fit you under it, though, would we? You'd have to hold it. Be my slave for a bit, eh?'

He looks away before she can see him blush. Tells himself that she just teases him for fun, and not for meanness. Reminds himself how many times she has stood up for him. Comforted him. Risked her career to back him up.

'Come on then,' she says, when it becomes clear he will not respond. 'Let's get wet.'

Pharaoh pushes herself off from the wall. Early forties, curvy, and habitually dressed in biker boots, knee-length dress and cropped leather jacket, she does not look much like the head of Humberside Police Serious and Organised Crime Unit. But she's damn good at a job she inherited under difficult circumstances, and she marshals the egos and neuroses of her team like an inspirational primary school teacher.

'She really didn't want to meet somewhere neutral?' asks McAvoy, squinting into the rain. 'She wanted us to come to the house?'

Pharaoh shrugs. 'I gave her the option. She said to come to her place. I warned her, if you were wondering. Said I didn't advise it.'

McAvoy nods. 'She knows what she's doing, I suppose.'

This time it is Pharaoh who remains silent.

They turn off Trinity Square and walk in silence until they reach the damp cobbles of Dagger Lane. It's only a minute from the Old Town and a quick sprint across the busy dual carriageway from the bobbing pleasure craft and empty pubs of the marina.

'One at the end,' says Pharaoh, nodding at the row of red-brick terraced houses that occupy this old street, the origins of its intriguing name lost to history.

'And she's sure?' asks McAvoy.

'Sounded it.'

Pharaoh leans on the bell outside the slim, nondescript terrace. Turns to McAvoy.

'Smarten yourself up, man. You know she fancies you.'

'Guv, I . . .'

The door swings open.

Leanne Marvell is forty-one years old, and though she no longer works as a bouncer or competes in the body-building contests that first tempted her into trying steroids, she remains a powerfully built and imposing physical specimen. Though she is not particularly tall, she has a masculine physique, and while her muscles are not as clearly defined as they are in the photographs that McAvoy has seen from her weightlifting days, she still looks like she could beat him in an arm wrestle.

Her large nose is the only wrong note in a relatively pretty face, which creases into a smile when she sees McAvoy on her doorstep.

'Aector,' she says, looking past Pharaoh, 'I wasn't expecting you as well.'

Self-consciously, Leanne begins to straighten her grey jogging trousers, and the belly that sticks out from beneath her workout top miraculously disappears as she breathes in and holds it.

'Let us in, Leanne,' says Pharaoh, rolling her eyes. 'And don't feel obliged to say his name in Gaelic. It should be bloody Eichann, if you're being picky. I read up on these things. Nobody else is called Aector. It's just him being bloody awkward.'

Leanne beckons them into the hallway. Presses herself against McAvoy's damp body as she pushes the door closed.

McAvoy begins to speak. Begins to outline the origins of his name, and the compromise his Gaelic-speaking father and English-speaking mother came to when they chose to name their second son. But he decides to close his mouth instead.

'You'll have to excuse the mess . . .'

Leanne opens the door and ushers the two officers into a joyless and compact living room. It contains a floral two-seater sofa, a cheap coffee table covered in pouches of tobacco and rolling papers, and a huge flat-screen TV. The old-fashioned stone fireplace that is set into the far wall contains no fire: just two wires gaffer-taped to the stone. The walls are papered in a swirl of peaches and pinks, and the only picture that stares down at them hangs askew. It shows a younger, fitter Leanne, flexing in purple bikini and fake tan, collecting an award from a man with a shaved head and too many teeth.

'Shaun's not expected?' asks Pharaoh, taking off her coat and hanging it over the back of the sofa, then reaching into her handbag for a hairbrush, which she uses to slick back her hair.

'Not for hours,' says Leanne to McAvoy. 'You taking yours off, Sergeant?'

'I'm fine,' says McAvoy, refusing to catch Pharaoh's eye.

'Sit down, Leanne. Tell us what we're doing.'

Leanne perches on the edge of the coffee table. She reaches under the sofa, and pulls out a formidable-looking dumb-bell. Begins to perform curls with her right arm. If the effort pains her, she does not show it.

'Tonight,' says Leanne, looking down at the dirty white trainers on her feet and the dirtier carpet beneath. 'I promise. It's going to be there tonight.'

'You sure?'

'I read his phone. He was passed out. I've been reading it all the time. I feel like I'm spying on him.'

'You are, love.'

'I know, but I don't like the feeling.'

'He doesn't know? He's got no idea?'

'He trusts me.'

'And you're sure? Really sure you want to go down this road?'

'I've got no choice.'

Pharaoh nods. Leanne has already made her decision. She made it months ago while leaning, wet-faced, against the wall of Hull Royal Infirmary, with blood on her clothes and Trish Pharaoh's cigarette at her lips.

Leanne has fallen far since the days she represented her country in weightlifting championships and landed rosettes and trophies for her bodybuilding. She's one of the Old Town's more colourful characters. Sober, she's caring, thoughtful and considerate. A good friend. A decent neighbour. Drunk, she's a demon. She's a ferocious ball of anger, who lost her two kids to social services and her job to her criminal record. She has convictions for dealing, possession, wounding, and only escaped a charge of attempted murder when her ex-boyfriend refused to press charges.

McAvoy has read and reread her file, and always found it difficult to reconcile the flirty, friendly woman with the photos of the damage she has caused when the steroids in her bloodstream exploded into rage.

It was temper that brought her to Pharaoh's attention. The night that the two Vietnamese drugs farmers were found at Hessle Foreshore, Leanne was in Accident and Emergency with boyfriend Shaun, handcuffed to two different police officers, having been arrested for attacking her partner with a corkscrew. She had managed to get the weapon halfway into his ear, and twice into his chest, before he managed to wriggle free by braining her with a brass ashtray. Quite what they had been arguing about they had been unable to tell the uniformed officers who broke their door down and carted them off to hospital. But it had clearly been important.

As they were being dragged into reception at Hull Royal, Pharaoh was standing at the nearby coffee bar, listening as one of the junior doctors gave her his appraisal of the condition of the two Vietnamese men. She had been scowling into her latte, wincing at the calmness with which he described the nail-gun wounds to the victims' hands and knees, the burns on their backs and torsos. A paint-stripper, he had speculated. Turned the skin to jelly . . .

The doctor had recommended both victims be taken immediately to a specialist unit in Wakefield, where their wounds could be better treated. Pharaoh had acquiesced. Made arrangements. Had the two men wheeled down from the ward, cuffed to the sides of the hospital bed. There was an ambulance waiting outside for them. A police escort too. Pharaoh had been taking no risks.

And then one of the Vietnamese men spotted Shaun. He was wrestling with two of the constables, trying to get his hands free, desperate to be allowed to speak to Leanne. He was shouting that he loved her. That he would kill anybody who came between them. That he forgave her the fact he was bleeding from his ear and his heart.

Then Shaun stopped. Fell utterly silent. The sudden cessation of noise was more potent than a shout. Heads turned, including Pharaoh's. And she saw the way Shaun was staring at the two men in her care.

The colour had drained from his face. The officers holding his arms found the strength had gone out of him, and wrestled him to the floor.

And both of the drugs farmers let fly with a stream of impassioned invective, a gibberish that meant nothing to anybody in the great open lobby, but which told Trish Pharaoh that her victims knew this man, and knew him well.

With the victims safely transported to Wakefield, Pharaoh played a hunch and insisted upon Shaun and the woman he was brought in with being kept apart.

She got their names. Pulled both their records. Acquainted herself with their criminal pasts. Shaun's rap sheet was petty. He had never done more than a week on remand. Had convictions for drugs possession and affray. She had been more impressed with Leanne's. She had done serious time, and was looking at more.

Pharaoh had found her in a private room, cuffed to a constable, a doctor stitching up the wound on the back of her head and asking that she do her best to stop crying, as it was making it difficult to keep the stitches small.

'He's going to leave me, I know it,' said Leanne through the sobs, talking to nobody and barely registering Pharaoh's presence. 'He's too young for me. He's got his whole life. He doesn't need this. I'm dragging him down . . .'

Pharaoh had asked the constable to slip the cuffs off. Asked the doctor if he was done. And then she had led Leanne Marvell outside and pressed a cigarette to her lips.

Vulnerable, scared and doped on a cocktail of painkillers and steroids, Leanne had been perfectly primed for careful questioning. And Pharaoh had obliged. Told her that two Vietnamese drugs farmers had been found tortured and mutilated at Hessle Foreshore, and that they had identified Shaun. Pharaoh had been careful to keep it vague. Had left most of the work to Leanne's imagination. And she had thanked her lucky stars that McAvoy was not there to tell her off.

Despite her formidable appearance and the time she had spent inside, Leanne crumbled. Told her what she knew and begged her to help keep Shaun out of prison.

She had promised to help Pharaoh however she could.

Now, safely registered as a police informant and fully briefed on what will happen if she lies, Leanne is about to earn her pay.

McAvoy, who is legally bound to appear at all meetings between Pharaoh and any of her registered snouts, has an affection for Leanne. She is almost schizophrenic in the change that comes over her when in drink, but here, now, she seems a good person, trying to do her best by her man.

'You can't ever tell him,' she says, though she has already had assurances on this point. 'You have to say you lost the evidence or something. He can't be the only one not to go down for this.'

Pharaoh puts a hand on her knee. Offers her a cigarette and then lights it for her. 'It's all taken care of, Leanne. We'll look after you.'

Over the course of several interviews, it has become clear that Shaun is a relatively minor player in the hierarchy of the gang which has taken over the cannabis supply. His job has been that of a glorified delivery man, overseeing the movement of crops from one factory to another, and transporting the remaining handful of the Vietnamese workforce around the various properties, where they have been reduced to virtual prisoners. He knows nothing about the muscle side of the business. Doesn't know where the orders come from. Even in drink has confided little in Leanne about his employers, save that they are white and scary as hell.

'I'm not a grass,' says Leanne, and it is a mantra she has repeated endlessly in their meetings. 'I know he's been a bad lad. But he wouldn't do that. He's not a violent person, not really. I don't know why they're pinning it on him . . .'

Pharaoh coughs, trying to move the conversation on. She knows McAvoy disapproves of the fact she is letting Leanne think her boyfriend is in the frame over the torture of his two associates. In truth, he is not a suspect. Through an interpreter, the victims had given only the sketchiest of details about their attackers, but they made it clear that the men who hurt them were higher up the food chain than the man who drove the van. The descriptions they had given were sketchy. Big. White. Well-built. Acting under the instruction of a smaller man, who seemed to be enjoying it all far too much . . .

'Do you think we could have a fresh start?' asks Leanne suddenly, putting her dumb-bell down to concentrate on her cigarette. She looks at McAvoy. 'Do you think you can start again?'

McAvoy tries his best to summon up an encouraging smile. Tries not to let his eyes linger on her paltry possessions, or the signs of frailty and abuse that are starting to creep into her physique.

'We'll take care of you,' he says. 'I promise.'

The words somehow seal it.

Leanne nods.

'The warehouse next to the Lord Line building,' she says. 'St Andrew's Quay. Where they used to fish from. Near the memorial.'

McAvoy holds Leanne's gaze as Pharaoh begins

dialling a number in her mobile phone. He pictures the location. The darkness. The nearness of the Humber and its cold depths.

Sees, in his mind, an area that has witnessed death enough times to make the waters run red.

CHAPTER 5

6.24 p.m. The car park at Peter Pang's.
Red glass lanterns clink and sway, disappear and then re-emerge from the shadow of the pagoda-like roof.

McAvoy looks. Listens. *Sees.*

The sound of waves slapping wood and stone beyond the grey sea wall; broad, brown Humber fading into cloud and drizzle.

The morning's storms have not blown themselves out, but instead hang heavy and threatening in a headstone-coloured sky. The river, swollen by the cloudburst, slaps against the rotting timbers of St Andrew's Dock. Dead flowers and plastic memorial cards skitter and tumble on the wind. Flowers are often left here. This dock was home to the Hull fishing fleet. It is the last glimpse of home that thousands of dead trawlermen ever saw.

On Pharaoh's orders, McAvoy has switched his phone off, but after two hours in this cramped vehicle with nothing to look at but car bonnets and brick, he needs to do something to keep himself alert.

The phone bleeps into life at the push of his thumb. Two hands shake on the blurry, liquid crystal screen. A moment later it vibrates to alert him to three new text messages. One is from Roisin, telling him she loves him and will be wearing nothing but the red leather jacket he bought her for Christmas when he gets home. The other two are from Pharaoh, telling him first that she is BORED, and second that she needs a pee. He presses his lips together to stop himself from laughing.

'Lemon chicken,' says DC Andy Daniells, sniffing the air. 'Maybe prawns in oyster sauce.'

'I'm sorry?'

'Black bean, definitely. Not satay.'

McAvoy drags his eyes from the distant bulk of the warehouse, looks across at his colleague.

Daniells, who had told him within the first ten seconds of shaking hands that the double L in his surname was originally Scandinavian and not Welsh, is new to the unit. He's an affable, likeable lad in his late twenties, with a bald head and healthy, ruddy complexion. In the month since he moved across from regular CID, McAvoy has only ever seen him in one outfit. He had clearly decided in his youth that he would never look better than in rumpled navy chinos, pale blue shirt and striped red tie, and had decided to stick with it.

The windscreen wipers squeak inelegantly across the glass of the Corsa, smearing the drizzle into streaks. McAvoy winds the window down, reaches out and uses the cuff of his jacket to try and make the glass better equipped for surveillance.

'You think this place has got owt to do with it?' Daniells asks, nodding in the direction of the restaurant.

McAvoy, pleased to be back on more familiar ground, gives a shake of his head. 'No, we've spoken to the owner. Clean as a whistle. Making a mint and wouldn't want to risk it. Did you know John Prescott's a regular here? Once got in trouble for parking in a disabled bay. Was in the papers . . .'

'Prescott. Deputy Prime Minister, wasn't he?' asks Daniells, without any hint of embarrassment.

McAvoy pauses for a moment, wondering whether he should instruct the detective on the importance of sound political and local knowledge, but decides that the cheerful, chatty young man will probably pick it up as he goes along. He's only lived on this coast for a year or so and his Midlands accent remains strong.

'Yeah, he was Blair's number two.'

'Must have done a lot for this city, then . . .'

'Yes, you'd think.'

They sit in silence for a moment, and McAvoy, who has never felt comfortable in one-on-one situations with colleagues, begins to feel self-conscious. He goes back to his notes, shuffles through the papers in his lap, and checks his watch again.

'Late,' says Daniells, lifting his left arm from the

steering wheel and showing McAvoy his cheap watch. 'She said six.'

McAvoy bristles. Can't help himself. 'She?'

'Pharaoh. She said six.'

McAvoy's mouth becomes a tight line. 'Do you mean Detective Superintendent Pharaoh?'

'Yeah,' says Daniells, not detecting the warning note in McAvoy's voice. He laughs suddenly, at a memory. 'Did you see her trying to get the stab vest on? Could put that on YouTube . . .'

'I beg your pardon, Constable?'

This time, Daniells spots the danger. 'Wouldn't want to mess with her though,' he says hurriedly. 'Great boss.'

'Yes. She is.'

He stares out of the window across the gloomy car park. Spots the rear tyre of the surveillance van. McAvoy tries to picture the scene inside: Trish Pharaoh, Helen Tremberg, Ben Neilsen and half a dozen uniformed officers, all sitting cramped and anxious in the half-light, extendable batons greased and palmed, jumping with each crackle of the radio . . .

'We've got movement.'

The voice on the radio belongs to Detective Chief Inspector Colin Ray, the second in command of the unit. He's a gangly, goggle-eyed and rat-faced man with a fondness for pinstripe suits. Pushing fifty, and with a greenish pallor to his skin, he is at once feared, respected and reviled. In the event of impending apocalypse and the collapse of the rule of law, he would find himself getting punched in the face by a lot of colleagues.

McAvoy tries to heighten his senses. Hopes Daniells will do the same.

A black Land Rover glides into the car park, tyres making an expensive-sounding swish on the wet tarmac.

Daniells appears to be about to duck his head below the steering wheel, but a warning hand from his sergeant holds him steady. *No sudden movements*, suggests McAvoy, with his eyes. Nothing to alert the occupant.

'Is it our guy?'

This time the voice is Pharaoh's.

'Too dark. Can't say.'

'Fuck.'

McAvoy can hear the frustration in his boss's voice.

'This them, d'you think?'

Daniells's voice sounds excited and nervous. McAvoy wonders how many of these operations the young officer has been a part of.

'We'll just have to wait.'

McAvoy wishes he were in the van with Pharaoh; able to give her the kind of encouraging smile that tells her he believes in her and that this will come good.

'Steady now,' comes Pharaoh's voice.

The Land Rover still has not moved. It remains at a stop, diagonally opposite where McAvoy and

Daniells sit. If they are lucky, two burly men will get out and walk across the five hundred yards of wasteland between here and the disused warehouse. Once they have entered, Pharaoh will give the signal and her team will move in to arrest everybody inside. McAvoy is here in case anybody slips the net: ready to block off the road if anybody flees in a vehicle. DCI Ray and DI Shaz Archer are hopefully shivering as they keep watch on top of the giant furniture store that marks the end of the retail park that the road winds through on its way down to this washed-out, rundown location. At the far side of the warehouse, two patrol cars from the Operational Support Unit are parked up behind a wall of containers, ready to block off the escape of anybody who makes it into the storage area of the still working dock.

Pharaoh's voice: 'Keep it together, children . . .'

Seconds tick by.

Minutes.

'Hell of a place, isn't it?' says Daniells broodingly, staring through the glass at the brick building opposite. 'All those fishermen . . .'

'Trawlermen,' McAvoy mutters under his breath. 'Fishermen stand on a bank with a rod. Trawlermen risk their lives in seas harder than you can imagine.'

'I'm just saying . . .'

Daniells does not get a chance to say anything more. In a shriek of rubber, the Land Rover roars out of the parking space.

DCI Ray's voice on the radio . . .

'Fucking hell . . .'

The vehicle tears out of the car park, but instead of turning left back onto the road through, it spins right, barrelling across the area of wasteland and rubble between Pang's and the nearest tumbledown warehouse.

'. . . what's he doing?'

McAvoy feels a fist close around his oesophagus. He grabs the radio, but in his haste it slips from his hand and into the footwell. He reaches for it, papers falling from his lap, scrabbling desperately until his fingers close around its bulk.

'Guv, get out of there, it's a set-up . . .'

McAvoy doesn't know why, but he is flinging open the car door. He could have instructed Daniells to drive. He will never know why he did not.

He has run only a half dozen steps when he sees the light. Sees the flame emerge from the dark glass of the Land Rover. Sees it flicker and bounce as the vehicle smashes its way over the ragged landscape. Sees a figure climb halfway out the window of the moving vehicle and draw back its hand . . .

The Land Rover spins 180 degrees and barely slows as it approaches the small outbuilding where McAvoy had seen the tell-tale smudge of a police van's back tyre.

His shout of warning dies in his throat. The light is momentarily airborne, arcing upwards, bright

against the dark sky, before it tumbles down, down
. . . and smashes against the double doors at the
back of the police van, stuffed to the gills with
police officers: sudden prisoners in a vehicle
clothed in flames.

CHAPTER 6

Home.

The back end of the Kingswood estate, a twenty-minute drive from the centre of Hull and near enough to the East Riding villages on one side to compensate for the nearness of Europe's biggest council estate on the other.

It's a computer simulation, this place: a sprawl of identikit houses and lawns the size of bath towels; of used cars bought on finance and square living rooms costumed with hand-me-down sideboards and January sale sofas, first-day-at-school photos and Ikea black-and-whites.

Here, on the curve of one nondescript cul-de-sac, all white paint and bare brick, a rusty blue Peugeot with two wheels on the kerb, tasteful ivory curtains and the slightest scent of baking . . .

Roisin McAvoy, pressing her head to her husband's bare chest, absent-mindedly tracing the ridged outlines of one of his many scars with her dainty, red-painted fingernails.

McAvoy barely registers her touch upon his dead skin. He can still smell flames. Twenty minutes in the shower scrubbing his face and hair with

Roisin's home-made rosemary-and-mint shampoo has not removed the acrid tang of petrol and smoke that clings to his skin like damp linen.

'Another?'

Roisin removes herself from his embrace and nods at her husband's mug, held limp and lop-sided between finger and thumb. The marshmallows have melted together and formed a rather pretty roof over the inch-deep sludge of hot chocolate.

'Aector? Another?'

'Not yet,' he says and doesn't know why. 'It was lovely.'

'It's the cinnamon,' she says brightly. 'Aphrodisiac, y'know.'

McAvoy does know. They've had this conversation before. Roisin knows this too, but in the past such chats have led to tickles and fun, so he is pleased she is trying to steer him towards that a goal once again, even if he has no energy for the helping of 'adult time' she has clearly been craving all day.

'You sure you didn't bump your head, darling?'

'I was nowhere near, Roisin. Didn't even get warm on the flames.'

Nobody was badly hurt in the blast. Ben Neilsen had tripped jumping from the van and cut his hand. One of the uniformed constables who had used too much hairspray before suiting up for the operation had found herself looking momentarily angelic when the flames took hold, but Pharaoh had had the presence of mind to push her headfirst into a puddle, and she had escaped without significant injuries.

The operation had not gone well. The four-by-four had managed to lose the patrol car somewhere in the maze of old buildings down by the docks. The helicopter, when it had finally turned up, couldn't pick up the trail. And when Pharaoh and her remaining team had burst through the sagging wooden doorway of the ramshackle warehouse, hoping to salvage the evening by at least seizing a few tonnes of marijuana, the place had been deserted. The long tables that lined the cold, dark space were covered in dirt and leaf: indicators that the building had indeed been used for cultivation of drugs, but whoever had used the place was long gone. Leanne has not answered her phone, and the uniformed officers despatched to her house said it was empty and unlit.

'She'll be fine,' says Roisin softly. 'Pharaoh. She's a big girl.'

McAvoy looks at his wife, trying to read her expression. She has not yet met his boss. Despite being married to a policeman, she is not comfortable in the presence of the law. She knows that Pharaoh means a lot to her husband and that there is no risk of him straying, but McAvoy has lately detected an edge in his bride's voice whenever Pharaoh comes up in conversation.

'Briefing in the morning,' says McAvoy. 'Debriefing, really. See what we can salvage from tonight. I'll go and try Leanne again first thing.

81

I'm sure she wouldn't be involved in any set-up. She's not a bad person. She's just, you know . . . it's a mess . . .'

'You'll sort it, Aector. Don't worry.'

They are in the kitchen, leaning against the work surfaces. Roisin has just finished the dishes. McAvoy, at her insistence, has not been allowed to help. The arrangement is in part due to her claims that men should not worry about housework, and partly because he has a habit of dropping things and making a mess.

'Oh, I got a call from an old friend today,' says Roisin suddenly. 'Can get us one of those Toyotas, the four-wheel-drive ones. Two grand and only three years old . . .'

McAvoy winces. Colours instantly. Wishes she had not brought this up. He does not know how to respond to her mentions of 'friends' and 'contacts' – least of all since this morning's embarrassments with the travellers. He does not believe that any such car will have been procured legitimately. Fears it may even be stolen. He is ashamed of his thoughts and what they say about his prejudices, even towards the person he loves more than any other.

'We'll see,' says McAvoy. 'The insurance could still pay out.'

Roisin barks out a derisory laugh. The McAvoys are locked in a battle with their insurers. Their people-carrier had been reduced to a burnt-out shell a week before Christmas, driven into a brick building by a killer who perished in the resulting blast. McAvoy had escaped with only minor burns. Those wounds have been a picnic compared to the resulting insurance headache. The company claims he is not covered for a 'work-related' accident. Refuses to pay up. They have passed him between a dozen different departments; all apparently peopled by twelve-year-olds who keep laughing when they read his description of what caused the accident.

A sudden, half-hearted cry from upstairs causes Roisin to close her eyes in frustration. She is looking tired. Lilah has been difficult all day, grizzling and sobbing, refusing to feed.

'I'll go,' says McAvoy, but Roisin waves a hand at him, insisting he go sit down. He does not want to, fearing he will fall asleep as soon as he closes his eyes. She brushes past him, too tired to notice him put out an arm for a cuddle.

McAvoy stands alone in the kitchen for a while. Looks in the bread bin and the biscuit barrel. Eats a couple of peanut-butter cookies and takes a swig of milk from the carton in the fridge to swill the crumbs from his teeth. He looks for some kind of chore. Spots his coat over the back of the small kitchen table, and picks it up to go and hang it in the cupboard under the stairs. As he does so, Roisin appears at the top of the staircase. Lilah is red-faced and wet-eyed in her arms.

'I'm throwing those trousers away,' she says,

nodding at the laundry basket by the bathroom. 'Horrible.'

She reaches down and picks something from the floor. 'Oh, this was in the pocket.'

She throws him the mobile phone.

McAvoy had almost forgotten it. He colours as he looks at it.

'Fancy model, that,' says Roisin, mid-yawn. 'You going to try and get it working?'

McAvoy runs his tongue around his mouth. Opens his mouth to justify his interest, and realises Roisin does not need him to. Just nods, and enjoys her smile.

An hour later.

An Irish voice, made snappy by tiredness.

'He fecking is.'

Roisin McAvoy is pronouncing that the man on the television is an arsehole.

McAvoy looks up, wondering whom his wife is talking about. He has been lost in concentration, safe in focused hard work. He takes off his reading glasses and lets his eyes focus on the giant flat-screen TV that stands in the corner of the room. He gives a shudder. It's the Thunderbird. Mr Popple-head. Wanchorman. *That Arsehole*, to give him his full title. A Hull institution, he has somehow been elevated to the status of a local legend without appearing to have a single fan. He is a slight, creepy, weaselly looking chap with a head too big for his slim frame and a moustache that has been shaved bootlace-thin and skin that has been sunbed-tanned to the colour of damp sand. To McAvoy he always appears to be trying to remember whether he has left the gas on. How he got the gig presenting the local news has been open to speculation for some time, but there are suggestions it involved a complicated ritual and the sacrifice of a goat.

'Oh God, turn him over,' he says, wondering how he has managed to blank out the man's voice until now.

'Can't,' she says. 'Help!'

Roisin is feeding Lilah, one breast flopping over the top of her nightie, poking out from the folds of her leopard-print dressing gown. 'The buttons are over there,' she says in mock desperation, nodding at the remote control. It sits taunting her at the other end of the sofa. 'I'm stuck.'

McAvoy takes the hint. He has a tea-tray on his knees, the mud-caked mobile phone and an assortment of screwdrivers, cotton buds and brushes laid out on the arm of the chair. He moves them all to one side and stands, padding barefoot to Roisin's side. He retrieves the buttons and hands them to her. She takes them gratefully, but does not yet change the channel.

'How's it going?' she asks, nodding at his tools.

McAvoy pulls a face. 'I don't know. It's almost clean. I've got an adaptor and I can charge it through the laptop. The battery from my old Nokia should fit it if that one's fried. SIM's clean, so maybe. I don't know. Wish I'd never found it.'

Roisin laughs. 'No you don't.'

McAvoy returns to his chair and Roisin, careful not to dislodge Lilah, fumbles with the controls. Before she can change the channel, Wanchorman introduces a story about changes to the make-up of the Police Authority.

'How did it go?' asks Roisin, remembering.

'It went,' says McAvoy. 'The new chairman has some interesting ideas. He could go far.'

'Sounds like you would like to throw him there.'

McAvoy shakes his head. 'I can't make my mind up. I guess it makes no difference what I think.'

Roisin laughs. 'You don't mean that either.'

McAvoy pokes his tongue out at her and turns his attention back to the broken phone, tuning himself out again as his wife makes herself comfortable and settles into her soap opera. He vaguely remembers that he has a cup of tea on the go, but figures that wherever he left it while bathing Fin and telling him his story, it will be too cold to bother about retrieving.

Ten minutes later, satisfied that the phone is as clean as he can make it, he disappears through to the kitchen and out of the back door to the shed. It stands on the nine-slab patio, next to the sandbox and mini-trampoline, and its mingled scent of sawdust and poster paints, linseed oil and solder, reminds him of his father. He has to cling to such links. The two do not speak.

McAvoy's tools are neatly arranged on the wall, each piece of kit outlined in black marker so he can know instantly when something is not in its proper place. He pulls open a plastic drawer and roots through the collection of wires and leads. He has a habit of collecting random things too interesting to be thrown away, a testament to the hardship of his youth.

He picks up a handful of wires and carries them back to the living room, stopping on his way to retrieve his laptop from where it is charging in the kitchen. Were his hands not so full he would scoop out another handful of lemon meringue pie from the foil tray that sits next to the microwave, but before he can consider sticking his face in the dessert, Roisin's voice cuts through from the living room.

'Leave it. You've had two slices.'

He comes back to the living room, his head bowed: busted.

'I wasn't going to have any more . . .'

'Fibber.' She raises an eyebrow, cat-like. 'Am I not feeding you?'

McAvoy looks down at his barrel torso, his chunky thighs and calves, bulging against his cut-off-denim shorts and rugby shirt as if he is halfway through a metamorphosis into the Hulk.

'It's soooo good . . .' he says, a child demanding more cake.

'I'll make another one at the weekend. You can't have everything you want all the time.'

The way she says it is enough to make them both laugh without need for a reply.

Some time later, after some gentle cursing and a skewered thumb, McAvoy has managed to create a makeshift adaptor out of an old phone cable and is plugging the phone into his laptop.

'Here we go,' he says and holds down the on switch on the keypad.

Roisin, who is yawning and trying to keep her eyes open for the final credits of her programme, can barely find the strength to pretend she is interested. 'Working?' she asks as she shifts Lilah into a more comfortable position on her lap.

McAvoy is too engrossed in fiddling with the laptop to reply. He has not used this software before, downloaded from a specialist site dealing in data retrieval and recommended by a colleague in the Technical Support Unit.

'Aector?' His name ends in a slur.

McAvoy looks up. Roisin is starting to doze off, sliding into a half-seated, half-lying down position, her legs drawn up childlike beneath her. McAvoy carefully moves the computer to the side and crosses to her, taking Lilah from her unresisting grasp. His daughter wriggles and grimaces a little, letting out a tiny cry of disapproval at being disturbed, but McAvoy presses her to his chest and shushes her back to the lightest of sleeps. He slides back into the armchair and watches the screen as the phone's memory is transferred to his desktop.

'Look what Daddy did . . .'

The flickering screen reflects on his daughter's face, turning her apricot cheeks and smooth, almond-coloured brow into a shimmering collage of images, of words, numbers, names . . .

Lilah wakes again. Reaches up and grabs her father's ear. She holds it, as if deciding whether there is anything to be gained by giving it a yank, and then lets go as she feels the backs of his knuckles stroking her jaw.

McAvoy props his daughter up so she can see the screen.

'I think this might have worked,' he says softly in her ear, as if sharing a secret. She looks at the screen wide-eyed, puzzled but fascinated. McAvoy smiles, starts to read. 'What have we got?'

He clamps a hand over Lilah's eyes. The movement is unexpected and Lilah gives a gasp of fright that turns into the motorbike-rev that signals her intention to cry.

On the sofa Roisin sits bolt upright. She sees her husband with his hand over their daughter's eyes, blushing furiously and signalling at the laptop with frantic nods of his head.

'Jaysus . . .'

Yawning, exhausted, too tired to sugarcoat, Roisin rolls onto the floor and crosses to him on her knees. She pulls Lilah from his grasp and holds her close, managing to croak a few words of song. With some rocking and a few soft shushes, Lilah settles, and Roisin achily manoeuvres herself upright.

'I'll take her up,' she says and there is more honey on her tongue than before. She meets her husband's eyes and manages a bone-weary wink. It's her apology for her sharpness, and McAvoy, never truly convinced of the source from which she draws her love for him, wishes she did not feel compelled to give it.

When the door closes, he looks back at the laptop screen. At the handful of legible messages he can make out amongst a fog of scrambled numbers, letters and computer code. The blush is getting redder. He feels the need to lock the door and pull the curtains tight.

'Bloody hell . . .'

A minute later Roisin slips back into the room. Her eyes find his and she raises her arms wide, indicating that she is all ears.

'The phone . . .' says McAvoy.

'You got it working? Well done.'

'Yeah, but . . .' he stops. Pulls an impish face.

'What?'

'"I want to take you inside me. Want to arch my back like a yawning cat, pushing back against your hardness, your manhood so deep inside me that it feels as if I am breathing for you . . ."'

'Fecking hell!'

Her tiredness momentarily forgotten, she all but runs across the room and throws herself over the arm of the chair and onto his lap, knocking loose the lead that connects the phone to the laptop. McAvoy doesn't care. This is fun.

'Is there more?' she asks, looking at the laptop.

McAvoy raises a hand to point at the screen and then stops himself. His wife, bright, witty, beautiful and gifted, had a traveller's upbringing. Her schooling was sporadic and disjointed. She is not a comfortable reader, despite the patience with which he has helped her develop a love of words. Instead he picks another phrase at random and reads it to her.

'"I am yours to abuse. I am a toy for your pleasure, a piece of meat to be pounded, clay to be moulded – a waiting receptacle for your frustrations and rage . . ."'

Roisin giggles and presses herself against him. They are two teenagers reading a friend's diary; naughty, wrong and loving it.

'"Want your breath against me, the cord biting into my skin . . ."'

'She's good,' says Roisin appreciatively. 'Bet he bloody loved it.'

'"Want my mind to sculpt your face; your identity to remain the desperate fantasy that first brought your tongue to my shoulders, your hand to my cock . . ."'

McAvoy stops short, and Roisin catches her breath. She gives a snort.

'It's two blokes?'

McAvoy catches himself pulling a face, and a guilty blush thunders from his brow to his neck.

His liberal self-loathing grabs a handful of his guts.

'Well, there's nothing wrong with . . .'

Roisin is giggling. 'You were loving it,' she teases.

'So were you,' he protests and then accepts there is no way to escape this with any dignity, so just starts laughing and buries his face in her chest.

'Did it get you going?' she asks seductively, trying to get a hand inside his shirt.

'No!' Then, sheepishly, 'A bit.'

'Me too,' she says and presses her face to his.

CHAPTER 7

'Slutty', he'd texted, when pressed for a preference on how she should dress. 'A dirty girl.'

Suzie hadn't really known how to interpret the instruction, but figured it hadn't included her Disney scarf or Care Bears rucksack.

Still, she has enjoyed playing dress-up, and her reflection pleased her when she looked in the mirror on the back of the wardrobe door. She has managed to find an outfit in her explosion of clothes that, to her at least, qualifies her as vaguely whorish.

She is shivering in a short blue dress and a second-hand leather jacket that reaches to her bare knees. Her hair is tied back and her make-up is thick enough to ensure there will be no facial damage in the event of a sudden fall.

The high heels her new playmate had insisted upon are on the passenger seat of the Fiat Panda. The stiletto points kept getting caught in the mat when she pressed the accelerator, so had been whipped off at the last set of traffic lights. She is now driving barefoot, unsure whether or not she likes this sensation of damp dirt and metal on the soles of her feet.

It is a miserable night. The rain is a damp net stretched across the black road. It does not seem to fall, but instead hangs, ghost-like and bone-soakingly omnipresent, in the chill, oil-dark air.

Suzie wishes Simon were here. She can picture him with no effort of will; can see him now, smoking a roll-up in the passenger seat and telling her she looks beautiful.

Such a wish is nothing new. Suzie's yearning for his return has become almost a prayer. But tonight it is more through some vague sense of unease over her safety than her usual eagerness to giggle and chat with her best friend.

It's almost nine p.m. This is her third visit to this location, but the first time she has driven here alone.

She remembers Simon's message when she first told him she had heard there was a popular spot for couples and singles on the coast road up to Bridlington.

'Coniston lay-by – where dreams are made.'

Ten miles from the city centre, between two mid-sized villages, a little side road has become, in certain circles at least, notorious. Though she does not particularly like the word, it has made the papers as a 'dogging spot'. Here singles meet, and couples put on participatory shows for the handful of guys who like to spend their spare time sitting in their cars in the dark: each hoping the next set of headlights in the rear-view mirror represents a blow-job rather than the police.

'What are you doing? Seriously, Suze?'

She asks herself the question as she slowly manoeuvres the tiny, battered car into the isolated, pitch dark of the entrance to the lay-by.

It is at least a mile from the nearest house.

There is a nervousness, an excitement, in Suzie's stomach and thighs, but to call the feeling arousal would be inaccurate. In truth she does not do this for the sex. Not really. It is perhaps just to prove herself alive. It is to be somebody who does not just fantasise, but who makes things happen. She does it because she thinks it is weak to deny your-self excitement.

In her years with her fiancé, sex was simplistic and routine. Life was OK. Middle of the road. Safe. When her heart was broken, Suzie lost herself. Did things she could never have previously imagined. Found reserves of lust and rage in equal measure, and made mistakes that catapulted her into a new way of being. She engaged in one-night stands and office flings: sweaty unions in nightclub toilets and in the backs of cars. She read and watched erotica. Bought herself toys with which to pleasure herself when she could not find a partner. Made it clear when starting conversations that she was not just a tease. That she was willing to play.

One such rendezvous introduced her to an attractive older man, who spotted in her a hunger for the unknown. He had introduced her to the websites and forums where like-minded people were able to enjoy grown-up fun. And she had thrown herself into the life. Had quickly come to view ordinary sex as somehow lukewarm and insipid in comparison. Had so grown to love the sordid nastiness of these couplings and triplings that she found herself turning down nights out with potential boyfriends in exchange for late-night assignations with strangers.

Simon was the only friend who knew about it all. Something had happened, shortly after they met, that bonded them together in a friendship without judgement. Both were free to be themselves, whatever that might be. They joined in each other's games and laughed about their adventures. She could not talk to her other mates about such things. Could not stand to be judged, or worse, analysed. Would not want to hear their aghast musings on what hole in her heart or bump in her brain forced her to subject herself to such abuses and degradation. She does not really want to think about any of that. Just knows that it makes her feel as if she is living life in colour after so many years in black and white.

'Wish you were here, Si. What am I bloody doing?'

There are two cars in the lay-by. A large estate car is parked up to Suzie's right in the shadow of

96

the mound of shingle and earth that blocks the area from view and gives it such appeal. Its lights, and engine, are on.

In the distance she can spot the shape of another car. It is dark and bulky, lights off, occupant obscured.

Suzie has been half-heartedly listening to the radio. There has been some sort of accident down at St Andrew's Quay. A police van has been petrol-bombed and two officers have been taken to hospital. She wonders if it was the speed-camera van and rather hopes that it was.

She takes a deep breath. Parks up on the opposite side of the lay-by to the estate car. Wonders who she is about to fuck.

In the beam of her headlights she can make out that the driver is quite tall. From this remove she guesses he is middle-aged, but cannot be sure. In truth, it doesn't really matter.

She closes her eyes and tries to calm herself. She has done more devilish things than this. She has played more daring games. But in the past Simon has been here to hold her hand.

'God, I miss you.'

The first few weeks without him she had had no appetite for such things. She didn't log on to any of the websites that used to bring her such fun. Didn't send a filthy message or put a single kiss at the end of an email. But as grief became bearable, so desire began to return. There were tears when she attended her first swinger party without him, but they had not flown so freely as to inhibit her. The night had gone well. She had enjoyed herself. Had made new friends. Had promised to return for the next gathering. Had even told today's playmate how much she hoped he would join her.

The phone on the passenger seat beeps and Suzie jumps. She picks it up and reads the message.

'Go and make him happy.'

The thrill of it all brings goose pimples to her skin. She reaches across for her high heels and slips her cold feet inside them, noting how her fingers tremble as she fastens the buckle. With a quick glance at her reflection in the too-dark mirror, she steps from the car.

A gust of wind pulls at the tails of her leather jacket and her legs feel unsteady as she totters across the tarmac on her high heels, closing the distance between herself and the vehicle in only a few strides.

The man in the car watches her approach. His head almost reaches the roof of the vehicle. He has a thin, pinched face, and rimless glasses. He is dressed in a nice suit, with his tie loosened almost to the middle of his chest. He is red-faced and there is a sheen of sweat visible on his thinning scalp. As he winds the window down, Suzie is hit by the smell of booze. Bending forward to talk through the glass, she sees the man already has his trousers undone.

'Want to play?'

The line sounds silly and false as she says it, but she can think of nothing better,

The man looks taken aback and Suzie wonders if he had genuinely expected to find sex here tonight, or had just driven here to see if the rumours were true.

'What you got in mind?'

His voice is slurred, but whether through drink or nerves she cannot say.

'It's cold out here,' says Suzie, trying to sound sexy.

'Do you want to get in?'

Suzie remembers her instructions. Wonders if her new friend is watching. Whether he is sitting in the distant car, smiling as she fulfils his fantasy without ever having seen his face.

'You can join me out here. The bonnet of your car looks soooo comfy.'

The man fumbles with the car door. He steps from the vehicle and a half bottle of Jack Daniel's falls onto the road. The man kicks it under his car and stands up straight. He has to reach out to steady himself, and his eyes slide halfway shut.

He is a good foot taller than Suzie, and twice the age.

She looks up at him. Decides they will not kiss.

She wonders if this is turning the watcher on. She is feeling only the slightest frisson of arousal, but that is to do with the sensation of being commanded, being watched, rather than by any desire to have sex with this man.

She goes straight to work. Reaches out and squeezes his groin. He moans and she wonders how long he has been turning himself on, here, alone, in the dark.

'Can I lick it? Lick you? Down there?'

She does not want him to, and tonight's architect had not commanded her to accept any such pleasures.

She shakes her head. 'Do me. Now.'

Suzie walks as sexily as she can to the front of the car. It is warm and throbbing as she lays herself upon it, face-first, listening to the hum of the engine. Without a word she pulls up the hem of her dress. The cold night air and faint mist of rain feels wonderful on her bare skin.

A moment later, he is behind her, pressing his still-clothed hardness against the backs of her thighs.

She wishes she had her phone in her hand. Wishes she could text him to ask if he is enjoying the show.

She hears the rustle of trousers falling to the wet ground. Feels rough and inexpert fingers between her legs and then a hand in her hair.

Suzie presses her face into the wet metal of the car. Feels him fumbling, trying to find the way inside . . .

'Get it over with,' mumbled into the back of her hand.

The sound of a car.

Big, powerful engine roaring into life. Fat, expensive tyres on wet tarmac. The sudden scream of a foot stamping on gas.

Suzie turns around. Stares past the grunting, thrusting man. Her eyes widen. It is a sensation of genuine terror.

The other car is screaming towards them, mere feet away and getting faster.

The noise she makes is a strangled squawk. It is an unnatural sound, gargled in her throat.

Desperately, she pushes back against the man, who pins her to the bonnet of his car. Hears him grunt and stagger as he tries to hold her where she lies.

'Get off me!'

Suzie knows she is about to die. Wonders if this is how Simon felt as he gave himself up to the noose.

And then she is squirming, shrieking, slipping out of his grasp: the roar of the car engine drowning her shouts to 'Move!'

She slips free. Throws herself into the dirt at the side of the road.

Turns, just in time to see the four-by-four crush the man, half-turning, against the bonnet of his own car in a crash of metal and flesh.

He is pinned between the cars, legs and buttocks still bare, shirt tails comically parted like stage curtains to reveal a dying erection.

Suzie cannot make a sound. Her throat has squeezed shut. Her eyes will not seem to close.

She stares, unable to yank her gaze away from the man's gulping, gasping mouth, opening, as if with the dying gasps of a fish, as his head falls forward onto the bonnet of the vehicle which pins him where he stands.

Beneath where Suzie lies, semi-sprawled, the ground is cold. Wet. Her knees are bleeding where she landed on stone. Her mouth is open as if in mimicry of the dying man.

Finally, she is able to raise her dirty hands to her face. To momentarily block it out. To stop her memory from absorbing any more.

She only looks up again when she hears the larger vehicle move. She looks up, watching as the four-by-four reverses back, pauses, and then turns in a semi-circle. It does not pause again. The sound of a boot stamping on the gas rings in Suzie's ears.

A moment later, she is alone, sitting in a ditch at the side of a lay-by, watching a stranger slide to the ground as if made of damp paper; his legs a ruined mess of skin, blood and bone.

She forces herself to move. Pulls down her dress as if suddenly terrified of being seen. Moves, in jerky increments, to where the man lies.

'I'm sorry,' she says, though the sounds do not come out.

She staggers back to her own car. Fumbles with the door. Cries. Tries a dozen times to get the key in the ignition. Breaks a heel as she presses the accelerator to the floor.

She has driven five miles with trembling hands before it occurs to her to call 999.

It is another two before she can find a phonebox.

She is nearly home before she has the presence of mind to go back and wipe her prints from the receiver.

CHAPTER 8

Lilah is whimpering. Thrashing. Kicking fat little limbs the colour of uncooked sausages. Turning her cheeks into cold, slapped flesh, with the power of her sobs.

'Please, baby girl. Please . . .'

McAvoy's giant hand is splayed upon his daughter's heaving belly, trying to soothe her with his gently massaging fingers.

He leans over the cot. Fills her world with his face. Tries to saturate his eyes with truth, to wordlessly convey to his frightened, agitated child, that she has nothing to fear. That Daddy is here. That she need never be afraid, or lonely, or sad . . .

He scoops her up. Holds her to his chest. Strokes the soft down that covers her warm crown. Shushes her, his stubbled cheek against her soft, untainted skin.

Gradually Lilah settles. One of her tiny hands finds McAvoy's lower lip, and she grips it territorially as she begins to drift back into sleep.

Content to let her keep whatever part of his face she wants, McAvoy leans back against the wall and stares through the glass. Takes in the symmetry and newness, the bland homogeny of the estate.

Allows himself a brief moment of memory. Recalls the gloss of condensation. The smell of smouldering turf. The chill stone floor of the family croft. That view: across the heather and peat of the undulating fields down to the glassy black waters of Loch Ewe . . .

He shakes it away. Concentrates on now. On Hull. Its sky and its streets.

McAvoy has never had cause to use the word in conversation, but he fancies the colour of the morning sky, as it bleeds from the orange-tinged black of night to the cloud-covered gloom of day, could be labelled 'isabelline'. It is a word he read in a book as a child, and its cheeky definition ensured it would lodge in his head forever. The word lends itself to the grey and yellow parchment hue reputed to be the colour of the underwear worn by Isabella, Archduchess of Austria, at the end of a three-year siege of her castle home.

It is a word that always makes his nose wrinkle, but it seems strangely appropriate for this damp and ghastly morning.

McAvoy checks his watch. It's just gone six a.m.

He listens for any other sounds inside the house, but there is silence save for Lilah's gentle snuffling against his chest. Roisin and Fin remain asleep. He has a moment to himself.

Soundlessly, he crosses back to the cot and

tenderly lays Lilah back down. Moving on tiptoes, he leaves the room and closes it behind him, conscious even as he does so how foolish he must look; a man of his size tiptoeing like a burglar, clad only in boxer shorts and suffused with the scent of smoke and too little sleep.

He retrieves his mobile phone from the pocket of the trousers which lie outside his bedroom door, alongside the tie, socks and underpants he has already picked out for the day. He is used to leaving at strange hours. Does not like to wake his bride by dressing in the bedroom.

McAvoy pads downstairs, checking the messages on his answering service.

He enters the kitchen. Pours himself a glass of milk and adds a squirt of strawberry syrup, then downs it in a gulp.

Within moments he is heading back upstairs. Pulling himself into his clothes and replaying the message that he wishes to God he had picked up when it was left for him at two a.m.

'McAvoy. This is Desk Sergeant Pulis from Queens Gardens. Your request just crossed my desk. I'm sorry, this didn't ring any bells before now. Shaun Unwin, yes? You're looking for him or Leanne Marvell, I understand. Shaun's been with us. In the cells. He's due to be released first thing, but I'll hold him if I hear back from you . . .'

Twenty minutes later McAvoy is walking briskly across Queens Gardens. The skies have not yet unleashed the lake they hold in their bellies, but the air is damp and the morning grey. He is grateful for the long woollen coat he took the time to pick up off the back of the sofa before silently slipping out of the house. He had pushed the car, hand-brake off, for two whole streets, before turning the ignition. He wants his family to sleep soundly.

He follows the paved walkway through the neatly tended landscape of duck ponds and grass and up the stairs to the glass and concrete frontage of Queens Gardens Police Station.

The sergeant behind the glass raises his eyebrows as the detective walks in, and swivels his eyes to look up at the clock behind him.

'My, you're up with the lark.'

'Shaun Unwin,' says McAvoy, crossing to the desk. 'Has he been released?'

The sergeant, whose name McAvoy recalls as having a military connection, opens a plastic folder and runs a finger along a list of names.

'Released at 4.40 a.m.,' he says. 'Pulis told him he could have breakfast before he went home but he was itching to get going.'

McAvoy closes his eyes.

Remembers the sergeant's name.

'I gave instructions, Sergeant Uxbridge. It was essential I speak to him . . .'

The sergeant bristles. 'I wasn't on shift, mate. Was it a paper request? Only they sometimes get misfiled, see. Now when it's on the computer, it should flash up to tell you not to let any bugger go if somebody still wants them, but even then it's a hit and miss business . . .'

Exasperated, McAvoy turns away. Runs his tongue around his mouth and rasps his hand over his unshaved face.

His mind fills with the snippets of information he was able to piece together on the drive over, in between phone calls to Pharaoh that had left his head ringing.

Shaun Unwin had been arrested for disorderly conduct at 3.15 p.m. the previous day: even as Pharaoh and her team sat planning the raid at St Andrew's Quay. He had been knocking back drinks in the Mission. Sparked up a cigarette and refused to put it out. Swung a punch at the barman and smashed his forearm into the Perspex frontage of the jukebox. Made a prick of himself, and told the owners that if they didn't like it, they should call the cops.

He didn't run when the police turned up. Seemed to give himself up without any of his usual aggression.

The constable who made the arrest said he could get nothing out of Unwin. Had got no reply when he, like so many others, tried to find Leanne Marvell to inform her of her partner's arrest.

McAvoy closes his eyes. Last night's bust was doomed to failure from the start. Leanne had told her boyfriend that she had told the police. He had gone and got himself banged up and, whether intentional or not, that news would have rung alarm bells with the gang who paid him. Calls would have been made. The cannabis relocated. And then some bastards in a Land Rover despatched to deliver a flaming warning to the coppers who had thought they were dealing with the usual class of scum . . .

His phone rings. Wincing in advance, he answers as quickly as he can.

'Guv?'

'I already know,' says Pharaoh, shouting above the noise of her sports car on the noisy road that leads from her home across the water up to the Humber Bridge. 'Fucking idiots. Have you tried the house? He's just thick enough to go back there.'

'No, Guv. I came straight to Queens Gardens . . .'

'Right. Well, fucking run. Why do these people think they can think? If he wanted to be out of the way, Leanne could have asked us. We could have planned it another way. He could have had nothing to do with any of it. To be sitting in the cells while we were sitting waiting for him – what does he think his bosses were going to think?'

The doors swing open as McAvoy walks back out into the cold. The rain is still holding off, and his feet are steady on the slick pavements as he jogs back across the gardens and over Parliament Street, down onto Whitefriargate, with its shuttered chain stores ands its full gutters stuffed with dead leaves, with empty bottles and polystyrene takeaway cartons.

He makes his way across Trinity Square and onto Dagger Lane.

Answers his phone as it vibrates against his thigh.

'Well? Anything? Shaun?' A pause. A note of real concern. 'Leanne?'

The street is deserted. The light from the street-lamps shows up the haze of moisture in the grey air, and McAvoy instinctively shivers as he looks at his coat and sees that somehow, despite the absence of rain, he is soaked through.

A voice in his ear: 'McAvoy?'

'Nearly there, Guv.'

'She'll be OK. You've seen her. She's hard. It's not her that told. They just put it together themselves . . .'

They both attempt to persuade themselves into happier, more positive thoughts. They fail.

'Not a sound, Guv. He wouldn't come here, though, and we've been trying Leanne all night . . .'

McAvoy stops.

Swears.

'Hector?'

The door to Leanne's terraced house is an inch ajar.

He closes his eyes for a moment.

'The door's open, Guv.'

'Fuck, Hector. Right, I'm on my way. Call for uniform immediately.'

McAvoy eyes the doorway. Reaches out a hand

and touches the wet wood. Pushes it open and steps inside.

'Hector, I'm not far off the bridge. I can be there in twenty-five minutes maximum. Don't you even think about going in there.'

McAvoy nods, steps back.

Then he smells it. Smells the soft, earthy scent of suffering: of tears and pain. It is an infusion in the air, a whisper of a taste. It catches in his nostrils and stuffs its fingers down his throat.

'Guv, there's somebody inside.'

McAvoy says no more. Ends the call and then switches off his phone. Moves, as if trying not to wake a child, back within the embrace of the house.

His feet make no noise as he takes the stairs. He moves slowly, but takes the steps three at a time so as to cut down on the likelihood of a creaking step.

He sniffs: a great stag checking the morning air.

He finds himself moving towards what he presumes to be the bedroom. The door, white-painted and featureless, has been pushed to but not closed fully. He inches towards it. Pulls the extendable baton from his pocket, and then puts it back. He has never swung the weapon. Has seen what it can do. Does not want to add his name to the list of officers who have found themselves disciplined or guilt-ridden after allowing their adrenalin to overtake them while armed with something so deadly.

He pushes open the door.

Shaun Unwin has been tie-wrapped by the ankles to a hardbacked chair. He is naked. His hands are palm down upon his knees; a gory mimicry of a well-disciplined schoolchild.

The room smells of blood. Of lighter fuel. Of burning flesh.

The skin on Shaun's torso has been melted down to bone.

His feet sit, unmoving, in a puddle of blood that runs down from where the nails have been driven through the backs of his hands and deep into his kneecaps.

His head lolls forward: lifeless.

McAvoy crosses the room. Lifts Shaun's head. Recoils as he stares into the slack-jawed ruination of the man's mouth. At the stumps of broken teeth. The blue-black blood. The perforations in his gore-lacquered cheeks.

Shaun's mouth has been filled with a fuel-soaked rag and then set on fire. His tongue is melted black.

McAvoy, fighting his instincts, reaches out a hand and presses his fingers to Shaun's neck.

Moves back to the wall and retrieves his phone.

Pharaoh answers before he can speak.

'He's dead, isn't he? Shaun. I bet the fucking idiot walked straight in the front door.'

'They hurt him, Guv,' says McAvoy, softly. 'Must have worked on him for a time. I can't see Leanne. Fuck, what a mess . . .'

A sound behind him makes him stop short.

Shaun would have been home by around five a.m. It's just after seven a.m. now. It would have taken time to do this. Could they still . . .

This time the noise is unmistakable. The bang of wood on brick, and then feet on cobbles.

McAvoy sprints across to the window. Peers left and then right, frantically searching for the source of the sudden sounds.

He catches a glimpse of three figures. A flash of black leather and bristled, porcine skin. Of broad backs and raised collars. A flash of auburn. An insinuation, in the chaos of the picture, of a smaller more delicate form, quicker than the others, a blur of colour and a flash of white.

And they are gone.

McAvoy finds himself alone in a missing informant's flat.

Finds himself sinking to his knees, bringing himself level with the ruined body of a man tortured to death, for allowing his woman to open her mouth.

'Nobody here,' says McAvoy, into the phone, and the words seem to make his tongue swell – make bile rise in his mouth.

He stops himself. Bites back the lies.

'Guv, I'm so sorry . . .'

CHAPTER 9

Home again. Tired and guilty, aching and sick.

It's not your fault. They were playing with bad people. It happened. Leanne could still be OK . . .

He has heard lots of soothing words in the past few hours, but none has helped him feel any better or cleansed his senses of the stench of Shaun's skin.

Pharaoh has taken over. A murder investigation has been launched, but the top brass have yet to decide whether it is to be folded into Pharaoh's existing investigation, or handed over to a separate CID team. McAvoy believes any attempts to remove it from Pharaoh's grasp would be madness, but knows, too, that his opinion counts for nothing. He's just the cop who found the body. The cop who has spent all day giving statements and having his clothes bagged by forensics officers because he went into the flat without a white suit on, and contaminated the crime scene.

He shakes his head, hating everything. Wishing he had listened a little harder. That he had run faster. Caught even one of them. They have nothing to go on. His description is even weaker than that given by the Vietnamese farmers who suffered the same injuries months before. The initial reports on the nails driven into Shaun's knees suggest they came from the same weapon as that used in the first attack, and the doctor's initial impression is that Shaun endured an hour of abuse before his heart gave out.

He has never been as grateful to leave the station. Never wanted to hold Roisin more.

She is upstairs now. Changing Lilah. Pleased to have her husband home early and hoping his presence in the house will allow her a few hours of proper sleep.

McAvoy should be enjoying it too. Should be up there, making them all giggle. Should maybe be getting his boots on and wandering around to pick up Fin from school. Should be revelling in the look on his son's face, the pleasure and pride at having the biggest dad in the playground.

With no instructions to follow or any ideas about where to look for Leanne, McAvoy had decided to have one last little look at the contents of the mobile phone he had fished out of the mud of the River Hull. He entertained a hope that, by looking at it again, he would satisfy his curiosity and be able to sling the damn thing away. Would be able to get focused. Get busy. Make amends.

He plugs the phone into his laptop. Begins to play.

Opening the contacts box, he scrolls through the

dots and numbers, whorls and compressed digits. He squints as he tries to make out something intelligible. Mc? MC2? Me?

McAvoy grabs a piece of paper from the pad by the phone and writes down the half-dozen variations that the numbers may be making up. He crosses to where his laptop is plugged in, and sits down in his armchair, his computer's battery pleasantly warm on his bare legs.

He logs on. Types in the first number that could vaguely fit with the jumble of numbers. Finds nothing but a string of serial numbers for a courier firm. Tries the next. 07969 . . .

Bingo.

There are three hits. The phone number is linked to a trio of sites.

McAvoy clicks on the first.

'Black cat, three years old, lovely temperament, missing from Anlaby area since last Sunday. If found, please call . . .'

McAvoy, hoping the animal turned up, clicks on the second link.

'New line-dancing club. All ages and abilities welcome. Experienced instructors and fun atmosphere. Every Wednesday at St Mark's Church Hall, Anlaby Common. Call Simon. 07969 . . .'

McAvoy nods. He is building a picture. Starting to care.

The third link takes him to playmatez.co.uk. He stares at the white screen, its gaudy purple banner;

thumbnail pictures of women in fishnets, and men showing off bare torsos, exposed genitals.

The Number 1 Hook-up Site on the Web! Swing When You're Winning!

McAvoy turns from the screen. Looks at the door. Prepares an explanation in case Roisin walks in.

Turns his attention back to the laptop, unsure whether he is prying or being a policeman.

He scrolls down until he finds the phone number.

FILL ME UP. MAKE ME YOUR SLAVE. YOUNG, SLIM, OH-SO-EAGER MALE SEEKING DOMINANT MAN. ANLABY AREA. Call 07969 . . .

'Has somebody hurt you?'

His words are said under his breath, but they are laden with the weight of a growing unease.

McAvoy copies the posting. Creates a file on his desktop and saves the link and the words. Does the same with the lost pet forum and the line-dance club. Wonders why this matters. Why he needs to know. Why he doesn't just put the phone in the bin and agree that it's none of his business unless a crime has been committed. Wonders just how he has convinced himself, with such certainty, that this warrants his time.

'You want to help me?'

The voice floats down the stairs with none of its usual music. Roisin is growing more tired and irritable. She told him earlier that it has been three days since she spoke to another adult. That she had found herself humming the theme tune to Wibbly-Pig while walking back from taking Fin to school. That she had to make a conscious effort of will not to ask for the cake in the shape of the 'moo-cow' when popping to the bakery last weekend. She is craving stimulation. Needing adult time. Needing to be a young woman rather than a mum.

McAvoy runs his tongue around his mouth to make sure there are no biscuit crumbs to give him away. Gives a slight nod. Makes up his mind.

'I've got an idea . . .'

He hopes she'll squeal when he tells her that this evening, they are starting a line-dance class in Anlaby.

'You have to hold me closer . . .'

The dancer smells of red wine and garlic bread, microwave lasagne and menthol cigarettes. She's angling her pretty face upwards, eyes heavy-lidded and sweat moistening her face at the temples. She is in her mid-twenties, and has clearly done this before. She is grinding her toes into the hard-wood floor and lifting her red dress above pink young knees to show firm calves and red-painted toenails. Her arms are shooting out with such ferocity that McAvoy wonders whether she is being operated by remote control. She is even managing to hum along to the music, which, to McAvoy's ear, would sound the same backwards.

He tries to ignore her nearness and warmth. Concentrates on his footwork. Counts in his head. Holds her hips as if she were made of glass. Tries to remember whether the hold he is about to place her in is called a hammerlock or a full nelson, and wonders whether the 'Suzy-Q' she is performing will lead to osteoporosis in later life.

'One, two, three . . .'

He squints over her shoulder at where his wife is having the time of her life in the arms of a seventy-year-old man wearing yellow corduroy trousers and a designer shirt. His hands are on her buttocks. He appears to be mentally testing a cantaloupe for firmness.

McAvoy and his wife came dressed for country and western. They found it was salsa night.

'Yes, it used to be Wednesdays, but we changed it,' said the nice middle-aged woman on the door. 'Salsa's more fun. Great for the youngsters. Beginners welcome. Only £5 each. Refreshments at half-time. And Mike used to be a county champion . . .'

Roisin had squealed and begged him to give it a go. Told him they could still go line-dancing another night if that was what he had set his heart on. Said it was a shame to waste the babysitter, and that he might love it.

He is not loving it. Salsa merely gives him indigestion.

'It's in the hips,' says Mike, rotating his own in a manner that, if performed outside the confines

119

of the church hall, could see him locked up for indecency. 'Excellent. Yes, grind it. Grind it!'

Mike is shouting this last at McAvoy's current partner, and she obeys, putting enough twist into her movements that he wonders whether her high heel will remain screwed to the floor when they separate and move on to the next person in the circle.

'That's it, my lovely. It's about sex!'

McAvoy looks as though he has been running in the rain. He is soaked through with sweat, his white shirt clinging to his skin and his jeans uncomfortably damp. His face is bright red with embarrassment and exertion, and exposed in its entirety due to Roisin's decision to slick his hair back from his forehead with her hand when she spotted him beginning to drip on his partners.

'. . . and rest.'

The sound of drums and Spanish guitar crashes to a stop, and the dozen people in the circle give a little cheer and clap one another.

McAvoy is breathing like a hot bull mastiff, and can barely even muster a polite smile when his partner squeezes him on his sodden arm.

'It takes some getting used to,' she says sympathetically. 'I took to it straight away but some people can take longer.'

'There are fish on dry land who dance better than me,' gasps McAvoy, bending over and placing his hands on his thighs as if he has just run a marathon. He feels her pat him on his broad back.

'Don't give up on it. You've got rhythm.'

He straightens up. Manages a little laugh. 'Just not the same one as everybody else.'

The girl extends her hand. McAvoy wipes his own on his jeans and takes hers in his palm. 'Mel,' she says.

'Aector,' he replies. It feels odd that he has introduced himself by anything other than his rank. He wonders why he has done so. Wonders if he is subconsciously reminding himself that he is not here as a policeman. He is not here on official business. That he's just a nosy bugger, lying to his wife . . .

'Aector, did you see me?'

McAvoy turns as Roisin excitedly bounds up to him. 'You were great,' he says instinctively.

'I know! This is awesome, Aector.'

'This is Mel,' he says, by way of explanation for the attractive, sweating woman at his side. 'I'm turning her feet into flippers. I don't think she sees me as a potential rosette winner.'

Roisin seems to notice her husband's dance partner for the first time. She looks her up and down. Red dress. Hair tied back into a ponytail and tethered with a silk red rose.

'We thought it was line-dancing tonight,' she says brightly, gesturing at her own red-and-white gingham blouse, tied above her belly-button, denim shorts and fawn, knee-length leather boots. 'This is so much better.'

'The line-dancing club's changed nights,' says Mel.

'So they said.'

'There aren't many people go to it now anyway,' she says, and she shifts the direction of her conversation from McAvoy to his wife. 'And they're all ancient. I went to it a couple of times when it was half-decent. Was a real giggle. These days they'll be lucky to get enough people to make an actual line. Not like it was.'

'People get bored with it, did they?' asks McAvoy.

Mel shakes her head. 'Different tutor,' she explains. 'Boring lady took over and all the people who used to come for the giggle packed it in.'

'The giggle?'

'Simon,' she says, and instantly breaks into a smile. 'He and his aunt used to run it. Was more of a cabaret night. Was such a laugh.'

'Has he gone to another club?' asks Roisin. 'We could maybe go there . . .'

Mel shakes her head. 'No,' she said. She looks away. 'It's sad.'

McAvoy pinches the sweat from his nose. Forces himself not to push it. Lets the two girls talk. Listens and takes notes in his head.

'We didn't know he was so unhappy,' says Mel.

'Quit, did he?' asks Roisin.

'Killed himself,' says Mel, matter-of-factly. 'Put a rope around his neck and hanged himself in his flat.'

McAvoy sniffs.

Blinks once.

'Poor lad,' says Roisin.

McAvoy nods. Tries to sound cool. 'What was his name?'

Mel pulls out her phone. Scrolls through. 'Simon,' she says sadly, and holds up the screen to reveal a grainy picture of a tall, thin, sweaty and smiling young man. 'Simon Appleyard.'

McAvoy looks at the phone number that is displayed across the young man's image.

He blinks once, like a camera taking a picture.

Files away digits he already knows.

CHAPTER 10

1 1.13 a.m. Courtland Road Police Station on the Orchard Park Estate. A pretty name for a shithole.

Used to be a decent area, this. Still is, in places. Still a few homeowners who give a damn and scrub their front step and pick up the crisp packets and empty beer bottles that roll on to their well-tended front lawns. Still people who give a damn, and who believe that once the empty high-rises are torn down and the druggies moved on, this community of tiny terraces and low-rent flats will be an address to brag about.

For the time being they're grateful for the near-ness of the cop shop.

The Major Incident Team operate from the first floor: a cramped warehouse of grimy computer terminals and coffee-streaked desks; of overstuffed files, bulging in-trays and mucky cups. A room joyless as a cell, decorated with crime-prevention posters, with overlapping memos and codes of practice, all spreading out from a streaky white-board where the names of active cases are scrawled illegibly in red marker pen.

Broken blinds fail to blot out the rain and the view. Strip lights buzz overhead and turn this oppressively quiet room the colour of gone-off milk.

McAvoy looks up from his borrowed desk.

Biker boots thudding on the thin blue carpet.

A waft of Issey Miyake perfume strong enough to catch the back of his throat.

Bangles jangling as if their wearer is rattling a tambourine.

Hair swishing sensuously against the collar of her leather jacket . . .

McAvoy feels disloyal for even thinking it, but Trish Pharaoh does not have a natural gift for covert surveillance. The other senses announce her presence long before the eyes take her in.

'Aector, my boy. Mummy needs a hug.'

She plonks her backside down on his desk, creasing the computer printouts he is carefully going through with a ruler and highlighter. She leans forward and puts her head on his shoulder, then proceeds to trundle it back and forth. 'I hate them all,' she says.

McAvoy looks around. There are three civilian support staff sitting at nearby desks, but there are no other police officers in the room. He lets himself smile.

'They being mean, Guv? The brass?'

'They are being wankers, Aector.'

'Wasn't it you that told me not to expect too much of people? That when an idiot is an idiot, it should not arouse surprise?'

Pharaoh removes her head from his shoulder and pulls a face. 'Did I say that? I don't think I said "idiots".'

'You said "tossers", I think.'

'Yeah, it's coming back.'

Pharaoh has spent the morning with the head of CID, Detective Chief Superintendent Andrew Davey. His underlings call him 'the accountant' though they occasionally drop a vowel. In truth, he's a decent enough career officer in his late forties whose life seems to involve nothing but form-filling, committee reports and a desperate and futile succession of spreadsheets designed to keep the holiday rotas from clashing. He does not tend to interfere in the running of the various CID teams. A small-framed, smartly dressed man with chronic indigestion and glasses that leave grooves in the sides of his long nose, he looks to McAvoy like a man who needs a good cry.

'How did it go?'

Pharaoh rolls her eyes. Her lashes momentarily stick together, and she pulls them apart with chewed fingernails that, though bitten to the quick, have been painted red.

'I've got a "watching brief", whatever that means. Shaun's murder's going to regular CID, but under my supervision, though they made it clear they wouldn't trust me to supervise the boiling of a kettle at the moment. They seem to think Leanne's at the root of it, but you and I both know that's bollocks. Davey made it plain that they think she

126

set us up, and Shaun too, but that's just the way she is. You know that. I know that. She's either so bloody frightened she's gone to ground, or they've got her too . . .'

McAvoy accidentally meets her eyes and quickly looks away.

'We'll catch them,' he says. 'Nail Gun and Blow Torch. They can't just . . .'

'They sound like a tag team, Hector. Or really shit superheroes.'

'And the third man,' McAvoy carries on. 'It doesn't feel right. None of it does. They've done these things to send a sign. We need to send one back. You will get them, Guv.'

Pharaoh smiles. 'We will,' she says. 'Well, somebody will. I won't. I'm being shunted sideways a little. Out of harm's way for a bit. They're asking me to look at some of the "peripherals" of the case, which has to be one of my favourite phrases of the day.'

McAvoy closes his eyes. Shakes his head.

'Colin Ray?'

Pharaoh smiles, ruefully. 'He's taking over as lead. Taking a fresh look at what we've done so far. I've got Daniells and a list of errands. Ray's the fresh pair of eyes this case needs, apparently.'

'You fought it, though,' says McAvoy, appalled. 'I know you fought it.'

Pharaoh holds up a hand and extends the index finger. 'I think I left a nail in his desk.'

McAvoy doesn't know what to say, so just stares at the carpet. Eventually Pharaoh gives a sigh and then straightens herself up. 'Come on,' she says brightly. 'It won't have much to do with you. You shouldn't be so wary of Ray anyway. He's a good copper, he's just a twat. You've got bigger things to worry about, like writing a report saying I'm ace and the MIT is rubbish and that they should give me more resources and money, and a daily bottle of Zinfandel.'

McAvoy rubs a hand over his face as he gives in to a grin. 'I'll do my best.'

'I'm not even going to ask you how it's looking,' she says, clearly asking. 'We're expensive, aren't we? The unit? You know we'll be the first to go in the budget cuts, no matter what the new chairman is saying. And we've had a couple of high-profile fuck-ups these last few days.'

'You weren't to blame,' he says and means.

She looks through the glass at the rain-lashed car park. Manages a smile.

'Thanks, Hector, but it wasn't my finest hour. Shouldn't have committed to the raid without being 100 per cent. I fought my corner, mind. Told them the pressure on us for results is going to lead to these balls-ups. They don't get it, though. They're too far removed. They don't know much more than they read in the papers, and according to the tabloids Hull's going to hell.'

'It's never been paradise,' says McAvoy, trying to make her smile. 'They exaggerate. That's what they do. It's a power struggle over a drug that will be legal in a few years. People are flexing their muscles. Somebody's trying to prove they're a big man, and people are getting hurt.'

'We could have had them,' says Pharaoh despairingly. 'Could have wrapped it up.'

'You don't really think these thugs are in charge, do you? They're just muscle. We catch them, there's still whoever is giving them their orders to worry about. And we know they must be serious. The Vietnamese don't play nicely. Whoever's taken over their operation must be one heck of a player.'

'That's not for us to think about,' says Pharaoh moodily. 'They may just be the hired thugs, but they're the ones we want. They're torturers. Now they're murderers. In the public's opinion, they're the ones we want off the streets – not the ones who have a fortune in the bank from farming bloody cannabis. It's not a drugs operation, any more. Not really. It all has to be accounted for, Hector. Has to be on the right fucking spreadsheet . . .'

McAvoy nods. Realises just what a balancing act it is to chase criminals without offending the other specialist units. Some of this investigation should be in the hands of the Drugs Squad. But Pharaoh, for now at least, is keeping their hands off it – much to the dismay of Detective Superintendent Adrian Russell, who has made his displeasure known. He's good at displeasure. He causes a lot of it.

'They could have killed us,' she says. 'They could have wedged the doors shut and burned us to death.'

'Don't think like that, Guv.'

'I'm not being morbid, Aector,' she says. 'I'm confused. These bastards don't think twice about nailing people's hands to their kneecaps and they get a chance to cook a van full of cops and don't take it?'

McAvoy considers. 'Maybe they didn't want that level of interest. Maybe it was a warning. There would have been uproar if anybody had been badly hurt.'

Pharaoh shrugs again. 'We've got a few leads to follow up, that's the main thing. The car park at Peter Pang's picked up their registration plate. Reported stolen from a high-class car showroom in Doncaster the day of the raid.'

'Donny?'

'Yeah, apparently people in South Yorkshire can afford £50,000 cars. Who'd have thought?'

'Anything else?'

'Yeah, there's a partial fingerprint recovered from the glass bottle they threw at us. Belongs to a bloke with a record long as your arm. Your arm, not mine. GBH. Embezzlement. Did years for armed robbery. Real piece of work.'

'Name?'

'Alan Rourke.'

'Doesn't ring a bell . . .'

'Bad sort,' she says. 'Connected to some real villains . . . Aector, look sharp!'

130

She jumps off his desk and stands up straight, dragging him to his feet by his collar and bodily spinning him to the door. Peter Tressider, the chairman of the Police Authority, has just entered the room, and is waving a hand in the general direction of Detective Chief Superintendent Davey, who is trailing behind him with the look of uncontrolled panic on his face.

Tressider looks around the room, completely ignoring whatever it is Davey is trying to say in his ear. He spots McAvoy, and his mouth opens in pleasant surprise. He crosses the room with his arms outstretched, and for a second McAvoy fears he is about to be taken into a bear hug.

'Sergeant,' he says warmly, and pumps McAvoy's hand with a vast, fleshy paw. 'Good to see you again. Heard about last night's excitement. Fun and games, eh? My word, I know we gave you a grilling but we didn't expect you to go and risk your life over statistics. Still, sometimes you have to rush in headlong, eh? I think I read that in a book about the samurai, or the like. Was it Ninjas? Anyway, excellent read. I'll lend you it. You ever read *The Art of War*? Fascinating stuff. Think I'll give it another once-over if I do make it to Westminster, eh? No shortage of bloody enemies there!'

McAvoy has to stop himself from physically recoiling in the face of the big, bearded politician's enthusiasm. 'It was a difficult operation, sir, but there are plenty of positives to take . . .'

Tressider waves a hand. It appears to be a habit of his. McAvoy wonders what political commentators will make of it should he get to the House of Commons. Whether they will applaud his earthy brusqueness, or dismiss him as an impatient dinosaur.

The chairman turns to Pharaoh. 'You must be the boss, yes? Pharaoh?'

Pharaoh smiles. Takes his hand. Manages not to wince as her palm is squeezed. 'Afraid so, sir.'

'Delighted you're still with us. Delighted! No shortage of people who would have taken a month off for stress, and yet here you are! Back at work and ready to lead. Impressive. Inspiring!'

Pharaoh gives a little half-laugh, unsure how to deal with this onslaught of optimism.

'I just want to catch the bastards,' she says, deciding to just be herself. 'Hope the powers that be let me do that.'

Tressider gives a nod of understanding. Taps his nose with a plump finger. 'We never spoke,' he says, winking. 'This conversation never happened. But don't you worry. I like your style.'

There is a moment's silence. 'Can we help you with something, sir?'

Tressider gives them both a warm smile. 'No, no, was just here for another meeting and thought I would show my face. Wanted to check you were all fit and healthy and raring to go. I hope I can trust you to keep me informed, and you can trust me to keep my nose out, yes?'

Both officers smile, and he shakes their hands again, even more vigorously than before. McAvoy glances over his shoulder at where Detective Chief Superintendent Davey is a picture of bewildered misery. As he looks back, he sees that the chairman's eyes have swivelled towards McAvoy's computer screen.

'Interesting?' he asks, nodding at the screen. 'A lead?'

McAvoy finds himself doing an odd thing with his mouth. Licks his lips. Twitches. Colours instantly. Remembers why he never plays poker.

'Just something I thought was worth checking out . . .'

'Show me.'

He clicks on the story he had tried to cover up when he sensed Pharaoh approach. The *Hull Daily Mail* article on the death of Simon Appleyard. Pharaoh, as in the dark as Tressider, reads halfway down and turns to McAvoy. He meets her eye purely through fear that, were he to look anywhere else, his view might take in her cleavage.

'Pet project?' she whispers.

McAvoy opens his mouth. Closes it again. Hangs his head. 'It's just something that doesn't feel right.'

He had found the story during a half-hearted Google search on his mid-morning break. It made him sad. The telephone's owner has an identity now. McAvoy has been reading the words of a real person. A loving, gregarious, confused young man who wrapped a cord around his neck and squeezed his own life away.

'The way he writes . . .'

McAvoy struggles to put it into words. Cannot explain why, from the outset, he has felt such unease.

'Writes?' asks Tressider.

'There's something about his death that troubles me,' he says, and he feels sweat prickling on his forehead. Can picture two men standing by the River Hull in the pouring rain. Can see the phone sitting on the mud. Can see himself slithering down the dock wall to pick up the device that has led him here. Wonders what the fuck he was thinking and how badly this will end.

'Follow your guts, my boy,' says Tressider, and he appears to lose interest. 'You can't go wrong if you do that. Anyway, it's been a pleasure. Mrs Pharaoh, I look forward to our next meeting, and Aector – did I get that right? – I'm delighted to hear you're unharmed. Do keep me posted.'

He turns away. Gathers up Davey the way a tornado snatches cattle, and bangs out of the door like a benign storm.

'I'm thinking about hurting you,' says Pharaoh eventually. 'I'm not going to do it, but there will be a part of me this afternoon that will regret not punching you in the head, I hope you realise that.'

McAvoy looks down. Keeps quiet.

'Were you going to tell me?' she asks.

'There was nothing to tell. Not really.'

She gives a frustrated sigh. 'Like we're not busy enough.'

'I can do it in my own time.'

'You haven't got any time, Hector. You're up to your eyes in drug dealers and babies. It was only yesterday that bugger told us he wanted violent crime stats down inside a quarter. And now you want to turn a suicide into a murder investigation?'

'It just needs a bit of a dig, Guv . . .'

Pharaoh throws her hands up. Looks at the closed door, as if Tressider were still there. She shrugs. Appears to reach a decision.

'Fuck it. I'm only on peripherals. And the boss said to follow your gut. Give it a dig. And if you balls up the crime statistics, it was all Colin Ray's fault. Deal?'

McAvoy smiles.

'Deal.'

The elements have made Hull a city of gargoyles. McAvoy has never seen so many faces locked in grimaces. Attractive office workers snarl into the driving wind. Shoppers popping to Marks & Spencer to pick up their evening microwave meal gurn angrily at the rain. The entire Old Town seems to be wincing.

It is just gone lunchtime. Whitefriargate, here on the periphery of the city centre's nucleus, should be bustling with shoppers. Instead the weather has forced everybody indoors. McAvoy has the broad,

135

attractive shopping street to himself. He's one of the few people who bother to look up. Lets his eyes roam past the first floor and enjoys the architecture: the handsome old mercantile palaces that lead down to the Museums Quarter and the waterfront. Enjoys the ornate frontage of the bank on the corner of Parliament Street. Lets himself daydream a little. To imagine this street when Hull was living its best days rather than remembering them.

He's glad he walked. Likes to feel the city beneath his feet. Wishes the destination was further away.

The files from the Simon Appleyard case have not yet been electronically input, and the paper copies are still at the Coroner's Court. He is enjoying the walk. Looking forward to an hour or two in a quiet room, immersing himself in the final moments of a prematurely ended life.

His booted feet leave large prints on cobbles that seem to have been dyed the colour of varnished clay by the incessant rain.

The smell of spit-roast chicken assails him from the butcher's shop. He realises he has not eaten since yesterday. Makes a mental note to admit this to Roisin when he gets home, so as not to be accused of hiding things from her, and then wonders if it would be kinder to conceal it so she does not feel pressurised into making him something as soon as he walks in. Wonders if she will think that he is trying to make her feel guilty.

Whether it would not just be easier to tell her that last night they went to the dance class so he could find out why somebody had buried a mobile phone.

He wonders if this is how other people feel. Wishes, just once, he had a clue how to live.

He continues to salsa in his mind as he makes his way to the attractively named Land of Green Ginger. The little side street is home to two pubs, a legal office, a beauty salon and a courtroom, though not all of these facilities are mentioned by the leasing agents who try to flog the seemingly endless apartment developments springing up in this part of the Old Town.

He prepares his speech in his head. Wonders if they could help him. Just needs a quick favour. McAvoy knows a couple of the ladies at the Coroner's Court and feels instantly embarrassed when he acknowledges that they will probably cooperate for no other reason than they like him.

He can feel the wind and rain doing him good. Breathes deeply. Enjoys the scent of distant sea spray and motor oil. Inhales the greasy aromas of the butcher's, the sandwich shops. Sucks in a lungful of the ever-present cloud of cigarette smoke that hangs outside the dark-blue door of the amusements as the punters spend their slot-machine winnings on tobacco and five-for-a-pound lighters.

He wonders if he loves this city or wishes it dead. The phone in his inside pocket rings and he ducks into the doorway of a trendy new clothes shop to take the call.

'DS McAvoy, Serious and Organised.'

'Sergeant Arthurs, Silly and Slapdash.'

McAvoy moves to one side to allow two teenage girls access to the shop. Despite the weather, they have bare legs beneath short, pleated skirts, and their hooded jumpers are soaked through. He wants to know whether they should be in school. Whether they are OK. How old they are. What they want. Whether they're safe . . .

'Thanks for calling me back, Sergeant,' he says, forcing himself to turn his eyes back to the street. 'It's about an incident you attended last November.'

'Yep, you said in your message,' Arthurs says brightly. McAvoy has not met the uniformed officer, but from his voice fancies he is in early middle age and almost certainly a dad.

'Simon Appleyard.'

'I'm sorry, can you give me a little more . . .'

'The hanging at Springfield Court. You attended.'

'Oh right,' says Sergeant Arthurs, recollection dawning. 'Yes, sad one that. The landlord found him, I think. Inquest was just a few weeks back. Open verdict, wasn't it?'

McAvoy nods, and realises the other man cannot see it. 'Yes,' he says. 'What can you tell me?'

'Well, it's not that exciting,' says the other policeman. 'The landlord needed to get in to read the meter. Couldn't get any answer. Let himself in and there he was. Dead in the kitchen. Slumped forward on his knees. I think the rope was tied to a knife rack on the wall. He'd been there a few days. Me and Shelley Dalston attended. WPC Dalston. You know her?'

'No,' he says, not wanting to be sidetracked. 'I'm on my way to look at your report right now actually. Can you give me the abridged version?'

Sergeant Arthurs gives a little laugh. 'The highlights? Well, he was naked, there's a start for you. Oh, and he was covered in baby oil. Proper covered in the stuff. What else do you want to know? There was no note, I can tell you that much.'

McAvoy looks up at the sky. The clouds remind him of kerbside snow; bulging and dirty-white.

'What's in the forensics report?'

'Well the whole thing went up to CID after we did our bit and they gave it about five minutes of their valuable time. When the inquest was coming up I asked a couple of questions on what had come of it all. Pathologist said cause of death was strangulation. Earned her money that day, eh?'

Across the road, a smartly dressed man appears from the glass-fronted doorway of a legal office. He pushes open a large gold umbrella that almost knocks over a middle-aged woman who is struggling with something heavy in an Argos bag. He wills the man to apologise. To admit his mistake and help her. To be good. Watches the man walk away.

'Was there anything on his computer, do you know? Was it sent to the tech unit?'

'No computer, as far as I can recall,' says the sergeant. 'That's almost a story in itself these days. I don't think he had much in the way of family, though. I seem to recall he was into dancing, if that's any good to you. What exactly is it you're looking into?'

McAvoy had hoped the question would not be asked, but was prepared for it. 'Another police service has been in touch,' he lies. 'CID in Berkshire have got two apparent suicides. There's a chance they were logging on to a website where people could share tips on how to bump yourself off.'

'And they think our lad might have done that? No, like I say, no laptop.'

'No phone?'

'Not that we could see. His next of kin lives miles away so it was another force that broke the news. His auntie came to ID him. Lovely lady . . .'

'Did you ask her about his phone?'

There is a pause, as if the other man is thinking. 'I'm not . . . oh hang on, yes. Yes, when we picked her up she said she had been ringing him for the few days before he was found. Hadn't picked up. Hadn't even texted back . . . yeah, I guess that means he must have had a phone.'

'Did you put that in your report? Did CID know that?'

'It will have been in my pocketbook, that's for sure. But no, I think I'd written up the incident report before I spoke to his auntie.'

McAvoy falls silent.

'The other lads gay as well, were they?' asks Sergeant Arthurs, his tone jocular.

'I'm sorry?'

'The other suicides. Gay as well?'

'How do you know he was gay?'

The man laughs. 'I'm not being a twat, mate. He was gay, that's all. You could kind of tell.'

McAvoy feels himself get hot inside his damp clothes. 'And how does one "just tell"?'

'Well, I don't know many straight lads with peacock feathers tattooed on their backs, do you?'

McAvoy is silent. Swallows. 'Well, no.'

'Anyway, it said in the paper, didn't it? At the inquest.'

McAvoy scratches his head. Watches the lady with the heavy shopping readjust herself, leaning the burden on a bollard. She puts her weight on a loose paving slab and dirty water splashes up her leg. Her face twitches. Tears begin to fall.

He asks his next question straight out. 'You think it was suicide?'

Sergeant Arthurs blows out a noise that suggests deep thought. 'I think so,' he says eventually. 'I didn't at first. Thought he was into that auto-erotic stuff. Maybe a game went wrong. But no, that was a lonely life. Was just a shabby existence. I think he bumped himself off.'

McAvoy thanks the other man for his time. Is about to hang up, already hoping the actual case file will be more useful.

'Oh, hang on,' says Arthurs. 'There was one thing

surprised me when I flicked through the file. There was no mention of the bruise.'

McAvoy stops. 'What bruise?'

'On his back,' says Arthurs. 'In among all the peacock feathers and the bloody baby oil.'

CHAPTER 11

Electric fire, lit to the third bar.

Glowing red: hot against his cheek.

No other light in this stuffy, airless room.

McAvoy, squinting, struggling to see the words he is scribbling in his notebook with a pen that tears holes in the damp pages.

'Do you think somebody killed him?'

The question comes from nowhere, and is asked in a voice that sounds like an enquiry into whether he would like another piece of cake.

McAvoy doesn't raise his head. He doesn't know what facial expression to pull. He does not know the answer. Does he think Simon Appleyard was killed? Her question forces him to consider his thoughts. He realises he has been behaving as such from the start. Acknowledges that, in his heart, he already feels he is hunting a killer.

Wonders why.

He is a procedural, methodical detective, given to only occasional flashes of instinct and hunch. He has nothing on which to base his feeling that a life has been taken before its time.

'I think there are questions to be answered,' he

says and hopes she will leave it at that. He is habitually beset by feelings of guilt and uncertainty, unsure who or how to be. Here, now, in this tiny two-bed terraced house with its unmowed front lawn and unfashionable wallpaper, its impersonal prints and half-hearted tidiness, he feels he does not deserve to be treated so warmly. He fear that he is, to all extents and purposes, trying to make her cry. He needs her to harbour fears and doubts. Wants her to tell him to dig and claw and kick until he gets her answers. Needs to feel that he is prying into her nephew's death for more noble reasons than his own macabre curiosity.

He looks at her. Nods to show the tea is lovely, and commits her image to memory.

Carrie Ford was probably very pretty twenty years and 5,000 cheeseburgers ago. Beneath a hefty layer of fat, McAvoy can make out what was once a willowy, elegant frame. Her green eyes and quick smile are anachronisms in a doughy, make-up-free face that sits atop a careless, dumpy frame.

She is dressed in her supermarket uniform. White polyester dress and green tabard, concealed beneath a plus-sized denim jacket. She looks her age. She looks as though six months of grief have carved a lifetime of wrinkles into her skin.

She had been on her way to work when he knocked on the frosted-glass door.

'Thought you were the taxi,' she says again, as

she pours McAvoy a second cup of tea. Then, for the third time, 'Work can wait, eh?'

She is a nice woman. She lives alone in this two-bedroomed semi-detached, a short walk from work and two minutes from where her nephew died bug-eyed and helpless on a blue cord carpet.

'That's our Simon,' she says, waving in the direction of the mantelpiece.

There are half a dozen birthday cards obscuring photo frames and ornaments and McAvoy cannot see whom she means. She crosses to the fireplace. Retrieves a picture in a cheap frame. Hands it to McAvoy with a smile.

'That's from the class. Our class. The line-dancing. See the smile on his face? That's when he was happiest. Performing. Helping people learn. Getting other people excited.'

In the poor light, McAvoy has to angle the picture as though trying to cast a shadow on the ceiling with the glass. Squinting, he looks at the picture of the lean, dark-haired lad. He is smiling broadly for the camera and the image, though far from flattering, is a happy one. Simon's fringe is damp with exertion and flopping over his eyes, and there is a sheen of sweat across his neck and chest where it slopes into a sleeveless sweatshirt, slashed provocatively at the collar. McAvoy angles the picture again. Sees his own face in the reflection. Hurriedly tilts it back.

'You had no indication?' he asks. 'Never felt he was depressed?'

145

Mrs Ford sits down on the high-backed armchair.

McAvoy, on the far corner of the matching two-seater sofa, wishes he had taken her up on her offer to hang up his coat. He is too hot, his damp clothes beginning to steam in the heat from the three-bar electric fire she had turned on instinctively as she led him into the tiny living room.

'He had his ups and downs,' she says, and looks at the picture in McAvoy's hands. Wordlessly, he hands it over to her, and is touched by the tenderness with which she looks at the photograph.

'There was mention at the inquest of difficulties with his father. With his sexuality . . .'

Mrs Ford pulls a face. Holds the photograph to her chest. 'Only person who had difficulties with his sexuality was his dad,' she says. 'My brother, before you ask. Always was an arsehole.'

'He didn't have much to do with Simon as a child?'

'Neither of them did. Mum or Dad.'

'That can't have been easy,' he says. 'Nobody to talk to . . .'

Mrs Ford waves her hands, dismissively. 'Simon knew what he was from being a kid,' she says. 'Never bothered him. He was outgoing, you know? Full of life. He never hid who or what he was. And his dad had no right to even comment.'

'But he did comment, yes?'

She sighs. Looks again at the birthday cards on the mantelpiece. 'They're from my class,' she says.

'Line-dancing. Not many left now. Not the same without Simon. He was the attraction, I know that. So funny. Would have been a great DJ. Was him that got the crowds in. They didn't come to learn how to line-dance.'

'I hear he was quite a dancer too.'

'Simon could do anything,' she says and her voice sounds far away.

'Everything I've heard about him suggests he was a lovely lad,' says McAvoy. Such lines often help.

'I raised him, you know,' she says, appearing to snap back into the present. 'His mum wanted nothing to do with him and his dad, well, he was bloody hopeless. He lived with me most of his childhood. Never had kids of my own. Never married, though don't be thinking I'm some spinster. There have been fellas. Simon was the only constant thing in my life.'

McAvoy realises he is talking to a woman who was all but a mother to the dead man. Tries to understand how that must feel.

'He grew up here?'

'No, love. I only moved in here a few years back. Always lived in Anlaby though. Him and me have lived in nigh-on every flat in the village. Gypsies, I think we are, though we never move far . . .'

McAvoy sits back in the chair and lets her talk. Tries to craft a person from her memories.

'His dad would come back now and then,' she says, scornfully. 'He'd ring, when he remembered.

Would sometimes send a few quid. But there was no closeness there. His dad wanted a lad he could take to the football and down the pub. Simon wanted to dance and write poetry. It was awful, watching him realise that everything about him was grotesque in the eyes of his own father. He was thirteen the first time his dad called him a poof. Can you imagine?'

McAvoy closes his eyes. Takes a sip of his cold tea.

'At the inquest there was talk of some text messages? An argument with his dad?'

Mrs Ford puts her hands together in her lap and her leg begins to jiggle. She is either nervous, or trying not to let her emotions get the better of her.

'Who hasn't done that? Who hasn't had a couple of drinks and sent some text messages telling the world you're pissed off? That's life. It is these days, any road.'

McAvoy nods. 'He texted a lot?'

'Fiend for it,' laughs Mrs Ford. 'Hundreds of them a day if you were daft enough to reply more than once. Him and Suzie almost starved themselves to death trying to get enough cash to buy one of those fancy phones. He was still saving when it happened. Silly lad. Should have spent it before he did it, don't you think? Go out on a high.'

McAvoy makes a show of looking through his notebook. 'Suzie?'

Mrs Ford pinches the bridge of her nose, as if suddenly beset by sinus pain. She looks down at her name badge. Reads it, as if looking for proof of who she is.

'Thick as thieves, them two.' She smiles. 'Wish I could tell you her last name. Awful, isn't it, not knowing, but you don't ask these days, do you? Lovely girl. Mad as a box of frogs, of course. The clothes! Looks like she's in fancy dress half the time, but would do anything for my Simon. Inseparable, they were.' She stops. Appears to be struggling with something. 'I don't think they were bad influences on one another, or anything. Just brought out the devil in one another. Suzie split up with her fella just before she and Simon became friends. Simon was a good listener. They had some silly idea for getting back at her ex. Made some silly mistakes. But they learned from them . . .'

McAvoy has only had time for the quickest of glances through the case file and has found no mention of any female friend. 'School pal?'

'No, they met on a writing course,' she says, with a touch of pride. 'That's what he would have liked to do, I think. Be a writer. Or a poet, in a different time. He had such a lovely gift with words. Even when he was texting he'd try and make it sound pretty.'

Placing his teacup down on the floor beside the sofa, McAvoy leans forward. 'Mrs Ford, it doesn't sound as though you think for a moment that he took his own life.'

She grimaces, and then breathes out a sigh that appears to have come from the heart. 'What do any of us really know about anybody else?' she asks. 'No, I wouldn't have thought of Simon as being that sort of person. He didn't smile all day like a clown, but he enjoyed enough of life to make the bad stuff OK. That's what it's about, isn't it? Life.'

McAvoy looks away so he doesn't have to answer.

'Mrs Ford, I need to ask you about Simon's personal life.'

'His sex life?' She smiles, warm and friendly. 'We'll both end up blushing.'

'He was promiscuous?'

'He was young.'

'He had a lot of sexual partners?'

'He enjoyed himself.'

McAvoy looks at his notebook. 'Mrs Ford, I need a little bit more. We have evidence that suggests Simon had made contact with a new sexual partner some time before he died.'

She shrugs. Looks at the photograph in her hands. 'Sergeant, I was his auntie. More of a mum than his real one. We had fun together and giggled more than most, but he didn't think to ring me every time some new bloke rolled off him.'

McAvoy instinctively pulls a face. She spots it. He tries to cover it up with a cough. Wants her to know it was her unnecessary crudeness and not the act that she described which caused him to shudder.

'So you didn't meet any boyfriends?'

'I met "friends",' she says, smoothing down non-existent creases in her uniform. 'Sometimes he'd get picked up from the church hall by a lad, or he'd tell me he'd been to see a play or for a drink or something and mention some bloke or other, but I didn't like to pry.'

'You indicated he was promiscuous . . .' he says cautiously.

She sits forward in her chair. It appears she is about to stand up and put the photo back on the mantelpiece, but she seems to decide against it and stays where she is.

'It's just things that Suzie and he said to each other,' she explains, waving a hand, vaguely. 'Maybe they were teasing each other, I don't know. They were like two kids. He'd make her blush, telling me to ask her what she'd been up to some night or another. She'd crack jokes about Simon being too worn out to give his all at some classes. Just the usual.' She glances at her watch. 'He wasn't shy, I know that much.'

McAvoy wonders if there is any more to be gained from this. Whether there ever was. He looks at his notes.

'He had tattoos, I'm told . . .'

'Oh yes,' she says brightly. 'Goodness, they were lovely. Got his first when he was just turned sixteen. Some lyric from a band he liked. Got a real taste for it after that.'

'I'm told his back was a work of art.'

She smiles. 'He'd have loved to hear you say that. They were in a magazine, you know. An advert in that glossy mag. I saw it in a doctor's waiting room, not long back. Simon would have been over the moon if he knew. I wasn't sure about it when he told me. You not being from round here you'll not know, but peacock feathers are awful bad luck.'

'They are where I come from as well.'

'Really? I thought it was a Hull thing.'

'No, I think it's the same everywhere.'

Mrs Ford sticks out her lower lip as though mulling over whether this matters. Decides it doesn't. 'Either way, I wasn't sure about them, but he was mad keen. He was going through his more, erm . . .' she searches for the word, before finishing with '"flamboyant" phase.'

'And this was?'

'Not more than a year ago. He and Suzie got their tattoos done the same day. They were both walking like they had sunburn for a few days afterwards but when he showed me I thought it looked lovely.'

'Why peacock feathers?'

'It was something he'd read, I think,' she says, looking at her watch again with a sudden expression that suggests work might not be able to wait much longer. 'Seemed to like peacocks for a while. It suited him. Just a phase, I suppose.'

McAvoy drums his fingers on his notepad. Taps his pen between his teeth. Wonders if he has

152

learned anything. Turns his face away from the three-bar heater and presses the backs of his hands to his too-warm cheeks.

'Do you think somebody may have killed him?'

He asks her the question outright, as she had asked him.

She does not answer for a time. Just looks at his picture and strokes the glass.

'I don't know,' she says eventually. 'In my heart of hearts, I suppose I'm frightened he died doing something a bit . . .'

'Yes?'

'. . . a bit mucky. I've read what people are into these days. I hope it wasn't that.'

He wants her to say it. Wants her to fear he was killed. Wants to turn his sense of disquiet into a sterile, official, evidence-led investigation, and needs her pain to make it so.

'Mrs Ford, do you have suspicions about third-party involvement?'

McAvoy is aware he's leaning forward, perhaps pushing too hard.

She meets his eyes.

'I'm not sure if I want to know,' she says, dropping her head. 'I can cope with him dead. It hurts, but I know how to grieve. If I thought somebody had hurt him . . .'

She looks back up.

Her eyes are wet but there is no danger of tears.

'"Dead" sounds so much more peaceful than "killed", don't you think?'

McAvoy doesn't answer.

He is certain he will soon destroy her peace.

Suzie is sitting at the kitchen table in the flat she rents above the florist on Anlaby Road. A fine rain mists the single-glazed window. The raffia blind and home-made curtains billow inwards as the breeze finds the cracks in the paintwork around the frame.

It is getting dark beyond the glass. Dark enough to switch the light on, should she find the inclination. The gaudy yellow of the street lights lends the view from the window an industrial, unnatural quality.

Sweet tea, that's what they swear by in the books. Good for shock. Calms your nerves. Better than Prozac apparently.

'Lying tossers,' she says, under her breath.

Suzie has drunk pints of the stuff since last night. Has put in enough sugar to give an elephant diabetes. And yet she still can't hold the mug steady as she raises it to her lips.

She looks again at the *Hull Daily Mail* website.

Three paragraphs and a phone number. Headline in blue, text in white.

Man Hurt in East Yorkshire Lay-by

A 44-year-old man is in intensive care after being involved in a suspected hit and run at an East Yorkshire beauty spot.

The man, visiting the area on business and said to be from West Yorkshire, was found by motorists at Coniston lay-by on the road to Bridlington late on Tuesday night.

Detectives are keen to talk to the person who made a 999 call from a nearby telephone box shortly after the incident. Anyone with information should call Humberside Police on 0845 6060222, or Crimestoppers, anonymously, on 0800 555 111.

It doesn't seem enough, somehow, but Suzie is pleased there is no more. Were it on the front page, she thinks she would probably buckle. She would call the number. She would admit it was her. She would tell them how she gets her kicks.

She stares at the laptop screen for an age. Reads the story over and over. Eventually the screensaver comes on. Herself and Simon, dressed for a Seventies night at Silhouettes night club. Orange afros, silver flares and huge collars. Big smiles.

Her head drops to her hands. She cried all she needed to when she got home last night and only lasted an hour at work this morning before telling them she felt sick and had to go home. She cried her last when she read the *Hull Daily Mail* story the first time. She has no tears left now.

She pushes the tea away. Crosses to the worktop and takes a packet of chocolate biscuits from a cupboard. Tears it open and stuffs two into her mouth as she leans back against the draining board. Wishes he were here.

She makes her way back to the table. She does not know what to do.

Flicks, distractedly, to the other stories on the site. There is a special article by the paper's crime reporter on the future of Humberside Police. It predicts swingeing cuts and redundancies. Suzie does not know what the sword 'swingeing' means, but it doesn't sound good. She reads a quote from the new chairman of the authority. He promises to secure all the funding he can during his tenure at the top, but warns that there are tough times ahead. The article says he is tipped to be the next MP for Haltemprice and Howden. Suzie wonders if people ever read this kind of shit for fun.

She opens another story. Skims through the details of a nasty-sounding attack on a man down Hessle Road. Anonymous 33-year-old beaten unconscious on his own doorstep. Neighbours claiming that he had been growing marijuana to help him deal with the pain of a motorcycle accident. Witnesses sought. Descriptions given of two heavy-set white men and a smaller, younger man, who left the scene in a four-by-four. Said to be the latest in a worrying explosion of drug-related violent incidents, and has been linked to the discovery of a body in the city's Dagger Lane . . .

Suzie loses interest. Turns away from the screen.

Next to the laptop her mobile sits dead and lifeless. She has not had the courage to turn it on.

Was it him?

The question is killing her. Was the man who insisted she perform for his pleasure merely setting her up? Was that his fantasy? To see her crushed beneath the weight of a half-naked stranger amid the sound of grinding metal and frothing blood? Or was it a mere accident? Was the man even there when it happened? Could he have seen something? Could he be a witness? Worse still, she thinks, what if he has already contacted the authorities and told them about her?

She looks at the door, imagining two uniformed policeman banging on it with angry fists, leading her away in handcuffs, her secrets pored over by all.

Suzie takes another bite of biscuit. Looks at the story one more time. At the newspaper's masthead. She remembers how the paper had dealt with Simon's death.

For no other reason than to change the picture on the screen, she types the name Simon Appleyard into the newspaper's search function.

Two stories.

One offering a name and age of the young man found dead in an Anlaby flat two days before.

The other from the inquest; held three weeks ago and too painful to attend.

A HULL woman has paid tribute to her 'gregarious and loving' nephew, who took his own life after sinking into a depression over his sexuality.

Hull Coroner Martin Duffy heard yesterday how 24-year-old Simon Appleyard was found dead at his Springfield Court flat in late November last year.

He had tied a length of rope around his neck and to a wall-mounted knife rack in his kitchen. He had been dead for four days when his landlord found his body.

Simon, who worked for a car valeting service in Wincolmlee, had won awards at a national level for line-dancing and ran a club in Anlaby.

His aunt, Carrie Ford, of Saffron Close in Willerby, told the inquest: 'He had times when he was down, like we all do, but it came as a shock to all who knew and loved him that he would be so unhappy. He had so much to live for. He was always so full of life and happiness. He was such a character, really outgoing and gregarious, with such a loving nature. I don't know what I'll do without him around to make me laugh.'

The court heard Mr Appleyard had been treated for depression as a teenager and had twice been prescribed anti-depressants. As a teenager, he had had difficulty accepting his sexuality and clashed with his parents when he came out as gay at the age of nineteen.

Although no note was found, text messages shown to the court by Mr Appleyard's father show he was feeling unloved and suicidal in the weeks before his death.

Kevin Appleyard, who travelled to the inquest from his home in Derbyshire, said, 'He said he was a disappointment. Said we were better off without him. Said I wouldn't accept who he was. I just wish I could hold him one more time . . .'

Suzie turns away from the screen, as disgusted now as when she had first read the stream of lies.

She feels sick that Simon's dad is even mentioned in the article. Disgusted that the man who battered and bullied her friend throughout his childhood would dare to suggest he had ever even hugged his son. Wonders whether, before he gave it to the coroner, Kevin Appleyard had the foresight to change his son's name in his phone to 'Simon' from 'poof'.

An email pops up in the corner of the screen. Instinctively she clicks on it.

Still on for Friday? Am already getting in the swing of things? Xx

The message is from a couple she knows as J & J. The male half of the relationship is an unattractive blond lad with Leeds United tattoos and poor spelling. The female J is a dumpy brunette with pierced nipples and glasses, who in Suzie's mind at least always seems to be wearing sticking plasters on her heels. They met at a party perhaps a year before. They were quite funny and lived near enough to Simon and herself to make them worth being friendly to. The strategy had saved them a fortune in fuel.

She wonders if she should ignore the message. Concentrate on her worries and woes. Manages to hold out for a full ten seconds before deciding she has nothing better to do than drop them a line back in return.

Hey you. Not sure about this time. Not feeling too good. Think I may bring the mood down. XX

She presses 'send'.

Gives it a minute, drumming her fingers on the table. Has another biscuit. Starts to reread the *Hull Daily Mail* report of the hit and run, then gets bored with herself and closes it down. She stares at the screen for a while as if debating, then clicks on one of the 'favourites' on her Internet browser. It takes her to the Xanadu homepage.

As ever, she feels a rush of excitement. In the

picture at the centre of the screen are a group of middle-aged men and women. They have blurred faces, thoroughly average bodies, and are unashamedly nude. With wide grins, they are all giving thumbs up to the camera.

Behind them, the flat green fields of Lincolnshire make the image look like a postcard. It just needs a slogan.

'We're fat and getting plenty,' she had once suggested to Simon.

Or, pointing at the thumbnail image of a 61-year-old woman in a love-swing and gimp mask, 'Does my bum look big in this?'

Go on, Blossoms. It's not a party without you. XX

Suzie can't help but smile. There's a birthday bash at Xanadu this Friday night. The owner, a tax inspector with matronly boobs and a liking for nipple clamps, is turning fifty. Christine and her husband, Big Dunc, have run Xanadu for eight years. As swinging clubs go, it's pretty plush. Set in three acres, two miles from the nearest house, it's Lincolnshire's best-kept secret. Christine and Big Dunc hold three get-togethers a week. One for couples, one for singles, and one where anything goes.

She flicks through the website, pulling faces and wondering what else she will do this Friday if she decides not to go along for her slice of cake and free glass of champagne. She's lonely. The thought makes her close her eyes. She has never really acknowledged it before. Since Simon she has been lost.

Suzie licks her lips. Prepares to type.

A thought occurs. Had she told him? Had she mentioned the party and the location? She has no way of checking without switching on her phone and scrolling through her messages, and she does not want to do that, so decides that she did not.

But last night . . .

It comes back again. The sound of the cars colliding. The crunch of bone. The splat of body hitting wet concrete.

Don't go, Suzie, she tells herself. *It's not the same any more.*

Would it be so bad? Were she ever asked to justify herself, Suzie would try and explain that there is a big difference between a swinging party and an orgy. The last one she attended at Christine's place she had spent most of the evening in the kitchen, helping the host make snacks and flicking through a copy of *Good Food*. She spent an hour nattering over a glass of wine with a nice woman from Dorset, talking about the best ways to iron a plastic bra.

Her fingers twitch above the keyboard. The story of the hit-and-run is open at the bottom of her screen. The report of Simon's inquest to the right. But the page that holds her attention offers freedom and fun; a Friday night of being young and hedonistic. A night of escaping from all the crushing reality.

You nearly got killed last night, she tells herself. The reply, in her mind, comes in Simon's voice. *All the more reason to live.* She nods. Makes up her mind.

What time are you leaving? XX

CHAPTER 12

'Is it two tees or two ells?' asks Daniells, his tongue wedged in his lower lip.

Pharaoh turns her head, slowly, a snarl already forming on her face.

'What?'

'Rottweiler,' he says, gesturing at his open pad with his biro. 'Double T or double L?'

For a moment she doesn't answer. Then she leans across, plucks the pen from between his forefinger and thumb, and with as much force as she can muster in the cramped confines of the little sports car, throws it at the side of his head. It bounces off and lands in the footwell.

Daniells pulls a face. Closes his pad and puts it back in his inside pocket. Then he mimes zipping and locking his mouth.

Pharaoh turns back to the window, where the larger of the two guard dogs continues to snarl, occasionally leaping up with an extra riot of barking to leave spit, steam and pawprints on the glass.

She would like to tell herself it had been a strategic and orderly retreat, but in truth she and Daniells had run for the car like Olympic sprinters when the dogs appeared and bared their fangs. It had been the right thing to do. The dogs had lowered their heads and torn after them in a gnashing fury and Daniells had lost the tail end of his coat when he slammed the passenger door.

'This is why we should have guns,' says Daniells, who has lost none of his cheer and appears to still be enjoying himself despite very nearly having his leg chewed off by an angry Rottweiler.

'What?'

'Guns,' he repeats.

She turns back to him. 'You'd shoot the dogs?'

He makes a gun of forefinger and thumb and mimes shooting the muscled, black-and-brown beast that is licking his window. He purses his lips, and blows on the tip of his index finger, as if it is smoking. 'Would be nice to have the option,' he says.

Pharaoh says nothing for a moment. Just stares. It's a look that makes him give an odd, nervous, half-grin. 'Get out,' she says.

'Pardon, Guv?'

'You're safer out there than in here.'

They sit in silence, broken only by the sound of the growling dogs and the thunder of rain on the glass.

'We could go,' says Daniells. 'Come back with the dog squad.'

Pharaoh has been thinking the same thing, but

the fact that Daniells has offered advice makes her bloody-minded. 'We're going nowhere,' she says.

The two-seater is parked on the driveway of Alan Rourke's bungalow. It's an attractive three-bedroomed property with imposing double-glazed bay windows framed by luxuriously gaudy drapes of crushed velvet and lace. The doorbell, when they pressed the buzzer, rang to the tune of 'Are You Lonesome Tonight?' They had been remarking on Rourke having a nice, albeit tasteless pad, when the two devil dogs emerged from the rear of the property and chased them back to the car.

'He must be able to hear them,' says Daniells. 'And his neighbours.'

It's a quiet cul-de-sac. A dozen detached properties with neatly tended gardens and leylandii trees; Mercedes estates parked on patterned red-brick driveways and well-tended hanging baskets next to uPVc double doors.

'They'll be used to it,' says Pharaoh, pulling down the vanity mirror and checking her mascara and lipstick.

She had not really given the animals much thought when she read through Rourke's file. The last contact the police had had with him was over a complaint that his two dogs had attacked a toddler who had been playing with a ball in his grandmother's garden. The file offered nothing more on the incident except to say the complaint had been withdrawn. Pharaoh could

166

only hope that the incentive to do so was financial rather than fear.

'Come on,' she says, more to herself than to her subordinate.

She stares at the door, as if willing it to open.

'Do you think he knows we're police?' asks Daniells.

Pharaoh gestures expansively, a display that takes in the tiny two-seater sports car and their plain clothes. 'I wanted the model with the flashing light but couldn't afford that and the CD-changer,' she says.

She blows out a sigh. Eases down the electric window a fraction.

'Mr Rourke,' she shouts. 'This is Detective Superintendent . . .'

Her words are lost in a cacophony of snarling and barking. Yellow teeth and frothing spit crash against the side of the car.

'For fuck's sake.'

She puts her head in her hands. Wishes McAvoy were here. Despite having the social skills of an excitable five-year-old, she rates DC Daniells as an officer. He is enthusiastic and eager. She has spent her working life surrounded by jaded cynics who can convince themselves that anything they can't be bothered to do is not worth doing. Daniells happily throws himself into the most skull-crushingly tedious tasks and is never less than grateful for the opportunity. She had been feeling well disposed towards him when she asked him to tag along for her chat with Rourke. He had called in a favour and managed to speed up the forensic results yielded by the shards of glass found at the scene of the petrol bombing. He had been so excited she almost offered to pull in at the service station to get him some sweeties as a tip.

She has to bite down on an involuntary smile as she imagines McAvoy, folded up and cramped in the passenger seat. She wonders what he would do. Presumes he would never have run from the dogs in the first place. Would have hummed them to sleep or banged their heads together. She wishes she had seen him talking to the escaped stallion. Can understand fully how he calmed the animal with his big eyes and soft words. Has experienced his almost other-worldly tenderness and empathy. She finds herself oddly jealous of the horse. It got the best of him. She wonders if the horse realises just what an annoying bugger her brilliant and hopeless sergeant can be.

'Nice place, isn't it?'

They are in one of the handsome villages that lie to the west of the city, Hull's version of a commuter belt and not the sort of place she would associate with a man like Rourke.

She reaches back onto the parcel shelf and grabs the printout of his record.

The mugshot shows a surly, stubble-cheeked man in his mid-fifties scowling out from beneath a shock of coiffed black hair turning grey at the temples. He is sporting a luxurious moustache she would associate with a Breton onion-seller, and his eyebrows could use a trim.

'Seven years,' she says, running her finger down his long list of offences and prison terms. 'That's a stretch.'

'Was that the GBH?'

'No, that was the armed robbery. Only got two years for the GBH. Provocation, apparently.'

'I'll bet.'

'He's been busy,' she says, and as she reads she finds herself growing more hopeful that she may have struck lucky. That the man she has come to interview is involved with the drugs gang she is so desperate to take down.

'Hang on . . .'

From the back of the property two men are emerging. One is unmistakably Rourke. He is dressed in black jeans, white trainers and an over-sized Fred Perry T-shirt that is too tight around strong, tattooed biceps and an impressive, over-hanging gut. With him is a younger man in bright green tracksuit trousers and an expensive leather jacket worn over a vest. He is thin and pinch-faced, and his hair, though recently shaved, is growing back ginger. He has a cigarette clamped between his lips and it rises skywards as he sneers angrily at the two occupants of the car.

'Mr Rourke, I'm Detective Superintendent . . .'

Her voice sets the dogs barking again, and the younger man laughs as she hurriedly pulls her mouth back from the slightly open window.

Rourke removes a tiny, unlit roll-up from his mouth. 'Ben. Dara. Cut.'

Both dogs stop their barking. They pad, obediently, to his side. He fondles their heads without taking his eyes from Pharaoh. Both dogs lick their muzzles happily. They could be different animals.

'Coppers?' Rourke asks the question.

Pharaoh nods.

Rourke gives a jerk of his head to indicate they are at liberty to get out of the vehicle. Pharaoh takes a deep breath and does so. As she hauls herself free of the low, cramped vehicle, her skirt rides up to reveal a large slice of attractive thigh. She pushes her hair back from her face and straightens her jacket, straightening her back with a movement that accentuates her figure.

Rourke does not change his expression, but the younger lad gives a leer.

'They should be locked up,' says Pharaoh, nodding at the dogs as she walks down the driveway and comes to a halt near enough to Rourke to encroach on his personal space. He smells of coffee, nicotine, hair gel and horses.

'They wouldn't hurt a fly,' he says, and his accent contains a tinge of Irish.

'I couldn't care less about flies,' she says. 'It's sinking their teeth in my arse that I'm not keen on.'

'That's a pity,' says Rourke, and the younger man laughs louder than the joke deserves. 'You look like the sort who'd enjoy it.'

Daniells has arrived at Pharaoh's side. He gives them all a big smile. 'Are they safe to stroke?' he asks brightly, seemingly having forgotten his desire of moments ago to put a bullet in their heads.

'They don't like coppers,' says Rourke. 'So yeah, stroke away.'

Daniells moves forward with his hand out but Pharaoh pulls him back.

Rourke smiles. 'He a bit soft upstairs?' he asks, jerking his head in the direction of the young, open-faced detective.

'He thinks the best of people,' she says, locking eyes with Rourke. 'We're chalk and cheese.'

Rourke shrugs. He pushes his damp hair back from his face with a dirty, cigarette-stained hand. 'What do you want?'

'Getting out of the rain would be a start,' says Pharaoh, looking up at the grey sky.

'Place is a pigsty,' says Rourke. 'We're grand here.'

Pharaoh doesn't push it. 'Who's your friend?'

The younger man takes his eyes off her cleavage and raises them to her face. 'I'm what you've been waiting for all your life,' he says.

If he means the words to be ironic, his face does not betray it.

'Really?' Pharaoh's voice oozes seductive menace. 'You don't look like a Lottery winner.'

Rourke gives a grin at that. His mood seems to soften. 'RJ here is doing a bit of work for me,' he says.

'Work? Heard you were allergic.'

Rourke gestures at his house. 'I'm doing OK.'

'Bank robberies pay well, I see.'

'All in the past, sister. I'm a good boy now.'

When he smiles, there is something endearing about Rourke. Although she has skimmed through his record, Pharaoh has to fight to remind herself that he is a violent criminal and not some lovable rogue.

'Tuesday night,' she says. 'Where were you?'

Rourke lifts his unlit, tiny roll-up to his mouth. Sucks on the end while thinking. 'Here,' he says. 'Like as not.'

'All evening?'

'I'll have been on the pop,' he says. 'Can't remember much after *Eastenders*. But aye, I'll have been here.'

'Can anybody confirm that? Your wife, perhaps? Your little friend here?'

'Doubt it,' he says, and his blue eyes twinkle with something Pharaoh can only think of as 'charm'. 'I aint seen the bitch in nigh on three years. And Ro here has business of his own of an evening. Treats the place like a hotel . . .'

'So you live alone?'

Rourke nudges the younger man with a meaty elbow and gives him a playful smile. 'I entertain the occasional lady caller,' he says, affecting an upper-class English accent.

Pharaoh nods. 'Do you want to know why I'm asking?'

'Not really,' says Rourke. 'But I don't really want you here, either, and that's happened, so chances are you're going to tell me.'

'Your fingerprints were found on a shard of glass,' she says.

'And?'

'Glass from a bottle that was filled with petrol, set alight, and thrown at a police van I happened to be sitting in.'

If Rourke is concerned he does not show it. He pulls a face and smooths down his moustache. 'I'm a bit old for petrol-bombing coppers. Young enough to do other stuff to them, mind.'

Pharaoh's patience snaps. 'Mr Rourke, try and imagine what's going on in my head right now.'

'Pretty picture?'

'It involves me ringing for a vanload of uniformed officers who will trample all over your front garden, kick in your front door, tranquillise your dogs, lead you out of here in handcuffs and throw you in a cell. Then we'll have this conversation again and you'll wish you'd just helped me out when you had the chance. So here's your chance. Why do you think your prints would be on that bottle?'

Rourke looks down at his dogs. Gives them a stroke and plays with their ears.

'Where did this happen?' he asks at last.

'Down by the Lord Line building on St Andrew's Quay. We were involved in a surveillance operation.'

'Surveilling what, love?'

'We believe a nearby warehouse was being used as a cannabis farm.'

Rourke scoffs. 'Cannabis? Who gives a crap?'

'I agree,' says Pharaoh. 'Couldn't give a chuff, to be honest. But the people who run it are very nasty people and they hurt somebody nice, so we'd like them to go to prison.'

Rourke nods. 'Fair enough.'

'So all you can tell me is that you were here on Tuesday night and you've no idea how your fingerprints ended up on the glass bottle thrown at the van.' Pharaoh smooths down the front of her jacket. 'Bit shit,' she says.

'The rain looks pretty on your tits.'

The younger man is staring at Pharaoh's chest. She gives an incredulous little laugh. 'Sorry, son?'

'Pretty,' he repeats, and raises his head to look her in the eye. 'Bet they don't look so bouncy when you take your bra off, you old bitch.'

Pharaoh opens her mouth, but before she can speak Rourke has slammed a meaty hand into the younger man's chest and pushed him backwards. He spins to face him, grabbing him by the lapels and pulling his face close. 'You can't help it, can you?' he spits.

'*Maraigh!*' shouts the younger man, his feet scrabbling on the drive. '*Maraigh!*'

Neither Rourke nor the two detectives have any time to react. The command, screamed in Gaelic, means nothing to Pharaoh or Daniells but the Rottweilers respond to it as if a bell has been rung.

174

Time seems to slow down.

To her right, Daniells is reaching into his pocket, trying to extricate his extendable baton from the confines of his battered coat.

Rourke is turning back to her, his eyes widening as his mouth drops open.

The young man is staggering backwards. Turning. Preparing to run.

In a heartbeat, the two animals transform into snarling, ravenous killers. Barking, jaws snapping, they turn on the strangers.

Jaws open, spit drooling from finger-long teeth, they leap.

Pharaoh's arms fly to her face but her eyes do not close in time to spare her the image.

Her vision fills with black-brown fur. Fangs. Pink tongue and yellow eyes.

As she falls, she knows with cold certainty, that the word means 'Kill'.

CHAPTER 13

'Hope the dogs have had their shots,' says Colin Ray, leaning across the table to take a chip from Helen Tremberg's plate and managing to drop a blob of ketchup on his mucky pinstripe suit.

'Yeah, would hate for them to get sick,' says Shaz Archer, taking a sip from her can of Diet Coke. She then gives a bark of a laugh. It sounds like the braying of an upper-class old man and not a petite young woman in an expensive dress and patterned tights.

Neither McAvoy, Tremberg or Ben Neilsen joins in.

'Cheer up, you fuckers,' says Ray, reaching for another chip and laughing when Tremberg pulls her plate away from him. 'She's all right.'

They are sitting in the canteen at Courtland Road Police Station. The news is flickering soundlessly on the TV in the corner of the room and two uniformed officers are playing pool on the table near the serving hatch, where a fifty-year-old woman in a tabard and hat is red-facedly offering a choice between cottage pie, lasagne, chips or going hungry, to a couple of visiting software salesmen in grey suits and name tags.

Detective Chief Superintendent Davey has just finished stumbling his way through the emergency briefing. Ray and Archer are now entirely in charge of the investigation. The cannabis factories, Rourke, and the attack on their senior officer have all been rolled into one. Ray and Archer are on their way to interview the one-time armed robber, who is busy going mental in the cells and threatening retribution against anybody who refuses to tell him what is happening to his two dogs. The rest of the Major Incident Team are circling, here to help, and ready to take over, if asked . . .

Pharaoh is in a hospital bed with bites to her chest, throat and hands. Daniells, fresh stitches in his palms, is painfully typing up his witness report on a borrowed desk in the MIT suite.

The teenager with the ginger hair, who gave the order to kill, has not been seen. Every patrol car in the division is out looking for him.

'New boy says she'd be dead if Rourke hadn't called them off,' says Ray chattily. 'Did the damage in about five seconds.'

'Long enough for the lad to leg it,' says Archer.

'We'll have an ID by morning, I promise you,' says Tremberg through a mouthful of chips. She is appalled at what has happened to their boss, but has an appetite that cannot be slowed by inner turmoil.

'We promise you too,' says Ray, blowing her a

kiss. 'Paddy will be singing in five minutes, I guarantee it.'

'He's not Irish,' says McAvoy with his eyes shut.

Ray pulls a face. 'Name like Rourke?'

'Irish descent. Born in South Yorkshire. Traveller family. It's all in his file. You should read it.'

There is silence for a moment. 'Gyppo, is he?'

Tremberg shoots McAvoy a look. He is staring at the ceiling, his face nearly grey. She knows about his wife's traveller roots and knows too of his sensitivity about such subjects. He had arrived at the briefing red-faced and panting for breath, clearly having run all the way from whatever he had been up to when the call came over the radio that Pharaoh had been hurt and that her team were required immediately at Courtland Road. As he heard what had happened, she saw something in his face that was at once bewilderment and despair. She has not yet seen him angry, but has no doubt the feeling is in there somewhere, and that Colin Ray would do well to stop talking.

'He's from a traveller family,' says McAvoy again deliberately.

'Gyppo, that's what I said,' says Ray, and he and Archer share a laugh.

The two are inseparable. There was a time, when this unit was first being formed, that DCI Ray was expected to get the top job, together with his hard-faced but extraordinarily attractive protégée as number two. Pharaoh had got the gig instead and the older man had not taken it well – and even less so when he was asked to be her deputy.

'Daniells gave us a good description,' says Ben Neilsen, piping up. 'Skinny lad, shaved ginger hair, little shit . . . can't be hard to find.'

'He says it came from nowhere,' adds Tremberg. 'The attack, I mean. Rourke was answering the boss's questions. Wasn't exactly friendly but nothing to worry about. The lad said something about the boss's boobs and Rourke gave him a clip. Then the lad shouted for the dogs to attack. Whether he wanted them to go for Rourke or the boss, Daniells couldn't say.'

'They would never go for their master,' says McAvoy quietly. 'Not in a million years.'

'So why set them on the boss?'

'Maybe he wanted to prove he had the balls.'

McAvoy rubs a hand over his face and looks at his watch. He is trying to stay in control of his emotions. He is furious not to have been asked to take over the investigation, but is also well aware that he has no right to expect it and that to even entertain such a hope is somehow to suggest he sees his boss's injuries as an opportunity. He holds himself still.

'Where were you, anyway?' asks Ray. He is twisting in his chair to watch the two lads play pool and does not turn as he asks the question. 'Thought you were pen-pushing for Everett or something. Was there a really interesting spread-sheet needed your attention somewhere?'

McAvoy finds himself colouring. 'I was taking a look at an old case,' he says.

'Cold case?' asks Ray, turning back to the table and giving a hand gesture that suggests he does not think much of the standard of pool-playing. 'That's Operation Fox, not us.'

'It's more recent than their remit. Just something that deserved some proper attention.'

Archer leans forward. McAvoy notices that the lacy design of her bra is visible through the white silk of her blouse, and turns away quickly. She is well practised in using her looks for effect and results, and seems to positively purr when she spots his discomfort.

'Picking and choosing now, are we?' she asks.

'Beg your pardon?'

'Forget it.'

Archer drains her can of drink and then stands up, taking her coat from the back of the hard plastic chair and pulling it on. Colin Ray pulls himself upright too and brushes the remnants of his sausage roll from his front. His pinstriped suit was probably expensive when he bought it but is stained on the lapels and wrinkled at the crotch.

'We'll be off,' he says, taking one last chip and winking at Tremberg. 'Call us if there's any improvement.'

'Yeah, we'll be worrying about those dogs all night.'

The pair are laughing as they push their way out

of the swing door, so don't hear Tremberg say, 'Wankers.'

Neilsen, Tremberg and McAvoy sit in silence. 'What's the case?' asks Neilsen eventually.

McAvoy looks at him. Tall and good-looking, he's from a Hessle Road fishing family who don't quite know whether to be proud or ashamed that their youngest is a policeman.

'Young lad,' he says, after a pause. 'Found a few months back hanging in his kitchen. Barely any investigation. I've got his old phone. It's full of messages from some sexual partner that there's no trace of in the report. They stop suddenly. It feels wrong. There's more to it.'

'Forensics?'

McAvoy pauses. Appears to make a decision. Reaches into his bag and pulls out the report and his notes. He pulls himself closer to the table.

'There's no doubt he died from strangulation,' he says, reading from his pad. 'Pathologist said the rope around his neck was definitely the one that cut off the blood to his brain. Fibres embedded in the skin, she said. He'd been sexually active at some point in the previous twenty-four hours. Had been anally penetrated. No DNA recovered. He was covered in baby oil, apparently. Had eaten a microwave tagliatelle and a Penguin biscuit around two hours before his death. Drank a glass of orange squash.'

'And then decided he'd had enough? Those microwave meals are awful, like . . . .'

'The file went up to CID and they gave it about thirty seconds. The coroner recorded an open verdict because there was no note, but there's been no investigation. The inventory of this flat's contents makes no mention of his mobile, even though he was on it nearly all the time.'

'But you've got it?' asks Ben curiously.

'I don't know. Maybe. If he kept his own number in his phone.'

'That doesn't matter,' he says, waving his hand. 'Look, I've spoken to his aunt today. She says there's no reason to think he would kill himself.'

Tremberg and Neilsen turn to face one another. Something passes between them and Tremberg is elected spokeswoman.

'Do you not think it would be better to keep our heads down?'

'I'm sorry?'

'It's just after the cock-up the other night, and now this with Pharaoh, do we really want to be saying CID missed something or didn't give a shit? Do we need to have a murder on the books when we haven't got a suspect? What's that going to do to the crime statistics?'

McAvoy looks at her with what looks like disappointment. He seems almost heartbroken.

'I really don't think that matters,' he says, and leaves it at that.

They sit for another few minutes. McAvoy tells them no more about Simon. He has made up his mind. Pharaoh's injuries are sitting in his guts like a snowball, but in her absence he cannot help but see opportunity. His line manager told him to take a look. And she's not around to be contradicted.

They say cheerful goodbyes and pull up their collars as they run across the darkening, rain-lashed car park. McAvoy throws open the door of his car and dives inside. Turns on the engine just in time for the seven p.m. headlines. A police officer has been hurt in a dog attack in Anlaby. Detectives have renewed their appeal for witnesses to a petrol-bombing incident which took place on St Andrew's Quay and which is the latest violent incident being linked to an escalation in drugs-related violence . . .

He watches Tremberg's car pull out into traffic. Gives a wave, obscured by the pelting rain, as Neilsen's Suzuki Swift follows. He gives it thirty seconds. Switches off the engine. Steps back out of the car and runs back across the car park.

He pulls the telephone from his pocket and holds it in a warm, damp palm as he makes his way to the Technical Support Unit. As he knocks on the white double door and tells them that Trish Pharaoh insisted that they get the results back asap, he hopes they put his blush down to his sprint in bad weather, rather than shame at his lies.

CHAPTER 14

Colin Ray holds the smoke in his lungs and feels his eyes begin to water. Feels the tickle in his chest.

Hold it, Col, hold it . . .

He's made it up the stairs without needing to breathe out.

Six, seven, eight steps down the off-green corridor.

Eyes streaming, chest thumping . . .

Turning the handle and entering into Interview Suite B.

He breathes out. Fills the cold, damp room with the smell of cigarettes.

'Thought you deserved a treat,' he says and then gives in to a fit of hacking coughs.

Police interview rooms have been no-smoking zones since 2007. Smokers are at the mercy of their investigators when it comes to a nicotine fix. Colin Ray is not feeling merciful. Left the interview to pop outside for a fag, and declined Alan Rourke's request to accompany him.

'Should give them up, lad,' says Ray, scraping the chair back from the desk and sitting down forcefully, wiping his eyes and then his nose with the heel of his hand. 'They're doing you no good. You look like shit.'

Rourke looks up. Shrugs. 'Must be like holding up a mirror.'

Ray gives a smile. He's enjoyed the past hour of verbal jousting with this hard, unshakable traveller. Rourke has given nothing away. Declined the offer of a solicitor with a wave of his hand, and launched into a variety of 'no comments'. He looks thoroughly unconcerned. Has the appearance of a man who will sit there forever rather than genuinely help the police with their enquiries.

The door opens again and Shaz Archer walks in on unfeasibly high heels. She's been to change her clothes, having failed to get Rourke's attention in her previous outfit. She's wearing fashionable patterned tights, an expensive mid-length skirt and a floaty polka-dot top over a black vest. She looks stylish, sexy and not at all like any of her colleagues. She's the opposite of Helen Tremberg. She emphasises her sexuality and is happy to give suspects a glimpse down her top if it means they start talking to say thank you. So far Rourke doesn't seem to give a damn.

'Looking hot, Shaz,' says Ray, pursing his lips approvingly.

'I was freezing. You could hang your hat on my nips.'

'I don't wear a hat.'

'Wasn't talking to you, Col.'

Across the table Rourke gives an appreciative, knowing smile. He doesn't bite.

'Smells like an ashtray in here,' says Archer, lowering herself into her seat and crossing her legs with a sensual, shushing sound of nylon on silk.

'Spray your scent, love. Give us a treat.'

Archer reaches into her handbag and pulls out a bottle of perfume. Gives it a squirt. Sprays some more on her wrists and then elongates her neck to dab it beneath her ears. She does the whole performance sexily, but Rourke pays no attention. Just carries on staring at the wall. Only turns to her when the smell hits his nostrils.

'Smells like a brothel now,' he says.

'That's Chanel,' says Archer tartly.

'Expensive brothel,' he says in reply, and gives an outlandish yawn.

Ray nods to his colleague. She swivels in her chair and turns on the tape recorder.

'It is 8.09 p.m. Detective Chief Inspector Colin Ray and Detective Inspector Sharon Archer interviewing suspect Alan Rourke. Now, Mr Rourke, where were we?'

Rourke rocks back on his chair. 'We were here, love. Having a ball.'

'Indeed,' says Ray, sucking his cheek and scratching at something unpleasant-looking on the lapel of his dirty pinstriped suit. 'We were talking about your fingerprints being found on the side of the bottle that was thrown at a police van. We were talking about your dogs attacking two police officers. We were sitting here, all ears, waiting for you to open your mouth and treat us to some of that fucking gibberish you pikey bastards speak.'

With the tape now recording every word, Ray should really be more careful what he says, but if he is concerned about repercussions, he hides it well.

Rourke says nothing. Gives a wry smile.

'*Go n-ithe an cat thu, is go n-ithe an diabhal an cat.*'

Ray and Archer look at one another. 'Come again?'

'May the cat eat you, and may the devil eat the cat.'

Ray scratches his face with his dirty yellow fingernails. Pushes his greasy hair back from his face. Chuckles noiselessly.

'That the family motto?'

'We're a dog family.'

'Yeah, we noticed. So did Pharaoh.'

Rourke nods, Looks down. Sighs. 'She OK?'

'Still waiting to hear more,' lies Ray. 'We're fearing the worst.'

Rourke stays silent. 'I stayed with her,' he says at last. 'Could have gone, couldn't I? I locked the dogs up. Called you. Held a towel to her throat . . .'

'You're all heart,' says Ray, pushing himself back from the table.

There is silence in the room for a time, Ray and Rourke eyeing one another up. Ray had begun the interview presuming it would be a matter of time before Rourke gave something up. Here, now, looking across the table into the retired armed robber's eyes, he is beginning to doubt whether he will ever give in.

'You've done long stretches, Alan,' he says, changing tack. 'You don't want to see another prison cell. We just need some answers. Some information. Let's start with the boy. Our missing teen. What's your connection?'

Rourke turns away again. 'No comment.'

'It doesn't sound convincing when you say it, Alan. You know you want to comment.'

'Honest to God, no comment.'

Archer reaches into her handbag and retrieves a piece of chewing gum, which she pops into her mouth. She holds the packet for both Ray and Rourke. Rourke accepts. 'Cheers, love.'

She smiles, friendly and warm. 'You understand how seriously we're taking this,' she says, leaning forward. 'Two incidents, Alan. The petrol bomb and a dog attack, both placing the lives of respected police officers in real danger. And you linked to both. You must know that this isn't going to go away. I understand completely that you have a code. You don't like the police. But I don't think you're the sort of man who would deliberately set fire to a vanload of cops. And I know it was the lad who gave the order for the dogs to attack . . .'

Anger flashes in Rourke's face. He curses in Gaelic. Apologises. Nods.

'They are your dogs, though, Alan. You'll be the one crying when they're put down.'

For the first time, Rourke's eyes show emotion. He bites down on his lip.

'We have some sway with all this, Alan. It's not a done deal. The dogs are being well looked after. They're safe with our specialist dogs unit. Having a little holiday. But they want to go home, and so do you. Just give us something to think about. Tell us why your fingerprint was on that bottle. Just a story, Alan. Something we can look into and discount you from our enquiries.'

Rourke yawns. Chews his gum. Looks up at the ceiling, as if the most interesting story he has ever read is written up there.

Ray loses his temper. 'You're going to give me something, lad. You're going to fill in the gaps for me one way or another.'

Rourke turns his attention to the senior officer. Gives a rueful shake of his head, as if considering a puppy who has once again failed to control its bladder. 'Always comes to that, doesn't it. You're all as bad as each other. Fucking thugs, all of you. All my life I've had you lot looking over my shoulder. Always comes down to the same thing. I've done my time, sir. Moved on. I've not been in trouble in a long time. And still I get you on my doorstep. I told the guy last month, you can threaten me all you want, I don't have anything to say to you . . .'

Ray sits forward suddenly. 'Last month?'

'Round face. Smart suit. One of your top dogs.'

Ray turns to Archer. Tells her to stay quiet without opening his mouth. Switches his attention back to Rourke.

'You were questioned recently?'

There is nothing on the database to indicate Rourke has had any dealings with the police in a long time.

'Don't know if it was questioned,' he muses thoughtfully. 'Given a talking to, more like.'

'In connection with . . .'

Rourke shuts up again. 'No comment.'

Ray slams his hand down on the desk. 'Which officer?'

Rourke appears to consider the implications of not giving away this snippet of information. 'Russell,' he says, at last.

Archer's body language gives away the fact that this is significant, and Rourke's eyebrows shoot up.

'Did he not put that on your little machine? Hardly a surprise. Would take some balls, that. Though I tell you what, sir, it takes some balls to threaten a man when his Rottweilers are by his side. He turned as green as these bloody walls. Don't think he really made his point the way he wanted to.'

Ray slumps back in his chair. Presses his lips together. Wonders whether the traveller is telling the truth. Adrian Russell is head of the Drugs Squad: the last surviving member of the corrupt team that had morphed into the Serious and Organised a year ago. He's also Colin Ray's friend.

'Did he talk to you about drugs?'

'No comment.'

'Robbery?'

'Ask him.'

'You will fucking talk to me . . .'

Rourke smiles, all teeth and eyes.

'No I fucking won't.'

11.41 p.m., Morpeth Street, Hull.

Flickering street lights and pouring rain.

A terrace of student bedsits and low-income flats, where every second window shows a poster for a club night, and where the small front yards are home to mountains of ripped bin bags, of pizza boxes and broken furniture. Where different styles of music hum and blare from open windows, and the shimmering colour of giant flat-screen TVs flickers from curtainless front rooms.

Nineteen-year-old Georgie-Lee Suthers sits on the front step of one of the better-looking houses on the street. She is smoking a cigarette and playing with her phone.

She is dressed as a dead bride: her charity-shop dress powdered with talc. There is a livid slash of colour at her throat. Panda eyes look out through a ghoulish white face, and her legs in ripped fish-nets are a canvas for an advancing army of ink spiders.

The rain is ruining her make-up, but the Mateus

Rosé and shots of rum have pitched her past caring.

She looks at her phone. Hopes there will be a message. An apology. Advance warning of a busload of guests.

Georgie-Lee bites down on the filter tip of her cigarette and pouts. 'Thanks a lot.'

It was supposed to be a party, but nobody could, in good conscience, call it anything other than a gathering.

Georgie-Lee has tried for the past three hours to make her housemate's birthday something special, but not even the cramped confines of their two-bedroomed flat can make the paltry dozen guests seem anything other than a disappointment.

She had worked hard at making the night a success. Arranged for friends to take Jen shopping while she set to work blowing up balloons and arranging chocolate crispy cakes and half-frozen sausage rolls on the coffee table. Even made a play-list for the iPod from their shared party tunes. Had a nice glass of wine and danced around as she covered the flat in fake cobwebs and skeleton silhouettes. Threw a bag of fake spiders around and drew pupils on ping-pong balls to drop in the 'witch's brew'.

With only half an hour to go before Jen was due back, Georgie-Lee realised that she should have made people confirm their attendance. The thirty or so university friends who said they would definitely try to be there have let her down. Jen has made all the right noises, of course, but even when she went and changed into the skimpy vampire costume that Georgie-Lee had picked out for her, it was clear she was neither in the mood for this, nor pleased that nobody else was either.

Georgie-Lee plays with her phone. Wonders whether she should update her Facebook status to read 'thinking of getting friends who actually give a shit!'

She won't, of course. Georgie-Lee cannot bring herself to be mean to people. She doesn't like conflict or an atmosphere. Instead, she logs on to the site and tells anybody who cares to read it that she is having 'the BEST time ever!!'

She rubs out her cigarette on the wall and thinks about going back upstairs. When she came down for some air, a mad professor and a werewolf were going through her DVD collection and demanding she apologise for the absence of any samurai movies. She does not particularly want to go and jolly everybody along and pretend the party is something it is not. She wants them all to go, now. Wants to give Jen her present, then watch a horror film with the lights off.

Georgie-Lee looks up. Tries to catch some rain on her face, but the awning of the doorway means she is relatively dry, even if the cold air makes her shiver. She looks down her street, wondering if she should knock on doors and ask anybody who looks even vaguely interesting if they would like to attend. She wonders whether the two lads who live at Number 57 are home, sitting watching DVDs in their downstairs flat, but her view is blocked by the presence of a large four-by-four, parked directly in front of the low wall that marks the border of her own property. It's an expensive-looking vehicle, but it has been in the wars. The front bumper is crumpled and the headlight cracked. She wonders whom it belongs to. It seems out of place.

She scrolls through her Facebook posts. Comments on a friend's photo. Wonders whether she can be bothered to change her relationship status again, and decides she'll leave it for now. She and her boyfriend break up and get back together every week or so, and the frequency of the changes is becoming embarrassing.

She flicks over to Hull Ink. Stefan has appointments free tomorrow. Devon is booked up all day, but he has uploaded some pictures of his old black and white stuff.

Indulgently, Georgie-Lee flicks through the various galleries, comparing the images on display. She finds herself wondering, again, who would go to the trouble of having Eeyore or Winnie the Pooh tattooed on themselves. Questions why somebody would walk into a tattoo parlour and ask to be branded for life with the lyrics from a Coldplay tune or the picture of a dead grandad. None of it is pretty, and to Georgie-Lee prettiness is para-mount. Her own ink makes her wriggle with pleasure, and to see it on the website, paraded for the masses, still gives her a genuine thrill.

She expands the picture. Looks at her own bare back. A solid brown branch, spreading from the top of her right buttock to the nape of her neck; curving, like a stream, into slender twigs and delicate flowers; a collage of overlying blossoms, against a shimmering lake of lilies.

The design is not really her own. Legally, she supposes, she should not even have it upon her skin. But she had subtly changed the design and added her own little motifs, and Devon had enjoyed the opportunity to perfect the image that he had inked on another girl some months before.

She looks through the various posts that accompany the image, secretly hoping that somebody will have added a compliment, but the four 'like' icons, and one 'love this' from an old schoolfriend, have not increased in number.

It had hurt less than she thought, and despite predictions that it would take four sittings, Devon had managed to finish in two. She watched him in the mirror as he worked, his face locked in concentration, the pirate ships on his forearms moving up and down as he drew, as if on gentle seas.

For a time she had planned to make her first tattoo a fairy castle; all daisies and scampering imps. But then she saw the ads. The glossy half-page in *The Journal*. The boy with the peacock feathers and the girl with the blossoms. She had booked herself in almost immediately, brandishing a copy of the mag and insisting that the tattooist who had created the vision do the same for her. He had told her about copyright laws and artistic rights, and she agreed to some tweaks to the design. Added a lily pad, and a tiny hummingbird on an upper branch. Asked if they accepted credit cards, and then stripped herself to the waist.

'You coming back up?'

She looks up. A head is poking out of their second-floor window: masked by cheap polyester afro and Michael Jackson Thriller jacket.

'Won't be a sec,' says Georgie-Lee and the head withdraws.

She takes a breath. Practises her smile. She is incapable of being the gloomy one in the room. Needs, always, to be jollying along and perking up.

She pulls herself up to a standing position and slips her phone into the elastic of her black mesh, elbow-length gloves.

She turns away from the street, stopped before she has taken two paces by the sound of a car door slamming. It is close. Close enough to suggest that perhaps another visitor has arrived, more party-goers out to salvage the evening.

She traces the sound to the stranger emerging from the four-by-four. Gives an accepting nod, and spins away from the road.

'Suzie.'

George-Lee wonders if she has misheard. On instinct, she turns in the direction of the noise.

In a moment she is crashing backwards; strong, powerful limbs bearing her to the ground.

A forearm, pushing up beneath her chin, forcing her head back onto the cold, wet tiles. Another hand, tearing at her wig, rubbing away the white powder, the black eyes.

She squirms. Tries to squeal.

And now she is being flipped. Rolled onto her belly. Feels as though she is being clawed open. Hands, nails, tearing at her dress.

Sudden cool air on bare skin; fingers ripping back the flimsy threads, wrenching her bra strap upwards so that the underwire digs in beneath her breasts . . .

'Help. Please . . .'

Her voice a gulp; a breath; an animal noise cut short by the sudden feeling of fists in her hair.

She reaches back. Squirms. Wriggles. Fights for her life.

Wet lips, next to her ear.

'I had to be sure. I'm sorry.'

Paving stones rushing towards her face.

Blackness.

And nothing.

CHAPTER 15

'They don't match.'

Roisin waves her hand in the general direction of McAvoy's feet.

'What don't?'

'Your shoes. One's a trainer. One's a boot.'

He looks at his footwear. Nods. 'Yeah.'

She turns back to the sink. Fills the kettle. Thirty seconds later she notices it is overflowing and manages to turn the tap off.

'What was I doing?'

'Tea, I think. Or were you sterilising?'

'It will come to me.'

Between them they got around four hours of sleep last night. Lilah had a fever. She screamed until her face was the colour of cherry tomatoes. Clenched her fists so tightly that she scored half-moon scars in her tiny palms. Brought both her parents to tears of impotence and exhaustion. Finally passed out through a mild overdose of Calpol around four a.m., laid stiff as a board on a pillow in Daddy's lap.

'You can't go in,' says Roisin. 'Not in that state, Aector.'

She is wearing her nightie and flip-flops, and is soaking wet. She tried to put her leather jacket on a dozen times before she walked Fin to school, but couldn't seem to find the arm-holes, and ended up taking him while still dressed for bed. She received sympathetic looks from other parents, familiar with the skull-crushing dishevelment that comes with being mum to a four-month-old baby.

'I can't call in sick for tiredness.'

'Work from home.'

'Roisin . . .'

'Nnnn.'

They are two zombies, communicating in slurred grunts, gestures and half-finished sentences.

'You need to sleep.'

'I got some sleep.'

'You got about five minutes and even then you were sitting up straight. Look at you.'

McAvoy pulls himself out of the hardbacked kitchen chair and lifts up the toaster. It's silver and polished to a gleam. He examines his face in the reflection. Unshaven. Dark circles beneath his eyes. A bruise starting to form on the orbit of his eye having spent too long resting his head on the heel of his hand. He notices his top button is undone. Fixes it. Straightens his red tie and checks the front of his black shirt and light grey suit for signs of porridge or baby spit. Finds nothing that cannot be remedied with a damp towel.

'It was like this with Fin. She'll be better tonight.'

Roisin nods. She is too tired to argue.

'You never got me told,' she says, lifting the kettle and wondering why it is so full. 'She ok? Pharaoh?'

McAvoy is engrossed in sifting through the cupboard under the stairs in search of his matching boot. After a few moments he spots it in his left hand.

'She'll be ok. Sore, but ok.'

'That's good.'

'Do you have any of that ointment left?'

'No.'

Roisin sounds quite final in her pronouncement. She is a gifted herbalist. There are few plants, trees, roots, berries or leaves that she cannot mix to create a poultice or pill. She would normally volunteer to make a fresh batch, her innate need to help and heal overpowering all other concerns. This morning she is too tired. She is snappy and nauseous and wants to fall asleep on her husband's chest and not wake up until both of her children are old enough to vote.

McAvoy does not get the opportunity to ask her if she will make something to help with the pain of Pharaoh's injuries. His phone rings.

'McAvoy,' he says, wearily.

'Sergeant?'

'Yes,' he says, running a hand through his hair. 'Just about.'

'It's Dan from Tech Support. Got something for you.'

Drowsily, McAvoy pictures the other man. Dan

looks barely old enough to have left university: small, wiry and with fashionably shaggy mid-length hair. He is usually dressed in a band T-shirt beneath his white coat and wears baseball trainers with suit trousers.

'Sergeant?'

McAvoy gives himself a little shake. He stands upright and screws his eyes up tightly, trying to bring himself round.

'Yes. Sorry. Terrible night with the little one. I'm listening.'

'Right. Anyway, we did it as a rush job. I'm trying to build up some lieu time so I was here overnight. Planning a Glastonbury trip but used my holidays . . .'

McAvoy bites his tongue, which is difficult mid-yawn. He resists the urge to tell Dan to hurry it along, all too aware of his own propensity for rattling on about things he presumes other people will be interested in. Eventually, the technician gets around to the phone.

'Yeah, well, like you said, it's knackered,' he says with an almost audible shrug. 'You did well to recover what you did. We've sent away the remaining soil for analysis . . .'

'There's no need for that, I know where it was found . . .'

'It's procedure,' says Dan.

'Right.'

'Took the SIM card out again and loaded it into another phone, but like you saw, it's just this mad stream of numbers and fragments. I did have more luck with the phone itself . . .'

'Yes?'

'Well, not all of the contacts were stored on the memory card. A couple were saved to the phone itself. Don't know why people do that, but sometimes they just hit the wrong button.'

McAvoy feels himself waking up. He pictures a chill breeze blowing through his skull, scattering the drowsiness and refreshing his thoughts.

'Well?'

'I've emailed you the numbers. Only a couple, and there's no way of working out which of the contacts they belonged to, but we've got some complete digits.'

McAvoy pulls on his boots as he talks. Unconsciously unfastens then refastens his tie.

'Have you checked who they belong to?'

Dan laughs. 'You did say it was Pharaoh wanted this doing, yeah?'

'Why?'

'I'm very eager to please, Sergeant,' says the younger man, in a way that McAvoy would have thought of as fun and relatively charming were he not so tired.

'Did you find anything, Dan?'

'Yeah,' he says, and there is a note of petulance in his voice. 'It's on your email. Let me know if you need anything else.'

Dan rings off.

'Bloody hell,' says McAvoy to himself, pulling his

laptop from his bag and logging on. He opens his email account and brings up the tech report.

'Interesting?' asks Roisin. She is holding a drinkable yoghurt and sitting on the floor, leaning back against the fridge.

'Could be,' says McAvoy, reading the two short paragraphs of detail. 'Got two full numbers in the memory. Dan's requested user details from the service provider but that could take some time. Ran the digits through a search engine and found them on a procurement committee report. Hull City Council.'

'That's nice,' says Roisin.

McAvoy runs his tongue around his mouth.

'Council,' he says thoughtfully.

The number is listed as being among a batch of phones ordered by the authority's procurement division for officers and elected representatives. McAvoy is not sure how he feels about this development. It could be utterly inconsequential. A telephone number listed as a contact in the phone of a dead man? Does it matter? He finds himself pondering how many hundreds of people have his own phone number stored. Whether he would feel angry were he contacted as a result.

Procedurally, he should not even be looking at the tech report. Dan's work will have to be paid for out of Pharaoh's budget. McAvoy is not officially conducting a murder investigation and no senior officer beside Pharaoh is even aware of what he is doing. But to make his previous deceit valid, he needs to bend the rules again. He feels the realisation settle within him. Feels his mouth begin to salivate, a prelude to sickness. Feels his skin prickle, as if the hairs on his body are being brushed the wrong way. Accepts this as both sacrifice and payment.

McAvoy pulls up the telephone number for Hull City Council. The Google search also brings up a page full of negative headlines. The authority has been bottom of just about every league table for as long as McAvoy has lived in the area. It has been slammed by every inspector to have found their way into the wood-panelled corridors of the Guildhall.

He dials the number and listens to the automatic prompts.

For enquiries about rubbish collections, press three. To apply for a council tax rebate, press four . . .

'If you want to find out why a phone number was stored in the phone of a dead lad, press six,' whispers McAvoy to Roisin. She does not reply. Her eyes are closed and she is spilling yogurt on her feet.

'Hull City Council,' comes a female voice, when he requests the 'any other enquiries' option.

'Procurement, please,' he says.

A moment later he is on hold, listening to something monotonously classical. He hums along, but finds his eyes closing, so opens them wide.

'Jacquie Carrington,' comes a high, bright voice.

'Hi,' says McAvoy suddenly unsure. 'My name is Detective Sergeant Aector McAvoy. I'm ringing from Humberside Police . . .'

'Yes?' She doesn't sound disinterested or particularly bothered.

'I'm trying to find out which council official was given a particular telephone.'

'The councillors' mobile numbers are all online,' she begins.

'Yes, well, I've rung the number and it's dead, but I believe it was among a batch ordered by the authority in July of last year?'

There is no reply for a moment.

'I think I may have to speak to my line manager about that,' she says, and it sounds as though she is reading from a script.

'There are obviously ways we can request this information formally,' says McAvoy quickly. 'I just thought perhaps you could save us some time. Did you say it was Miss Carrington?'

The lady repeats herself. Tells McAvoy she will speak to her line manager and call him back. Takes his name, number, and thanks him for his time. Promises she will not be long.

McAvoy hangs up and puffs out his cheeks. He turns and looks at Roisin and feels his heart swell at how adorable she looks, snoring softly on the floor with her damp clothes clinging to her goose-pimpled skin. Smiling to himself, he crosses to her and scoops her up with the ease he carries their children. He carries her to the living room and sits her down. She is flopping like a rag doll and makes no protest as he peels off her wet clothes. He lays her down and returns to the kitchen to retrieve a blanket from the tumble dryer. Comes back and covers her up. Presses his lips to her cheek, and whispers, 'Love you,' in her ear. Fancies he sees the faintest of smiles.

His phone rings again. Roisin opens her eyes at the sudden noise and he frantically shushes her, answering the call as he dashes out of the living room and closes the door behind him.

'McAvoy.'

'Detective Sergeant McAvoy?' The voice is nasal. Young.

'Yes. Is that Procurement . . .?'

'Sergeant McAvoy, my name is Ed Cocker. I wondered if you would be free to talk about one or two matters of a politically sensitive nature.'

McAvoy colours. 'How did you . . .?'

'Sergeant, I'm led to believe you are looking into the activities of Councillor Stephen Hepburn. Can I ask you the nature of the investigation?'

'I'm sorry, I'm not sure . . .'

'A source at the Guildhall has informed me that his telephone number has come up in connection with an investigation into an ongoing case. I also have some interest in the councillor. Perhaps we could share some information.'

McAvoy is silent for a moment. Wonders just what he is doing and, more importantly, what he will do next, if not this.

'Perhaps we could.'

* * *

They are in the Green Bricks, a pub named after the emerald tiles that adorn the building's frontage. It offers a decent view of the bobbing pleasure craft that moor at Hull Marina, and the city centre is only over the traffic-clogged main road. It should be a bustling area even in the face of today's harsh gales. Instead it is an open grave. McAvoy has seen old black and white photos of the area in its prime. The fruit market, with its hurly-burly of trade and activity, its carriages and wagons, its chain-smoking men in their dirty jeans and overalls, treading clementines and too-ripe bananas beneath tyres and welly boots. Profitable chaos. Trade. Life.

He has seen, too, images of the nearby waterfront. Has read of how the waters, now calmed and framed by the walls of the marina, once rushed haphazardly into the open estuary and provided a living for the captains of many small vessels who would take passengers and produce to New Holland on the opposite bank. Two minutes away is Victoria Pier; the main terminal for ferries to Lincolnshire. McAvoy has heard the stories. Enjoyed the tales of passengers and livestock sharing space on cramped vessels, spending uncomfortable nights stuck on a sandbank midway into the crossing, claimed by the treacherous tides.

He stares out through the glass. Tries to picture it. Tries to give the area new potential. Fresh life. Today most of the units carry 'to let' signs, or are home to hairdressing salons where bored stylists read magazines and paint their nails.

To his right, just visible through the dusty, rain-lashed windows, is the stern of the Spurn lightship; a smudge of black against the grey sky. It is one of Hull's most distinctive landmarks and seems to embody the city and its fortunes. For almost fifty years it sat five miles off the East Yorkshire coast, a floating lighthouse which served as a navigation marker for the thousands of vessels that steamed in and out of the Humber each year: its towering acetylene light visible for more than ten miles against the ink-black waters and skies. It was retired in the mid-seventies, around the same time the city's trawlermen were being told to fuck off home, and has since been turned into a floating museum. Today day-trippers and bored locals are the only ones to clamber inside and try to imagine how it must have felt to live and work in its claustrophobic embrace. It sits at the edge of the marina, black and joyless. As uninviting as its reality.

'Did you order food?' asks Ed Cocker, raising his hand and manfully trying not to wince as it is taken in McAvoy's great paw.

The man, whose business cards declare him a 'political consultant', is as tall as McAvoy, but only half the size. He is skeletally thin, with cadaverous cheekbones and sunken eyes. His flesh is stretched so tightly over his skull that McAvoy wonders whether his shaving cuts ever nick bone, and his dark grey, old-fashioned suit covers legs that put McAvoy in mind of a stilt-walker. He is perhaps thirty-five years old, and if he is earning a good living, he is not spending the proceeds on his appearance.

McAvoy shakes his head. 'I'm not stopping long.'

Ed nods. Sips from his bottle of lager. Reaches down and picks up a sheaf of printed pages from the seat next to him. 'You've been involved in some very high-profile cases,' he says, respectfully flicking through the papers.

'What do you mean by that?' asks McAvoy, colouring. Instinctively, childishly, he presses his cola glass to his cheek.

Cocker brushes past the question. 'Gets its fair share of big cases, Hull. Bad business last year with that poor girl in the church.'

McAvoy realises his leg is jiggling.

'New problems too, I hear. Some new outfit getting in the faces of the Vietnamese? You don't want to go upsetting them, do you? Crazy. What is it about this city?'

McAvoy breathes out. He is on safer ground here.

'There's a thesis to be written on that,' says McAvoy. 'Socio-political doctorate.'

'On why it's a shithole?'

'It's not a shithole,' says McAvoy, and his words surprise him. 'The fishing industry died. Nobody had any work. And the Germans bombed the hell out of the place in the war. No investment. Culturally, a historic lack of impetus on education. And from a geographical perspective, it has a sense of isolation. It's the last stop on the line. It has to deal with more than most. That leads to high crime . . .'

Cocker is listening. He appears to be taking it in.

McAvoy stops. Wonders if he should shut up. Wonders how to explain this city to a stranger.

He turns to stare through the dirty windows. A teenage couple are wincing into the wind and rain, trudging past the glass with their arms folded and faces set in grim determination, their blue jeans made black by the downpour. They are not holding hands. Not talking. Just making their way in grim, resigned silence. McAvoy thinks it would be easier to answer Cocker's question were he just to point at them and tell the southerner to take a look.

'It could be so much,' he says, turning back to Cocker, 'this place. This city. Used to be. You know that. Biggest fishing port in the world.'

Cocker pulls a face. 'Doubt it made the working man a millionaire.'

'No,' says McAvoy thoughtfully. 'But it was something. Something to cling to. An identity. That's what it lacks now. Something to be.'

'You got any suggestions?' asks Cocker through a smile.

'I leave that to the politicians,' he says, turning away. 'I have to hope the people who get paid more than me know more than me.'

They catch one another's eye and smile, though for different reasons.

'Anyway,' says Cocker.

'Councillor Hepburn,' says McAvoy. 'You have an interest.'

'In him? Not very much. In who he's friends with? Yes, quite a lot.'

McAvoy decides to stop dancing around the subject.

'Why are you here, Mr Cocker? What's your job?'

Cocker gives a nod, as if making a decision. Shrugs. 'Your new boss. Peter Tressider. Chairman of the Police Authority.'

McAvoy says nothing. Waits for more.

'You must have heard the rumours that the Party is interested in him. He could be set for great things.'

'He may run at the next election, you mean.'

Cocker nods. 'And if that goes well . . .'

'People have plans?'

'Indeed.'

They sit in silence, both eyeing each other up. McAvoy speaks first.

'And you're seeing if there are any skeletons in his closet.'

'In a manner of speaking. I'm a political consultant. I dig. I find out whether we should be worried down the line.'

In his mind, McAvoy quickly runs through the many political scandals he has flicked through in the red-tops these past few years. He pulls a face. 'There always seems plenty to be embarrassed about in politics.'

Cocker gives a grin. 'I can't be everywhere.'

'And what is it about Councillor Tressider that worries you?'

'Councillor Hepburn.'

'I don't understand.'

'No. You don't.'

Cocker reaches into the inside pocket of his jacket. He pulls out a crumpled roll of paper, covered in photocopied newspaper articles and scribbled notes.

'Let me read you something,' says Cocker, clearing his throat. 'If you don't mind, that is . . .'

'If it's important,' says McAvoy.

'Important? Possibly. Interesting, certainly.'

McAvoy waits. Wonders when the other man will make his point.

Cocker reads the words on the page. 'He's the politician who has made a fortune from the pink pound – and who swings to the left, the right, and straight down the middle . . .'

McAvoy closes his eyes. 'Classy. Where's it from?'

Cocker stops. 'Political website. One of many. They'd tone it down for a broadsheet feature but the few times he's been in the national headlines, the tone hasn't been far away from this tripe.'

McAvoy nods at the papers. 'Carry on.'

'Stephen Hepburn, forty-seven, is the flamboyant, colourful and rabble-rousing independent councillor and gay-bar owner who is shaking things up in the Guildhall in Hull. He's also the man who saw a hole and decided to fill it – and who has yet to hit a bum note on his rise to power. A local boy who was involved in the music scene during the Manchester explosion of the early nineties, he managed bars in London for a time before coming home to Hull a decade back. Hepburn purchased a rundown gay bar not far from the city centre and planned to make it the biggest, boldest and campest club in Britain. Apparently the idea for Slammers came to him in the night. Hepburn faced fierce objection from locals and various civic dignitaries, but despite recommendations that they block the proposals, Hull Council's planning committee allowed him to proceed with the application. Yes, they bent over and took it. Rumours have since abounded that the authority feared accusations of homophobia, and that Hepburn played on those fears during the consultation process. The high-profile case turned out to be the making of Hepburn, who gave several interviews on radio and TV in which he came across as charming, bold, determined – and very funny. He had the presenter in tears of laughter as he ploughed into the objectors and the different members of the committee: mimicking their mannerisms and questioning their motives in a speech that was full of double entendres. The opening night of his new club saw several big names from the music scene put in an appearance, and high-profile gay rights activists applauded his victory – bringing him to national attention. Slammers has gone on to become a hugely popular venue, attracting clubbers from across the country and revelling in a reputation for controlled hedonism where people can gleefully dance on the bones of Hull Council's cock-up . . .'

McAvoy stops him, holding up a hand. 'This is vile.'

Cocker spreads his hands. Takes a drink. 'This is politics.'

'It's not. It's—'

'During the dispute, Hepburn clearly tasted something he liked,' continues Cocker. 'He swallowed the plaudits, and so much more. When the next local elections came around, Hepburn put himself forward as a man with something big to offer. Due largely to a low turn-out and the fact that the sitting Labour councillor didn't bother to try and drum up any support, Hepburn was elected to the council. When the ruling Lib-Dems of the time needed an extra vote to get through a key part of their manifesto, they persuaded Hepburn to join them in a loose coalition that gave him a position on the authority's cabinet. He has since been sticking it to the cabinet on every occasion, making political allies along the way, impressed with his silver tongue . . .'

'Stop.'

'Horrible, isn't it? But people read it.'

McAvoy screws up his face. Tries to remember who he is and what's he's doing.

'And what has this to do with Peter Tressider?' he asks.

'I'm getting to that. Look, known about Hepburn for ages,' he says. 'His name has come up once or twice. He's a playful man. Every bit as flamboyant as he pretends. That's not what worries us. It's the shadier side. The money. There are questions over where it came from. It wasn't cheap, building that club.'

'Shady?'

'Loan from a criminal associate, perhaps,' says Cocker, speculatively. 'Or perhaps somebody with dough to spare who might not like being linked to that sort of place.'

Realisation dawns. 'You've been through Tressider's financial records, haven't you?'

Cocker does not look away. 'That's basic. That's the first job on the list.'

'Hepburn's name came up?'

'In a roundabout way.'

McAvoy makes no attempt to hide his contempt. 'Has anybody done anything wrong?'

Cocker puts his hands flat on the table. Looks away. 'That's not the point.'

McAvoy waits for more. 'Tressider's a business man. What are you getting at? What does this matter?'

Cocker loses patience. 'Look, in this business rumour can kill you. A whiff of impropriety, you're out on your ear. It doesn't matter how good you are, or even if you've done anything wrong. It's what people think. And the Party has got wind of whispers about a business relationship between our new paragon of virtue and a gay trouble-maker, and it's up to me to see if that is something we can swallow.'

'You don't care about the truth?'

'I care about the appearance of truth.'

McAvoy has to remind himself to breathe. He wants to see if he could fit the man into the empty lager bottle. Wants to pummel this walking embodiment of all he despises about the world.

'And this is a job? A real way to make a living?'

'A good living,' says Cocker unashamedly. 'And I'm worth every penny.'

McAvoy scowls as he puts together the chain of events that have brought him here.

'You slipping cash to some of the officers at Hull Council? Asking to be told about anything involving Hepburn?'

Cocker grins. 'That would be frowned upon, I imagine.'

'Mr Cocker?'

'I have sources.'

McAvoy nods.

They sit in silence for a minute. Cocker looks at his watch and then in the direction of the pub kitchen. From the state of him, he could have been waiting for this meal since the mid-seventies.

'There will be eyes on this place soon,' he says, gesturing out of the window at the dismal, half-empty marina. 'The national media will be taking an interest in Tressider if he gets the nod. Right sort of man. Successful. Straightforward. Beautiful wife. Right background. Could go far.'

'If you let him.'

'Yes.'

Silence falls. The sound of glasses being stacked and plates laid on sticky, varnished tables occasionally rises above the relentless patter of the rain on the glass.

McAvoy runs his tongue around the inside of his mouth and wonders if he has missed something. Whether the past half-hour has been worth his time.

'We're not investigating Councillor Hepburn,' says McAvoy eventually. 'I don't think you should be either.'

'What were you ringing about this morning?' asks Cocker, appearing not to register the firmness of McAvoy's gaze.

'It's nothing. We're trying to find out why a certain telephone number was in a certain telephone . . .'

Cocker sits forward, like a jockey planning on giving a horse a few extra kicks towards the finishing post. He can clearly smell a story.

'Hepburn's phone, you mean?' he asks, all smiles.

'I can't tell you that,' replies McAvoy, willing himself not to blush.

'The number you gave my contact,' Cocker muses to himself. 'That was Hepburn's phone. Only had it a month then reported it lost. Got a new one from his own pocket.'

McAvoy looks away before his face betrays him. 'And?'

'And what?' says Cocker. He is not in the least bit deferential in his manner. He is talking to McAvoy as if they are mates. McAvoy bridles a little.

'I think we're done,' says McAvoy, and begins to stand.

'Are we going to mention it?' asks Cocker. 'The thing we both know?'

McAvoy sits back down. He had not wanted this conversation to reach this stage. Yes, he knows about Hepburn's record. Flicked through it as he sat in the car outside the pub. He knows that, as a twenty-something, he was arrested for the alleged rape of a teenage boy. Knows, too, that the evidence was circumstantial and that the case collapsed well before trial.

'He hasn't been convicted of a thing,' says McAvoy. 'He hasn't done anything wrong. You're out to get him just because you don't like what he stands for.'

'What does he stand for?' asks Cocker, incredulous.

McAvoy colours. 'Alternative lifestyles,' is the best he can do, and he is embarrassed by the pomposity of his tone.

Cocker does not disguise his laugh. He shuffles his papers and looks as if he is about to read some more. 'You want to hear how the papers reported the case?'

This time McAvoy does stand. 'If you try and pay off any more council officers I'll arrest you,' says McAvoy, walking away.

'I'll be in touch,' shouts Cocker at his departing back.

McAvoy pulls open the double doors to the pub and all but throws himself out into the gusting wind and rain. It takes all of his willpower to say the word 'tosser' only in his head.

CHAPTER 16

Going for the three-course lunch today. Bag of peanuts, packet of crisps and a pickled egg. All swilling, like croutons, in the red wine Colin Ray has been pouring down his neck for twenty minutes.

It's 1.24 p.m.

He and Detective Superintendent Adrian Russell are sitting by the hearth in the George, representing two-fifths of today's clientele. Warming themselves on the open fire. Ray's got his back to it. There's steam rising from his damp clothes, as though from compost.

It's an unashamedly old-fashioned pub, this. Dark. The smell of fag smoke still lingers even now. It has atmosphere. Style. It's a proper boozer, all fingerprints and greasy brass. All leather-studded seats and dust-caked light-bulbs.

Ray looks around. Breathes it in. Wishes he could smoke. Closes his eyes and plays his game. Tries to bring the scene to life in his memory. To paint the picture in his mind and then compare it to the reality. To see how much he can remember.

Hardwood floor, darkened and scuffed.

Mahogany walls, almost black.

Thick, frosted windows.

Old newspaper articles on the wall. Dartboard, more holes than cork. Drawing of something obscene on the blackboard by its side. Warm. Friendly. Comforting. Like crawling inside a hamster's cheek and lighting a fire . . .

Ray opens his eyes. He has every detail memorised. Could draw this place, if asked.

It sits at the bottom of the Old Town, on a deathly quiet cobbled street that carries the most unlikely of names. Land of Green Ginger, the street signs declare. A narrow road which was named either for the profitable trade in exotic spices that brought money to the area centuries back, or in honour of a Dutch joiner who had a yard here once upon a time. Nobody is really sure, but the street name is an interesting enough discussion to knock back and forth over a few drinks.

'Should have come to us in the first place,' says Russell. 'Drugs bust. The Foreshore. You could have had the collar, but when it comes to a bust that's our territory. That's what we do.'

Colin Ray is uncharacteristically diplomatic in his response. He knows that now is not the time to criticise Pharaoh. She's just had her throat torn open by a pair of Rottweilers, which buys her some goodwill among the troops. Has decided to be sympathetic, at least until Russell lays his cards on the table.

'Order came down from on high, Aidy. Don't think she wanted it in the first place. And you've had plenty of results this year, if the *Hull Daily Mail* is anything to go by.'

Russell gives a begrudging nod. 'Yeah, we've had some wins.'

'We're going to put it all back together,' says Ray. 'Shaz and me.'

Russell takes a swallow of his second pint of bitter. 'You're a lucky boy, having Shaz to play with.'

'She's lucky to play with me,' says Ray as he sips his wine. He drinks lager in the evening.

Russell waits for a juicier titbit, but when none is forthcoming he picks up his drink again. 'Should have come to me in the first place,' he says again. 'It should never have come to this.'

Ray nods his assent. Has the sense to keep his mouth shut. Just picks his back teeth with his tongue and wonders if it would be taking the piss to claim the senior officer's drinks back on expenses. He lets it play out. Doesn't push. Keeps his temper.

'It wasn't that I wouldn't have shared,' says Russell slightly petulantly. 'Just nobody asked. We're supposed to be the fucking experts . . .'

The boundaries that separate the roles and responsibilities of the different units within Humberside CID may as well be written in water. For every specialist section in the service, there is another team who feels better placed to do their job. For every case that goes to a particular unit, there are half a dozen disgruntled officers who believe the crime comes under their own remit. The Drugs Squad is unsure how to feel about the Serious and Organised team. Their duties frequently overlap, but rarely to anybody's satisfaction. The balls-up during the failed cannabis factory raid at St Andrew's Quay has given the officers on the Drugs Squad a reason to feel a little better about themselves. They felt they should have been given responsibility for the raid – rather than being reduced to a peripheral role. And their boss, Adrian Russell, has made no secret of the fact. The only thing he has made a secret of is how much he could have helped, had he so chosen.

Despite his rank, Russell is neither liked nor trusted by the majority of the CID team. He is one of the few members of the old CID to have survived the internal enquiry into the corruption so endemic on Doug Roper's team. Nobody really understands how he scraped through it all – or landed a promotion and a cushy number running a headline-grabbing team. The consensus is that he has friends in low places.

Ray considers him. Russell is in uniform today. Despite being one of the most senior plainclothes officers, he has been called to HQ for a meeting with some local dignitaries and been told to wear his best blues. He and Ray met a decade or so back when both were unwilling participants on a 'community assurance' training course. They were so vocal in their contempt during the two-day seminar that they might as well have stood up and pissed on the course tutor. They had hit it off. Found enough in common to form a half-hearted friendship based on drinking, football and in-depth discussions about breasts. It was Russell who suggested Ray get on board when the top brass announced the formation of the Serious and Organised Crime Unit. Ray has sometimes wondered whether it was Russell's recommendation that cost him the top job and instead reduced him to Pharaoh's understudy.

'If she'd only asked . . .' says Russell again, and looks away. Once upon a time the action would have caused a ripple in his fleshy face. These days he's leaner and a damn sight more presentable. When Ray first met him, his gut was spilling over his beige suit and there was a sheen of sickly looking perspiration on a jowly face that sloped upwards to a shock of bristly grey hair. He hasn't been much to look at, but a routine medical had given Russell enough reasons to clean himself up a little, and he had started hitting the gym. He's still a large specimen, but there is now more muscle under his shirt than fat.

Ray finds himself drawing crosses on the hard-wood floor with the sole of his shoe. He wants to tell his friend to get on with it. To shit or get off the pot. To give him what he's come for.

'If it had been you running the show, Col . . .'

Ray gives an understanding nod. Condones his

senior colleague for being deliberately obstructive. For holding back. For not telling Pharaoh what he's about to spill to one of the good old boys . . .

'Just a steer, Adie,' says Ray, turning away at the sound of the front doors opening. A man in a suit pokes his head in. Takes a look at the virtually empty bar and then withdraws. The door bangs again. 'We all know it should have gone to you. But it came to us and Pharaoh played it her way. Maybe she didn't know how much you know. I won't make that mistake, mate. Straight to the horse's mouth.'

Russell knows he is being flattered, but the smile on his lips does not suggest that he minds. He takes a longer swallow of beer, and then leans forward, bringing himself closer to Ray.

'I've skimmed the operational reports,' he says and then sneers. 'She didn't know half of what she was dealing with. They were never going to be there. This snout she had? This lass who told her where to raid? She's bottom rung, mate. And if she had any sense, she'll have told her bosses what she told Pharaoh the second she had the chance. They'll have cleared out about thirty seconds after she told the brass she had located the latest farm. They're too well connected. We only raid what they can afford to lose. There's a system here and she's messing with it.'

Ray wrinkles his brow. His eyebrows meet in the middle and he blows air into one cheek, as if he has toothache.

'There's a deal in place? An arrangement?'

Such things are not unknown. During his career he has worked with plenty of senior officers who view their criminal targets as little more than professional associates. He has known officers who have turned a blind eye to wholesale criminality in exchange for being allowed to nab some headline-grabbing, mid-level dealer.

Russell waves the suggestion away. 'It's not like that. Not like it used to be. You and I both know the Vietnamese have been looking after cannabis for years. It's almost their national dish. Nobody else even bothers. That's what they do. It's like Colombians and cocaine. Some people have just got a gift for it.'

'So who's making waves?'

Russell sighs. 'Pharaoh knew a bit of this, but she's only scratched the surface. You think those blokes who got nail-gunned were the only ones? Man, the shit we've heard! We don't know much about where they've come from or how far their ambitions stretch, but there's a new outfit which has got the Vietnamese running scared.'

'The Vietnamese don't scare.'

'Maybe it's not fear,' says Russell irritably, gesturing with his pint glass. 'Maybe it's more pragmatic than that. We know these new lads have muscle but maybe they have money too. The Vietnamese farmers don't make enough money to even pay the electricity bill on the places where they set up shop. They've got bosses. Paymasters.

Maybe our new boys have bought the local labour and are backing it up with a few demonstrations.'

Ray raises his eyebrows, expecting more. 'That's a lot of maybes, Aidy. You're in charge of the Drugs Squad, mate. Come on, now.'

Russell bristles. 'You seen the last quarterly reports? You want to know how many raids we've successfully carried out this past few months? It's almost daily. The scale of the operation is enormous. Somebody with a bit of vision has realised that most of the force don't give a damn about cannabis, and they've taken advantage of that to make some serious money.'

'Where's your intel coming from?' asks Ray. 'The raids? Your targets?'

'Some we get from street dealers who've got an ear to the ground. Deals with people trying to shave a few months off sentence.'

'And the bigger raids? The ones that make the papers?' Ray fancies he already knows the answer.

Russell looks into the bottom of his empty glass, but Ray makes no move to fill it. The senior officer sighs. 'Anonymous tips,' he says. 'Good ones. Straight through to the mobile phones of me or a couple of my lads. They're never on the blower more than a few seconds. Just give us an address and a time. We hit the place and the cameras start flashing. Nice picture opportunity and the Chief Constable is happy.'

Ray sips his wine. Decides it hasn't taken the edge off what he's feeling. He finishes it in a gulp.

'They're pacifying you,' he says. 'Either that or taking out the competition.'

Russell shrugs. Looks at his glass again. Ray turns to the bar and nods to the young, skinny lad in a black Ramones T-shirt, who is fiddling with his mobile phone behind the bar. Signals for two more drinks.

Russell doesn't speak again until he is wiping beer from his upper lip. 'It's all part of the business these days,' he says. 'You know as well as I do we can't get drugs out of our lives. We can't get them off the streets. We can't get them out of bloody prisons. It's about showing that we're trying. And we are trying, Col. But with the resources I'm putting into cannabis raids, the smack-heads and coke dealers are having a ball. And how do I know the lads who've taken over the Vietnamese workforce aren't looking after the harder stuff too? I know bugger all about them except they're hard as nails, very good and very well informed.'

Ray purses his lips. Holds his tongue until the barman has brought him his change. Pockets it and then places his palms flat on the table, as if taking part in a seance. He appears to be thinking.

'Alan Rourke,' he says. 'I don't take him for some criminal mastermind.'

Russell gives a smile. 'He's hard, I'll tell you that much. Nearly as hard as his old running partner. The stories I could tell you about him and Giuseppe Hamer—'

Ray waves a hand. 'Tell me the story I want to hear. Why are Rourke's fingerprints on the bottle that smashed against a police van outside a bloody cannabis factory?'

Russell squeezes one hand with another. 'The travellers aren't much different to the Vietnamese,' he says, rapping the table with his knuckles to emphasise the words. 'They do their thing. They stay in their own community. They fracture some laws and they cause us headaches. That's always been the way. But we live in a multi-cultural society, Col. Sometimes they branch out.'

'And Rourke has branched out? He's connected to this?'

Russell shrugs. 'He's a known commodity. He's a tough guy with respect and back-up. You've seen the witness reports. It was white guys. Big white guys. What's to say it's not the gypsies who've moved up in the world?'

Ray considers it. Thinks of Rourke: brimming with confidence and utterly unafraid as he kept his silence across the interview table, with a look in his eyes that suggested he would rather bite his tongue off than give up his secrets.

'Where is this coming from, Aidy? I wouldn't even have known you knew the fella if he hadn't mentioned your name. He only did that to see if I'd bite. To show he knew more than me. Made me look a right cunt. Why did you pay him a visit?'

Russell takes another swallow of his drink. Says nothing.

Ray gives a nod of understanding. 'You got another call, didn't you? On the mobile. Same voice that tips you the wink on which factories to raid is now telling you who to put the frighteners on. Bloody hell, Aidy, they may as well have you on the payroll. What did they tell you?'

Russell looks down at the numbers on his arm. The flashes on his uniform that remind him he is a very senior officer. 'Just told me that Alan Rourke was worth a look. That if we had a bit of a lean on him, we might get a few more phonecalls and a few more raids. He's got some lad staying with him. The voice on the line said that we should leave him alone. The teenager. That we should remind Rourke that he's not the boy's father, and that the lad has friends.'

Ray pushes himself back from the table. He is always pissed off. Always aggressive. Can only hold himself back for so long. It's taking an effort now.

'You may as well be on the payroll.'

Russell reddens. 'How can I be working for somebody when I don't know who they are? It was the right decision. A professional decision. I passed on a message, marked his card, and the phonecalls kept coming.'

Ray isn't listening. 'The lad,' he says. 'It's the same one. The one who set the dogs on Pharaoh. Yes?'

Russell nods. Takes a swallow of beer. 'Soon as I saw the description and Rourke's name I decided

230

to call you. You just called me first. I would have rung, Col. Now you're looking after this we'll get somewhere.'

Ray rocks back, the chair on two legs. 'How did Rourke react when you went to see him? What did he have to say?'

'Did all but laugh in my face,' he says. 'Didn't scare. Didn't flinch.'

'And the lad? He was there?'

'Turned up as we were leaving. Climbing out of some flash bloody four-by-four as if he was a Lottery winner or Wayne fucking Rooney.'

Ray drains his glass. His gaze meets Russell's. The senior officer looks away first.

'I know why you didn't tell Pharaoh what's going on with the Vietnamese,' says Ray softly. 'It's because you didn't have much to tell without making yourself look like a bloody gopher for some drug dealers. I even get why you went to see Rourke. What I don't get, Aidy, is how you can't see what's going on.'

Russell narrows his eyes. 'Go on then, smart-arse.'

'The lad's the bloody player. The teenager. He's the one who's valuable to your friends at the end of the phone. Rourke's up to his eyes in all this, but he's overstepping his boundaries. It's the lad who's connected. It's his gyppo connections that are causing your friends the headache.'

Russell seems unconvinced. 'You're a fucking long way from proving any of that.'

'I just need to know it, not prove it,' says Ray, putting all four chair legs flat on the floor.

'What's your move?' asks Russell, looking at his watch and clearly deciding that four pints is enough. 'The lad's top priority, yes?'

'He set the dogs on Pharaoh. So we want him. But we want to know what's in his head too. It's all linked. I'm getting a fucking headache here . . .'

Russell gives a smile, and any tension that existed between them seems to evaporate. Both are old-school. Ray would never even consider grassing another officer up. But he does at least recognise that he suddenly has a useful ace up his sleeve.

'The next time you get a call from your friends . . .'

Russell's face drops back into a scowl.

'Go on.'

'I want in on the raid. I want to talk to whoever you pull.'

Russell seems to think about it. Gives a quick nod. 'It could be sooner than you think. It's been a few days . . .'

'Whenever. I'm not planning on getting much sleep.'

'Where are you heading next?'

Ray gives a little smile, pulling his phone from his pocket. He punches in a number with long, yellow-stained fingers.

'Shaz? Roll off whoever you're on and get yourself in the car. We're going on our holidays, love. Off to visit a few lovely little caravan parks.'

From the other end of the line, comes a barrage of confused questioning. Colin Ray shushes her. 'The ginger lad. He's run to what he knows. He's back with his people. And we're going to go and make him unwelcome.'

CHAPTER 17

4.14 p.m. Ha'penny Bridge Way, on the Victoria Dock estate.

McAvoy, resting his head on the steering wheel, listening to his wife cry. Her sobs sound in tandem with the rain that beats on the glass.

'Come home,' she gasps. 'Please.'

McAvoy looks out through the waterfall of rain that runs down the windscreen. The air is slate grey, the sky reaching all the way down to the deepening puddles and burst drains that are starting to obscure the roads and pavements.

'One stop, Roisin,' he says again. 'One more stop and then I'll come and take over.'

'She won't stop crying,' she says again, and the desperation in her stabs into his chests like an icicle.

'An hour,' he says, closing his eyes.

'She's screaming,' begs Roisin. 'I can't . . .'

She hangs up. She has never hung up on him before.

He begins to call her back. His phone rings again. 'Roisin . . .'

'No, lad. DCI Ray. Where the bloody hell are you?'

McAvoy winds the window down a crack. Lets some air into the vehicle. Watches the reeds sway in the tatty duck pond that separates the two modern apartment blocks that loom over the patchwork of semi-detached properties.

'I've been—'

'Don't care,' says Ray. 'Anyway, Tremberg's been bending my ear about getting in touch with you, so I am because it might make her shut the fuck up. Got her well trained, that one, ain't you? We spoke to Alan Rourke. Gypsy bastard barely said a word. No ID on the lad who set the dogs on her highness, but Shaz is in with Rourke again now and is promising to stop his dogs getting the chop if he's a bit more helpful. We've got fuck all on the Vietnamese or the petrol bombing. Nowt that would interest you, anyway. Reckon we should be checking the England cricket team from the way they threw that thing. Bloody awful bowling action. Anyway, Ben Neilsen's over in Doncaster rounding up CCTV from when the Land Rover was nicked. Turns out they've got other vehicles missing too. Merc, Audi, a Lexus or two. In Doncaster! You feeling in the loop now? Right. Fuck off. Bye.'

McAvoy is too tired to subject the exchange to analysis. He just nods to himself. Eventually closes his phone.

Beyond the glass, the storm is getting worse. The news headlines on Radio Humberside were starting to sound a little hysterical when McAvoy tuned in on the drive here. It is only a few years since Hull suffered near-biblical floods. There are still people living in mobile homes in their front gardens. Every time it rains the city holds its breath. The weather was top story, ahead of an appeal for witnesses following a nasty attack on Morpeth Street last night. A nineteen-year-old girl is in hospital with severe head injures after being set upon by an unknown assailant around 11.30 p.m. Friends have described her as a happy-go-lucky girl who would do anything for anyone. A spokesman for Humberside Police said it was too soon to speculate whether the incident could be linked to the escalation of violent crime in the city, rumoured to be linked to the drugs trade.

It had made McAvoy grimace. Made him wonder, too, why he was chasing so hard after answers about Simon Appleyard when the living were being mercilessly persecuted.

With some difficulty, McAvoy hauls himself from the car. He is far too big for its cramped confines. Feels as though he should cut a hole in the roof to poke his head through. Worries he will pull the door off every time he grips the handle.

The wind and rain refresh him briefly. He looks up at the slate sky and allows the downpour to soak his face. Slicks back his hair and licks the collected droplets from his lips.

The flat he is after is on the ground floor, offering a decent view of the dense mess of reeds which all but obscure the water of the large rectangular pond. McAvoy and Roisin had considered getting a place on this estate when they first moved to the city. It is only a ten-minute walk from the centre and was designed with upwardly mobile families in mind. The houses are small but neatly built and well looked after, but the sense of inner-city community that the developers had been aiming for when they called it an 'urban village' has never truly materialised. Many of the properties are let to young flat-sharers by distant landlords, and there are too many 'for sale' and 'to let' signs to suggest it is a place where people are desperate to stay. It is beginning to look tired, not least because of the moonscape that many of the streets are beginning to resemble thanks to the widely predicted subsidence. A former working dock, it was in-filled to make way for the housing development. There are fears that the whole estate is beginning to sink.

McAvoy takes care on the damp timbers of the footbridge. Looks for signs of life in the duck pond. Wonders if there are any ducks hiding in there or if they, too, have left the estate for more comfortable accommodation in the East Riding villages.

He checks his notepad to confirm the address. Realises he is already standing outside the doors to the apartment block and cannot put this off any longer. He rings the bell.

Seconds go by. Water drips down the back of his neck.

A burst of static from the intercom.

'Hello?'

'Councillor Hepburn,' says McAvoy, louder than he had intended. 'I'm a policeman. Could I have some of your time?'

There is another pause.

'Come in.'

The door buzzes and McAvoy pushes it open. He finds himself in a wide, grey-carpeted, buttermilk-painted atrium. There is a set of stairs at the far end, and three brown wooden doors set in the remaining walls.

Number 29 is opening.

He recognises the man in the doorway from the newspaper and TV appearances. He is in his late forties, with dyed blonde hair swept back from a long face that nature has made unremarkable, but vanity has coloured. The tuft of hair beneath his lower lip is dyed peroxide blonde and his sideburns are razored to a neat, almost devilish point. He has two rings in his left ear, and McAvoy doubts that his eyebrows are naturally as jet black as they appear.

He is smiling broadly, a politician's grin. He is wearing a purple V-neck jumper and loudly checked trousers that are more Rupert the Bear than Harris tweed. He is in relatively good shape, but the outline of sagging pectorals can still be made out through the material of his sweater.

'Plain clothes, eh?' Hepburn asks warmly. 'Intriguing.'

McAvoy looks down at himself, standing in a puddle, all but raining on the floor.

238

'Still drizzling?' asks Hepburn.

McAvoy forces a smile.

'Come in,' Hepburn says. 'I'll get you a towel.'

He steps back inside the apartment and holds the door open. McAvoy wonders if he should offer to remove his boots, but remembers the fuss he had getting his shoes on this morning, and very much doubts that his socks match.

He follows the councillor inside and down a short corridor decorated with black-and-white prints.

He is led into a large living room, painted terracotta and designed in a vaguely Javanese style. The blinds are raffia, and the prints on the wall are of elephants and traditional fishing skiffs, pots of spice and gentlemen's club antique maps. There is an expensive-looking rug on the cream-carpeted floor, and the red chesterfield sofa gives the place the feel of a British Empire hotel gone slightly to seed. The two-seater table at one end of the room supports a huge vase of lilies. The other end of the long room is given over to a large flat-screen TV.

'Paula, can you bring me a towel, love?'

Hepburn shouts this last as he throws himself down on the sofa. There is a laptop computer on the middle cushion, and a mobile phone on the floor.

'What can I do for you?'

McAvoy is about to speak when a woman appears in the doorway. She is around the same age as

Hepburn, and almost as imposing a physical specimen as McAvoy. She is pushing six feet tall, and broad across the shoulders. Her hair is a collage of different shades of blonde and is cut in a choppy, neck-length bob that looks to McAvoy's inexpert gaze as if it was expensive. She is wearing a white blouse and cropped trousers with wedged high-heels. She hands McAvoy a fluffy yellow towel, which he takes gratefully, and uses to dry his face and hair.

When he has finished, he does his best to smooth down his curls, and is grateful that he is facing away from the mirror that dominates one wall.

'Paula,' says Hepburn to the woman in the doorway, 'this is . . .' He pulls a quizzical face. 'Did you tell me?'

'Detective Sergeant McAvoy,' he says and is embarrassed by the squeak in his voice.

'McAvoy,' says Hepburn thoughtfully. Snaps his fingers, as if placing the name. 'Indeed. This is Paula.'

'How do you do,' says McAvoy, extending his hand.

Paula gives a curt nod. Raises an eyebrow at Hepburn.

'Coffee,' she says, and it does not sound like a question. She turns her back. Leaves them to it.

'So,' says Hepburn again. 'What can I do for you?'

McAvoy realises he has been pressing his lips together. Takes a breath.

'Councillor, I probably shouldn't be here, but today I received information that suggests you are the target of some kind of journalistic investigation designed to discredit you.'

He stops. Hepburn widens his eyes, and the playful smile on his face seems to grow.

'Really? Do tell.'

'I had reason to speak to a reporter from a national newspaper about another matter. He informed me they are planning a story looking into some criminal connections in your past.'

Hepburn gives a whistle.

'Anything else?'

'There is some suggestion that your nightclub has been financed by drug money.'

Hepburn is openly laughing. McAvoy feels sick.

'Councillor Hepburn?'

The other man pulls himself off the couch. Stands up straight and gives a wide grin. 'And you're bringing this to me because . . .'

McAvoy allows himself to look baffled. The answer should be obvious. 'Because that's not right.'

Hepburn pulls himself together. 'But you don't know me,' he says, looking straight at McAvoy. 'People get shit written about them all the time. I got elected by people who either wanted a drink at midnight or liked the idea of pissing off Labour. Seriously, Sergeant, another story about me being a bad boy is not going to destroy me. Might even be good publicity. Come on, what's the ulterior motive?'

McAvoy feels his cheeks flush. He had not expected to have his integrity questioned. Is appalled to have been seen through so easily. Fears what it says about him that he could so easily be identified as a liar.

'Come on, Sergeant,' says Hepburn.

McAvoy meets Hepburn's gaze. There is a fierce intelligence in his blue eyes. He remembers his TV appearances. His quick wits and sharp tongue. Realises he was wrong to blunder in here so ill-prepared and cack-handed.

'Simon Appleyard,' he blurts and then has to all but wrestle with himself to stop his right hand coming up to his face in a childish show of regret.

Hepburn narrows his eyes. 'And who might that be?'

'Simon Appleyard was found hanged at his home last year. We are looking again at the circumstances surrounding his death. I'm going through the numbers in his telephone. Your number is among those that were stored.'

Hepburn shrugs, and it is not an unfriendly gesture. 'I'm sorry, but I really don't think I know the name. I'm a public figure. I run a club. I change phones quite a lot . . .'

'This is the telephone you were given by the city council.'

'Ah,' says Hepburn, with a grin. 'Right. Had that about a fortnight then it went missing. Probably nicked from the club. Felt a right fool reporting it missing. Been using my personal one ever since. Got two SIM cards in it. Really snazzy . . .'

'And you don't know the name Simon Appleyard? He was in his mid-twenties. Tall. Ran a line-dance class . . .'

Hepburn shakes his head.

McAvoy ploughs on.

'. . . peacock feathers tattooed all over his back . . .'

For a fraction of a second Hepburn's smile seems to die at the eyes. Then it is back. Wide. Charming. Naughty.

'Leave me your card, Sergeant,' he says, still being friendly. 'I'll have a think. Get in touch with you.'

Paula reappears at the door. She is not holding coffee cups. She is not smiling.

McAvoy looks at Hepburn, whose raised eyebrows represent a friendlier version of Paula's hard stare. He is being invited to leave.

'My card,' says McAvoy, handing the councillor a damp rectangle of blurred ink. 'I'm sorry to have bothered you. I just thought you should know about the reporter . . .'

Hepburn is nodding as he gets to his feet. Makes a show of shaking the officer's hand. Is only a pace behind him as he corrals him out of the door, past the bulk of his unfriendly companion, and into the hall.

'If I hear anything more . . .'

'Thank you, Sergeant,' says Hepburn.

The door shuts behind him and McAvoy finds himself back in the lobby.

He feels his cheeks burning, but this time it is with temper instead of shame. The way she looked at him. The playful little smirk on Hepburn's face. He had felt like a teenager caught out in an untruth. Had been made to feel a fool.

He would have taken such feelings as penance, were it not for that moment, that flicker of recognition, that caused the councillor's grin to lock in fleeting falsehood.

McAvoy came here in the hope of unearthing something to vindicate his instincts. Hoped to find a whiff of something that means he is not wasting his time. For a moment, here in the heat of tired irritation and embarrassment, he feels he may have found it.

The rain is less furious as McAvoy lets himself out of the doors and into an ankle-deep puddle. He barely pays it any heed. He pulls his phone from his pocket. Calls Roisin.

'Darling,' he says, when she answers on the eighth ring. 'I'm on my way home. I'm so sorry.'

They talk for five minutes. Her apologising. Telling him she understands. Him begging forgiveness for his remoteness. His uselessness. Telling her, excitedly, about his five minutes in the home of Councillor Hepburn, and his suspicions that the man knows more than he is willing to admit. That there is a case here. A real investigation.

He is still talking when his phone beeps, and he tells Roisin he will have to go. He will see her soon.

'Sergeant McAvoy,' he says. 'Serious and Organised.'

'Sergeant. This is Assistant Chief Constable Everett. I want you in my office right away. There has been a complaint that you are harassing a senior member of Hull Council.'

The colour drains from McAvoy's face. He closes his eyes.

He can already hear the tears in Roisin's voice.

The man in the tan leather jacket is losing his temper. Suzie is no expert in body language, but from the shape of his shoulders and his white-knuckled grip on the counter, she senses an imminent explosion of anger.

'Am I speaking a different language here?'

Suzie, sweating despite her damp clothes and beginning to feel a little feverish, shares his pain.

She looks at her own cashier. Tries her sweetest smile. Hopes her exasperated grin will find a kindred spirit. Gets nothing in response. The lady behind the glass is younger than her, but has the sour face and unmoving expression of a lifelong doctor's receptionist.

'It was 18p,' says Suzie, again. '18p! That's how much I was overdrawn by. You charged me for the letter you sent to tell me that, and then charged me for three days of unauthorised overdraft use. I would have cleared the 18p, but the charge put me £15 into the red, and then the extra charges . . .'

She stops. It is the fourth time she has tried to persuade the cashier behind the glass that she is being treated unfairly. She can feel the back of her neck getting hot and prickly. The injustice of it is making her words catch in her throat. Misery sits in her stomach like a snowball.

'It's my money,' says the man in the leather jacket and his voice has increased in volume. 'You look after it for me. That's your job.'

The neighbouring cashier is equally intractable. 'Without a passport or driving licence, we can only give you £5,000.'

'But it's my money!' he shouts.

Both debates have been going on for some time and the lengthening queue in the bank is watching the two exchanges with a mixture of impatience and interest.

Suzie stands in silence, shaking her head and trying to think of another collection of words that might make the cashier change her mind. She fears that her eyes are on the verge of filling with tears.

'It's an issue of your security,' says the adjacent cashier.

'The charges are all explained on the website,' says Suzie's tyrant.

The man in the leather jacket is looking around, as if for an ally who can help explain to him the workings of this insane and alien world. He looks at Suzie. Their eyes meet. He is a handsome enough man, pushing forty, and his clothes are casual but expensive. His face softens a little as he takes in her red face and sodden hair, damp clothes and watery eyes.

'Can you believe this?'

Suzie shakes her head. Turns to the cashier.

'I'm having a bad time,' she says softly. 'It was 18p. And now it's pushing £100. Just with charges. Can I give you the 18p? Or a token gesture, or something. I can't get back into credit until payday . . .'

'The charges are all explained on our website.'

Tears come. Unbidden, Suzie realises her eyes have overflowed.

Salt water runs down her powdered cheeks and her shoulders start to shake.

'I'm sorry,' says the woman behind the glass, with the same expression she has worn since Suzie reached the front of the queue and asked for a little leniency.

'I'm on my lunch,' sobs Suzie, as if this might make a difference. 'I normally sit in a little garden . . .'

She cries openly into her hand. She hates the pathetic picture she knows she must be presenting. Hates being so feeble. Wants to turn and run, to hide until somebody finds her and promises that it will all be better soon.

She has still not had the courage to turn on her telephone. Has heard nothing more about the man she left to die.

'We own you anyway,' says the man in the leather jacket, turning his attention from his own cashier to Suzie's. 'The taxpayers. You belong to us.'

He looks around at the queue behind him, as if trying to drum up support for a revolution. He gives a sigh as he takes in the collection of damp shoppers and office workers, shivering in wet clothes and waiting for their turn to go and shout impotently at the staff.

'The rules are there on the website.'

Suzie stiffens as the man moves closer. He ducks down to place his face in her line of vision. He is looking into her eyes. It is a caring stare, devoid of malice or threat. He wants to see if she's ok.

'They won't listen,' he says to her quietly. 'Charges, is it?'

Suzie tries to smile. She feels wretchedly miserable.

'How much to get back in credit?' he asks, leaning in close enough for his words to tickle her wet earlobe and neck.

'Nearly £90.'

The man gives a nod. He puts a hand in his pocket and takes out a roll of notes. 'Take it,' he says, handing her five £20 notes.

'What? No . . .!'

Suzie's chest constricts. She begins to protest. To tell him that it's not his problem. That he has problems of his own.

The notes have found their way into her hand. A damp smile has made its way to her face.

'Please,' says the man softly. 'Let me.'

'I don't—'

'I don't want these bastards taking another penny off anyone. Please.'

Suzie, flustered and unsure, turns to the cashier, who is struggling to keep the grimace off her face.

'Here,' she says, through a face of tears and snot. 'I'd like to make a deposit.'

The man does not return to his own cashier. He leans against the counter, and looks at Suzie with amused affection.

He looks her up and down. Likes the view.

'Does that buy your phone number?' he asks.

Suzie freezes. Gives a girlish, embarrassed smile that Simon would have mocked her for.

'I know,' says the man, raising his hands. 'It spoils the selfless gesture.'

'I'm not sure . . .' she begins.

'Take mine,' he says, and writes a scrawl of digits on the back of a paying-in slip. 'No pressure.'

Suzie looks up again and finds herself blushing.

'I don't know if I'll call,' she says, picking up the number.

'I'll be hoping,' he says and turns away.

'Bye,' she says, shocked and embarrassed.

'Bye, Susan,' he says and is gone.

Suzie stays at the counter for a few seconds, wishing she had somebody to share this odd moment with. She wonders who she will tell about the handsome man who came to her rescue.

Whether she will log on to Facebook and tell her friends. Thinks of pulling out her phone.

Freezes, as paranoia strikes.

Her name. He knew her name!

She turns from the counter and pushes through the crowd, down the half-dozen steps and through the double doors onto Whitefriargate. She looks this way and that, squinting in the rain, trying to make out the shape of the leather-jacketed man.

Cautiously, taking care in her flip-flops on the cobbles, she splashes through a puddle and runs up the street.

'Hey,' she shouts, and finds herself giving a peculiar little laugh at the indignity of the scene. 'Hey!'

Up ahead, outside the record store where she and Simon had bought the Twilight box set and then argued over custody, she spots him. She half falls into his back, clumsily grabbing his shoulder.

He turns. Surprised at first, then pleased.

'How did you know my name?' she asks, breathlessly. 'You said, "Susan".'

The man rubs a hand over his face and screws up his eyebrows.

'What?'

'My name. You knew my name.'

He looks around him, almost as if searching for a hidden camera crew. When he finds none, he looks at her and closes one eye as he speaks, as if wincing at the words.

'It's on your bank card,' he says, gently but confused. 'What's wrong?'

Suzie breathes out, hard. Fresh tears prick her eyes.

'I'm sorry,' she says, looking down at the floor.

The man stands there for a moment.

Suzie is a statue. Looking down at wet cobbles and her own soaking, dirty toes.

Then she feels his arms around her.

Her shoulders shake and she weeps against his chest: clinging to a stranger in the pouring rain.

CHAPTER 18

I t is pushing eleven p.m. when McAvoy opens
his front door.
Home, he thinks gratefully. *Thank you.*

He is so tired he can barely lift his feet. Too
drained to notice that the rain has stopped or
comment on the brightness of the near-full moon,
which hangs like a disc of crumpled parchment
in a blue-black, cloudless sky.

Too exhausted to remark upon Roisin's absence.
She is normally here, smiling in the doorway,
waiting for him. Waiting to kiss him home and
slide herself into his embrace.

'Roisin?'

He finds her in the darkened living room, curled
up on the sofa. Finlay is wrapped around her, face
to face, snoring softly into her open mouth. He is
wearing a woollen hat, pulled down over his ears.
McAvoy takes it as a sign that his eldest child has
grown tired of his sister's cries.

'I'm so sorry,' he whispers, and hopes that it will
cover his multitude of sins.

Quietly he heads upstairs, avoiding the creaking
steps.

Lilah is laying spreadeagled in his bed, prisoner in a rectangle of pillows. She is healthily pink-faced and her sleep looks a lovely and peaceful thing. He wants to kiss her. To smell her head. To say sorry for not being what she needs. He persuades himself not to wake her. Tiptoes back downstairs.

Roisin is disentangling herself from Fin. She looks up as he appears at the door.

'Hi,' she smiles drowsily. 'What time is it?'

'Too late,' says McAvoy, crossing to her. 'I'm so sorry.'

He bends down and crushes her in an embrace.

'Aector, easy . . .'

He is holding her too tightly. Lets go. Tips her face upwards with his index finger and stares into her eyes. Again. 'I'm so sorry.'

Her smile, though tired, is warm and genuine. She kisses him.

He tastes the sleep in her mouth. Tastes the blackcurrant juice she and Fin have shared. The tang of hand-rolled cigarettes.

The last few hours have been torture, made worse by the cold agony of separation.

Everett swallowed his story about wanting to warn Councillor Hepburn about the newspaper investigation. McAvoy had even been commended by the tall, ferrety man for his diplomacy and foresight, and had managed to keep his mouth shut about Simon Appleyard. He had been starting to let himself think he could still make it home in time to bath the little ones when he had been asked to cast his expert eye over a speech Everett was due to present. It took hours. McAvoy has many times rued the day he first put together an expenditure report for a committee briefing. It had been coherent, simple to follow and correctly spelled. In Everett's eyes, it had marked him out as a borderline genius and the go-to guy for any job that required somebody who doesn't move their lips when they read.

'How was it?' Roisin asks quietly, leading him into the kitchen so as not to wake Fin. 'You a naughty boy?'

McAvoy manages a little laugh. 'I think Hepburn has friends in high places,' he says.

'Let's hope they're going to jump,' she replies, setting to work making him a sandwich with fresh bread and home-made jam.

'I can't have been out of there thirty seconds before he made a call,' he says, taking a swig of the glass of milk she hands him. 'He was ok when I was there.'

'Arsehole.'

She hands him his sandwich. Watches him take a bite. Seems pleased with his grunt of appreciation.

McAvoy notes she is wearing the same clothes she had on this morning.

'I could bath you,' he says through his dinner. 'Candles. Wash your hair. Shave your legs. Paint your nails.'

Roisin grins. 'Sounds lovely,' she says. 'But let's just go to bed. I've got a surprise for you.'

McAvoy wonders if he has the strength to keep pace with whatever surprise she has planned. He is about to suggest they just hold each other, when she gives a bright smile. 'Wait here,' she says and runs from the kitchen.

Puzzled, McAvoy finishes his sandwich. Drains his drink. Takes a chocolate biscuit from the tin by the microwave and polishes it off in a bite.

Like a deflating bouncy castle, he folds himself into the kitchen chair and drops his head to the table. He closes his eyes. Treats himself to a moment devoid of thought.

It hits him then. Just how reckless he has been. How disloyal and vain. He has been pursuing proof of his own instincts. He has been trying to vindicate a feeling. While he has been trying to prove that he can sense a crime the same way his father can smell the nearness of snow, a real investigation has gone tits up and the only colleague who truly believes in him has been attacked by dogs.

Simon Appleyard.

He decides it's time to make the case more official. He will approach one of the detective superintendents in regular CID tomorrow. Tell him there is a case to be looked into. Take the withering looks and jaded sighs and simply insist that the investigation is carried out, and properly.

'Don't be cross.'

Roisin is standing in the doorway. She is smiling

and has changed into a silkier nightdress. Her hair is piled high on top of her head, exposing her dark, scented neck.

McAvoy blinks a few times, muzzy-headed. He smiles as he takes her in.

She holds out her hands.

On her left palm is a mobile phone.

'You got him one, did you . . .?' begins McAvoy, then stops, his smile freezing, as a picture surfaces in his addled memory.

'I'm sorry I was so mean,' she says, and walks towards him, waiting for her hug.

McAvoy's mouth falls open and the colour bleeds from his face.

His wife is holding an unfamiliar mobile phone.

He doesn't know whether it is instinct, or simply the hopeful, helpful look on his wife's face, but he knows at once it belongs to Councillor Hepburn.

'That's him,' says Suzie, pointing through the railings. 'Trevor, say hello.'

Beside her, in the dark, she can hear Anthony smiling. It is an odd feeling. She can sense him staring. Grinning at the side of her face. He has been looking at her with affectionate bemusement much of the evening, and now appears to be enjoying the note of sleepy drunkenness that has entered her voice.

'That's where I sit,' she adds, pointing at the bench in the courtyard garden. 'Every day. Me and Trevor, setting the world to rights. I do most of the talking but he's a great listener.'

Anthony scratches his stubbly chin and gives her an encouraging smile.

'He's a lovely tree,' he says, and then has to stifle a little grin. He has never really imagined having to use such a phrase, and wonders what his mates would think to this strange, colourful girl. He finds himself hoping they will find out.

Their date has gone relatively well. Suzie called him from the work phone mid-afternoon, to apologise for being weird and to reassure him that she wasn't mental. He had laughed and insisted she could only make it up to him if she met him for a drink.

It is now just gone eleven, and they have the Old Town to themselves. The endless rain seems to have swept the city clean, and there are no raised voices or passing cars to break the perfect silence that exists here in this darkened pocket of Hull.

Suzie is wearing a long blue dress onto which she has embroidered a large felt heron. She is wearing a beret and her earrings are owls in cages. It took her a long time to get ready. She was excited and scared, and wished she had somebody standing behind her telling her she looked nice, would have a good time, and that there was very little chance of having to jump out of the way of a speeding four-by-four while mid-fuck.

The alcohol in her system coupled with the bracing night air is making her feel teary and tired.

She is over-emotional. Confused. She has talked endlessly. Managed to keep the conversation away from one-night stands and casual sex without really knowing why. She wonders if she is ashamed. Or simply cautious about driving away this nice man by revealing who and what she really is.

She had been pleased he wanted to meet Trevor.

'I tried to persuade myself he was Simon,' she says suddenly. 'But he couldn't be, could he? Trevor's been here for years. Simon hasn't been dead long. What do you think? Could it have sucked up his soul?'

As she asks the question, she leans her forehead on the damp brick. She closes her eyes. She has drunk too much, eaten nothing, and feels truly intoxicated on the newness of this evening. She has enjoyed talking. Letting her mouth run away. Unburdening herself. She feels somehow free tonight. Anthony is nice. He seems to find her interesting.

Anthony puts an arm around her shoulders and gently pulls her back from the wall. He bends down a little to better look into her eyes.

'I'm sure he's happy, wherever he is.'

Anthony has not followed her stories perfectly. Suzie is not the most linear of narrators. He understands that her best friend died some months ago and that, since then, she has felt isolated and alone. He is not sure how to ask more without prying, or what he would do with the answers.

'Do you think?'

He nods as solemnly as he can.

'You're nice.'

She wonders if this is what dates are usually like. Her life has not been like this. She was with her first boyfriend from childhood, and segued into promiscuity at the relationship's end. She has never been romanced. Tonight, sharing a couple of bottles of wine in the attractive Russian vodka bar at the bottom of Whitefriargate, has felt pleasantly bizarre. She feels more nervous, here and now, than during her countless trips to sex clubs. In that environment, she has never found herself timid or unsure. Each patron came with one goal in mind.

Here, on a regular date, with a nice man who wants to know more about her, she feels twitchy and confused. She doesn't understand what he wants.

'I'm nice?' he asks, pretending to be offended. 'Just what every man wants to hear.'

Suzie smiles. She is feeling tired. 'Nice in good ways, I mean. You wanted to see my tree . . .'

'It's a grand tree.'

'He.'

'He's a grand tree.'

Drunkenly, impulsively, she leans forward and kisses him. She catches him just below the lips, and presses too hard, hurting both of their faces.

'I'm sorry,' she says as she pulls back.

'Don't be,' he replies, laughing and rubbing his lips.

They look at each other, awkwardly, for a moment. Anthony is thirty-nine years old and, up close, it is clear he shaves his head because he is balding anyway. He is wearing the same brown leather jacket he had on in the bank, and smells faintly of some kind of aftershave balm. He is an attractive man, and had looked embarrassed while telling her that he makes his living hiring out play equipment for children's parties, and renting out mobile discos. He has two children from a failed marriage, and lives alone in an apartment on Victoria Dock. They are walking distance from his home.

'I'm sorry I've prattled on,' says Suzie, suddenly unsure what to say next.

'I like the way you talk. It's soothing.'

Suzie looks at him again and wonders what to do. If this were a club night, she would simply take him by the hand and lead him to a private room. She is willing to have sex with him. But this feels different. She would quite like to kiss him too. Wants to know how it would feel to have his arms around her and her head on his chest.

'I have more wine at home,' he says with a slight smile. 'It's not far . . .'

Suzie looks down at her feet. She is wearing her flip-flops, and is standing in a puddle. It feels nice. If she wriggles her toes, she can feel grit on the soles of her feet.

The sensation feels familiar.

She is suddenly back on the layby at Coniston.

She is being fucked over the bonnet of a car by a stranger, while somebody slams their foot down on the accelerator . . .

She is at the sex club. She is spreadeagled on the floor; one man inside her, three more waiting their turn. Simon, leaning against the wall with a rolled-up cigarette, talking to a handsome man with grey hair and a flamboyant shirt, open to the waist.

She is crying into her phone, unable to hear Simon's auntie's words of condolence as she tries to digest the news that her best friend is dead and had never trusted her enough to share his pain . . .

Suzie flops back against the wall. Her eyes fill with tears. She does not know what she wants or who to be. She just knows she misses her friend and that her life has felt empty and lonely ever since he hanged himself in his kitchen.

'Nobody understands,' she murmurs.

She needs to feel alive. She needs to close her heart and open her legs. She does not need love, she tells herself. Does not need to be held, or kissed, or praised or romanced. She needs to take her pleasures and please those who want her, and she needs to close herself down to all the anguish that threatens to spill in and out of her if not controlled.

'Suzie?'

'I'm sorry,' she says, with her eyes closed 'I'm not ready for a relationship.'

Anthony's face flashes with confusion. 'I didn't think I was offering one,' he says and, when he realises how harsh that sounds, adds: 'I just offered a drink.'

Suzie cannot really hear his words. The blood is rushing in her head, and she is feeling dizzy. Sick, suddenly. Her whole sense of self has become a finger painting; all intermingled swirls of contradiction and insecurity.

Anthony is a nice man. She has enjoyed his company. He is funny and charming and seems to care. And she knows he could do so much better. She knows that she is not right for him. Not built for satisfying the heart.

'Just do what you want,' she says dozily, and turns her back on him, pulling up the hem of her dress and then stumbling to one knee.

She lies there, face against the brick, tears rolling down her face.

Anthony looks down at her, bare leg and thigh exposed, dirt and brick-dust streaking her pale skin; the tail end of a tattoo upon her flesh.

For the briefest of moments desire fills him. The sight of bare, youthful skin thrills him. And then it is gone, replaced by pity. More than that. Tenderness. Affection.

He sits with her and strokes her hair until the taxi arrives. When he tells it to take her to her own home, and not to his, it is with only a hint of regret.

He hopes there will be other times with this odd,

kooky, pretty girl, who talks to trees and mourns dead friends and draws peacocks on beer mats with tears in her eyes.

In her drunken sleep Suzie knows there will not.

11.18 p.m. The Kingswood estate. The kitchen of a cardboard cut-out house made wedding-cake white by three days of rain.

Aector and Roisin McAvoy, angry and disappointed with one another for the first time in their lives.

Even as they argue, their voices are whispers. Their row does not get loud enough to wake the baby. Their tempers do not supersede practicalities.

'I'm a policeman! This is theft. It's burglary. You robbed a member of the public . . .'

'You said he was a suspect! You said . . .'

'But I don't tell you things so you can go and do this! I tell you because I've got nobody to talk to . . .'

'I wanted to help. I'd been so grumpy and you've been working all these hours and I thought if you caught somebody maybe you could come home . . .'

'But I'm a policeman!'

Roisin's face is flushed. McAvoy cannot tell if she is angry at him for being so pathetically moralistic, or for not just saying thank you and giving her a kiss.

He is trying to control his panic. He feels as though the back door could be kicked off its hinges by internal affairs officers at any moment. He tries to picture himself as anything other than a policeman. Wonders whether he will be kept in a special wing in prison to save him from the other inmates . . .

'I'll have it taken back,' she says sadly, and McAvoy realises she is upset purely because she had tried to something nice and he does not like his present.

Even now, his heart thundering in his chest, his hands trembling, he cannot maintain his anger at her. He crosses to her. Pulls her in close. Feels her resist and then acquiesce. She looks up at him.

'I'll phone my pal,' she says. 'He'll drop it off.'

McAvoy gives a nod. Tries to calm himself. He wants to ask her who took it. Wants the name and address of this criminal whom his wife seems to have no compunction about contacting.

'I don't understand,' he says softly, moving away. 'I never ask, Ro. Never ask you what you do to make money or the people you know. I'd never want to hear the answers. But I wouldn't know who to ring to get a house broken into, and I'm a policeman . . .'

Roisin shrugs and moves herself onto one of the kitchen chairs. When she raises her head, she is looking at him as though she is talking to a child. He is a decade her senior and has spent his adult life chasing killers, but sometimes he thinks she sees him as extraordinarily naive. He suddenly questions whether she stays with him not because he is her big, strong protector, but because she pities him as an unworldly innocent.

'Everybody knows somebody who can do that kind of shite,' she says. 'It's just a phonecall. He took it from his pocket . . .'

'He?'

'My pal. It was supposed to be a nice surprise.'

McAvoy cannot help but smile. He pinches the bridge of his nose and looks again at his wife. She has put the phone on the kitchen table. It sits there invitingly.

He bends down and kisses the top of Roisin's head. Turns her face and kisses her pouting mouth.

'Next time could you just make me a lemon meringue?'

Roisin giggles.

'I knew you'd be a bit mad,' she says, still grinning. 'But go on, admit it, you're pleased.'

McAvoy pretends to look indignant, then gives in.

'I can't look at it,' he says and wishes he were somebody else.

'Oh, for God's sake, Aector,' she says exasperated, and picks up the phone. She starts pressing buttons and pulling faces. 'Ooh. Wow. Wait until you see this.'

Laughing, despite himself, he takes the phone from her hand. 'Go on up,' he says, nodding in the direction of the stairs. 'Five minutes, I'll join you.'

She raises an eyebrow. 'I put this on for you,' she says, gesturing at her short nightie. She puts her bare legs and feet on the kitchen table. 'Don't let me fall asleep.'

McAvoy blows her a kiss as she stands, and feels a wonderful warmth inside himself as she flashes him her bum on the way out of the door. He loves her enough to go to jail. Would die for her. Would rather break the law than let her think he doesn't appreciate her present to him.

He takes a breath. Locks the back door and moves to the living room. Checks on Fin, still snoring peacefully on the sofa. Removes his coat and sits down in his armchair. Closes his eyes, as if in prayer, then turns his attention to the phone.

It is an HTC Wildfire, its touchscreen as awkward as all others McAvoy has tried to get to grips with. His big fingers prod at the surface, and he navigates his way to the phone's message facility.

He reads through the last few texts Hepburn has received. There is one unopened; obviously sent since the phone was taken, sent from a contact named Gwen. He flicks through those that have already been opened. Reminders about a meeting the following day from somebody named Carl. A query from Tim about whether he can run an Artois Cidre promotion at the club. A string of half a dozen messages for P.

McAvoy reads backwards, from apology to insult.

I'm sorry. So grumpy. Not your fault.
Too much pressure, sometimes. Talk
soon. Xx
   You don't give a damn about anybody
but yourself.
   I have so much wrapped up in you. I
couldn't just stand by.
   What are friends for? xx
   You've got enough on. I wasn't trying to
make you cross. You don't understand.
   You break my heart when you are like
this. I hate you.

McAvoy carries on scrolling through the inbox.
The messages were sent between five and six p.m.
He flicks to the 'sent items' and finds only two
messages in return.

Wish I could be what you need. Xx
I give a damn about you. Xxxx

He opens the phone's diary function. Leafs
through Hepburn's schedule. Council meetings.
Officer reports. Interview with *Mixmag*.
Then:

Plmtz, 8pm, Saturday. Birthday bash.

He closes his eyes again. Wonders if it is the right
thing to stop now. Asks himself, in all seriousness,
whether Hepburn deserves to have his personal

details pored over like this when he has done, so far, nothing wrong.

He opens his photo files. Flicks, quickly, through hundreds of party-night pictures; all neon lights and shadows; sweating shapes and amplifiers, half-empty glasses and screaming girls.

Opens another file. Pictures from a holiday. Hepburn, in blue Speedos, on a sun-lounger with something exotic and fruity. Two young men, grinning for the camera: shirtless and tanned. A figure on a jetski, far out on a blue sea . . .

McAvoy cannot help it. He opens the file marked 'Fun'.

He does not look for long. The images are clear in their content.

Naked male flesh. Hard cocks and bare buttocks, wet mouths and body hair.

Men making love.

He recognises Hepburn. All smiles. A man having fun.

Opens another file. More of the same. So much skin.

As he watches, a message flashes up on the screen.

He can't help it. He opens it.

Needed you tonight. You said you would call. X

The message is from a contact called MC. McAvoy jots down the number. Picks up his laptop. Enters it in Google with one hand, while keying Simon Appleyard's number into the mobile phone with the other.

There are no hits on Hepburn's phone. Nothing that links him to the dead man.

He looks at the laptop. Closes his eyes.

MC is Hull City Councillor Mark Cabourne. Vice-chairman of the Planning Committee, and member of the Police Authority. Portfolio holder for health and equalities and executive member of the Yorkshire Flood Defence Committee. A face. A name. A former council planner turned politician.

He tries to make sense of this. Tries to diminish the impact of his string of semi-discoveries and fresh questions. Two colleagues texting? So what? Perhaps the kiss is an accident. Perhaps the message is non-sexual. Perhaps none of it is any of his fucking business.

He switches off the phone. Makes a decision.

Achily, exhaustedly, he pulls himself out of his chair. His wife is waiting for him to thank her properly. Tomorrow is a new day. The rain has blown itself out and none of his crimes so far cannot be remedied.

He feels a sudden tremble against his chest. Feels like crying as he pulls out his phone.

'McAvoy? It's Helen. Helen Tremberg. I just bumped into Shaz Archer. Detective Inspector

Archer, whatever. Colin Ray's been following a lead. Reckons the lad we're after is with the gypsies on the playing fields. There's a link to Rourke. He's been gone ages. He didn't take back-up. She's going up there after him. I think you should come . . .'

CHAPTER 19

Midnight. Dead on.

McAvoy runs across the wet grass, mud splashing his trousers and lapping at his boots, acid belching into his throat.

He can hear dogs barking. Raised voices. The crackle of throaty laughter.

He squints ahead at the semi-circle of caravans. There are black figures etched against the darkness, the lights spilling from the curtained mobile homes and the melee of parked cars making the picture dance and flicker.

Tremberg filled him in on the way here, shouting into the phone he held guiltily to his ear as the little car whined its way to seventy mph on the dual carriageway.

It was pure luck that Colin Ray had made the connection between Alan Rourke and the makeshift traveller camp that had caused McAvoy so much embarrassment on the first day the rains came. Ray had been taking a break from the endless 'no comment' interview and had used it to go through the report of Rourke's known associates that one of the civilian workers had left on his desk. He had been looking at a printout of an armed robber by the name of Daragh Fitzroyce when Helen Tremberg had come back to the office and recognised the mugshot as the leader of the gypsy gamp causing chaos up at Anlaby. 'Buttercup's owner,' she had told the confused DCI, smiling, only to find out that the tall, grey-haired, scowling detective inspector had not heard about the incident, nor, as far as she could tell, the invention of the Internet. She had filled him in on McAvoy's horse-wrangling of a couple of days before.

Ray didn't believe in coincidence. Reread Rourke's own file.

Suddenly convinced of some gypsy conspiracy, he retrieved Shaz Archer from the interview room and headed off to the playing fields. That was some time ago and he has not yet checked in.

'McAvoy!'

He spins his head. Helen Tremberg is running towards him out of the darkness, having parked on a nearby side-street and waited for his arrival. He recognises her shape and instantly feels bad for it, while noting that she, too, must have identified him from his mass.

'Nice timing,' she says, as she gets close enough for him to make her out. The front of her pinstripe suited is covered in mud and her face is flushed, though she is not out of breath.

'Have you called for uniform back-up?' he asks.

Tremberg shakes her head. 'What if he's fine? He'll go bloody spare. He's our superior, not the other way around. He can go in guns blazing if he wants.'

McAvoy can see her point, but knows that procedurally they are in serious trouble. 'What if he's not fine?'

'That would be a mixed blessing,' she says, meeting his eye. 'I'm sorry for calling you out. I just thought . . .'

'I know. It's ok.'

They stand in silence. 'They wouldn't hurt a policeman . . .' he begins.

'Let's see,' Tremberg says, and nods in the direction of the caravans.

Sighing, unsure, hating himself, McAvoy nods, and together they walk briskly towards the lights.

The dogs bark more loudly as they get nearer, and moments later figures are emerging from caravans and cars; lifting themselves from the sofas that sit in the centre around what looks, at this remove, like a selection of patio heaters.

'Police,' shouts Tremberg at the approaching crowd.

'Serious and . . .'

McAvoy falls silent.

Half a dozen men are approaching the two officers. Their faces are angry and territorial. McAvoy recognises one of them from the other day and tries a half-smile, but gets nothing but anger in return.

'We've done nottin',' says one man, over shouts and protests from the others.

'We're not fucking going anywhere, I'll tell you that!'

'Leave us be, ya Guard bastard.'

'Jaysus, look at the size of the fucker.'

McAvoy raises his hands, as if trying to pacify an angry dog. He pushes through the crowd into the centre of the clearing.

'Detective Chief Inspector Ray! Detective Chief Inspector Ray!'

He wonders what he will do next. Whether he will start opening doors and checking under caravans. Wonders what the fuck is the point of thinking of himself as an asset.

'Christ, it's the Highlander!'

On the sofa, next to the patio heater, Colin Ray and Shaz Archer are sitting as if in their living room. Ray is drinking from a bottle of Newcastle Brown Ale. Archer is sipping tea from a mug. Opposite them, on a leather recliner, lounges the man McAvoy now knows as Daragh Fitzroyce. He is drinking from a glass bottle of fresh orange juice, and welcomes McAvoy and Tremberg with big smiles.

'Mr McAvoy,' he says warmly. 'Buttercup's been missing you!'

There is laughter from the rest of the group, who assemble like Roman senators to watch what will follow.

'What are you two after?' asks Ray angrily. 'And how do you know McAvoy?'

Fitzroyce grins, mischievously. 'Just for his cowboy skills, Mr Ray, just for his cowboy skills.'

Ray nods, suddenly remembering the connection. McAvoy breathes out, relieved beyond explanation that his wife's name has not been mentioned. He tries to catch Fitzroyce's eye to see if this omission has been deliberate, but the camp leader has turned his attention back to the two people on his sofa.

'If we'd known there would have been this many of you I'd have got the wife cooking,' he says. 'Does the best cottage pie. Can do a Sunday dinner on a two-ring hob. Wonderful woman.'

On the doorstep of the largest caravan, the woman who was sitting with Fitzroyce the day the horses escaped is smoking a cigarette and raising a mug of tea, as if saluting her husband's words.

'Can I get you a drink? Beer? Cider? Got some crème de menthe if you're partial.'

McAvoy stands still, unsure how to steer the situation. He is suddenly conscious of how he looks. The mud on his clothes, the redness of his face.

'By Christ, you're wearing some funny stuff for jogging,' says Fitzroyce, and there is laughter from the crowd.

He turns to Ray. 'Am I going to have to say all this shite again?'

Ray glowers at the two newcomers and Shaz Archer gives a condescending shake of her head. 'You've said nowt as it is, Fitzroyce.'

The other man grins warmly. He turns to McAvoy. 'Your boss man reckons I'm hiding me a dangerous fugitive,' he says. 'Reckons a lad I used to do a bit of naughtiness with has told him I'm looking after somebody you want. Ginger little scrub-headed bastard, by the sounds of it. Set another man's dog on a woman? Wrong. Just wrong. If them dogs are destroyed . . .'

He shakes his head, tailing off.

'I told your man here I ain't seen Big Al in bloody years. Your man says he lives around here. That's grand. Pint would be nice some time. But I haven't seen him, and I don't know nothing about this lad you want. I've got enough problems . . .'

McAvoy is watching the crowd. There must be thirty people here now. He tries to put his finger on what is bothering him, besides the hell of it all.

Fitzroyce beats out a little rhythm on his thighs and finishes his juice. He looks as though, were they not already outside, he would like to politely show them all the door.

'You want a few more of the bottles?' he asks Ray, gesturing at the ale. 'Got plenty. Take them away with you. Make sure it's not a wasted trip . . .'

'Kids in bed?' asks McAvoy suddenly, looking at Fitzroyce. He realises what is wrong. He has been to many traveller sites and has never seen one without children, even at this hour. Indeed, he can only see a couple of women. The rest are aged between their mid-teens, and mid-fifties.

The moment of concern that ripples across Fitzroyce's face is soon replaced with a smile. 'Tucked up warm,' he says. 'Been cold. It's late.'

'Must be tucked in cupboards, if all these lads are sleeping here too,' says McAvoy, gesturing.

As he looks around, he takes in the various vehicles parked around the camp. There is only one that looks expensive, a black Lexus. He squints. It has been here some time.

'We're good at making room,' says Fitzroyce, though his eyes flick to where his wife sits.

Colin Ray notices the gesture and glances at McAvoy. He levers himself out of the chair and motions to Shaz Archer to do the same.

'Nice motor,' says McAvoy, pointing at the Lexus. 'Yours?'

'I wish,' laughs Fitzroyce. 'Belongs to a pal. Letting me have a play.'

'Insured?'

McAvoy says it playfully – two mates having a laugh. Fitzroyce gives a grin. 'Of course, sir, of course.'

McAvoy nods. Scans the crowd again. Reaches into his jacket and finds the clunky radio he had the presence of mind to pick up on his way out the front door. Flicks it on and fills the sudden silence with static. 'Control, this is Sergeant Aector McAvoy. I need a PNC check on a vehicle . . .'

'Oh now, Mr McAvoy, there's no need . . .'

'Close the lips, fella,' says Ray, holding up a hand. 'Let the officer do his job.'

Fitzroyce looks again at his caravan, then back into the crowd.

McAvoy moves around as he talks into the radio. Changes his position.

'You,' he says and points at the crowd. 'Name?'

The man in front of him is tall and heavily built with a shaved head. He is wearing a black T-shirt over large muscles and his forearms are covered in amateurish prison tattoos.

He looks McAvoy up and down. Gives a little snort of laughter, full of contempt.

'Fuck this . . .'

McAvoy's feet slip from under him as the man pushes him in the chest and muscles past him. As he falls, he hears a thud from the caravan. He turns and the air leaves his body as he hits the ground. He hears shouts. A scream. Glances up and sees Fitzroyce's wife sprawled on the floor. A scrawny ginger lad is struggling to get past her.

Through a mass of bodies, he sees the man who had pushed him over sprinting for the Lexus. He hauls himself up, begins to run, but a shout behind him pulls him up short.

He turns back. In front of him stands a ginger teen. He is unmistakably the weaselly little bastard who set the dogs on Trish Pharaoh.

Behind him, Colin Ray is on his knees, holding a hand to his head and struggling to gain his feet.

McAvoy blocks the lad's way. 'Don't you fucking try it . . .'

The lad, clad in white vest and tracksuit trousers, suddenly swings wildly with an object in his left hand. It is a large crucifix, and McAvoy only just manages to dodge backwards as it arcs up towards his chin.

Helen Tremberg, trying to grab him from behind, is not so lucky. He chops down with the crucifix and there is a sickening thud as it cracks into her kneecap. She goes down, roaring.

Triumphant, furious, the teen turns back to McAvoy. 'Out of my way, ya Jock shite . . .'

He swings the wooden crucifix like it's a hatchet, and McAvoy has to fight to keep his feet as he steps backwards. He looks up and sees Fitzroyce tending to his wife. Sees Ray and Tremberg on the floor. Sees Shaz Archer disappearing into the darkness, sprinting after the disappearing lights of the Lexus, which roars, wetly, into the distance . . .

'Come on then!'

The ginger lad is screaming in his face, spittle hissing from bared teeth. He lunges, the crucifix hacking down as if he is chopping wood. McAvoy sees the blow coming and dodges backwards, his gait that of a boxer, his hands becoming fists. He throws out a right hand, and snaps it back just before it collides with the young lad's face.

The lad, furious to know he could have been so easily knocked out, snarls again and begins to turns away.

McAvoy lunges forward. He barrels into the

young lad with all of his weight, a rugby player to his core, and plants him in the dirt.

'Backup urgently required . . .' he begins, fumbling again for his radio.

'We'll kill you,' screams the lad, squirming underneath him. 'We'll fucking kill you all . . .'

CHAPTER 20

There is milky breath in McAvoy's face.

He kisses Lilah on the eyebrow and she snuggles in closer. He looks up and locks eyes with Fin. His son is lying on his tummy at the bottom of the bed, laid out across McAvoy's legs. He is reading a photocopy of McAvoy's report into the mess at the gypsy camp. There are pages all over the bed.

'What's a crucifix?' asks Fin quietly.

McAvoy smiles at him. 'Tell you later,' he whispers. 'Put that down now, son. You go play.'

Fin does as he's told. Shuffles off the bed and heads to his room, where moments later McAvoy can hear the sound of a five-year-old boy telling one of his toys not to mess with Detective Sergeant Finlay McAvoy, and then pretending to fight a bad man.

McAvoy snuggles into the blankets. He looks at the clock by the bed and realises he has been asleep for nearly thirteen hours. It feels good. He is warm and contented: happier than he has been in a while.

He has no right to feel this way, of course.

Yesterday was a catastrophe. The well-muscled man in the Lexus got away. A search of the database showed it had been stolen from a car showroom in Doncaster.

The lad with the ginger hair has been named by Fitzroyce as Ronan Gill, though the traveller is giving no further information, and only volunteered that much through gritted teeth. Ronan is sixteen years old, a minor in the eyes of the law, who can only be interviewed in the presence of an appropriate adult. He is not cooperating. Has not stopped screaming and swearing yet, forcing every attempt at interview to be abandoned. Grabbed the left breast of one of the well-meaning volunteers who had agreed to sit in on the interview in the absence of a parent or guardian.

A psychiatric consultation had been ordered by the force's medical examiner, but so far they have not been able to find anyone who is available. As a result, time is ticking on, and they have no answers about who the man in the Lexus was, why Ronan set the dogs on Trish, or why Alan Rourke's fingerprints were on the petrol bomb.

Rourke was released last night, having stuck to his 'no comment' answers throughout, breaking his silence only to thank Shaz Archer with all his heart when she revealed his dogs were still ok, and were being cared for at a nearby shelter until a decision could be made as to whether they were to be destroyed.

The plus side of having such a busy day of

form-filling, paperwork and desk-bound enquiry, was that McAvoy was able to get home at a sensible hour. He had come home to cottage pie and a four-pack of bitter. Drank one. Watched his bride polish off the other three. Had told his children stories.

He hears a faint buzzing sound. Wonders if there is any chance of him reaching his mobile phone. Manages to disentangle himself and climbs out of bed. Finds his trousers on the bedroom floor and curses, silently, as the call ends.

He looks at the number. Tremberg. He pulls on a pair of rugby shorts and a hooded top, and pads downstairs, intent on making breakfast before doing anything that might upset Roisin on his day off.

Entering the kitchen, he has the vaguest of memories. Last night. Just after nine p.m. Giggling, here, by the sink, as she held aloft a rolling pin like a club. Roisin telling him that her contact couldn't be trusted to put Hepburn's phone back, and suggesting they smash it up instead. Him, knowing that it was the right thing to do, but unable to acquiesce.

He picks up the phone from where it lies on the counter. Switches it on. Fills the kettle as he lets the phone pick up messages and calls. Looks again at the screen. A dozen texts and seventeen missed calls.

He would like to give the phone to the tech unit. Wants them to go through it and make it evidence.

To make it clinical and somehow policeman-like. At the moment it is still prying.

Half-heartedly, lips pursed, he glances through the messages.

More, from Mark Cabourne.

> ARE YOU IGNORING ME?!
> He's rung again! What is it he wants? Please. Xx
> Have I done something?
> Why are you being like this? I need you.
> I need this. Please text. Xx

McAvoy rubs his face, the peace of sleep evaporating. He cannot help himself. He cannot stop now.

He makes a mug of tea and opens the back door. The day is clear, bright and blue-skied, and the cold air feels good on his bare legs. He sips his tea, and winces, as if it is too hot. It is not. The grimace is the result of making up his mind.

He dials a number. Waits only three rings.

'Councillor Cabourne? This is Detective Sergeant Aector McAvoy . . .'

The noises coming from the cell seem to be a mixture of English, Gaelic and Demon. Spits and shouts, screams and cries, all made unintelligible by the fury with which they froth from Ronan Gill's mouth.

'And he thinks he's angry now . . .' says Colin

Ray grimly to himself, as he passes the custody desk and makes his way to Cell Four.

He takes a breath. Winces. His ribs ache. There is mud caking his suit. He has a headache where his teeth slammed together, and he can taste blood. And he's feeling pretty good.

From within the cell comes another series of crude screams and threats.

'He'll have you. All of you. And him! Fucking cunt! He'll take you down. All of you!'

A noise behind him makes Ray turn. He is surprised to see the tall, imposing shape of Helen Tremberg. It strikes him as odd to have a female companion other than Shaz Archer. Shaz has gone home to get changed, but Tremberg is less concerned about the dirt on her clothes and has made little effort to sponge her knees or face clean. She wants to be here. To be involved. To see what happens next.

Ray seems about to tell her to piss off. To ask why she's here and not busy putting antiseptic on McAvoy's poorly grazes, telling him what a big brave soldier he is.

He loses interest in insulting her. Just gives her a shrug, as if to warn her that he's about to do things his way and it's up to her whether she stays or goes.

'Where's my fucking solicitor? I'm not speaking. Not a fucking word. You know how much my brief costs? He'll have you all. All your jobs . . .'

Ronan Gill has learned nothing from his

guardian in terms of keeping his mouth shut. None of Alan Rourke's stoic silence has rubbed off on the teen. He has been like this since the uniformed officers dumped him on the cell floor and began stripping him of his clothes. The sergeant in charge, who finished the job with a bleeding lip and bruised knuckles, said that putting him in the paper suit was like trying to put a lobster in a rubber glove, though Ray doesn't know who did his research.

'I'll have you all . . .!'

Ray bangs his palm on the metal door.

'Shut the fuck up, son. Back it up.'

The warning prompts another burst of Gaelic. Ray finds himself smiling back at Tremberg, who pulls a face. It is the warmest moment that has ever passed between the two.

'I need to talk to you, lad. I can come in with a dozen uniformed officers and we can do this in a way that hurts.'

There is silence for a moment, then Ronan's voice, thick with rage. 'I'm bleeding! They assaulted me. That's assault. When my brief gets here . . .'

'Easy now,' says Ray, and reaches up to open the viewing flap in the metal door. A moment later a comet of spit shoots through the gap, and Ray thanks experience for not having been in the way.

'Feel better now?'

'Fuck you!'

'I can stay out here if you like. We can talk from here. You obviously enjoy your privacy.'

There is another stream of spit.

'You're gonna dehydrate, son.'

Quickly, deftly, Ray glances through the viewing window. Ronan is bouncing on the balls of his feet, fists at his side, face crimson, like a baby with wind. He has torn the paper suit to shreds which hang off him as if he has burst out of them from within. The mattress from the bunk is propped against the far wall with fist-shaped dints at its centre. The toilet pipe is leaking water, as if it has been booted again and again.

'I've been going through your things, Ronan,' says Ray. 'You're going to have some explaining to do.'

The silence from the cell is longer this time. Without looking, Ray beckons Tremberg closer. He reaches into his pocket, and hands her a slick, expensive mobile phone, and a handful of bits of scrap paper. She takes them, without asking why. *Read them*, he mouths at her.

'You break my phone and I'll break you,' says Ronan, though his voice has taken on a slightly more whiny tone.

'I'd have thought you'd have wanted me to break it,' says Ray. 'Thought you'd have wanted it smashed.'

'There's nothing in it,' says Ronan, but there is a note of uncertainty there now.

Ray smiles at Tremberg as she looks up from going through the ragged scraps. She looks puzzled. Doesn't seem to know whether it would make her look an idiot to admit she doesn't know what she's looking at.

Ronan had fought like a tiger to keep the phone. He was brought into the custody suite with an officer holding each limb, screaming and roaring, and any attempt to book him in properly would have ended in somebody's blood. He should have been asked his name, age and address, and been given a list of items that were in his possession at the time of arrest. Instead he had been dragged to the cell, forcibly stripped, and the contents of his pockets stuffed into a carrier bag to be given to Colin Ray as soon as he arrived.

Ray's fears that any messages in the phone's history would be in Gaelic were unfounded. He had made sense of it all pretty swiftly. It was clear that Ronan did not use the gadget for personal reasons. There are no messages from girlfriends or mates in the in or out boxes. It's all business.

'It's not even my fucking phone,' shouts Ronan.

Ray grins, and in the lurid half-light of the corridor it's a ghoulish thing.

'You gonna stand back so I can open the door, son? Gonna play nice and let me in for a little chat?'

'I ain't speaking until my brief gets here. I told you.'

'We'll do the interview, Ronan. We'll go do it all properly, you'll see. Be super-official and very polite. You'll follow your brief's advice and keep

288

your trap shut. I can see it all now. Don't worry, we'll follow procedure. I just wanted to have a little parley – two grown-ups together. But we can leave it. Don't fret. You have a nice time smashing your cell up and tearing your clothes to confetti. We'll talk later.'

'Fuck you,' comes the reply.

'Like auto-pilot, isn't it?' says Ray to Tremberg. 'Pavlov's dogs. They hear me speak and start salivating swear words.'

Tremberg looks up from where she is scrolling through the half-dozen messages in the phone's history. She can't make much sense of what she sees. Letters. Numbers. The occasional smiley face. It seems more gibberish than code.

Ray takes the phone from her hand. Holds it up. Looks at the most recent message.

He reads aloud. '11. H4. 9. Agreed. Two crew. 401. Transfer H6.'

There is silence in the corridor.

'I just sunk your battleship,' says Ray through a grim smile.

'I don't know what that fucking means.'

'No,' says Ray. 'Neither did I at first. Code of some kind, I reckon, because I'm smart like that. And I reckon that if I spent the rest of my life trying to break it I'd only get a headache. Thing is, son, I don't need to, do I?'

There is silence from the cell.

'You took that illegally . . .'

Despite the pain in his ribs, Ray starts laughing.

'Always hide behind the law, these fuckers,' he says to Tremberg.

'You don't know what you're doing,' says Ronan, and there is desperation in his voice.

Ray takes the handful of paper scraps from Tremberg. Holds one up; a lined page scrawled with biro.

'H4 – Division Road,' he says clearly. '9 = Movement of crops. Nips know. Pick up by Lee. 401 plants. Transfer – New Bridge Road. Before weekend.'

There is silence in the corridor.

'I'm surprised you remember much from your schooldays, Ronan, but it's nice to see you show your workings out.'

Ray slams the viewing window shut to muffle the screams and threats and pounding fists that rattle against it. He gives Tremberg a nod and walks past her, favouring his left side.

'Sir?'

Ray turns back. 'Stupid prick couldn't remember the code. Wrote it down in English for us and shoved it in his pocket. Little shit thought he was untouchable.'

Tremberg throws her hands up. 'I don't understand.'

'He's running the Vietnamese crew for somebody. He's moving the crop before the weekend. The farmers know to expect him and a crew of two and take it all to the next house on the list.'

In the poor light, it takes Tremberg considerable

effort to show her shock and scepticism. 'He's just a little thug.'

'They all started out like that, love,' he says, and for the first time he does not sound as though his every word is spraying bile. 'Ronan was on the ladder.'

'Was?'

Ray rubs a hand over his unshaven face. 'I don't think they'll fast-track him once we raid Division Road.'

Even if he were not already a vaguely familiar face, McAvoy would still recognise the councillor as he enters the diner. There is an air of dread and panic about him; a cloud of anxiety that dampens his face and slicks down his hair.

The man scans the room. Takes in the mono-chrome baseball and Rat Pack photos on the wall; the black-and-white tiles on the floor, the expensive flowers by the till and the open grill at the back of the room, where white-suited chefs toss pancakes and grill bacon.

McAvoy waves a hand. Beckons him over.

'Detective?' he asks, approaching. He lifts his hand to shake, drops it to his side and then lifts it again.

McAvoy begins to stand. Smiles through a mouthful of breakfast. Realises that, even in this half-crouch, he towers over the other man, and is quick to sit down again so as not to be instantly intimidating.

Cabourne slides into the seat opposite him. He is full of nervous energy. Drumming his hands on the table. Playing with the salt cellar. Jiggling his legs.

'That your partner?' Cabourne asks the question with what is intended as a little laugh, but it comes out as a strangled, high-pitched giggle. He is nodding at Lilah, fast asleep in a car seat at McAvoy's side.

'Saturday parenting duty,' says McAvoy. 'You got children?'

Cabourne looks away.

McAvoy already knows that his brunch companion is a father. A married man. Homeowner and former council officer turned politician. Fourteen years on the local authority. A member of the Police Authority and face on more committees than he could name. This is an important man, and he looks like a child summoned to the headmaster.

'Nice here,' says Cabourne distractedly. 'Chain, is it.'

McAvoy nods. Approves. Wishes they would switch back on the Italian jazz they had been playing when he arrived.

He and Cabourne are among only a handful of customers in this imitation American diner. It sits between the hamburger joint and the fried-chicken chain that constitute a major part of the 'retail and leisure' end of the Kingswood estate.

Roisin has taken Fin to see a Disney film at

the nearby cinema. There is talk of slush puppies and bowling afterwards. It could yet be a nice family day within walking distance of home. There has been no need to tell Roisin that his offer to take Lilah for breakfast is not entirely selfless. He is not sure how he would have arranged things if Cabourne had not agreed to meet him here.

As it happened, Cabourne had been only too willing to help – happy to meet the detective whenever and wherever he wanted, and not once asking what it was about.

'Can I get you something?'

McAvoy passes the brunch menu across the table. He takes a sip of his chocolate milkshake, and skewers another pancake with his fork, teaming it with a half-rasher of bacon and enough maple syrup to fossilise a woodpecker.

'Erm, coffee would be nice. And water, please. I'll get them . . .'

Cabourne plunges his hand into his pocket and tries to retrieve some change. As he does so he seems to get his sweaty palms stuck, and as he wrenches his hand free change spills onto the hard-wood floor.

'Shit!'

A waiter in black trousers and shirt comes to help as McAvoy levers himself out of the booth and starts retrieving coins. The councillor just sits there, arms folded, looking down at the black lacquer of the table, seemingly unsure what to do or say.

'Coffee,' says McAvoy to the waiter, as they both deposit a handful of change in front of Cabourne. 'And water, please. Tap.'

As McAvoy slides back into his seat, Cabourne gives him a grateful smile. 'I've always been clumsy,' he says.

McAvoy looks him up and down. He is around six foot. Late forties to early fifties. Grey hair swept back from a thin face, made stern and bookishly intelligent by rimless glasses. He is dressed in thick mauve shirt and chinos, and his only adornments are a simple gold wedding ring on his left hand and a thin silver chain at his throat. To McAvoy, he has the air of a foreign football manager. He looks like he can afford his own breakfast.

'I appreciate you coming,' says McAvoy, pushing his plate away. 'As I explained, we are at the very earliest stage of an investigation and I am talking to you purely out of courtesy . . .'

Cabourne holds up one hand. He closes his eyes. Takes off his glasses and rubs his eyes.

'I think I already know,' he says quietly.

They sit silently, as the waiter leaves the coffee and water on the table.

'Councillor?'

Cabourne sips his water. Puts the glass down. Lifts it and gulps some more.

'I didn't know it was illegal,' he says.

McAvoy sits in silence, content to let things play out.

Cabourne's eyes are darting, flitting from booth to booth, table to table, although whether for familiar faces or a way out McAvoy cannot say.

'Why don't you get it off your chest?'

The older man seems to sag. It is as if he has been punctured. When he looks up again, McAvoy has removed Lilah from her car seat and is sitting her, floppily, on his knee. Deep down, he knows he is using his daughter as a prop: putting the councillor at ease by making this a chat between fathers rather than an interview with a policeman, but to acknowledge it would be an admission of manipulation, and that is an admission he does not want to make.

'Hepburn's ignoring me now,' Cabourne says. 'I think he's more scared than he's letting on. That's Steve, though. Always the same.'

McAvoy strokes his daughter's cheek with the back of his knuckle. Dips his finger in the dregs of maple syrup and lets her lick it, while nuzzling her head with his nose.

'Councillor, I know you want to tell me something. You'll feel better. You're not under caution. This is just a chat.'

Cabourne seems to galvanise his resolve. Gives a nod.

'He's left me so many messages. This Ed Cocker. Some sort of political fixer. I don't know what he wants me to say.'

McAvoy gives an encouraging nod.

'Some people get sports cars or motorbikes when they hit middle-age. I did this.'

'This?'

Cabourne looks suspicious suddenly. 'Can I see your warrant card?'

McAvoy raises his eyebrows. Pulls out his card from his shirt pocket and slides it across the table. Cabourne studies it. Nods.

'This Ed Cocker. He won't take no for an answer.'

McAvoy sighs. 'What's the question, Councillor?'

'He says Hepburn's the story, but he's not, is he? Not when he finds out.'

McAvoy runs his tongue over his lips and strains his brain. Thinks of the desperation in Cabourne's messages to Hepburn's stolen phone. The kisses. Looks now at the father of three, sweating and panicking in the seat opposite him.

'Councillor, your personal life is your own. Whom you have relationships with is not police business.'

Cabourne sags again. 'It's not a relationship,' he says. 'It was just one of those things.'

Something that you wish would continue, thinks McAvoy. 'And the journalist from the *Hull Daily Mail* knows about it?'

'I don't know. Steve would never tell, no matter how much he likes the limelight. And I haven't told anybody. But we've made mistakes. And I've hardly been discreet.'

McAvoy raises his hands to stop the councillor's flow. Takes a breath.

'Councillor, I'm obliged to inform you that I am here to talk to you about the circumstances surrounding the death of a young man named Simon Appleyard. Simon died in November last year. Hanged himself. There are reasons to consider looking again at his death. Your name has come up in connection with the investigation.'

'Oh God!' The councillor collapses in on himself, his face red, his mouth open. 'I knew,' he says, hugging his arms. 'I knew.'

McAvoy does not know how to respond, so simply kisses his daughter and waits for Cabourne to meet his eye.

'Do you know Simon Appleyard?'

'I don't know,' hisses Cabourne angrily. 'Fuck!'

McAvoy gestures in the direction of his daughter. 'Don't swear.'

Cabourne, rubbing his face, apologises. He sips more water. Has his face in his glass when McAvoy slides a picture of Simon across the table. It is a photocopy of the image that the dead man's aunt had given him.

Cabourne shrugs. Looks away.

'Do you know Simon?'

Cabourne forces himself to study the photo. 'It was dark.'

'When?'

'Every time!'

They look at each other, each trying to gauge what the other knows.

'You have been meeting men for sex,' whispers McAvoy, conscious of Lilah's nearness. 'Am I right?'

Cabourne sips his coffee. Meets the detective's eye. 'Men, not boys.'

'Simon was twenty-five.'

'I didn't mean that. I mean it's not illegal.'

'No, it's not.'

Cabourne breaks first. 'I love my wife,' he says, suddenly pitiful. 'I think I do, anyway. We've been together so long. It was just—'

'One of those things?'

'Exactly. I've never cheated with a woman. Not really.'

'Not really?'

'Only when they've been there too.'

'Where?'

'The parties!' he says exasperated. 'The clubs. The dates.'

McAvoy puts Lilah back in her seat. Scratches his head. Lets the pieces drift together.

'Sex parties. That is what Ed Cocker is investigating?'

'It must be!'

'Parties that Councillor Hepburn organises?'

'He doesn't organise them,' says Cabourne defensively. 'Why would he? He can have what he wants. Take what he wants.'

Cabourne sniffs. McAvoy passes him one of Lilah's wipes, which he takes gratefully and uses to clean his face.

'Councillor Cabourne, my brain is starting to hurt. What is it you're frightened of?'

Cabourne looks up, blinking.

'Playmatez,' he says, under his breath. 'It was just to try it out. I'd always had this fantasy . . .'

McAvoy nods, keeping his eyes impassive. Non-judgemental. 'You went on a website, yes? A dating site?'

'I wanted to try it. Everybody was there for the same thing. It was free. I must have been drunk when I signed up. Just put a bit about myself and what I liked. Didn't even think about it at first. Linked it to my private email.'

'And?'

'And I got loads of responses. Men and women! I didn't even say I wanted girls and there they were, turned on just at the thought. I emailed a few of the lads back. Said I was a novice. Didn't know what to do or what I wanted. Said discretion was everything . . .'

'You met?'

Cabourne finishes his coffee and looks away. 'Cheap hotel near Goole,' he says. 'A married man, out for the same thing as me.'

'And?'

Cabourne shrugs, all pride lost. 'I wanted more. Met more.'

'When did this begin?'

'A year ago, maybe. No more.'

'Simon,' says McAvoy, nodding again at the picture. 'Did you ever meet Simon?'

Cabourne picks up the picture again. 'No,' he says at length. 'I'm sorry. No. This is the dead man?'

'Did you ever read this post?'

McAvoy slides a piece of paper across to Cabourne. The councillor's lips twitch as he reads the words on the page. It is Simon's posting on the Playmatez website. An invitation to fill him up and a phone number.

'It rings a bell,' he begins, noncommittal.

'Did you respond to that posting?'

'Possibly,' he says, with a shrug that is far from uncaring. 'I replied to so many.'

McAvoy looks around him. There are balloons on a table to his left, already laid out for a party later in the day. Beyond the wooden blinds the rain is holding off temporarily. Shoppers and diners walking past the glass are coatless. Some have bare arms. He wants to be in that sunshine now. Not here, where the clouds are gathering and the air smells of rain.

'Councillor Hepburn,' says McAvoy, deliberately vague, 'explain how that happened.'

Cabourne closes his eyes. He pulls his phone from his shirt pocket and looks nervously at the screen, as if checking for messages. 'We had friends in common,' he says, and appears to be watching footage of the night in the cinema of his memory. He is almost smiling.

'Friends?'

'I let my mouth run away with me. Told a guy

my real name. What I did for a living. I don't know why. Just trying to impress.'

'And he knew Hepburn?'

'Everybody knows him.'

'And?'

'And even though I begged him to forget what I said, it wasn't long before I got a text from Steve telling me he knew I'd been a bad boy.'

'That must have been a difficult moment.'

'Horrendous. I panicked. Told him I had no idea what he was talking about.'

McAvoy reaches across and takes a sip of Cabourne's water. He can think of no other way to show the other man that he is not disgusted. That he does not feel repulsed by these admissions and is still a safe listening ear.

'He didn't believe you?'

'We were only colleagues, not friends,' explains Cabourne. 'We'd had a few rows in council meetings. Been in the same bars after meetings. I'm Labour, he's an independent, but he wasn't exactly a political enemy. Nor was he a great mate. Just a guy I kind of knew. A guy famous for his lifestyle choices, who now knew everything about me.'

'What did you do?'

'I didn't have to do very much,' he mutters with a half-smile. 'Hepburn didn't make a big deal of it. After those couple of texts he was just his usual self. Said hello when we passed on the stairs, gave me a grilling at committee. Usual stuff. I didn't see anybody else for a while. Then one day he just asked me, out of the blue, if I fancied a drink. He was casual about it. Just said it one day as were coming out of committee. I panicked. But I said yes.'

'And?'

'And we talked. He didn't try and put pressure on me to admit what I'd been doing, but I just blurted it out. Told him it all. He just listened. Let me be myself.'

Cabourne purses his lips. Distractedly brushes at the front of his shirt. Looks at his phone and puts it down again.

'You had an affair?'

Cabourne shakes his head. 'We just became friends.'

McAvoy looks sceptical. 'Friends?'

'He made my life more interesting. He knows everyone. Has been living the right kind of life for an age.'

'The right kind of life?'

'Fun,' he says bombastically. 'Alive.'

'You went to parties together? Sex parties?'

'Nothing round here,' says Cabourne, as if trying to prove he has not been a complete fool. 'We'd go to London. Manchester. There's one in Blackpool . . .'

'All men?'

'All sorts.'

They stop talking. McAvoy stares hard at the other man. He is trying to decide how he feels

302

about him. He wonders if he has done anything wrong. What 'wrong' even means.

'You really don't know Simon?' asks McAvoy at length.

'I could have emails from him,' Cabourne says, trying to be helpful. 'So much of this stuff happens online. Most times it leads to nothing. Some people leave their mobile numbers on the site but I could never do that. Too risky. I could check . . .'

McAvoy waves him into silence. 'Dial this number,' he says, flipping open his notebook and showing Simon's digits to the councillor. 'Dial it and show me your phone.'

Obediently, like a child, Cabourne does as he is bid. The councillor punches the final digit, and waits for it to ring. Before the warning message flashes up to tell him the number is unavailable, the phone does the hard work for him. The number is linked to a contact called 'Peacock'.

Cabourne's mouth drops open. 'Him?'

McAvoy looks at the other man with an expression that says he does not appreciate being lied to.

'I swear I just took the number down,' he says desperately. 'I've contacted so many people on there. I just kept the numbers when they gave them. Look, look . . .'

Cabourne is turning the phone around, scrolling through the contacts. Names flash by.

'Paul T,' he says, pointing. 'That's for "throat". He said he liked having his neck squeezed.

And there, look. Vampire. He said he was into biting. They're just for me to help remember who is who . . .'

'And Peacock?'

'I think he said he had tattoos.' Cabourne stops, memory dawning. 'He emailed me,' he says, eyes wide. 'There was a line of poetry on the bottom of his message. Something he said he liked. Peacocks and lilies.'

McAvoy drops his head to his hands. He has more questions than answers.

Suddenly he looks up. 'He emailed you? Not texted?'

'Definitely.'

McAvoy begins rummaging through his papers. He is trying to find a mention anywhere in the various reports that suggests Simon owned a computer.

'I'm an idiot . . .' mumbles McAvoy.

'I'm sorry?'

'Were the emails from a smart phone?'

'I'm sorry, I don't, I don't think so . . .'

McAvoy stops. He realises the man in front of him is guilty of betrayal. Of confusion. Of weakness and lust. But he does not see a criminal.

'Keep your head down, Councillor Cabourne,' he says, sliding himself out of the booth and picking up Lilah's car seat. 'Ed Cocker isn't after you. He's after somebody much bigger.'

Cabourne looks up at him, unsure whether to

give in to the magical sense of relief that threatens to flood him.

'I'll check my old email account,' he begins. 'I'll do anything I can to help you.'

McAvoy nods. 'Yes. You will.'

CHAPTER 21

1.47 a.m.

A blue twelve-year-old Vauxhall Frontera, steamed up and idling on the double yellow lines that edge this quiet side street off old Hessle Road.

Four cops inside – damply smouldering, jittery with unused adrenalin.

There's a brightly lit takeaway to their left. It's all glass and white paint, cartoon characters and gaudy lettering. The relentless rain jewels the large, dirty windows and turns the skinny, fifty-something woman behind the counter into a fragmented caricature of herself: mechanical, joyless, shaking spice into paper bags full of fries.

There's a barber's shop to their right. Black gloss – bought in bulk and applied too thickly, collecting in rivulets in the gaps between the bricks.

Shutters down today. Down most days.

Helen Tremberg sits in the back of the unmarked car. A sergeant from the Drugs Squad stares out of the window beside her, watching the raindrops dribble haphazardly down the glass. He hasn't spoken since giving her a grunt of acknowledgement as she slid into the back of the car and wiped the rain from her face with a warm palm. He smells faintly of stale beer and wet dog.

DCI Ray is sitting in the front, passenger side, sucking the chocolate off a Twix.

At the wheel is Detective Superintendent Adrian Russell. Everything about his manner suggests he is in a foul mood. He is moving chewing gum around his mouth, but the look upon his face is more in keeping with a man trying not to acknowledge the gone-off oyster under his tongue.

There is silence inside the vehicle, save the drumming of rain on the roof, and the occasional swish of damp tyres as cars pass by on Hessle Road.

Tremberg feels uncomfortable. Out of place. Unwelcome. She has never worked with Russell or his underlings, and has no bond with her DCI. She is here because the opportunity arose. Here because she is an ambitious officer who wants to be there when a high-profile raid goes down. Here because Shaz Archer can't be rustled up, and because with Pharaoh out of the picture and McAvoy out on a limb, she is feeling lost. There has been no fanfare to welcome her return. No hugs or tears. She came back after risking her life to catch a killer, and was very nearly on fire before the end of her first shift.

'Should have parked ourselves in Rayner's,' says Ray chattily, throatily, while jabbing a thumb over his shoulder at the legendary pub across the street. 'Could have bought you a Babycham and a packet of peanuts.'

Ray angles the rear-view mirror until he can see into the back. A bite of Twix moves around in his mouth as he talks.

'Never been in,' says Tremberg, turning in her seat to stare across at the building on the corner. 'Doesn't look welcoming. They do scampi in a basket?'

'Proper pub,' says Ray. 'I read up on it when I moved to this shitty city. Hessle Road was already on its arse by then but, fuck, that place had character.'

It is not the first time Tremberg has heard about this boozer, or its place at the very heart of the old fishing community. This is where the trawler-men drank on their three days home, their refuge after six weeks risking their lives in distant waters. It is where scores were settled and where tensions erupted into bloody violence. Where feuds ended in bloodshed or in forgiveness. Where men tried to dilute the ocean in their veins with pint after fucking pint. It was a hard man's watering hole. A place of mourning and of celebration. A place that numbered countless dead among its regulars, and where it was said that the ghosts of recently dead trawlermen would call in for a drink before sailing on to purgatory.

'What's it like in there now?' asks Tremberg, for something to say.

Ray shrugs. 'Only been in the once. Decent pint. Few old boys with a story to tell. Bit sad really, when you think what it was. What all this was . . .'

Ray stops talking as he realises he is sounding soppy. He gestures at the run-down side street beyond the glass. Waves an arm half-heartedly at the cut-price furniture shops and the empty greasy-spoon cafes.

'It was probably all shit in the good old days too,' he says, by way of antidote to his display of nostalgia. 'Fifty years from now Hull folk will reckon life nowadays was fucking peachy.'

Silence again.

Adrian Russell, chewing his gum.

The sergeant beside her stifling a burp and then blowing out the faint smell of last night's beef madras . . .

Tremberg wondering if she should text McAvoy. Tell him what Ray has arranged. Ask him if he knows why the fuck the detective superintendent seems to have ceded operational authority to his junior officer, and appears to be swilling sick around his gob.

They all jump as Russell's phone rings, the riff from Gary Numan's 'Cars'.

A look passes between Ray and the detective superintendent.

Russell closes his eyes. Answers in little more than a whisper.

'Russell. Yes. Yes, as a matter of courtesy . . . No. Well, obviously. I do appreciate that. No. It's not my call. There are limits, you understand . . . I'm not sure that would be wise . . . No, I realise that. Different breed, you might say. Of course I understand the benefits. Yes. If you're sure . . .'

Russell hands the phone to Colin Ray.

Ray is all smiles.

'Detective Inspector Colin Ray. Very Serious and Vaguely Organised.'

He puts the phone onto loudspeaker. Seems to take pleasure in the other officer's shiver of discomfort.

The car is filled with a stranger's voice: tinny and robotic.

'Mr Ray, I'm sorry we have not had a chance to be properly introduced before now. I would have made it my business to do so, but I was unaware of your existence till today.'

The voice is almost accentless. The enunciation clear but giving nothing away.

'That's OK, son, I don't much about you either. Know you're going to have a bad day though.'

Ray's words seem not to register with the speaker.

'In the past hour I have remedied my aberration. I have acquainted myself with several of your personal details. Allow me to express my sadness that such an experienced officer should find himself so poorly remunerated at such a time in his career. You have given up so much for this job, and you are rewarded with a childless existence, and more ex-wives than a man can afford. To be only a few years from retirement, and still to be an underling . . . it saddens me. A man of your experience should be better rewarded.'

In the mirror Tremberg watches Ray's face for any glimmer of discomfort. Sees none.

'Aye, you're right there,' he says, as if chatting to an old friend. 'I'm surrounded by fucking ingrates and incompetents. I'm sure you know the feeling. That's what you get for working with Chinks and pikeys. You should put your hand in your pocket, son. Bring in some lads who can think and tie their shoes at the same time.'

For an instant there is no reply. Then the voice continues, as though Ray has not spoken.

'The house on Division Road is not expecting you, Chief Inspector. The details of my arrangement with your colleague were clearly miscommunicated.'

Russell reaches out to take the phone, mumbling words of protest. Ray raises his arm and splays his fingers. Keeps the phone beyond the other man's reach, until Russell sinks back into his seat.

'Like I said, son, bad day for you.'

'I have experienced bad days before. What happens today will be of significance to you, but of little or no consequence to me and the people I represent.'

'And yet you took the time to ring . . .'

'If inconvenience can be avoided, I believe it to be worth the gesture.'

'You're not going to avoid this inconvenience, boy. One of your little helpers took a swing at me with a fucking crucifix. That doesn't buy you much in the way of goodwill.'

Ray catches Tremberg's eye. Winks. He seems to be enjoying this.

'Some of my associates are spirited individuals,' says the man. 'They have unique character traits and skill sets that we attempt to harness. I am not one to stand in the way of youthful exuberance.'

Ray laughs. 'That what you call it when you nail somebody's hands to their knees? When you petrol-bomb a police van? You're no fucking big-shot, whoever the fuck you are. You run a few cannabis factories. You've scared a few Chinks. You think you'll make my memoirs when I retire?'

Now it is the other man who emits a chuckle. 'I presume that you are recording this conversation, Chief Inspector, so I will refrain from unburdening myself with regards to my regret for recent incidents. But to presume my associates are limited to such matters represents a degree of short-sightedness that they will find amusing.'

'Did you actually want something, lad? Only I've got a drug den to raid and a couple of fucking Chinks to arrest.'

The man does not speak for several seconds.

Finally he gives a little sigh.

'Your colleagues,' he says. 'The large gentleman who looks like he should be carrying a claymore. The lady in the biker boots and breasts. Tell them not to feel guilty. They had a job to do. Miss Marvel was big enough to make her own decision. And do tell Detective Superintendent Russell that I will be in touch.'

The call is terminated. The speaker begins to emit slow beeps, like a life-support machine.

Ray looks at the side of Russell's face for a spell. Looks as though he is about to spit.

'Sir?' Tremberg is the first to speak. 'Do you think that bloke runs this lot, then? That he's the boss? He didn't sound right. Didn't sound like just some drugs thug . . .'

Ray picks his teeth for a spell.

Says nothing.

Finally picks up the radio from between his legs. 'Go.'

A dozen car lengths ahead, the double doors open swing open at the back of a white van. Half a dozen uniformed officers emerge, fast and furious.

Further up the street, four plain-clothes Drugs Squad detectives step into the rain.

As one they descend upon a deceptively large town house halfway up the street.

Tremberg opens her own door. Puts her left foot down in a puddle. Pulls her extendable baton from the pocket of her waterproof. Listens, above the foot-steps and the resurgent rain, for the sound of the police dogs as they pour into the property's backyard; straining at the leashes of their handlers . . .

Watches a burly officer muscling his way to the front of the pack.

He hefts the Enforcer, the rubber-ended metal battering ram that can deliver three tonnes of kinetic energy in a single swing.

Brings it forward: expert and practised.

The wooden door at the front of the house is smashed back off its hinges.

She hears shouts. Warnings. Watches the officers streaming forward – a blur of colour and rain – as they surge through the busted door.

Colin Ray puts out a hand.

'No point being in there first, love. Being last out, that's what you want. Slapping the cuffs on and watching as the bastards take their last look.'

Tremberg looks at him. At the rain running down his sallow, unhealthy-looking face. At his stained teeth and sodden, stained pinstripe suit. Wonders whether, if he could just be a bit less of a cunt, she could learn a lot from this man.

More shouts. A roar, full of frightened energy.

'Fuck! Fuck!'

One of the detectives emerges from the property. He is breathing hard. Puts out a hand to steady himself against the red brick wall.

Tremberg follows Ray as he walks briskly up to the house.

'Well?'

The officer is around Tremberg's own age. Fleshy-cheeked and earnest, all supermarket suit and inoffensive haircut.

'Fucking forest up there,' he says, wheezing. 'Got one lad. The other did a bunk out the back.'

The radio in Ray's hand crackles. The dog unit has cornered an Asian-looking gentleman in the backyard.

'Job well done then,' says Ray, about to step into the property.

The constable shakes his head. Something is wrong.

'There's a woman up there, sir. Big girl. There was a report, couple of days ago, a misper . . . missing person . . . I think it's her . . . fuck, sir, what they've done . . .'

Tremberg steps inside the house. Pushes past the throng of uniformed officers who line the hallway and staircase, uncomfortable in their damp waterproofs, and makes her way up the stairs.

The carpet beneath her feet is patterned with swirls, and her head spins as she pushes open the doors to room after room set up for the cultivation of the finest quality marijuana. Here blocks of resin, stacked like house bricks, set up for collection. There sacks of leaf, dried out and also ready for collection, sitting like bags of Christmas presents against white-painted walls.

She follows the sound of foreign shouts. Of brutal curses and angry threats, frothing on a tongue bitten bloody by gnashing teeth.

Sees a young, dark-haired Vietnamese man, in vest and shorts, writhing on the ground, tie-wrap cuffs behind his back, an officer on his legs and another pinning his shoulders.

Looks past him. Past the detective leaning against the door-frame of a bedroom wrapped in plastic sheeting and hemmed with snaking wires.

Takes in, briefly, the plants in their varying stages

of growth: some flowering, verdant and glossy, beneath yellow hydroponic lights.

'In here.'

Tremberg approaches. Looks inside.

The woman is alive, but barely. She lies on her side, hair plastered to her face, an officer's uniformed jacket covering her naked, foetal form.

'We've called an ambulance. We didn't like to move her.'

Tremberg crosses to the woman's side. Gently pulls back the coat.

The heads of the nails scarcely protrude an inch from the putrefying entry wounds in the back of her hands. The tips are buried three inches into her knee-caps. Blood has run down her legs to her ankles and blackened her feet. She was sitting up when this was done to her, before being thrown down here for more blood to trickle and congeal upon the lumpy, linoleum floor.

Her bare breasts appear, at first glance, to be covered in a matted, sticky hair.

Tremberg peers closer.

Sees the horror of the mutilated flesh. The blackening and burning of her skin.

Tremberg, face grey, turns back to the door. Colin Ray is standing there, smile gone.

'Pharaoh's snout,' says Tremberg through bile. 'McAvoy's admirer.'

Ray scowls. Turns away.

Tremberg brushes Leanne's hair back from her face. Feels the big, well-muscled woman shiver and pull away. Her eyes flicker open and closed. Her lips move. Tremberg has to place her ear next to her mouth to make out what she is saying.

'Shaun – is he OK? Shaun? They wouldn't tell me. They kept asking me where he was, then laughing when I said I didn't know.'

Tremberg, despite herself, feels tears prick at her eyes.

She wonders who will have to tell this tortured, broken creature that the man she has been protecting is already dead. That she has been mere practice, and sport.

CHAPTER 22

The reporter is in her thirties and plain as a cheese sandwich. She has brown hair, glasses, and her waterproof coat betrays no flair or sponsor. She's BBC to her bones.

Helen Tremberg tries not to let the sauce from her bacon sandwich drip as she stands in the canteen and watches the bulletin.

The reporter is being lashed by a heavy, gusting rain, and winces slightly as she talks to camera.

'I'm here on Division Road, just off Hessle Road in the west of the city, where residents were this morning witness to the latest in a series of city-wide raids by Humberside Police. We're told that this morning, in an operation involving the force's helicopter and a dozen officers, Drugs Squad operatives smashed their way into the property you see behind me and recovered hundreds of cannabis plants, along with equipment used for their cultivation. There are reports that one of the suspects removed from the house was transferred immediately to a medical facility, though where they sustained their injuries remains unknown.

'I'm joined here by Detective Superintendent

Adrian Russell, who oversaw the hugely successful operation.'

Tremberg takes a bite of her sandwich and watches as the senior officer enters shot. He has pulled on a coat and made an attempt to slick back his hair, but the unhealthy pallor of his skin and fretting of his hands betray his discomfort.

Tremberg finishes her lunch in two bites as the reporter asks a series of bland questions, to which Russell gives anaemic answers.

She tries to pay proper attention. Focuses in on what he is saying.

'It's too early to say at this stage whether this set-up has anything to do with a larger organisation, but this is clearly an important result. These drugs would have a street value of hundreds of thousands of pounds. We found seedlings and plants in thirteen rooms in this abandoned house, as well as a complex set-up. Corridors between the rooms were snaked with electric wires and pipes to vent the smell of the drugs out of the building. The energy to heat the equipment came from a generator that had been custom-built to hide the noise. The front of the property appears totally derelict—'

He is interrupted by the reporter, asking the only question that matters.

'And the two men you arrested?'

Russell looks as though he wants to be sick. 'I can only tell you that a fifteen-year-old youth and a thirty-year-old man, both believed to be

Vietnamese in origin, have been arrested and are currently being questioned by senior detectives.'

Tremberg smiles to herself. Wipes her face with a napkin. She likes being called a senior detective.

Throwing the napkin in the bin, she pushes through the swinging canteen doors and heads for the interview room. She was grateful when they took a break for a mid-afternoon lunch. She was starting to worry that the vein in Colin Ray's head was about to pop. He is truly struggling with the concept of people not really being able to speak English. Seems about to reach across the desk and do some serious harm.

As she nears the interview suite, one of the doors bangs open and Colin Ray stomps out, furious.

'Fucking Chinks!' he screams at nobody in particular, and then glowers at Tremberg when he sees her. 'They understood Ronan easy enough, and he sounds like he's drowning half the time. And they don't understand me? They can say "solicitor" well enough, lying bastards. Where you been, anyway? Fucking part-timer . . .'

Tremberg bows her head as she is bawled out, and suddenly feels an extraordinary rush of affection for McAvoy and Pharaoh. She wishes to high heaven they were here. Wishes they were running this. She has seen Colin Ray get results today. Seen him, somehow, twist people inside out. And yet it only added to the acid in his gut and the distaste on his face. There is something vile within him. A genuine, bona fide malevolence. She realises he is dangerous. That if he were not so damned obsessive about catching crooks he would be one.

'Is the translator on her way?' asks Tremberg at last.

Ray spits on the linoleum floor of the corridor. 'Hours away. And the assistant chief constable is sniffing around. Talking about procedure.'

This morning's brief sensation of victory is souring. The two Vietnamese farmers are saying nothing. If they speak English, they are hiding it well.

Ray stares into space for a while.

'Ronan's picture,' she says. 'Anything?'

Tremberg had stayed with the older man in the interview room while Ray worked on the younger one. She has not yet heard how it went, though from Ray's face she can guess.

'Knows him, course he does,' says Ray viciously. 'Eyes like bloody saucers when I showed him. Then it was all this Vietnamese shit and plenty of 'No, no, no.' Same with the picture of Shaun Unwin. And the two other Chinks from the Foreshore. Christ, you'd think they'd want to help their mates. Don't they know what they're looking at? Even if they didn't do the harm to Pharaoh's informant, they've been busy growing weed while she lay there rotting and begging for help.'

Ray slams a fist into his palm. 'They're not going to talk, are they?'

Tremberg doesn't answer.

'Neither's Rourke. Or Ronan. His brief's got him to shut his trap. Shaz can't get a word out of him.'

They stand in the corridor, and for a moment neither knows what to do.

Within seconds of each other their phones begin to ring.

They turn away. Ray to Archer. Tremberg to McAvoy.

'Hello, Helen. Are you ok? I heard about the raid. What's happening? I thought you were going home last night. I would have come with you. Were you with Ray? And Leanne, she's ok, yes? Does Pharaoh know? Are you ok?'

Tremberg gives in to a smile.

This is the most appreciated she has felt all day.

'Could you butter these, please, Suze?'

The middle-aged lady nods at a tray of bread rolls. The gesture comes as a relief to Suzie. The lady is wearing a plastic apron over what appears to be a basque paired with school socks, and Suzie had momentarily feared she was going to be asked to do something unusual with a tub of margarine.

'Don't go mad,' she says as Suzie sets to work. 'Just a scraping.'

This is the aspect of swinging and wild sex that Suzie finds most pleasantly surreal. Underneath the costumes and the impromptu blow-jobs, these gatherings are little different from a normal house party. Although most of today's guests will spend the day naked, the owners are putting on a finger buffet, and so far everybody who has arrived has brought a bottle, a plate of home-made cakes, or a card for the birthday girl.

It is four p.m. on a bright but cold Saturday afternoon. Suzie has gravitated towards the large, old-fashioned kitchen of the white-painted farm-house that stands in a dozen acres of private fields and woodland. She is dressed in a short denim dress, thigh boots and a Venetian mask, which sits on her head as she sips from a plastic beaker of lemonade and helps the host and her best friend make snacks.

'Throw a few cherry tomatoes on the tray,' says the woman. She shakes a bottle of home-made salad dressing with enough force to send her lopsided breasts jiggling. 'Make it look pretty.'

Suzie is pleased she came. She is not planning on staying all evening, and has no hopes or ambitions for how the party will play out, but she is enjoying the feeling of relaxed escapism that always settles upon her when she finds herself in the company of people who, to some degree at least, understand her.

'I wish I'd brought a cake or something,' says Suzie as she gaily drops cherry tomatoes on to limp-looking ham sandwiches. 'It was just a last-minute thing.'

'Don't you worry,' says Christine. 'Just nice to see you.'

Suzie turns. Adjusts her glasses so she can slide

the mask back onto her face. Smiles at the hostess. 'Are you having a nice birthday?'

'Ask me again when a few more turn up.' Christine laughs. She had greeted Suzie with a big, full-breasted cuddle and a kiss on both cheeks.

'Are you expecting many?' asks Suzie, taking another drink. 'Maybe the weather will put people off.'

Christine looks out through the thick glass. The sky is a rich blue, but the trees that bound the paddock are shaking in a chill breeze.

'We'll see,' she says. 'Got a party with the family tomorrow anyway. This is just a normal club night, even if I do get a few extra presents.'

'I like your outfit,' says Suzie.

'Took some getting into,' says Christine. 'It's not real leather. You have to cover yourself in talc to get it on, and when it comes off you can still see the shape of it on your skin. Hopefully be too dark for anybody to notice by then.'

Outside, Suzie hears the sound of a car pulling up on the gravel driveway. She heads to the back door and steps into the cold air; her boots precarious on the uneven cobbles.

On the patio four or five couples are lying, in various states of undress, on deckchairs and sun-loungers. When she came here with Simon, Suzie had thought it funny that wicker chairs were also laid out. They had laughed uncontrollably when she had nudged him and pointed at the back and

324

buttocks of a sixty-year-old man who had recently vacated one armchair. 'Crinkle cut,' she'd said.

There are smiles all around as she is noticed on the patio. None of the people who have turned up so far are particularly attractive, but all have enjoyed dressing up. Unfortunately the cold weather and muddy fields have rather spoiled their ensembles. On one striped deckchair, a woman in her early thirties is wearing a waterproof parka over a crotchless body-stocking, while her fifty-year-old partner is holding his lighter as if it were a portable heater, cupping his hands around the flame as he shivers in jeans-shorts and tight-fitting T-shirt.

On the other side of the patio, two couples are chatting animatedly about the rising cost of fuel. The tall, dark-haired man who arrived with a younger, bespectacled girl in a PVC catsuit and red knitted cardigan is complaining that it cost him eight pounds more to fill up the car than it did the last time they made the drive over here from their home in Morecambe Bay. The younger, stockier man he is talking to looks genuinely interested. He is complaining that he just spent £20,000 on a new car, but that it has no cup holder, and beeps at him when he doesn't wear his seat belt. It is a pleasant conversation, and neither of the men seems to mind that the younger chap is wearing an unfastened white dressing gown and wellies.

Later they will pair up and team up. They will

drink and smoke and giggle and splash in the hot tub that sits at the bottom of the far field, next to a cheap, imitation Hawaiian bar. Those brave enough will stride naked to the small stream with its half-hearted waterfall that bisects the apple orchard half a mile from the house, where Suzie and Simon once sat and smoked a joint with a gay couple from Leeds.

'Everybody, this is Jarod and Melissa. Say hello.'

Big Dunc, the homeowner and husband of birthday girl Christine, is introducing two newcomers to the rest of the group. Jarod is no more than twenty-five years old. He has short blond hair and an unremarkably pleasing face. He is wearing a black muscle vest that shows a slim but well-defined physique, and looks happy, if slightly ill at ease.

The lady is older. Larger. Expensive and imposing. Black hair, cut short. She could be his mum, were it not for the fact she is holding his hand.

'Just the one single,' says Christine, smiling and pointing at Suzie. 'Plenty of couples to pick from soon enough. We're really pleased you could join us. Now can I get you a drink?'

Suzie takes a sip from her glass as the newcomers look at her. Jarod smiles. Melissa does too, but it comes a moment later and is not so wide.

'Where do we put our stuff?' asks Jarod of the lady in the waxed jacket. He gestures at his sleeping roll and overnight bag.

'Big Dunc will sort all that,' she says. 'Just leave

it there for now. You can trust everybody. There's nobody comes up unless they're here for this, so there's never any thefts.'

Jarod smiles a thank you. The woman in the parka, who Suzie seems to think might well be called Karen, gives the man a once-over with her eyes. She looks at her partner and they share a grin.

'First time here?' she asks the newcomers.

'Yeah, thought we'd try,' says Jarod. 'Game for anything, us.'

'Couple are you? Or just a swinging couple?'

Melissa turns to her. 'We're just here to play,' she says, and there is something in her voice that suggests no further questions are welcome. Those present respect her wishes. Such gatherings are based on trust. All participants in these parties have told some lie or another about where they are going. Some are with playmates they met on the Internet. Others lead completely separate lives with other partners and spouses, only coming together with their 'swinging partner' for such parties and club nights as these. And others are here with their husbands and wives, keeping their relationships fresh and exciting by fucking strangers, and terrified at the prospect of their kids finding out what Mummy and Daddy were up to when they went away for the weekend.

Suzie feels a bit of a spare part. She had not felt in the mood to be chauffeured by J & J, and so has driven here on her own. If they turn up later, she will apologise and if needs be make it up to them. She is resisting the urge to drink alcohol so she can drive herself home if and when she feels like it, but is beginning to feel an eagerness to claim a glass of wine.

She has not switched her phone on yet. Does not know if Anthony has called. Has vague memories of him putting her in a taxi and sending her home, but the thought of switching on her phone and sifting through the last four days of messages and voicemails fills her with dread. She's thinking of him though. Remembering the puzzled little smile with which he listened to her ramblings. The tenderness with which he had held her in the street as she wept in his arms. The way he stood his corner in the bank and saved her with his white-knight generosity.

'Here.'

Suzie has been staring across the flat green fields and trying to work out if she can see Lincoln Minster in the distance, and is startled when Melissa places a bottle of beer in her hand.

'I'm sorry' she says nervously, taking the drink. 'Miles away.'

Melissa looks at her. There is an intensity to her gaze. 'I like your mask,' she says. 'That would have been a good idea. Do people usually wear them?'

'Only if they want to,' says Suzie, absent-mindedly sipping the beer that she had not asked for but is grateful to receive. 'It's not about secrecy. Everybody knows everybody.'

'Yes?'

Suzie thinks about it. 'Well, no. I guess everybody trusts everybody.'

'These people know you?'

'They know my face.'

Melissa gives her first real smile. 'I bet they know more than that.'

Suzie takes another drink, and points with the bottle at where Jarod is talking to another couple of newcomers about the difficulty he had in getting this location to show up on satnav. 'Jarod, was it? Interesting name.'

Melissa shrugs, as if to suggest that not much about Jarod interests her at this moment. Suzie feels vaguely uncomfortable under the older, larger woman's stare. She has played this game before, of course. She has experimented time and again. She did not think she was averse to doing so again tonight, but at present there are no stirrings of desire within her. She is just enjoying looking across the fields and not really existing for a while. The events of the week are a mound of cold coins in her gut. She feels weighted down and toxic. She fancies she can taste blood when she swallows. She is existing in moments of exhilaration and numbness, unwilling to let any of her thoughts develop into questions. She knows she cannot ignore what happened. Knows that she left a man to die. Knows, too, that she feels somehow fearful for her own safety. But she cannot distinguish this feeling from the loneliness and solitude that have been constant since Simon died. More than anything her thoughts keep returning to Anthony. It has been a long time since she had these feelings. Is feeling the lovely terror of wondering if somebody likes her . . .

'You've polished that off,' says Melissa, pointing to Suzie's empty bottle. 'I'll get you a proper drink.'

Suzie lifts her mask then drops it again. She likes being half-hidden like this. She readjusts her dress. Exposes the lilies inked on her skin.

'Hi,' comes a voice, close enough to her ear to goose-pimple her skin.

She turns. Sees Jarod staring into her eyes, his own a piercing green.

'Beautiful ink,' he says, tracing a hand over the design. His touch makes her tremble.

'Thank you.' Her voice catches. In her throat.

A half-smile on the young man's face; his eyes on her tattooed skin.

'I feel like I've been looking for you.'

Night-time. A shapeless landscape in northern Lincolnshire; green fields and neatly tended apple trees. Two figures laughing: stick drawings etched in tar.

'Are they ok with this?'

'Of course,' laughs Suzie. 'They're ok with everything.'

This is a pleasant drunkenness. Suzie does not feel sick, and the dizziness is that of a carousel rather than a fairground waltzer. She feels light.

Not content, but happy enough with this sensation of giddiness.

'You cold?'

'I'll live.'

The night sky is the colour of bruised fruit, but remains cloudless, and though the air is cold and close the wind has dropped.

Both Suzie and Jarod are wearing dressing gowns over naked skin. Until a few moments ago they had been drinking wine in the hot tub with a married couple who had driven up from Reading, and a large Asian man with an extreme amount of body hair who nobody seemed to know.

Suzie has been drinking for seven hours. She has long since given up the notion of going home. Here, intoxicated, giggly, excited, she can see nothing to rush home for. Cannot bear the thought of the empty flat. Shudders at the thought of sitting at her kitchen table, trying to think of something wholesome to do, before giving in and searching dating sites and porn channels for something that will divert her attention from the fact that somebody tried to kill her, and that her best friend took his own life . . .

'Down here,' she says, holding open an old wooden gate and pointing to the six stepping stones that lead to the river.

'Pretty,' says Jarod, touching her hip with his palm. He takes the lead and follows the sound of tumbling water.

'Anybody there?'

He and Suzie pull expectant faces as they listen for answers, then giggle at the silliness of it. Suzie feels her insides warming. Enjoys herself, throwing herself into silly games with this young, attractive, playful man. Imagines, for the smallest of moments, that the past few months have not happened. That she is giggling with Simon and that death has not touched her life.

'Is it deep?'

The stream is at its widest point here, beneath the miniature waterfall. It is perhaps six feet across. The riverbed is silt and stone, and sandbanks slope upwards to soft, damp grass.

'Up to your waist,' says Suzie, cautiously tiptoeing to the water's edge. She is cold – the water from the hot tub turned icy cold on her flesh during their walk across the fields.

'I can't believe we're doing this,' says Jarod and laughs. He leans in and gives Suzie a light kiss on the cheek. It is friendly and not sexual. They may have been naked in the hot tub together, but there has been no suggestion so far of anything happening besides giggles and laughter. They have enjoyed one another's company. They are the youngest people here. Have laughed themselves drunk at one another's gently barbed comments about the other guests. Have talked football and music, stayed away from anything that matters.

'Do you think she saw us?' asks Jarod, peering into the darkness. 'She's like a bloodhound.'

Melissa, the lady he came with, has not been

a popular party guest. She has barely taken her eyes off Jarod or Suzie all day, and anybody who has approached her with an offer of finding a private room, or a place to get to know one another better, has been rewarded with an icy stare. Suzie does not want to know the dynamics of her new friend's relationship with the older lady, but fancies it is not destined for marriage and kids.

'Ooh, it's freezing!' Suzie has dipped a toe in the water. She winces. Takes her glasses off and lays them on the bank. She pulls up the hem of her borrowed dressing gown and steps, ankle-deep, into the water.

'I'm game if you are,' says Jarod. He doesn't look particularly game. In truth, he suddenly looks cold and reluctant.

'It was your idea,' says Suzie, and her laugh rings out, the only sound besides the tumbling water.

'How did we end up here?' asks Jarod thoughtfully. He appears to be trying to distract Suzie from making him make good on his skinny-dipping promise.

'You said you wanted a plunge pool. You said you were too hot in the hot tub. Which you would be. That's its job . . .'

'No, here,' he says, casting an arm around. 'What did you say you were? Twenty-five? I'm twenty-two. They're all, like, old.'

Suzie frowns at him. 'They're just people having fun,' she says. 'You're not going to get Angelina

Jolie at a place like this.' She pauses. 'You might, actually. She seems into all sorts.'

'I didn't expect it to be like this.'

Suzie pouts. 'You not having fun?'

Jarod waves in the direction of the house. 'We're not a couple,' he says a little drowsily. 'We've done it a few times. Met her on the Internet and it turns out she lives near me. I don't fancy her, or anything. I don't even know how we ended up in bed.'

Suzie is shivering now, up to her knees in the water, not really listening.

'This is her fantasy,' he says. 'She says she wants to see me do it to somebody else.'

Suzie shrugs. 'She doesn't seem like she wants to.'

Jarod nods, enthusiastically. 'I'm not really called Jarod, by the way. I'm Luke. I just liked the name Jarod.'

Suzie smiles. 'I'm really called Suzie. Some people call me Blossoms.'

'It suits you.'

'Thanks. Jarod is a good name. You're more a Jarod than a Luke.'

They smile at each other, half-drunk, half-happy, here, knee deep in a silted-up stream.

'Fancy getting soaked?' asks Jarod, looking at the water.

Suzie is not sure, now. She knows it will be exhilarating to plunge into the water, but it suddenly seems too cold. Too dark, even. Her thoughts turn to Simon before she can stop them. To the last time she threw herself into this water, hand in hand with her best friend.

'Next time,' she says, and begins to inch her way back to the bank.

Above the sound of the falling water she hears voices. She looks up the slight slope to see a naked couple and the Asian man in a giant bath towel appear at the top of the stepping stones.

'Hi,' shouts Jarod, to alert the newcomers. 'Water's lovely.'

The trio of fellow bathers wave and laugh. 'Is it freezing?' comes a woman's voice.

'Too cold for us,' says Jarod.

They pass one another, awkwardly, wet and naked, on the stepping stones. Suzie gets a whiff of beer and marijuana. The fat Asian man gives her a smile that is guileless and innocent. She wonders if he has turned up here by mistake.

Suzie and Jarod begin to walk back towards the house. They are barefoot and the wet grass feels nice on their feet. Behind them, they can hear fading shrieks of alarm and excitement as the three bathers enter the pool.

'Do you think Melissa is making friends?' asks Suzie quietly, as they pass under the low-hanging branches of an apple tree and Suzie lets the leaves play through her fingers.

'Doubt it,' says Jarod, with a laugh. 'Here, did you—?'

He does not get to finish his sentence.

Suzie turns at a sudden movement in time to see Jarod falling to his knees. He is crumpling as if demolished from beneath. Even in this darkness, she can see the sudden explosion of crimson that colours his expressionless face as he folds in on himself.

Suzie begins to shriek, but finds no words. She spins, her world chaos and movement, darkness and noise, and then there is a hand in her hair and she is being pushed to the ground.

Her face is in the grass, her mouth full of dirt. There is pressure on her back, now. Strong arms upon her shoulders, a fist in her hair.

She feels a frenzied tugging at her clothing and, for a moment, she knows what will happen. Knows she is to be raped. Knows that without Simon to protect her, her fears are coming true . . .

She is yanked back and down again as the dressing-gown belt is tugged free. Suzie tries to throw elbows backwards, to claw at the pressure upon her, but she is suddenly aware of her weakness, her glasses pressed painfully into her face, the sudden taste of blood in her mouth as she mashes her teeth on her tongue.

Now the belt is free. Her bare stomach and breasts are pressed into the grass. There is more dirt on her tongue.

A hard yank, her hair tearing at the roots, and now the belt is around her throat: a hissing sound fighting the blood in her ears as her neck is squeezed shut.

Simon. Please. Simon . . .

'What the fuck?'

A chorus of shouts. Sudden protests.

'Who . . .? Get off, you bastard.'

The pressure suddenly loosens. She can breathe. She can breathe!

'Come here, you fucker . . .'

'Stop!'

Suzie: coughing up blood and earth, gasping for breath, trying to turn herself. To see who did this to her. To see who it is that is trying to end her life.

Tears in her eyes. Blood streaking her face.

Suddenly feeling lighter than air. Flying. Rising high: a half-drunk rapture.

Being picked up in the arms of a fat Asian man. Her face pressed into a wet, hairy chest. Heart thudding, masking the sound of running footsteps, and distant shouts . . .

CHAPTER 23

Sunday, mid-morning. A leg of lamb roasting in the oven and the smell of garlicky meat and fat filling this small, two-bedroomed house.

McAvoy looks at his wife. She is wearing a purple velour jogging top and shorts. She has taken her make-up off, and her dark, tanned skin looks kissably soft in the half-light of the bedroom, illuminated only by the ghost-shaped lamp that sits on Fin's chest of drawers.

'You happy, darling?'

Roisin gives her husband a huge grin. Then playfully shouts, 'Catch,' and pretends to throw him their daughter. He adopts a rugby player's stance, and they share a laugh together over his instinctive response.

'Are we going to watch the film now?' asks Fin.

The lad had been upstairs, playing with his toys, when he had asked if his sister could come and join him. Roisin had taken Lilah up and told him he had to play nicely and not let her near the toys that can come to bits. Ten minutes later Fin had shouted for his parents and told them his sister had given a noise that was a definite laugh. His parents had needed proof, and set about putting on a comedy routine. Lilah had not responded to silly voices or Roisin's star-jumps, but had started showing signs of mirth when McAvoy plucked his wife out of the air and threw her on the bed.

'Sure, Fin, we'll put it on. You finished playing?'

McAvoy is interrupted by the sound of a Shakira pop song. Roisin fumbles in her cleavage for her phone, and puts Lilah on her hip as she speaks.

She rolls her eyes at McAvoy as she asks who it is.

Her smile fades. She stops looking at her husband. Turns away from him.

'Daddy, can we—?'

McAvoy shushes his son. Crosses to his wife and turns her to face him.

'But that's mad,' his wife is saying. 'It's not an honour thing now. How can it be? He'll never say yes. He's a policeman. No. that's . . .'

McAvoy is rubbing his wife's forearm. Trying to get answers. He has a feeling between his guts and chest, an uneasiness. A queasy feeling of foreboding.

'Tell him "no",' says Roisin. 'No.'

She hangs up the phone. Turns to McAvoy. Her face is pale. The dark lines beneath her eyes, invisible when she was laughing just moments ago, seem suddenly to have deepened to a bruise.

'Fin, can you watch your sister for five minutes? There's a good lad.'

Roisin's voice has a slight tremble. Its tone is grey.

She settle Lilah back on her play mat, and takes McAvoy's hand as she leads him from the room and into their own bedroom. She switches on the bedroom light and sits down on the bed, looking up at him with wide eyes.

'Did you hurt Ronan?'

McAvoy, the nervousness inside him threatening to make his hands tremble, is too bewildered to answer. He tries to predict what he will be told. Cannot think fast enough.

'There's a new halting site at the playing fields in Anlaby,' she says. 'Some of the lads from Cottingham have set up there.'

McAvoy spreads his hands, eager to find out how much he needs to worry. 'Yeah, I was there a few days ago, there was an escaped horse, I told you . . .'

'You were there a couple of nights ago. You arrested Ronan.'

McAvoy frowns. An image of the ginger lad fills his mind. Sees himself, pinning him to the dirt and wrenching his hands behind his back. Hears, again, the hissed threats. 'Do you know him? He's the one who sets the dogs on Trish.'

Roisin waves the question away. 'I think we were once at a wedding together. That's not the thing.' She stops. 'Aector, do you know who his godfather is?'

McAvoy's mind is struggling to keep up. 'What? No.'

'Look, Aector, people know who you are. They know you're the big ginger copper that Roisin Byrne ran off with and got herself married to. They know your name.'

'What does that matter?'

McAvoy's voice betrays his feelings. They have not had to discuss such things in many years. His wife's past and heritage are things they have both long since assimilated into their union. They have been a couple since she was seventeen. Their first meeting was on a halting site just outside of Carlisle. She was a girl, giggly and raven-haired, entertained but not enthralled by the giant, young, uniformed policeman who blushed so furiously as he spoke to the men on the site about a spate of petty thefts. It was only later that their passing knowledge of one another was cemented. Bonded by fire. Turned into something deep and unyielding in a moment of violence that left McAvoy with blood on his hands, and a weeping girl in his arms: she rescued from her attackers by luck, providence, and a giant man with flame-red hair and furious righteousness in his eyes.

'Aector, Ronan's godfather has heard about what you did. Ronan's called him somehow. Told him you beat him up. Tied his hands and battered him.'

'That's insane,' splutters McAvoy. 'I would never . . .'

'It doesn't matter,' she says, her eyes pricking with tears. 'He believes it. And he wants a straightener.'

McAvoy opens his mouth. Pulls a face. He breathes out, relieved that the problem is no bigger than the ones he is already facing.

'A straightener? I'm a policeman! You told them that, yeah?' He pauses. Furrows his brow. 'Who was that on the phone?'

Roisin looks at her phone distractedly, as if it doesn't matter. 'Just somebody giving us warning.'

'Friendly or unfriendly?' asks McAvoy, and there is an edge to his voice now.

'Aector, there are still people who care for me. I'm not dead to everyone.'

McAvoy sees the flash of temper in her cheeks and sits next to her on the bed. He puts an arm around her slim, toned shoulders. 'I didn't mean that,' he says.

He knows how much she has sacrificed to become his wife. Knows that her mother and father can barely bring themselves to acknowledge that their youngest daughter has married a policeman, in a simple registry office ceremony. Her two brothers deny her existence. Roisin was brought up believing in family above all else. He knows that part of her soul was fractured the day she told her parents that she had fallen in love with the policeman who had twice arrested her dad.

'Aector, his godfather is Hamer.'

McAvoy searches her face, waiting for more information. None comes.

'Hamer?'

'Giuseppe Hamer. Beppe.'

McAvoy stands again. There is a half-full glass of water on the bedside table, and he takes a sip, swilling around his mouth until it is warm.

'I'm a policeman, Roisin. We don't have fights. We deal with dangerous people all the time.'

Roisin stands now, coming close to her husband. There is a genuine fear in her expression.

'He won't care about that,' she says. 'It's a traveller thing. An honour thing. Ronan's told him you hurt him and that's that. The uniform won't matter.'

McAvoy sighs. He could do without this. 'Roisin, seriously, he can't expect me to go and have a bare-knuckle fight . . .'

'He does! That's what he's demanding.'

'Well, he hasn't demanded anything of me.'

'This is how it works, Aector,' she says patiently, as if explaining to a child. 'The word gets out. A message gets to you. A time and place is arranged. You meet and you fight. And you keep going until one of you gives up.'

'Dead?'

'No, not dead. There are rules. There's a ref. He keeps it from getting—'

'Deadly?'

'Yeah. But people get hurt. Really hurt. And they get hurt by Giuseppe Hamer.'

McAvoy finishes the glass of water. Sits back down and pulls Roisin to his knee. In truth, he is not overly concerned. He is sad that his wife is upset, and knows that he will probably have to deal with this situation at some point, but in terms of what he has to deal with at present, he will not be giving Giuseppe Hamer much thought. He mentally puts a circle around the name. Makes a note to check him out, and cross-reference for any links to Vietnamese drugs gangs.

'I can look after myself,' says McAvoy. 'This is what I do.'

Roisin does not seem pacified. 'Would you fight him, Aector? If you had to? For honour?'

McAvoy looks at her. He realises he has been wrong. Her fear is not that Hamer will hurt him. It is that he will not fight.

'There's no honour in this,' he says coldly. 'I'd die for what I thought is right. But this? Is that what you think I am?'

Roisin drops her face to her hands. 'I don't know what I want. Sometimes I feel like a stranger. The way things are, the way you all behave?'

'Who's "you all"?'

They sit in silence. For a moment, McAvoy entertains the notion of agreeing. Of standing his ground and taking his bruises from a bare-knuckle fighter. He laughs under his breath. Reaches out and strokes his wife's hair.

'I'll be whatever you want me to be, Roisin. I'd die to make you smile.'

She shakes her head. 'I don't want that. I don't even want you to fight. I want you to be you. To be good and brave and caring. But then I see my mam's face and how she would sneer if one of her boys said no to a straightener and I don't know who to be myself.'

McAvoy pulls her close. Holds her. They were married when she was so young. Her life was among the travellers, and she took to his world without a backwards glance. There are times they both feel they married somebody from a different age.

He tries to make her smile.

'Lilah was awesome, wasn't she?'

With an effort of will, Roisin manages to let herself be steered into more pleasant thoughts.

'She's got my laugh, not yours.'

'That's a relief,' says McAvoy. 'She'd scare people.'

Fin appears in the doorway. He is scowling and clearly ready to watch the film.

'Go on down with Mammy,' says McAvoy. He eases Roisin into a standing position. 'I'm going to make a call or two, then I'll be down too.'

She looks at her husband. Ruffles his hair and bends forward to stroke the rasping stubble on his cheeks. 'You're my hero.'

The family head downstairs, leaving McAvoy alone in the bedroom. He picks the laptop up from where it has been charging by the bed, and places it on his knees as he shuffles back against the headboard. The machine had run out of power when they were looking at holiday destinations in bed the night before. The picture is frozen on an image of a lake in Sweden. It is the view from the remote log cabin he hopes to be able to afford to take his family to for a week or so in the winter. Whether they make the trip or stay at home will depend on whether the insurance company pays out for the people-carrier. He is not getting his hopes up.

He logs on to his work email, using his remote access code and password. Checks his messages. Nothing from the tech unit yet, and a brief line of thanks from ACC Everett for rewriting his speech. It had gone well.

Pursing his lips, unsure whether he is simply inviting more worry, he accesses the Police National Computer. He enters the name 'Giuseppe Hamer' and breathes out through a tight mouth as the screen is filled with the criminal activities of the 48-year-old repeat offender. He scans the various crimes. Armed robbery. Wounding. Receipt of stolen goods. He has served four different lengthy sentences. Was only released from a stretch last September and has not kept any of his parole meetings. A warrant for his arrest is currently active.

McAvoy brings up the mugshot. Maximises the image until it fills the screen. Looks into the face of a thick-set, bovine man with close-cropped hair and piggy eyes, his jowls and jaw covered in a grey stubble. McAvoy checks his height. 6ft 2ins. He gives a little nod.

'OK,' he breathes.

He is about to close the screen when it occurs

to him to check Hamer's associates. He does not know whether he expects to find Ronan's name, or Roisin's.

Scrolling down, he looks for familiar names. Stops at Alan Rourke. The pair did an armed robbery together in 1993. Held up a post office in a village just outside Leicester. It had been a straightforward raid: lots of noise and shouting and a shotgun shoved in the postmistress's face. They would have got away had Hamer not realised, on his way out of the door, that he had used the name 'Al' when shouting instructions at his partner. Despite Rourke's protestations, he had climbed out of the getaway car to go back in and silence the witnesses. The decision was costly. Rourke and Hamer were still arguing on the pavement over whether or not they should add murder to their list of crimes when the police turned up. The chase was a short one. Rourke crashed their stolen Toyota, and both men were sent down. They served seven years of a twelve-year sentence.

McAvoy jots down a couple of notes. Closes his eyes, aware he is about to be shouted at, then picks up his mobile. Calls Colin Ray.

'What do you want?' The voice is tired and grumpy.

'It's about Alan Rourke,' says McAvoy, determined to simply say what he has to, and then get off the phone. 'One of his associates. A Giuseppe Hamer. He's worth checking out.'

There is silence at the other end of the phone. McAvoy wonders where the other man is. Realises he knows precious little about his life. Knows only that he is twice divorced and lives in an apartment somewhere in the city centre. He tries to picture his life. Finds it hard to imagine the older man without Shaz Archer in his shadow. A thought crosses his mind. He wonders if there is anything more to their relationship than the master and protégée dynamic. Realises that many of his colleagues must have questioned it before him. Wonders, briefly, whether such rumours would ever circulate about his own bond with Trish Pharaoh.

'It's Sunday morning, lad. I'm busy.'

'Oh yes?' McAvoy tries to sound chatty. Can't help but be curious.

'Picking up the lads, as it happens. Football match.'

'Yes? Who's playing.'

'We are, you daft bastard. Bridlington away.'

McAvoy vaguely recalls some conversation he had with Colin Ray when he first joined the unit. Remembers that the older man coaches one of the divisional police football teams. Remembers too, the detective inspector's expression when he told him he was a rugby and boxing man, and did not follow football.

'Are you driving? 'McAvoy is about to offer to call him back when it is safe to take the call.

'What do you fucking want?'

McAvoy feels the blush. Wishes he could talk to people with some degree of comfort or aplomb.

'One of Alan Rourke's past associates. He's a real villain. A Giuseppe Hamer. He's also the godfather of Ronan.'

A pause at the other end of the line. 'Hamer?'

'Yes. Armed robber.' He thinks for a second about whether to reveal more. Realises he must. 'Traveller.'

Ray gives a bark of a laugh. 'You don't say.'

McAvoy falls silent. 'I thought it might be worth checking out, that's all.'

He has done his best to maintain an interest in the Rourke investigation, but knows only that the old armed robber kept his trap shut during the interview. Gave 'no comments' all the way. Young Ronan gave only slightly more. Lost his temper, shouted and screamed his way through questioning. Neither Ray nor Archer had managed to get a useful word from either of them and, though they made a fuss when both were given bail, they had expected little else. Ronan gave his address as Rourke's place, and the older man was put down on paper as being his current guardian. Social services went away happy. And Ronan fucked off the second he walked out of the door.

'I know the name Hamer,' says Ray quietly, appearing to be struggling with a memory. 'Fighter, isn't he? Bare-knuckle stuff.'

McAvoy isn't sure how to respond. Starts

Googling Hamer's name for something to distract himself. 'A boxer? I don't think . . .'

'Traveller fighting,' says Ray. 'Bare-knuckle stuff. I think he's part of that crowd.'

McAvoy finds a link to the gypsy's name. Clicks it. Feels himself closing down inside as he presses play on a video showing Hamer stripped to the waist, knuckles taped, pounding right hand after right hand into the ribs of a younger man while a crowd of lads form a rough circle around the fight. A muscular man in a white T-shirt tries to separate them. To keep some kind of order. He is struggling.

'That's illegal.'

'Piss off, lad,' says Ray. 'Everything fun is illegal. And the gyppos have been doing this shit for centuries. Straighteners, they call them. Honour fights. Big business now. They're arranged like pro fights. Big crowds. And the DVD sales are massive.'

'I'm watching him fight now,' says McAvoy. 'How can I be watching an illegal fight? I just clicked one button . . .'

Ray gives a joyless little chuckle. 'I'd love to see the world like you do, lad. Fucking hell.'

McAvoy pauses the video, just as the camera pans in on Hamer's snarling, blood-spattered face. His bound knuckles, too, are caked in red.

'The interview,' says McAvoy. 'Ronan.'

Ray laughs again. 'Fuck all so far,' he says. 'Had to sedate the little bastard. Every time he went in his cell he lost it. Started bouncing himself off the walls. Not happy with you.'

'Me?'

'He's feeling a bit miffed that you put him down like a sack of shit.'

McAvoy isn't sure whether to preen or be humble. 'I'm a policeman.'

Ray says nothing for a moment. Then, as if it hurts him to say it, adds, 'You did good, by the way. Taking him down. I lost my feet. Little shit got me right in the jaw. Landed on a rib. Hurts like hell . . .'

McAvoy knows that if he were to speak, he would spoil the moment, so simply nods. 'Any news on Pharaoh?' he manages.

'Back tomorrow, so she reckons,' says Ray, equally glad to have had the subject changed. 'She could have strung this out for months, silly cow. Obviously needs to come and make sure we can still wipe our arses.'

McAvoy lets the other man talk. He is wondering what Pharaoh's return means. Whether he has done enough wrong to get more than a telling off. Whether he will be able to get the report back from the tech unit in time to present her with evidence of the need for a genuine murder enquiry. Whether he should just do what he's been told. Wonders, for a moment, why he is not trying this hard to catch the two shaven-headed thugs who have out-muscled the Vietnamese, and caused a spike in the violent crime statistics.

'Enjoy the match, sir,' says McAvoy. 'Hope you win.'

'Enjoy whatever it is you fucking do,' says Ray and ends the call.

McAvoy stares for a moment longer into the eyes of Giuseppe Hamer. Shakes his fears away. Calls the tech unit and asks for Dan.

'Sergeant,' says the young man when he comes to the phone. 'All good?'

'I was rather hoping to have your report this morning,' says McAvoy. 'Superintendent Pharaoh did specify that it was very urgent.'

'I know she did,' says Dan. 'I was up till three for her. She's worth an all-nighter, don't you think. That's why I sent her the report.'

McAvoy closes his eyes. 'You sent it to Superintendent Pharaoh?'

'Yes. And?'

I asked for it to come to me. I said!' He sounds exasperated. Childish.

'Does it make any difference? I wanted her to know how much effort we'd gone to . . .'

McAvoy is spared the effort of trying to formulate a sentence by the sound of the doorbell. He takes the phone away from his ear and listens to the muttered conversation from downstairs. A moment later there is the sound of footsteps on the stairs.

'I'll call you back,' he says into the phone.

He looks up, ready to smile for his wife, as the

door opens. His face freezes, locked in place, colour falling into his shirt.

In the doorway of his bedroom, gauze strapped to her throat, hands bandaged, dressed in jeans, too-tight vest and leather jacket, stands Trish Pharaoh. Her eyebrows are raised almost to her hairline.

'Guv, I . . .'

He is suddenly aware that he is wearing nothing but shorts. That he has a laptop balanced on his lap. He shuts the screen like a guilty teenager looking at porn.

Pharaoh raises a fist full of computer printouts.

'Time for a chat?' she asks.

Her voice could shatter steel.

'Your missus is a looker,' says Pharaoh, leaning against the bedroom wall and making no attempt to look away as McAvoy pulls on a hooded sweatshirt and smooths down his hair with the palm of his hand. 'Not what I pictured.'

McAvoy wonders what his wife made of his boss. What she will make of him, when she is gone.

'Thank you,' he says, distractedly. He waves an arm vaguely to indicate her injuries. 'How are you?'

Pharaoh's expression does not change. She continues to watch him with wide-eyed detachment. 'Sore. Getting attacked by Rottweilers will do that to you.'

'I wish I'd been there . . .'

'I know you do.'

McAvoy stops. Stands, next to the bed, and meets her gaze. 'I was worried,' he says.

Pharaoh softens. For a moment she is an indulgent mother accepting a thank-you fridge-drawing from a naughty toddler. 'Daniells stepped up. Kicked one of them right in the nuts.'

'He got hurt too.'

'Poor lamb.'

'He did good.'

'He's not you,' she says shrugging, and what she means by it is left unsaid.

McAvoy cannot help himself. He points at the papers she clutches. 'Tech report?' he asks, wincing.

'Yes, emailed to me at three a.m., together with a little note from some computer geek who wanted me to know how hard he had worked on this, along with all the info I requested and assigned to my budget.'

McAvoy rubs his face. Realises he is biting the webbing between forefinger and thumb.

'It's the case I told you about, Guv,' he says. 'You suggested I have a look.'

Pharaoh runs her tongue around the inside of her lower lips. Despite her injuries, she is wearing make-up. He wonders whether she applied it herself. Why she bothered, if only to come and shout at her sergeant.

'Does the expression "bane of my life" mean anything to you, Hector?'

McAvoy grabs the question like a lifeline. 'Bane is an old English word for murderer. That morphed into meaning "something that causes death". That's where you get the name for poisonous plants from, like wolfsbane and henbane . . .'

'No, Hector. *You* are the bane of my life. I spend a lot of time deciding whether or not to stab you in the head.'

McAvoy stops talking

She looks at him hard. Gives the room a quick once-over. Lets her gaze linger, for the tiniest fraction of a second, on the leopard-print silk nightdress that hangs from the foot of the bed.

'I hesitate to ask this of your big brain, but is there a landlubber word for a Jonah?'

'Are you really asking?'

'No,' she says. 'But I am implying that you seem like a magnet for shit.'

McAvoy looks at the papers in her hand as she gesticulates. Is desperate to unroll them and read the hidden words.

'I thought it was important.'

Pharaoh smiles, rolling her eyes. 'It is important. You were right. You're nearly always right. Doesn't mean I don't think about hurting you.'

McAvoy's skin prickles. He does not know how to comport his face, so stands still, looking expectant. 'I was right?' He is hesitant to ask which if his half-formed theories and vague gut instincts have been vindicated.

'Right about Simon Appleyard,' says Pharaoh,

crossing the room and sitting down, unasked, on his bed. He stands up, in turn. He has to fight the urge to turn scarlet at the intimacy of the moment. His boss, here, in his bedroom. Family downstairs. Words to stroke his ego in her hand.

'He was murdered?' asks McAvoy, instinctively, leaning back against the wall in the position she has just vacated.

Pharaoh shrugs. 'You're right that he could have been. I've spoken to the pathologist again. She emailed me through images of the body and the post-mortem exam. Pretty boy, wasn't he?'

'His back, you mean? The tattoos?'

'Yeah, lovely work. Will have to show you mine some day. Anyway, I can see why she didn't see it, but she'll be getting a bollocking at some stage.'

'See what?'

'The bruise,' says Pharaoh, rustling through her papers.

McAvoy crosses back to her. Sits next to her on the bed. Catches a hint of her perfume. Notices that she is wearing open-toed shoes instead of her usual biker boots, and that her feet are not as pretty as his wife's. Wonders why he is even thinking about such things.

'You can see it here,' she says, holding up a colour printout.

McAvoy looks upon the photograph of the boy whose death has so troubled him. Simon is laid out naked on a steel table. The clinical aluminium and white of the mortuary frames the exotic colours of his body. Makes his slim frame appear almost skeletal. McAvoy stares into the mass of ink. Squints, between the eyes of the tattooed peacock feather, at the slight blur of discoloration.

'Sergeant Arthurs told me about that,' he says. 'Said he was surprised the pathologist missed it.'

'Nothing surprises me,' says Pharaoh. She hands him more pictures. Simon, kneeling forward, slumped and lifeless, his skin a mottled red and blue. A rope trailing from his throat, tongue hanging forward from between open lips, a black slug.

'He had been there some time,' recalls McAvoy.

'Heater was on the whole time too. Decomposition started quickly. She'll have a good reason for not seeing it.'

'If it's anything at all,' warns McAvoy.

'True,' says his boss. 'But it looks like a footprint to me.'

'Or a knee,' he says, looking again at the image.

They look at one another, close as lovers on the edge of the bed. McAvoy looks away first.

'Why did you contact the pathologist, Guv?' he asks.

'Boredom?' She laughs. Then her face turns serious. 'No, Hector, I trust your instincts. You've made your usual balls-up of going about it all, but there's something here.'

McAvoy is torn between feeling flattered and insulted. Tries to ignore both feelings and just ends up jiggling his leg. His mind is trying to work out how much she knows. Whether she is already further ahead than him.

'Dan's report?'

'I'm pleased it came to me first. You'd have had a heart attack. But you're right. I think we made a right cock-up looking into it.'

'I've spoken to his aunt,' says McAvoy. 'She doesn't know what she thinks. Doesn't know if she wants to know. But she says he was living life to the full, if you get my meaning. And had a friend who went everywhere with him. I haven't started tracking her down yet.'

'What else?'

McAvoy looks skywards. Realises he has no real justification for sharing more, but does not want to hold anything back. 'Two city councillors,' he says, at last. 'Cabourne and Hepburn. They're connected. They're lovers.'

'Lovers! Christ, the way you talk. They're both blokes, yes?'

'Yes. Hepburn's the one who . . .'

'Yes, I know him. Character, yes? Some shady stuff in his background but nothing he hides.' She waggles her tongue thoughtfully. 'And have they got a connection to Simon?'

'Cabourne has been meeting men for sex – using the same dating site that Simon posted his details on. Simon's phone number is on there.'

'And does Cabourne remember Simon?'

'He thinks they shared some messages but nothing ever happened.'

'But?'

McAvoy shrugs. 'Hepburn knows more than he's letting on. And I think Simon might have met somebody on that site who didn't want his secret getting out.'

'Cabourne?'

He considers it. 'I don't know.'

They sit in silence.

'Anyway, turns out Dan's more of a technical genius than you are. He's got plenty more info off it than you managed.'

She hands him another sheaf of papers, made almost illegible by the amount of creases.

'What's this?' He looks at the images. Turns it around. Widens his eyes.

'Yep,' says Pharaoh with a smile. 'That appears to be a picture of our dead man having a little bit of fun with himself, though quite why Dan thought I'd want that to be the picture I looked at over my breakfast is anybody's guess.'

'He sent these?'

McAvoy looks at the images. They are unmistakably of Simon Appleyard, naked and pleasuring himself.

'Bloody hell.'

'Yes. And they were sent as picture-messages at about nine p.m. on the day Simon was last seen.'

'That's . . .'

'Yes, about an hour before the pathologist reckons Simon died.'

'So he was sending this kind of stuff at nine p.m. and then hanging himself at ten?'

'Doesn't mean he didn't bump himself off,' says Pharaoh, taking the pictures back. 'Just means there is a hell of a lot to explore here.'

'What else?'

'Some more poetry. Messages he sent . . .'

McAvoy takes the report. Reads Simon's words out loud.

'You move inside me as a puppeteer. Take ownership of my body. Fold me into your vision of desire . . .'

'You say the nicest things. Look at what he was getting in return. These were in the inbox.'

McAvoy turns the page. 'Am going to hurt you. Take you. Make you my bitch . . .'

'They were my wedding vows.'

'Will scratch my mark on you, tear open the ink on your skin . . .'

'Yep, I do.'

McAvoy stops. 'So they knew he had tattoos? Had they met before? Or did he send him pictures of his back, too?'

Pharaoh sighs. 'What we can get is in there. Simon's poetry, and this other person wanting to hurt him and dominate him.'

'Is it just a game?'

Pharaoh raises her eyebrows. 'I'm not the expert,' she says. 'I know people go online a hell of a lot looking for sex and I know people have fantasies they want to come true and those that they don't. Anyway, this is all just maybes. I'm not here on a Sunday for maybes. You haven't got to the interesting bit, yet.'

McAvoy turns to the last page of the sheaf. Reads the words underlined in red. The words Simon Appleyard received the night he died.

Want you on your belly when I arrive. Naked. Body waiting for my touch. Hold the rope in your hand. Leave the door unlocked. Show me your ink as I arrive, then let me take possession of you. Let me make you feel pretty . . .

McAvoy looks up. 'Fuck.'
Pharaoh smiles. 'Yes indeed.'

CHAPTER 24

The water tastes of early mornings. Of last night's booze.
Dirt.
Grass.
Blood.
'Thanks.' She grimaces. Her throat is full of cold stones. 'Lovely.'

She shuffles herself into a more comfortable sitting position. Watches the sunlight stream in through the conservatory glass. Dazedly soaks up the view. The flat green landscape and the swaying trees, the painted-on symmetry of the distant apple trees and the blueness of the clear sky.

'Still sore?'

Suzie winces again as she finishes the drink. 'Will be ok when it opens up a bit. Christ, I sound like Louis Armstrong.'

She is in the large, L-shaped living room of a remote Lincolnshire farmhouse that, two nights a week, becomes a sex club. This morning it is just a home, and she is an injured guest, convalescing, wrapped up in a blanket on the sofa and with her hair stuck up on one side.

'Did you have bad dreams?'

Suzie gives a shrug. 'I don't remember,' she says. 'Maybe. Doesn't matter if you don't remember, does it?'

Christine is up and dressed. She looks comfortable in old jeans and a rugby shirt. Big Dunc is doing something onerous out on the shingled drive. She can hear the scrape of a rake on the pebbles.

'You must be hungry,' says Christine. 'Yoghurt? Fruit?'

Suzie screws up her face. 'I'm going to get off this morning. I'll stop at a McDonald's on the way home. I'm fine.'

'Suzie, you can stay as long as you want.'

'Honestly,' she says. 'I need to go.'

Christine seems unsure. Suzie can understand her feelings. Here, on the sofa in the living room, she can be watched. She can be gently spoken to and nursed. She can be persuaded of the benefits of chalking Saturday night down to experience, and keeping her bloody mouth shut.

'Really,' says Suzie, stretching. 'You've been good to me. I'm ok to go.'

Christine's still looks worried, but she forces her lips into a tight smile. 'I'll make you a sandwich for the journey,' she says and takes the empty glass from Suzie's hand, before heading back to the kitchen.

Suzie rummages around in her thigh boot and finds her watch. It's just gone lunchtime. A McDonald's breakfast is out of the question.

She fell asleep just after three, just as the last vehicle left the grounds, and as news filtered back from the hospital that Jarod had a fractured skull, but was going to be ok. He'd been smashed across the head. Suzie did not have much to say about that, or anything else. She was on the sofa, knees curled up beneath her, sucking an ice cube, some of Christine's hand-cream turning the redness of her rope-burned neck into something ghoulishly shiny.

Last night is coming back to her in stages. Nobody had wanted to call the police. There had even been dissenting voices when Big Dunc said he was going to take Jarod to hospital. Were it not for the fact that she could barely swallow and that her heart was still racing, as if to justify its reprieve, she would have found the discussions of the previous evening comical. Even in her dazed, drunken, semi-throttled state, she could feel a bizarre giggle building inside herself as she took in the scene. A score of men and women – some in white dressing gowns, like Greek philosophers, and others with towels around their waist. One man entirely naked, sitting on the edge of a wicker chair with his shrunken manhood sitting on his balls like a hat. Jarod laid out on the patio in a mess of mud and blood. Angry voices and fist-shaking accusations.

The man who carried her back to the house said his name was Matt. He was a chartered accountant from Bradford and spoke with a thick West

Yorkshire accent. He did not let her go until she was ready. Held her in his arms as if comforting a child. Placed one large hand over her left ear and pressed the other ear to his chest, while the argument raged about what had happened and what should be done.

Suzie does not judge the others for wanting to keep their secrets. Few would be proud to have their names and addresses taken by detectives in connection with an attempted murder at a sex party. Fewer still would want their lives pored over by sniggering police officers, or their wives and partners to be questioned over their movements and bedtime habits.

Suzie's attacker had not been found, having vanished into the shadows with barely a sound; the shouts of their pursuers roused the rutting couples who were enjoying the party, and resulted in a hastily convened, babbling argument in the conservatory about what was for the best.

'My life will be over! This can't get out. There'll be interviews. Police. The papers. My wife!'

'It's about right and wrong. Somebody's attacked him. He could die!'

'No, it's too important. Secrecy, remember. That's what the website says. Discretion assured.'

'This changes things. It's life and death. It could be one of us.'

'He probably slipped. She might have had too much to drink. It might even be her who did it.'

Like a tennis umpire, she watched the debate go

back and forth. At length, they had convinced Suzie that her attacker was probably a local teenager. Big Dunc revealed that their website had received a few emails from youngsters who had heard there was a sex club open on their doorstep, promising to pay a visit next time there was party. Suzie had merely nodded. Kept her own counsel. Swallowed painful mouthfuls of blood and picked the dirt from between her teeth.

Here, now, she knows. Knows full well that she has been running from her own thoughts. Knows that Simon did not hang himself. That she never truly believed that he did. Simply refused to let her fears take her to a conclusion that terrified her. She knows, more than anything, that whoever killed him is now after her.

Filling herself with a deep, painful breath, she rummages through her handbag and finds her phone. It has been switched off for days. She half expects her hands to tremble as she turns it on, but is surprised to find that she is in control. She feels detached somehow. Not numb, but somehow separated from what she is doing. She did not feel her soul leave her body as her attacker strangled her, but now she almost feels as if she is looking down on herself from above.

Suzie disentangles her legs from the quilt. She is still wearing the dressing gown. Somebody has brought her clothes from the side of the hot tub, but she is in no mood to dress as yesterday. She stuffs them in her handbag after removing a long, blue dress, spotted with snowflakes and with an owl on her left breast. She pulls it on and wriggles her feet into her boots as the phone begins beeping. Spewing out messages and missed calls.

Closing her eyes, preparing herself, she moves to the conservatory door and slides it open. Takes a lungful of cool, fresh, air. Plugs back into her life against a soundscape of chattering birds and scraping gravel.

The message she seeks was sent ten minutes after the car ploughed into the man she had been ordered to fuck.

> So sorry. Can't make it. Will you still go play for me and tell me how he touched you? Wish I could see what a dirty girl you are. Xx

Suzie swallows again. Sneers, ever so slightly, and makes fists with her hands.

His next message was sent early the following morning.

> Were you a bad girl last night? xx

Then:

> You've gone quiet on me. Did you pussy out on me? Are you a tease?

There is a hiatus of a few hours. Then, angrily:

Knew you would be just like the others.
Knew you were all talk.

She scrolls onwards. Finds his next missive.

Sounds like you had a lucky escape. Bad
accident at the layby. Lucky girl. x

Finally:

May make an appearance at the party
you mentioned. Lincolnshire, you said.
Googled it and sounds a ball. Would I be
welcome? x

Suzie stares out across the fields. Watches a fat,
purple-throated pigeon walk delicately along the
wooden fence. Squints, and wonders if the brown
creature she can see near the hedgerow is a rabbit,
or somebody's discarded Ugg boot from the night
before.

She sifts through her other messages. Nothing
from the police about the accident, but plenty of
enquiries from work, from friends, about where
she is and what she's doing. A Facebook alert from
her mum.

Her eyes close, almost involuntarily. The sensation of dislocation is dissipating. She is coming
back to herself, guided in by the pain in her
throat and the cold emptiness in her gut. She is
unsure, right now, how she feels about herself.

She knows that she has let Simon down by accepting his suicide without question. Believes herself to have cheapened their memory by giving in to fear, and never demanding a less palatable truth.

It was the shabbiness of his life that Simon hated. The smallness of it. The inability to shine as brightly or as brilliantly as he wanted to. But such miseries would not claim his life. No, he was killed by somebody he wanted to make happy, and Suzie wants to cry at the thought.

'Somebody wants to kill me, Si,' she says, under her breath. 'Somebody who killed you.'

She opens eyes that threaten to fill with tears. 'I'm so sorry.'

'Beg your pardon, love?' Suzie turns. Christine has entered the conservatory with a fat ham sandwich and a mug of tea. 'Made you a little something,' she says, putting it on the stout table that has been cleared and wiped down sometime between the party and today.

'Oh, I'm sorry, I don't think . . .'

'You need to eat,' she says. She puts an arm out and gives Suzie a squeeze. 'Lovely dress,' she says.

Suzie can barely find the strength to smile. She wants to run suddenly. Wants to get away from these old people, with their sagging flesh and foul-tasting skin and their desperation to touch her and make themselves feel alive. She hates herself now. Hates seeing herself as this link to vitality. This young sacrifice being fawned and pored, tongued and tasted, by men and women fleeing the grave. She feels disgusted with herself. Here, now, she feels the wrong kind of dirty. Feels the wrong sort of whore.

'I have to go,' she says, bundling out of the conservatory door, spilling yesterday's knickers from her bag as she fumbles for her car keys.

'Dunc!' Christine is shouting her husband's name. 'Dunc, she's going . . .'

The big man appears suddenly from behind a white-painted outbuilding. He is all smiles.

'Yoo off, sweetie? There's no rush. I'll give you a lift later . . .'

Suzie can't think of anything to say. She just pushes past him. Runs to where her crappy blue car is parked on a patch of grass. Pulls open the door and climbs inside, willing the engine to work. Now her hands tremble as she turns the key, and she laughs with relief as it bursts into life.

She turns the car in a ragged semi-circle, scattering the neatly raked gravel, and puts her foot down. She feels alive suddenly. And so very scared of death.

The trees and hedgerows fill her windows as the car bumps and jerks down the rutted path. She is barely looking at the road. Instead, she fiddles with her phone. Scrolls through her numbers. Finds the number she could have called six months ago.

Rings the auntie of her dead friend.

Doesn't even manage a hello.

'Simon was murdered,' she says.

And in this moment, a sluice gate opens inside of her. The tears finally come.

CHAPTER 25

'Are you not going to eat it?'

McAvoy holds the plastic Tupperware box on his lap as if it is a ticking bomb.

'Maybe on the way back.'

'It'll get cold.'

'It's nice cold. It's fine.'

'If you'd done as I'd said, you could have sat down to dinner with the rest of us.'

'I wasn't that long. I just wanted a quick shave . . .'

Pharaoh has a little smile on her face during the exchange. She is not deliberately trying to embarrass him, but is enjoying having a little play with his shyness. Likes these married-couple chats that they too rarely have the opportunity to indulge in.

'She wasn't cross, was she?' he asks, his eyes closed, like a toddler trying to make themselves invisible.

'Hector, I don't think she could be cross with you if she found you nuts deep in a squirrel.'

McAvoy is grateful he is already looking out of the window. This way he does not have to disguise his blush or his smile.

Pharaoh stayed for lunch. Sat down to roast lamb

and minted peas and potatoes while McAvoy was upstairs showering, shaving, and slipping into a brown, tweed-effect, three-piece suit. He is not wearing a tie. It is his concession to working on a Sunday.

'There's a lot to hate about your wife,' says Pharaoh chattily, as she turns the little sports car onto Anlaby Road and slams down the clutch with her bare left foot.

'I beg your pardon?'

'Gorgeous. Slim. Lovely. I should hate her.'

McAvoy, who had swivelled his head towards his boss, looks away again. 'Oh.'

'Seriously, Hector. If that lamb knew how well his body would be treated, he would have handed himself in at the abattoir. I have never had gravy like that. Could I take a slice home for a sandwich?'

McAvoy holds the lunchbox a little tighter. Of all the crimson hues that his cheeks have taken this past week, none was as deep as that which exploded in his face when his wife handed him a Tupperware box with his roast dinner inside it, kissed him on the cheek, and told him to have fun.

'We had a nice chat,' says Pharaoh devilishly. 'Can't believe we've let it go this long without ever properly meeting.'

McAvoy splutters a little. 'Yeah, well, next pub quiz, or something . . .'

'No, I owe you a dinner now. We'll have you over to ours.'

He does not know how to reply. Has never been able to picture his boss's home life, or felt comfortable enough to ask about it. He knows only that she has teenage children, and a wheelchair-bound husband, though whether his condition is from injury or disease he has never ascertained.

'What's your speciality?' he asks her, by way of conversation.

'The wine list,' she says, her eyes on the road. 'Up here?'

McAvoy gives a nod. 'Yep. Second right, then pull in.'

In the past two hours Simon Appleyard's death has become a murder. They are taking the first tentative steps towards telling the top brass in CID that the violent crime statistics for the year are going to show another unlawful killing. They have only briefly mentioned the discovery of Leanne Marvell. Neither wants to address it. Neither wants to question whether they could, or should, have done more. They will visit her, together, when this is done. Help her somehow. Make it better . . .

'These are all right,' says Pharaoh, pulling into a space and looking up at the properties. 'Small, but neat enough.'

'£350 a month, or thereabouts,' says McAvoy. 'One-bedroomed, but properly looked after. All the same landlord.'

They disentangle themselves from Pharaoh's two-seater sports car. It is as close-fitting around

McAvoy's bulky frame as a tailored suit, but Pharaoh adores the vehicle and wears it far more comfortably than her sergeant.

'Going to be a nice one,' says Pharaoh, looking up at the blue sky. 'Any more rain on the way, Farmer Boy?'

McAvoy smiles. Gives a sniff of the air. 'Maybe a bit of drizzle tomorrow.'

'And what perfume am I wearing.'

He inhales again. 'Issey Miyake. And roast lamb.'

McAvoy straightens his clothes and checks that his notebook is open on a fresh, dated page.

They stand for a moment on the pavement outside the little apartment block. Springfield Court in Anlaby. A nice enough neighbourhood with decent schools and a couple of 24-hour supermarkets. Flats for young couples saving for a deposit on a starter-home, and for singletons content to rent.

'Still nothing from the landlord?' asks Pharaoh.

McAvoy checks his phone, and shakes his head. He has left a message for the property owner, but has heard nothing back. A quick search of the electoral register indicates that Simon's old flat is now occupied by a Mr Paul Essex, though how precise the information is they cannot say.

'Flat 2b, yeah?'

'Or not.'

'What?'

'Hamlet. Forget it.'

Pharaoh rings the bell. They stand for a moment on the step, staring at the white paint. Out of habit, Pharaoh tries the door handle. It doesn't move.

'In bed or out, you reckon?'

McAvoy considers the crisp blueness of the day, and doubts that the door will be opening any time soon.

'Try the neighbour,' says Pharaoh, stepping back from the door to peer up at the first-floor window. Net curtains obscure the glass.

McAvoy moves around to the other side of the building. Rings the next bell. Stands for a time, tapping his foot, then rings again.

'Luck of the Irish, you, aint' you?' says Pharaoh snappily. She sighs. Cocks her head. 'Can you hear that?'

McAvoy listens. He can hear guitar music coming from inside the ground-floor flat. He struggles to place it. It sounds Spanish. Classical. '"Asturias",' he says, nodding.

'What?'

'The piece.'

'Hector, you're a fucking idiot.'

Pharaoh pushes him aside and hammers on the door with her fist. The music stops. She lifts the letterbox. 'Police,' she yells, then looks at McAvoy. 'Sort of.'

A moment later the door is answered by a lad in his early to mid-twenties. He is short and thin with curly red hair and a pale, freckly complexion.

He is wearing a faded black shirt and tight jeans with baseball trainers, and he holds a battered guitar in his right hand.

'Seriously?' he asks, halfway between a curse and a sigh. 'Does this have to be now? I was caught up in the moment.'

'That's ok,' says Pharaoh. 'I get like that when I'm Hoovering.'

She puts her foot on the step and muscles him back into the cramped hall, which is littered with discarded trainers and a mountain of takeaway leaflets.

'We just need a moment,' says McAvoy by way of explanation. He follows Pharaoh down the hall, the bewildered lad following with much huffing and protestation. They arrive in a small, busy living area that does not appear to have been decorated to the occupant's own tastes. The carpet is a grey cord, and the wallpaper is patterned with floral swirls. A pink, two-seater sofa covered in sheet music and draped in drying T-shirts, is pushed back against one wall, and the open-plan kitchen to their right is home to a mountain of dishes and polystyrene chip cartons.

'If you don't like the mess you can tidy before you leave,' he begins, aggressively.

'It's ok, sweetheart, I'm not your mum.' Pharaoh looks around her. Decides she will not sit down. It's not overly dirty here, but she feels like she is in a teenager's bedroom, and is wary about sitting on anything that will not rub out with a wet cloth.

'What's this about?'

'Your neighbour,' says Pharaoh, turning to him, with a bright smile. 'Bit on the dead side.'

The boy looks strangely relieved. Gives a shrug. 'Lad from 2b?'

'Simon,' says McAvoy. He feels claustrophobic in the little room. Is grateful the electric heater is not switched on.

'You know him?' asks Pharaoh.

The lad sits back down on the sofa. Holds his guitar comfortably in his lap. His expression is unreadable, but not unfamiliar. McAvoy has seen it too many times. He has interviewed too many youngsters who truly do not give a damn about anybody but themselves. He has looked into the eyes of too many people who truly do not give a damn.

'How long have you lived here, Mr . . .?'

'Woodmansey,' he says. 'Darren. Been here just under a year now.'

'So Simon was your neighbour.'

Woodmansey gives a grunt. Sighs, like a teenager being asked if he has done his homework. 'Haven't we done this? Back when it happened?'

'You've spoken to a detective before?' asks McAvoy.

'Dunno about detective. He was a copper. Fella in uniform. Told him I barely knew him.'

'You knew his name was Simon?'

Darren looks up, mulling this over with exaggerated wariness. 'Yeah, I think so. I mean, I know

now, what with the inquest and everything. But yeah, he introduced himself.'

'What was your opinion of Mr Appleyard?' asks Pharaoh, crossing to the window and looking out at the neatly tended grass verges and hedges that border the little group of properties. She watches a pigeon pecking at a discarded piece of takeaway fried chicken. Wonders if it qualifies as cannibalism. She turns back. 'Did you get on?'

Darren smiles a little and plucks at the guitar strings. 'Can't say I had much of an opinion of him at all,' he says. 'Not in a bad way, like. He was just there. I was just here. Y'know? People come and go. Who fucking cares?'

'Ever go in his home?' asks McAvoy, watching the young lad and trying not to let himself imagine putting him over his knees. He suddenly remembers he hasn't showed him his warrant card, and does so now, if only to remind himself who he is and what he does.

'Round for dinner, you mean?' asks Darren, with an attempt at a laugh.

'Round for whatever, sweetheart,' says Pharaoh. 'It's like this one, isn't it? Same layout?'

Darren shrugs. Appears to think. 'I helped him carry a mini-oven up there about a month after I moved in. Was struggling with it when I got home so I gave him a hand.'

'Neighbourly of you,' says Pharaoh.

Darren shrugs again. It is an irritating habit – a display of affected nonchalance that McAvoy considers inappropriate. 'He spotted me. Asked. I couldn't get away.'

'And his flat? Layout like this, yes?'

'Far as I can recall,' says Darren and strums a complicated-looking chord.

McAvoy nods. Moves into the kitchen. Looks at the knife rack screwed into the wall next to the drainer. According to the crime-scene photos and the incident report, it was a mooring just like this that Simon Appleyard hanged himself from. Tied a belt around his neck, the other end here, and leaned forward until he was dead.

McAvoy taps the plasterboard wall with his knuckles. Catches Pharaoh's eye. She nods, and reaches into her pocket for her purse, retrieving a £20 note and wordlessly handing it to the guitarist. 'Sorry,' she says.

McAvoy grabs the knife rack and pulls. There is barely a moment's resistance before the screws are wrenched free and the object clatters onto the draining board: knives and ladles spilling noisily over the linoleum floor.

'What are you doing?' asks Darren, angry and shocked. 'This place isn't mine. It's rented.'

'Bit of grout and a deeper screw and it will be ok,' says McAvoy, distractedly. 'It can take a bit of weight.'

'But not a body?' asks Pharaoh.

'No.'

McAvoy and Pharaoh hold one another's gaze. McAvoy takes over.

'We're trying to find out a little more about Simon's death,' he says, crossing back to the seating area and deliberately looming large over the small, seated young man. 'There is evidence to suggest he might have been murdered.'

Darren looks from one officer to the other. He appears genuinely bewildered.

'What? Who?'

'That's what we're trying to find out. We're led to believe that Simon was promiscuous. Do you remember seeing many other people calling at his home?'

Darren puts the guitar down. 'I'm not the Neighbourhood Watch,' he says, masking his discomfort with a mild attempt at aggression.

'Mr Woodmansey . . .'

'Yeah,' he snaps. 'Yes,' he corrects himself, looking up at the towering police officer. 'There were knocks on the door sometimes. And I'd see the odd soul come and go, like.'

'Do you remember faces? Dates?'

'Of course not,' he says, incredulous. 'Just blokes.'

'So you were you aware that Simon was a homosexual.'

Darren snorts. 'Er, just a bit,' he says, sarcastically. 'He couldn't have been any gayer, really. Not that I'm bothered, like. Whatever, y'know.'

'And you didn't mind him entertaining people on your doorstep?'

'I might have had something to say about it on my doorstep,' says Darren, attempting to stand up and then sitting back down again when he realises he is only as tall as McAvoy's chest. 'I don't give a shit what he did in his bedroom. What's this got to do with me?'

Pharaoh moves beside McAvoy. 'Were you sad to hear he had died?'

Darren looks appalled by the question. He leans over the arm of the sofa and picks up a glass ashtray that looks like it has been stolen from a pub. He pulls a cigarette from the packet on the floor and lights it, taking a breathless drag. 'Whatever. Tough break, man.'

'And you didn't suspect foul play?'

'I didn't think about that side of it.'

Pharaoh pulls a face. 'A man dies next door and you don't think about it?'

'I thought it was a shame he had died,' says Darren, examining the end of his cigarette. 'He seemed a nice enough fella. But, y'know . . .'

McAvoy's face is impassive. 'I know what?'

'People's lifestyles,' he says, grasping around for a way to explain himself. 'You don't know what they get up to behind closed doors, do you? For all we know he was into all that auto-erotic stuff . . .'

'Oh, so you do have one theory,' says Pharaoh acidly. 'Any others?'

'I don't mean that,' he says, uncomfortable in the ferocity of her sudden glare. 'I mean, what am I allowed to think, these days? I vote Liberal. I mean, I would do. If I voted. And if the Liberals were still liberal. I don't mind what people do. I used to be in a band with a gay bassist.'

There is silence for a moment. McAvoy looks at the young man and wonders how many years there are between them. How different their view of the world is. Wonders how it would feel to look out on the world with such disinterest.

'I know that song,' begins Darren, as a Curtis Mayfield tune blares out from Pharaoh's handbag.

Pharaoh waves a hand at him, shushing him while reaching for her phone. 'Did you think he could have been murdered?' she asks.

Darren turns to McAvoy. Seems to think for a moment. He shrugs. 'Maybe for a minute. I don't know.'

McAvoy sighs. 'The time he died. Not the day, I know you can't remember. Just vaguely around the time. Did he have any visitors that you can recall?'

'There were always people coming and going.'

McAvoy arches his back and his chest muscles strain against his shirt. He is getting tired of nobody giving a damn. 'Mr Woodmansey, I appreciate that it is a Sunday afternoon and that this was not what you were expecting when you answered the door . . .'

'Bollocks to it,' says Pharaoh. Her phone stops vibrating before she can take the call. 'McAvoy, leave the lad alone.'

She turns on the youngster, suddenly a mum, furious with her son. 'Did you, or did you bloody not see or hear anything that I might find even vaguely fucking interesting?'

The young man backs himself into the sofa as though retreating from punches. He looks desperately up at McAvoy, and then appears to start thinking hard.

'He had a friend,' he says. 'A lass. Bit odd-looking. Smiley. She picked him up sometimes . . .'

'Anything else? Ages of his visitors? Anything?'

Darren gives up. Looks at the end of his cigarette. 'I guess they didn't look gay.'

McAvoy's shoulders sag. 'What does gay look like?'

'Like Simon! These were blokes. Like, just blokes.'

For a moment there is silence. Wordlessly, Pharaoh takes back the £20 note. 'You haven't done anything wrong,' she says quietly, as McAvoy stomps from the room. 'I just don't like you.'

She follows him down the corridor and finds her sergeant leaning against the brick wall, shaking his head slightly and looking cross.

'Nobody cares,' he says. 'People die next door and their neighbours just think it's none of their business.'

'He helped him carry his oven,' she points out.

'It's hardly the same.'

'McAvoy, people don't want to think about it. That lad could barely afford decent fags. He sure as hell couldn't afford to move. He's not going to want to let himself think his neighbour's been killed.'

'You were as hard on him as I was,' he says defensively.

'I'd have happily been harder.' She smiles. 'I got bitten by a dog this week. I'm not in a happy place.'

McAvoy leans his head back. Closes his eyes. 'I'm not sure if I should ever have started this. I feel like a bloody amateur . . .'

Pharaoh is about to offer some words of comfort when her phone begins to ring again. She answers, and listens for a moment.

'Right,' she says, into the mobile. 'Send me the number.' She takes the phone from her ear. Looks at the screen. 'Got it. You sure? Right.'

She hangs up. McAvoy looks at her expectantly.

'Dan's managed to unlock some of the mobile's call history,' she says. 'Knows his stuff that lad, even if the kisses on his emails are in capitals. And the specialist lab he sent it off to reckons there are two different types of dirt present in the phone's insides. Silt and sand, as you would expect, but also mud. Seeds that have no business in a tidal river. It looks like it was buried twice.'

McAvoy says nothing. Takes it in. 'The call history,' he says, at last. 'Tell me.'

'It called a taxi firm the day Simon died. Made no calls afterwards. And it belonged to Simon.'

McAvoy pauses. Thinks. 'He stored his own number?'

Pharaoh nods. She is already dialling the taxi firm. Introduces herself and asks for the manager.

385

Explains what she needs. Uses the right amount of sweetness and snarl. Hangs up and motions for McAvoy to follow her back to the car. She leans against the bonnet, waiting for another call, and breathes out with a whistle.

'Exciting, police work, isn't it?'

McAvoy despite himself, manages a little grin. He watches as she unlocks the car, removes his Tupperware box from the passenger seat, and starts eating the cold roast lamb and gravy. 'If you want this, you're going to have to fight me for it,' she says, licking her fingers. 'And be warned – I bite.'

Her phone rings. Between mouthfuls, she answers. McAvoy hands her his notepad and pen. She scrawls down the address, and says thanks.

'The taxi company says according to their records they received two calls at that time, on that day. One was a cab between the Empress in town and the Tiger in Cottingham,' she says, one half of her mouth curling up and the other still chewing a roast potato. 'The other was a pick-up from Morrison's going to Beck Lane. Welton.'

'Near the Dale?'

'Near enough.'

'Address?'

She nods. Swallows. Pulls her police radio from her handbag and contacts the control room.

'This is Trish Pharaoh,' she says. 'I need you to check an address for me. Beck Lane, Welton. Thanks.'

They stand in silence. It feels like they are waiting for a diagnosis.

McAvoy frowns. 'He wouldn't get a taxi home, would he? You don't kill somebody and then call a cab . . .'

Pharaoh shrugs. 'Morrison's is a minute from here. Could have bumped Simon off and walked it. Ordered a cab, dumped the phone when they got near home. Would never have expected anybody to find out. Nothing sinister in getting a cab home with your shopping.'

'Did the passenger have shopping? Did we get a description?'

'Driver's in Marbella, apparently. They're trying to rustle him up on the mobile.'

Moments pass. McAvoy, for something to do, plucks a leaf from a privet hedge and folds it into quarters. Pharaoh presses her knuckles into her forehead.

Both police officers jump as her radio crackles. 'This is control, Guv. We've got the details you asked for. That property belongs to a Peter Tressider. Councillor, it says here . . .'

Pharaoh and McAvoy stare at one another. After a moment, Pharaoh switches off the radio.

'It could be nothing to do with all this,' says McAvoy instinctively, but even as he speaks his mind is soaring back to the riverbank: to the two stick figures in the distance, and the phone, winking up at him, from the mud.

'No,' says his boss, quietly. 'But.'

'Yeah. But.'

Pharaoh drops her head to the car bonnet. Wonders if her injuries are sufficiently well healed to remove her bandages.

She wants to look her best when she goes to question the new chairman of the Police Authority in connection with a murder.

CHAPTER 26

On sunny days all roads lead to the Country Park Inn. It sits no more than a few hundred yards from where the Humber Bridge stitches Yorkshire to Lincolnshire, and offers the best view in the county of the towering road and its metal harp strings, albeit from virtually underneath. *Mole's-eye view*, McAvoy had said when he brought Roisin here. She had been good enough to laugh.

The tables and chairs on the patio area at the front are constantly occupied, families and friends sipping iced cider and flicking cigarette butts onto the shingle beach that leads down to the coffee-coloured waters. Across the water is another strip of mud leading up to Barton. There's a wildlife sanctuary over there that McAvoy has yet to get around to visiting. An art gallery that was once the longest tiled building in Europe, and which used to be a rope-making factory before it fell to ruin. McAvoy read once that they made the ropes for Hillary's conquest of Everest. It is a snippet of information that refuses to leave his brain.

Could be another country, thinks McAvoy, staring

across the water. North Lincolnshire remains somehow 'over there'.

The river that separates the two counties is the same stretch of mud and swirling currents which, centuries earlier, halted the Romans in their march north. Today it is still a barrier. 'Humberside' was reviled on both sides when the government tried to create a new county that included towns north and south of the water.

Yellow-bellies. That's what the Yorkshiremen call people from Lincolnshire. *Miserable, tight-arsed bastards*, is the rather less poetic riposte from across the water.

There had been rejoicing all around when the boundary lines were put right. Hull became Yorkshire again. Humberside Police has yet to change its name to something more popular. It still polices both banks.

McAvoy likes it here. So do plenty of others. Although the wind still whips in cold from the east, the glimpse of blue sky has been enough to persuade the county's drinkers that they should be outside, and there are perhaps fifty people thronging the outside of the pub, wrapped up warm and holding glasses and bottles, as McAvoy and Pharaoh cross the car park.

'Bloody mad,' says Pharaoh, nodding at a girl in her late teens who appears to have dressed for a tropical beach, and who is turning a shade of blue that matches her bottle of WKD.

'Inside, yes?'

'Too right.'

They enter the large, brightly lit bar. On the walls are posters advertising tribute acts and local singers. They sit uncomfortably next to mass-produced abstracts on canvas, and blackboards advertising the daily restaurant specials.

Pharaoh orders herself a double vodka with lemonade and lime, and McAvoy decides that half a pint of bitter would be a welcome anaesthetic. They take their drinks to a corner booth circled by glass, and sit opposite one another.

'Cheers.'

They clink glasses.

'Here's to following your nose.'

McAvoy looks down, ashamed to be the victim of the sarcastic toast.

Eventually Pharaoh gives a snort of laughter, then shakes her head. 'They don't like me anyway.'

'Who?'

'Top brass.'

'Oh.' McAvoy looks out of the windows. Watches the green channel marker bobbing on the swollen waters of the estuary. 'I'm sure they respect you.'

She shrugs. 'I don't know. No black and whites, are there? They like it when I catch villains. Don't like it when I don't.'

'Your clean-up record is top-drawer,' points out McAvoy, gulping half of his drink and then surreptitiously spitting some of it back in the glass. He has no more change in his pocket. He has to make his drink last.

'My predecessor's clean-up was nigh on 100 per cent,' she says.

McAvoy bites both lips. Any mention of Doug Roper makes his scars hurt. 'It was all lies,' he says.

'Yeah.' She pouts. 'Wish I could tell some.'

They drink their drinks. Watch the channel marker. Think their thoughts.

'You going to tell me what's happening in there?' asks Pharaoh, making a gun of her forefinger and thumb and pointing it at her sergeant's forehead.

McAvoy rubs his hands together. Wonders if he should just keep his trap shut. Realises that he can't.

'It's a sex thing,' he says, looking away, and realising as he does so just how feeble and prudish it makes him look. 'Simon Appleyard had been meeting men off the Internet for sex. One of those men killed him. They set him up to be lying on the floor of his living room when they arrived. Even made him pick his own noose. Strangled him to death. Made it look like suicide. Took his phone and his laptop. Dumped them.'

Pharaoh is nodding thoughtfully. She clinks the ice in her glass. Runs a short, jewelled finger around the rim.

'Were they killing Simon specifically, or just anyone they could get their hands on?'

McAvoy picks up a beer mat. Starts spinning it on its end as he thinks. 'They wanted to kill

Simon,' he says, and hearing it out loud makes it seem more real. 'He knew something. Saw something . . .'

'Based on what?'

McAvoy gestures with his hands, casting around as if trying to pluck the right answer from the air.

'So far, three councillors' names have come up in connection with this. I wish one of them hadn't, but it has. Fuck, just saying that makes me need to pee. Why did it have to be Tressider's place? Anyway, fucking hell. So . . . yeah . . . three councillors. And that's just with my tiny bit of digging. None of them would want their secrets coming out.'

'Hepburn got himself elected by playing the gay card,' says Pharaoh, warming to her role of devil's advocate. 'He wouldn't care.'

'And Cabourne looks like he wouldn't say boo to a goose.'

'So.'

They meet one another's eyes.

'Tressider,' says McAvoy.

'Bloody hell,' says Pharaoh.

They sit in silence. McAvoy's mind turns to the day by the river. Himself, damp to the bone, the smell of horses on his hands, and two stick figures talking by the water. Could one have been Tressider? Could the big, bearded, future MP really have come straight from the Police Authority meeting and then thrown Simon Appleyard's phone into the mud of the River Hull?

Pharaoh finishes her drink. Looks at McAvoy's. 'Drink it, you girl.'

He does so. She goes to the bar and comes back with the same again for both of them.

'So, if he's just got himself a high-profile job and he's on the fast track to Westminster . . .'

'Then maybe he has reasons to make sure all the skeletons in his closet are very much dead.'

They look at one another. 'We're being harsh on him,' says Pharaoh at last. 'He's a big lovable bugger, after all. Likes you. All we have is the fact that somebody took a cab from Morrison's to his house on the day Simon Appleyard was murdered. Called the cab on a mobile that was very likely used to set up the murder of a practising homosexual . . .'

McAvoy finishes his first drink and starts on the next. 'It's not exactly damning.'

'No. Nor does it look good.'

After a moment, Pharaoh starts tapping her fingers on her teeth. 'Show me the website.'

'Guv?'

'This Playmatez thingy he was on. Where all these people seem to meet to get their kicks. Cabourne was on it, yeah? And I bet Hepburn's no stranger. Let's see how it all works.'

McAvoy looks around him. The pub is almost deserted. He pulls his laptop from his bag and opens it up. Searches for the website.

'Come round this side,' says Pharaoh. 'We're not playing Battleships.'

McAvoy slips in beside his boss on the other side of the table and spins the laptop to face him. The desktop wallpaper is a photo of Roisin, laughing, as a baby Fin closes his pudgy fingers around one of her gold necklaces.

'You take that?'

He nods.

'Pretty. She looks young.'

'Eighteen,' he says.

'And you were?'

'Twenty-seven,' he says, not looking at her.

'Girls mature quicker than boys,' says Pharaoh, looking at the side of his head as if willing him to glance in her direction.

He says nothing. Intends saying nothing more.

'Go on then,' says Pharaoh, sighing, and pointing at the screen. 'Show me some bummers.'

He finds the website. Blue background with toned bodies and lustful glances superimposed.

'Women too?' asks Pharaoh, looking at the images.

'You click your preferences,' says McAvoy. 'Tell them whether you want a man, a woman, or you're not particular.'

'And they say romance is dead. Show me something.'

McAvoy gives her a quick guide around the site. Shows her how to create a personal profile and where to post messages.

'So if you're feeling randy you just pop on here, tell the world you're after a bit, and then you get an email from somebody who wants to pummel you from behind, yeah?'

McAvoy bites down on his embarrassed smile. 'Something like that. There are different categories of membership. You can just log on and post a message, like you can on craigslist or Gumtree or any of those . . .'

'I've heard of them.'

'Or you can become a member, create a profile, and then it's more like a dating site.'

'Or?'

'Or you can become a gold member, pay a membership fee, and have access to even more stuff.'

'Like what?'

'Well, you get to see all the other member profiles. Pictures as well. And you can message them direct. That might be what happened with Simon.'

'But Simon's phone number was on here. That's how you found him.'

'It's against the rules, but it's not run like some big multinational company. It will have an administrator who checks for things like pictures of kids or threats or anything, but it's easy for things to slip through.'

'So how do we see Simon's profile?'

'We'd need to know his user-name.'

'And we don't?'

'No.'

'Could we try a process of elimination? Look for

members between twenty and thirty, local to this area, certain body type, into certain things, tattoos and whatnot?'

McAvoy smiles, pleased that she has picked it up so quickly. 'There are thousands of members. It's still a needle in a haystack. If we had even a part of his name we could narrow it down . . .'

He stops. Closes his eyes. One picture flashes into his mind whenever he thinks of Simon. Of his inked skin and flamboyance. His love of words.

Types, slowly, into the website's search facility.
P-E-A-C-O-C-K

Four matches are revealed. Each has a user-name that contains the name of the bird. Only one belongs to Simon. The image that accompanies his profile is a close-up shot of a hard, firm torso. The other three profiles are illustrated with erect penises.

'Distinctive,' says Pharaoh, peering at Simon's picture. 'Skinny as a rake. What did he have to say for himself?'

McAvoy brings up the member details of Peacock1990. The information is scarce.

Young, slim, tattooed male, seeks dominant master. Want to be hurt and controlled. Non-smokers preferred.

'Non-smokers?' laughs Pharaoh. 'Fucking hell.'
McAvoy looks at the section of the profile that

details sexual preferences. All relate to being controlled and dominated.

'What's that?' asks Pharaoh, as he scrolls down the page. She puts her finger on the screen. Reads aloud. 'Remember that the most beautiful things in the world are the most useless: peacocks and lilies, for instance.' She pauses. 'That's nice.'

'That's his profile signature. He must have been on the forums. You can give yourself a signature. Some line from a film or something so people know it's you. That's his.' McAvoy squeezes his fist with the palm of his other hand. Thinks for a moment. 'That must be what his auntie was talking about. Poetry. Some line that meant the world to him. That must be what he put on the messages he exchanged with Cabourne.'

'So it was definitely him?'

'As definite as it can be.'

'Can we go on the forums, then?'

McAvoy looks at her. He is suddenly aware that his cheeks are no more flushed than usual, and wonders what to make of it. He is not embarrassed. He is looking at a sex site, crushed against his boss in the corner of a secluded pub, and he feels more like a policeman than he has in days.

'You need to be a member,' he says. 'You have to pay.'

She shrugs. 'Pay.'

'I haven't got my credit card . . .'

'Oh, Hector.' She pulls her purse from her handbag. It's designer and looks expensive, but when she opens it, it's filled with receipts and battered business cards. 'Here,' she says, handing him a Visa card. 'Shall we do you or me?'

Now the blush comes. McAvoy's face turns scarlet.

'Christ! Fine, we'll make somebody up. Relax.'

For the next fifteen minutes they enjoy themselves crafting a sub-dominant twenty-something pretty boy with big muscles, tattoos and, at Pharaoh's giggled insistence, ginger hair. They choose not to upload a picture, and tick the same preferences boxes as Simon. They give themselves the user name ruffstuff69, which McAvoy hopes is in reference to his boss's date of birth rather than anything else. Moments later, Pharaoh's phone buzzes. An email has arrived activating her account.

'Nice one,' she says, smiling. 'Go on then. Show me.'

McAvoy navigates them onto the discussion forums as Pharaoh brushes past and heads back to the bar for more fuel. In her absence he checks his phone. He has a missed call from a withheld number, and an 'I love you soooo much xxxx' from Roisin.

'What's he got to say for himself?' asks Pharaoh, sitting back down. 'He leave any messages saying he was bummed then strangled to death by three local politicians?'

McAvoy takes another sip of beer. He can feel it doing him good. Types Simon's user-name into the forum to see what he has posted on. Pulls a face when he gets nothing back.

'Not very chatty,' says Pharaoh.

'I'll try some of his areas of interest.'

They try line-dancing. Hull. Anlaby. Dominance.

All bring up discussion threads but none that Simon contributed to.

McAvoy drops his head to the table and gives a moan as Pharaoh takes over on typing duty.

'The spelling is shocking. I suppose it can't be easy to care when you've only got one hand to spare.'

McAvoy listens as his boss murmurs ideas. Feels the vibration in his forehead as her fingers thunder on the keys. 'Hey, Hector, I've got a message. Wahey, somebody loves me!'

He looks up. In the corner of the screen is an icon indicating the arrival of new mail.

'Open it,' he instructs.

Pharaoh reads: 'No picture? You tease. Bet you're pretty in the flesh. Want to meet?'

McAvoy shrugs. 'Nothing.'

'Dunno,' muses Pharaoh. 'Sounds quite nice.'

'Click that one,' says McAvoy suddenly, looking at a discussion title. 'Go on.'

Pharaoh does as she is told. The discussion is titled 'All talk, no action – left me lying.'

'Scroll down. Click that. There.'

They read it together. It is little more than a chat between two members, with occasional comments from observers. The first posting was made in August of last year: a missive from a member called Adams71 furious at having been led on by a potential partner, only to be left wanting. A reply, from RedKen1960, details a similar experience.

'Was so embarrassing,' reads Pharaoh, from the screen. 'Days of texts, getting me so horny and hard, I did everything he wanted, and he just left me there.'

'Ditto, mate,' reads McAvoy. 'Feel sick thinking about it. Just took a look at me and left. I thought it was part of the game.'

'He's online now,' says Pharaoh suddenly. 'Look.'

A red icon is flashing on the screen. RedKen1960 is logged on.

'Let me,' says McAvoy, grabbing the laptop. Quickly, he types: 'Hey you. Read about your problems with that no-show tease. What happened? xx'

They say nothing for a moment. Just stare at the screen. Tap their fingers on the table. Inhale, in unison, ahead of the dejected sigh that will come if there is no reply.

'There,' says Pharaoh, first.

She clicks the message icon. Opens it up. Reads aloud.

Still fuming about it! Met some teases but that was just cruel. Even thought about reporting him, but he'd closed down his profile by the time I came back on the site

401

to give him a telling off. Spent the day emailing me, getting me so horny, all these things he wanted to do to me. So kinky. Wanted me naked, waiting for him when he got there. Was just going to take me without a word. Even asked me to get a belt so he could tie my hands. Did everything he wanted, he came in the room, and then just sodded off without touching me. Soooo embarrassing. Anyway, was his loss. Am over it now. Wot about you? See we're into the same things. You got any playmates you can recommend?

Pharaoh pushes herself back from the table so she can look at McAvoy without his face going blurry through nearness. As expected, he has his eyes shut.

'I can think and keep my eyes open at the same time, y'know,' she says sweetly. 'Multi-tasking, they call it.'

His eyelids flick open. He sees her staring at his face and looks away. When he finds the courage to return her gaze, she is looking back at the computer screen.

'He was looking for Simon,' says McAvoy quietly. 'He wanted to see if they had tattoos. When they didn't, he left. When he found the right man, he killed him.'

Pharaoh sucks in her cheeks. Blows out. Crosses her legs, then lifts one by the ankle and angles it across the other. The material of her clingy dress shows the shape of her thighs, and McAvoy has to fight the impulse to commit the image to memory.

'Am I replying?'

Pharaoh nods. 'Tell him to see if he can find the original user-name of the person he got in touch with. We need the messages too. If we do take this further, we'll need it all to give to the website administrator.'

'If?' asks McAvoy.

Pharaoh nods, openly. 'Yeah, if. At the moment this is just Hector McAvoy's intellectual exercise. It's not a murder investigation. It's you and your boss knocking theories about and trying to decide whether there's enough here to take it further.'

McAvoy widens his eyes. Shows his frustration. He feels as if he is running over breaking ice. 'I thought you agreed with me.'

Pharaoh smiles indulgently. Puts her hand on his knee, as if he is an angry teenager refusing to accept her advice. 'I do agree with you. I agree CID didn't look into this when they should have and I agree there is a bloody good chance Simon Appleyard was murdered. But the lad has been cremated. The only evidence we have are some knackered mobile phone and some theories. I've got to think about the likelihood of a conviction. If not, there's just another unsolved murder on the books.'

McAvoy turns his face to her. He is flushed and

prickling with sweat across his back and shoulders. 'So what does that make us? If we're more concerned with numbers than justice then who holds it all together? What are we here for?'

He has raised his voice more than he intended, and Pharaoh's face turns angry. 'Don't count me in with the number crunchers, boyo. When somebody does something wrong I want them caught and I want them punished. When somebody has been hurt they deserve to know that there has been some kind of payback.'

'And when somebody has been murdered?'

'We catch who did it,' she says, then adds, 'if we can.'

They sit in silence, looking past one another, unsure of whether to make up or take the argument further.

'What next?' asks McAvoy.

Pharaoh shrugs. 'Next, we take a step back. We see what else Dan can find on the phone. We wait for a description of the taxi passenger. We try and find out why they took a cab. We learn more about Simon. Then we have a think.'

McAvoy nods sullenly. He can see the sense in the suggestion.

'What if he's trying to hurt somebody else?' he asks.

'You said it yourself, he was after Simon. He's got him.'

McAvoy cannot meet her gaze, so turns back to the computer screen. Starts flicking through

Simon's details again. Looks at the 'friends' section of the site.

'You think any of those are Suzie?' he asks Pharaoh, highlighting some of the female contacts that Simon has listed on his page. 'Should I email them? See how they knew him?'

Pharaoh nods. 'Good idea,' she says.

'It's a whole world we don't know about,' says McAvoy thoughtfully, as he ploughs through the endless profiles. 'People must be so lonely.'

Pharaoh looks at him as if he's from outer space. 'Not everybody has what you have,' she says at last. 'People need excitement. Some people drink. Some smoke. They gamble. They meet strangers for sex. They put themselves in the hands of a sadist because it makes their heart beat faster. Life's so tame sometimes, Hector. People just need badness sometimes.'

McAvoy wishes he had something else to drink. 'I just can't imagine spending my evenings having sex in the back of a car with a stranger.'

'You wouldn't fit in a car. You'd need to go dogging in a van.'

McAvoy takes no notice of her words. He just hears 'dogging' and has a moment's flash of inspiration.

He clicks out of the website and finds a search engine. Types 'dogging, East Yorkshire' into Google.

'Good job your missus doesn't check your search history,' says Pharaoh.

Moments later, he is on a website called

swingingheaven.co.uk. He scrolls through dozens of postings left by members with names like luv-bstolik and trev69, until he sees one that mentions East Yorkshire. Opens up the discussion thread and finds a score of messages mentioning the A46, Coniston lay-by.

He goes back to Google. Types in the road name. Is taken straight to a story on the *Hull Daily Mail* website.

Man Hurt at East Yorkshire Lay-by

A 44-year-old man is in intensive care after being involved in a suspected hit and run at an East Yorkshire beauty spot.

The man, visiting the area on business and said to be from West Yorkshire, was found by motorists at Coniston lay-by on the road to Bridlington late on Tuesday night.

Detectives are keen to talk to the person who made a 999 call from a nearby telephone box shortly before the incident. Anyone with information should call Humberside Police on 0845 6060222, or Crimestoppers, anonymously, on 0800 555 111.

As he turns to Pharaoh, her sigh is powerful enough to tickle his damp fringe. 'Guv?'

She pulls out her phone. Rings through to control. Asks which uniformed officer dealt with the incident and whether they are working today. As she waits for an answer, she mouths, 'I hate you,' at McAvoy, who scowls and then gives a nervous laugh.

'Really? I think I know him, yeah. Radio through and ask him to ring me on this number. Thanks.' She hangs up. Turns to McAvoy. 'It's gone up to Tony Laws at Bridlington. Control are asking him to get in touch.'

'Why don't we know about this?' asks McAvoy.

'We're just a little unit,' says Pharaoh. 'We look after very specific crimes. You remember the regular CID workload, Hector. You can't keep track of it. And nobody knows you and I are doing this. We're supposed to be finding out which bastards nailed lots of people's hands to their knees. They probably don't think we have time for dogging.'

Her phone rings. She answers politely.

'Tony, hi. Yeah. No, I know. I won't keep you. Forget all that ma'am stuff. Guv will be fine. Or Trish, once you've bought me a drink. Look, Coniston lay-by, I'm told somebody got a bit carried away . . .'

McAvoy listens as his boss learns more in five minutes of charm and chat than he has in days of solo grandstanding and analysis.

She hangs up, having made a new friend.

'Right,' she says, as he looks at her expectantly. 'Victim was one David Stoneleigh. Letting agent from Morley. It's near the Ikea roundabout, before you ask. Leeds way. Over here looking to link up with another letting firm, or at least that's the story. Tony Laws reckons he came all this way to meet somebody up the lay-by. Apparently it's endless up there. They ignore most of it. Do the occasional sweep of the area but tend to turn a blind eye. Anyway, they got a call last week from a phone box in the next village. Female voice, told ambulance to get to the lay-by. Somebody badly hurt. Police were alerted automatically. Patrol car arrived. Found this bugger flat on the ground, pants around his ankles, legs smashed in and hips broken. Death's door. Got him to hospital and he was unconscious for two days. Operated on Friday and he's lost his spleen, but he's conscious again. Not talking very much. Probably shitting his pants trying to think of something to tell the wife. She's used to it, mind. He was cautioned for kerb-crawling in Bradford in 2003.'

McAvoy digests it all. 'Nasty business. But I don't see any connection.'

'No, neither did I. Was about to go back to being sensible and doing this cautiously. Then he gave me the other news.'

'Yes?'

'They've fingerprinted the bonnet of his car. His own prints, and another set.'

McAvoy looks at her expectantly.

'Susan Devlin. Twenty-four. Arrested two years ago for an attack on her partner. Criminal damage.

Attacked her boyfriend when he was tied up. Sex thing.'

McAvoy tries to link the information, but cannot put it together. Pharaoh is smiling.

'Received a suspended sentence when it went to magistrates' court. So did her co-accused.'

'Co-accused?'

Pharaoh grins. 'Simon Appleyard.'

CHAPTER 27

7.17 p.m. Welton. Councillor Peter Tressider's big, white house: screened by leylandii trees and tall black railings, so as to be almost invisible from this wide, quiet, street.

Trish Pharaoh, pulling in to the driveway in her two-seater sports car, sucking two extra-strong mints and smoking a black cigarette.

She looks up at the property. Gives a grudging nod. It seems tailor-made for an aspiring politician. It suggests wealth without pretentiousness, success without pomposity. Pharaoh would use the word 'tasteful' if asked.

She steps out of the car. Checks her reflection in the window. Ensures there are no errant herbs between her teeth, and then grinds her cigarette out with the heel of her boot. She's been home. Changed into a lemon-yellow blouse and black skirt. Put a scarf around her neck and brushed her hair. Slipped into her biker boots and pulled on a suit jacket, which she has since discarded and thrown on the passenger seat. It was a long drive, just to make herself presentable. Sixty-mile round trip, over the bridge and back. But she's pleased she made the effort. Feels less self-conscious about her bandaged cuts and scars now she is dressed for her day job.

A slight pause. A breath and a moment of darkness, hiding behind her eyelids. Then up to the front door. Two taps with the brass knocker, followed by a ring of the bell.

Five seconds. Ten.

She tries the handle. Nothing. Listens for sounds from inside the property. Fancies she can hear activity somewhere past the glass conservatory that marks the western boundary of the long, brick-built property.

Pharaoh crunches over the gravel and onto the deep green grass. Is silent as she moves to the back of the house. Pushes open a wooden side gate and emerges in a long, well-tended garden. A raised patio area gives way to a hundred yards of landscaped lawn. At its centre is a Chinese-style pagoda, overlooking a large, teardrop-shaped pond. On a raised platform above, water shoots from an ornamental fountain to splash merrily across polished, coloured rocks.

Peter Tressider is sitting with his feet in the pond. He is wearing a white short-sleeved shirt with a jumper folded like a cape about his neck. His trousers are rolled up and he is reading from a sheaf of A4 papers while sipping beer from a can.

'Councillor Tressider, sir?'

He looks up, eyebrows knitting together, as Pharaoh crosses the grass. He's a burly,

411

square-shouldered chap with a dark, thick beard that looks as though it would regrow within the hour if shaven.

'No, no, this is my private residence, I'm afraid I . . .'

He starts getting up, pulling a pale, fleshy right foot out of the water and bracing his hands on his thigh to lever himself into a standing position. He recognises her as she gets closer. Gives a show of surprise.

'Pharaoh, isn't it? Aector's mate?'

She nods, happily accepting the description. 'Yes, sir. I'm so sorry to intrude . . .'

He waves a hand. Lowers himself back down.

She stands at the water's edge, watching her reflection being distorted by the water falling from the fountain. Catches sight of a large orange-and-white carp moving slowly in the depths of the pond.

'You're welcome to have a dip,' he says warmly, pointing at the pond. 'Wonderfully refreshing once you get used to the cold. I used to go for a dip every New Year's Day at Bridlington, y'know. Very bracing. Don't think the heart would stand it now. Will settle for getting chilly to the ankles.'

Pharaoh notices a wooden fold-up chair in the gazebo and brings it down to the side of the pond. She erects it and sits down carefully.

'You ok with that chair?' he asks. 'I notice you've hurt yourself.'

'Bit of a scrap with a couple of dogs,' she says matter-of-factly. 'They came off worse.'

Tressider frowns. 'Are you the officer involved in the gypsy case?' He catches himself. Looks around, feigning guilt. 'I can't say that, can I? Gypsy? What's the politically correct term for them? It was you, though – yes? A suspect set his dogs on you and another officer? Am I right in thinking it's all linked to the drugs business? Yes, yes. Goodness, how you keep it all in one head I'll never know. You're having quite a time, aren't you? All this just to keep the spreadsheets looking pretty. It's a world gone mad. Can't wait to change it! Glad you're back on your feet.' He stops. Looks suspicious. 'This isn't about compensation, is it?'

Pharaoh pinches her nose and sits forward in her chair. It's nice here, with the tumbling water and the lowering sky. She looks back up at the house. There is a lot of glass and expensive-looking, pleated curtains. She fancies that from the balcony you would be able to see down to the Humber from the first floor.

'It's actually quite a delicate matter, sir,' she says, conspiratorially. 'I'm sorry for intruding and turning up here unannounced, but I was keen to be as discreet as possible.'

A half-smile plays at the corner of Tressider's mouth. He takes a sip from his can of beer. 'Now I am intrigued,' he says and stifles a burp. 'Pardon me. Goodness, my insides are disintegrating. Can you overdose on antacids? I've taken about twenty today.'

'I used to suffer,' says Pharaoh companionably. 'Too much white wine. Doctor put me on pills that made me feel like I was full of polystyrene. Decided just to live with it. Friend of mine's wife knocked up a herbal potion for me, actually. Don't know what was in it. Tastes of cardamom and wet dog, but it does the job when you're struggling.'

'Sounds like a good friend to have,' says Tressider. 'Could use something similar myself. I'm 90 per cent bile.'

Pharaoh tries to steer the conversation back where she had intended it to go. 'Councillor . . .'

'Peter, please.'

'Councillor, I'm looking into a case from last year. Some questions have been raised. I'm talking about the death of Simon Appleyard, a man in his twenties who was found strangled in his flat in Anlaby last November.'

Tressider looks at her, open-faced, awaiting more. 'I know that name. Aector was having a ponder, wasn't he? On his computer screen when I popped in at Courtland Road? Small world, eh? Right, yes, well, what else?'

'The coroner recorded an open verdict because there was no suicide note. But evidence has since come to light that suggests Mr Appleyard may have been murdered.'

She has Tressider's full attention, but his

expression still shows nothing more incriminating than intrigue.

'Councillor Tressider, this is not a proper investigation yet. We're just taking a look. And out of courtesy I wanted to tell you face to face.'

Tressider wrinkles his brow, confused. 'Well, I know I asked you to keep me in the loop, but I trust CID to investigate cases as they see fit. You don't need to worry about the authority peering over your shoulder . . .'

Pharaoh looks down into the deep, dark water. 'Councillor, I'm not talking to you in your role as chairman of the authority. I'm here to ask you some questions about your own knowledge of the case.'

There is silence for a moment. Tressider's brow is so creased as to be almost knotted.

'I'm sorry, am I somehow a suspect in all this?'

His voice is quiet. There is no menace. Just a genuine enquiry. He looks confused. Bewildered. Lost.

'Councillor, we have evidence that suggests you took a taxi on 14 November last year. It took you from Morrison's in Anlaby to your own front door. The mobile phone that called for that taxi belonged, as far as we can tell, to Simon Appleyard.'

Tressider's face pales. 'I don't have a bloody clue what you're talking about,' he says, and throws himself angrily backwards from the water – hauling himself into a standing position.

Pharaoh stands. 'Councillor, I wanted to talk to

you here, privately like this, so we could clear up any misunderstandings. As I said, this is not an investigation. Not at this stage.'

Tressider is windmilling his arms now. Looking around him as though expecting more enemies to jump out of the bushes.

'You've made a big mistake here. A big bloody mistake. Is this the best they've got?' He steps close to Pharaoh, face right in hers. 'Do you think I'm a bloody idiot?'

Pharaoh holds her ground. Her heart is beating hard, but she is careful to remain calm. Professional.

'Councillor Tressider, did you take that taxi? Did you know Simon Appleyard? He was a practising homosexual. Was involved in online dating. We believe he was known to one or two of your colleagues over on Hull Council.'

Tressider turns away. Drops his head to his palm. Appears to be tugging at his hair.

'I'm not having this,' he says when he spins back. 'I've got nothing to hide. I've only been chairman five bloody minutes. The selection process for the next candidate doesn't start until next year. Who's so bloody scared of me they have to resort to this? I told him and I'll tell you, I don't even know if I want the nomination.'

'Told who, Councillor?' asks Pharaoh, reaching out to put a gentle hand on his arm and not letting go when he tries to shake her off.

'That slimy bastard. Cocker, or whatever. Upset Paula. Made me look a prize berk.'

'I don't understand.'

'Cocker,' he says again angrily. Then he screws his eyes closed and throws himself back down to the grass, thrusting his feet back in the water.

'Cocker is the political fixer, yes? Guy who checks for skeletons in the closet of Party members?'

Tressider rustles around in his top pocket. Pulls out a couple of receipts and then a business card. Hands it to Pharaoh. She takes it and looks at the logo, and Ed Cocker's name and job title. 'What did he want?'

Tressider casts around with his hands. Picks up his empty beer can and tries to find a drop of comfort. He looks exhausted suddenly.

'Stephen bloody Hepburn,' he says, and it almost pains him to say the words. 'Cocker seems to think he's a story. Could ruin my chances at the election. Not the Authority one, that's a done deal. The real election. If I stand. If they let me. If my heart doesn't pack in first. The git turned up here last Saturday . . .'

'Hepburn?'

'Cocker. Knocked on my door, bold as brass. Told Paula he wanted to speak to me. She said I wasn't home. So he started on her. Asked her if she knew Hepburn. Whether she had any knowledge of his business dealings. Whether he knew that I had invested significantly in his club . . .'

'The gay bar? In Hull.'

'It's bollocks,' he says dejectedly. 'I never invested in any bloody gay club. I loaned a business

417

associate some money to assist with the marketing of a new club he was buying into. It happened to be Hepburn's.'

'Much money?

'£15,000. A pittance, really.'

'Who was this friend?'

'That's not important. It's all there in this paper trail Cocker says he's got. It's enough to bugger things up for me. Enough to give the Party the jitters about me. Cocker's the guy who will see if there's enough there to be scared of.'

Pharaoh pulls a face. 'Councillor, I don't think that's a story. Not these days. I don't think anybody would care.'

Tressider looks up at her. 'He upset Paula. I called him when she told me. Tried to be polite, but I lost my temper. Told him to leave us alone. Said I had done nowt to be ashamed of and they either wanted me or they didn't. But he's on good money to do this stuff. Has a job to do, so he says. A report to write. Reckons there are enough positives about me to make me worth digging a little deeper into . . .' He pauses. 'Flattered me, I guess. I mellowed a bit. Said I didn't like his methods but that I was listening.'

'How did he take that?'

Tressider looks down into the pond. Raises his feet and looks at his toes, as though confirming he is real.

'He seemed confused, I suppose. Said he wanted to explain properly. Wanted to meet up.'

'And?'

'And then he started asking questions about my family life. Even about Paula. Told me it was common practice to compile reports like these – about prospects and their partners. I lost my temper. I put the phone down. Tried to forget about it. And now you're on my bloody doorstep.'

Pharaoh feels suddenly sorry for the man. She cannot explain it, but there is something about the tenderness with which he describes his wife that she connects with. She squats down next to him.

'You're going to have to get used to people prying, Councillor. If you're going to be an MP. If you're this rising star . . .'

Tressider snorts. 'I'm fifty-six,' he says. 'I go to the toilet three times a night. I'm not on the bloody rise, love. I'm a decent councillor. I'm a good businessman. I could be a good MP and I promise you I'll be a good chairman. But I don't know how much of it I actually want.'

They sit in silence for a spell.

'Simon Appleyard,' says Pharaoh at last.

Tressider looks away. Turns back to face her with his eyes still closed. 'I don't know anything about that, love. I don't know the name. I haven't taken a taxi in bloody ages. I don't shop at Morrison's. I've got one mobile phone and it's in my pocket. You can look if you want. I've had the same number for years.'

He fumbles in his trouser pockets, and his wallet falls to the ground. Pharaoh picks it up. It has fallen open, and the front flap shows a picture of a smiling, blonde, middle-aged woman, holding a glass of wine and with candlelight catching in her blue eyes.

'She's stunning,' says Pharaoh, though in truth the woman is little more than well-groomed.

Tressider looks at the picture. 'He really upset her,' he says, almost to himself.

'Is she home?' asks Pharaoh. 'We could ask her if she wants to make a harassment complaint . . .'

Tressider blusters. Brushes it away. 'She's a tough lass. She can take it. We breed them hardy. She's from Lancashire to begin with but I don't hold that against her. One of ours now.'

Pharaoh considers him for a moment. Wonders how far to push it. Whether all she has succeeded in doing is alerting him that they are investigating a murder that he may have his fingerprints all over.

'I'm sorry to have troubled you, Councillor,' she says, at last. 'You can imagine how difficult it was to know how to proceed . . .'

Tressider nods, lips thin, eyes glassy and dark. 'You have a job to do,' he says. 'I appreciate you being so discreet.'

Pharaoh stays crouching for a moment longer. Then she extends her hand. Shakes the one that is offered in return, and while doing so, scoops up one of the receipts that has fluttered to the damp grass. She slips it into her boot.

She turns and begins walking across the damp grass.

'Simon,' he says suddenly. Pharaoh spins.

'Pardon, sir?'

'The boy,' he says. 'Did he suffer much?'

Pharaoh considers it. Looks up. Clouds are rolling in. Against the darkening sky they turn the heavens into a muscled back.

'I think he always suffered,' she says. 'But his death was no relief. It was murder.'

From this remove, she cannot see the councillor's expression. But she can tell that his head has dropped, and his feet, in the water, are still.

CHAPTER 28

9.43 p.m. Tranby Rise, Anlaby.
A police van, swaying erratically past nice middle-class houses and neat lawns.

Two angry Rottweilers making a racket in the back. Two animals in the front, hungry for blood . . .

'Shut the fuck up!'

Colin Ray twists in his seat and instantly regrets it. Pain grips his ribs; a bony handful of flesh and gristle. He winces, then covers it up. Curses. Hopes Tanner didn't see.

'Fucking gyppo,' through gritted teeth.

He hopes the pain is muscular, left over from his tussle with Ronan. He likes pain to be the result of something tangible. An impact or collision. He can understand the notion of cause and effect. Illness perplexes him. He is disquieted by syndromes. He wants his rib to be broken because that would explain why it hurts so much. The alternative diagnosis involves his heart, and he does not believe there is good news to be found in that line of enquiry.

'You ok, boss?'

'Little git definitely potted a rib. Thought it would have worn off by now.'

'You should get yourself on sick. Have a few months. Bit of compo.'

'And who'd look after you lot, eh?'

Ray looks across at his travelling companion. Malcolm Tanner is a sergeant in the dog section of Humberside Police. He is a round-faced and affable man, with thinning brown hair and a tendency to swallow his top lip with his lower one when smiling. The habit makes him look a little like a sock puppet and, as such, he answers to Socko around his football buddies. He's a better man than his presence here suggests. He has drunk too much and recklessness has made him willing and cruel.

Ray considers his friend and for once he is grateful that he is not in the company of Shaz Archer. She's busy tonight. Up to no good with one of her pretty boys. He'll want details from her in the morning and she'll be willing to oblige. He'll be glad to have her back by his side. Tremberg was happy enough to get stuck in, but if he needed some feminine wiles to get the Vietnamese to talk, he'd have been better off slipping into a dress than asking that fucking brontosaurus to act sexy.

Tanner's good company, even if he's not much to look at. For tonight's adventure he has changed back into his uniform, but the collar of his goal-keeper jersey is poking out above his white shirt and his knees are grass-stained and muddy beneath his creased navy blue trousers.

They are sitting together in the front of a dog van, two streets from the home of Alan Rourke. They have the radio up high in a bid to drown out the Rottweilers' incessant barking. The noise of the animals is muffled by the panel that closes off the driving area from the back, but the dogs are in a fury and the noise cannot be completely eclipsed.

Ray is almost grateful for the din. It keeps him angry. Keeps him looking forward to the moment, mere minutes from now, when he can put the gun barrel against the first dog's skull, pull the trigger and watch a lying gypsy bastard cry.

He looks down at the object in his lap. Enjoys its shape and heft. Its sleekness. Its clarity of purpose.

'It's called a captive bolt stunner,' Tanner had said beerily, as he reached under one of the panels in the back of the van and pulled out an object wrapped in a hessian bag. 'Most humane thing there is.'

Ray had looked the man in his eyes to see if he was taking the piss. 'Why you got one of these, lad? You're meant to be a fucking animal lover.'

'That's why,' he'd said, removing the gun from the bag. 'You know the places we get called to. You seen animals screaming, boss? Did you know animals can scream? Sometimes you can't wait for the vet. Just can't listen. They'd have my warrant card if they knew, but I'm not the only one. Quick blast with this, it's over.'

'And you can do that, can you?' Ray had asked. 'These dogs aren't dying, son. They just belong to a cunt who needs to talk.'

Tanner had laughed off the suggestion he would not be up for whatever was required.

'They went for a copper, boss. And besides, it's you who'll be pulling the trigger, if it comes to it.'

Ray feels the stun gun's weight in his hand. He has absolutely no doubt about his willingness to make good on the threats he is about to make. Can feel bile and venom rising up his chest as they get nearer to the target. Can already see Rourke's face in his mind's eye, pleading for his dogs' lives and giving them chapter and verse . . .

They move off, quickly, slewing right as Tanner pulls onto one of the quiet side streets and narrowly misses a parked Mercedes.

'Fucking Italians,' says Ray.

'German, aren't they? Mercs.'

'Dunno.' Ray considers it. Tries to remember who he is mad at. 'Make good cars.'

Both men are too drunk to be driving. A couple of hours ago, furious at the command from on high that both Ronan and his uncle be released due to lack of evidence and the insinuation that Ray had broken plenty of rules in dealing with the younger prisoner, this had all seemed a superb idea. They had sunk half a dozen pints of dry cider apiece as they celebrated their team's 5–2 victory over Bridlington. The rest of the lads had called it quits after a pint or two, sloping off home to watch a period drama with the missus or pick up a curry and a six-pack ahead of a night in front of a DVD. Ray and Tanner had shown no such compunction. Ray has nobody to go home to. Dad-of-three Tanner merely doesn't want to go home.

If asked, neither man would be able to decide accurately which of them had taken credit for their current course of action. The idea was born around teatime, in a pub called the Coach and Horses on the road back from Bridlington. It's only a short drive from an area known to be popular with swingers and doggers looking to get their kicks, and where an out-of-town businessman was nearly crushed to death while cruising for sex a few nights ago.

Alan Rourke's Rottweilers are due to be returned to him tomorrow. His solicitor presented an emergency petition to the city magistrates, who ruled there was insufficient reason to have the animals destroyed. Rourke's brief said the dogs had never harmed anybody before and were only defending their owner. What's more, they had been responding to an order to kill given by a third party. The magistrates had taken mere moments to rule that the dogs be returned to their owner from the police-approved kennels where they were being held.

Ray had told the story to his goalkeeper over

their celebratory ciders. Some time later they decided to take the dogs. They sank more alcohol. Talked about gypsy bastards and ginger cunts. And then Tanner had told him about the little tool he kept in the back of the van in case of emergencies. And Ray had risen from the pub table like a monster, teeth clamped and finger already twitching to caress the trigger.

The van pulls in to Tranby Rise. Behind thick curtains, tasteful lighting and TV screens glow. This middle-class street of bungalows and wind chimes smells of roast-beef dinners and family get-togethers. It is a place for families who all have the same surname. Colin Ray does not like the fact it is home to Alan Rourke.

'That one. Like a bloody cartoon house, isn't it?'

They park on the road, blocking the driveway and crushing two well-tended bushes that bloom beside the neat lawn.

The dogs, perhaps sensing themselves near home, double their frenzied barking. Listening to their angry, frothing cries, Ray wonders that they were able to get the dogs in the back of the van without losing important body parts. He had marvelled at the way Tanner had corralled the snarling animals into the specialist vehicle, using only a long pole with a slip-knot noose, and some well-placed swear words.

Ray steps down from the vehicle. Arches his back and winces again at a second stab of pain.

'Tasteless bastard,' he mutters, looking at the

large bungalow and the two large Honda four-by-fours parked on the red-brick drive.

'Bet he's got chandeliers,' says Tanner, appearing at his side. 'They always bloody do.'

A light comes on beyond the frosted glass door of Alan Rourke's home. The door swings inwards. Rourke is silhouetted on his step, a can of beer in his hand, wearing only jogging trousers and leather slip-on shoes.

'Them my dogs?' he asks, advancing down the drive. 'Jesus but you've got them worked up. That you, Mr Ray?'

They have left the vehicle lights on, and the glare of the headlights means Ray and his friend are hard to see. Rourke raises an arm as he approaches and squints his eyes.

'Mr Ray? Jesus, I didn't expect personal service, sir. My brief said to just go pick them up tomorrow meself. By, you're a grand fella, so you are.'

Ray runs his tongue around the inside of his mouth. He feels angry and sick. It is a feeling he is used to. He suffers with stomach ulcers that would be enough of a reason for retirement. He sometimes feels as though his insides are decaying. When he is drunk and melancholy, the gases that belch up into his throat are rank with the taste of corruption. Of the grave.

'Couldn't expect you to put yourself out, Mr Rourke,' says Ray, sneering. 'That's what we're here for, lad. To serve people like you.'

Rourke stands in front of them, hand veiling his

eyes. He looks from one to the other with a half smile on his face that fades a touch when it is not returned. Both men are looking at him coldly. His excitement at being reunited with his dogs begins to fade.

'You want to reverse into the drive so you can let the animals straight in the back?' he asks chattily. 'May be easiest, eh? They'll be over-excited and we don't want to wake this snooty bunch up, eh?'

His attempt at making the two men warm to him gets nowhere, so he shrugs. Returns to the sullen unhelpfulness he exhibited throughout his interviews.

'The lad wrapped up warm, is he?' asks Ray.

'Ah, Ronan will be out with his pals, sir,' says Rourke. 'I'm not his jailer. He'll be home soon enough, and pleased to see my dogs back safe and sound.'

Ray hopes that Rourke can smell the beer on their breath. Hopes he can tell how they feel about him. The stungun is in his pocket, cumbersome but reassuring.

He turns to Tanner. 'Nice night for it, eh, Tanner? Would love to be out for a wander with my pals. Having a drink or two. Packet of fags. Fingering some tart round the back of the skips. Christ, he's living the life, eh? Must be great coming to stay with Uncle Alan.'

'Uncle?' asks Tanner, as if they have prepared the exchange.

'Oh, not his real one. Friend of the family, like. Isn't that right?'

Rourke spits. Shrugs. Has heard enough. Wants his dogs.

'He's got an uncle though, hasn't he? Godfather, or whatever these godless bastards call them.'

Rourke's jaw tightens. He sips from his can of beer, then throws it into his garden.

'Scary bastard, from what I've heard,' says Tanner quietly.

'Aye, he is that. Big man in Ronan's world, though. Big name.'

'What was it again, boss?'

Ray cocks his head. Looks skywards. Appears to be thinking. 'Italian-sounding, I reckon. Can't bring it to mind. You want to help me out, Mr Rourke?'

Rourke considers the pair. Looks back up to the warmth of his own front door.

'You got any more you want to get off your chest or can I have my dogs?'

Ray gives a tight-lipped smile. 'That's the thing, son. That's the thing.'

Rourke considers the detective. Looks closely at the fifty-year-old man in his dishevelled black raincoat over soft cords and golfing jumper. Looks again at the face that has snarled at him across an interview-room table time and again these past days. There is nothing new about the distaste and contempt he sees in the policeman's eyes, but tonight, away from the police station and accompanied by the sound of enraged barking, it is an undisguised malevolence.

'The magistrates—'

Ray laughs. 'You hiding behind the law now, boy? You bomb a police van. You set your dogs on an officer. You spend days making me look a prick . . .'

'Sir, I told you what I knew, and it was nothing . . .'

Ray is shaking his head now, getting angrier. He does not know what he truly expected to happen when they arrived.

'You made me look a prick, lad. But that's going to change.'

'Give me my dogs.' Rourke's voice is rising.

'I'm going to appeal to your better nature.'

'My dogs, sir.'

'I'm going to ask you the same questions I've asked you all fucking week . . .'

'Ask what you like!'

'And if you don't tell me what I want to know, I'm going to kill your fucking dogs and throw them in the river. And if anybody asks what happened to them, we'll say it was gypsies.'

Rourke's face twitches. He shows teeth. Pushes his hair back from his face. 'You ok, girls?' Shouts this last at the side of the van, and is rewarded with a cacophony of barking.

Ray has had enough. He pulls the gun from his pocket and Rourke instantly backs away.

'Don't you worry,' says Ray through a grimace.

'It's not what you think it is. I'm not going to put a bullet in your knee, though God knows I'd fucking love to. No, this is for your little darlings. You seen one before?'

Rourke is shifting his weight from one foot to the other, looking in turn at the officers and the weapon in Ray's hand.

'Abattoir gun,' he says, his teeth locked.

'Give the man a prize,' says Ray, his voice high and unhinged. 'I think they call them a stunner. They fire a metal bolt several inches into the brain. Render an animal unconscious in a heart-beat, to give you a bit of time to enjoy slitting their throat.'

'They're illegal.'

'I give a fuck?'

'You wouldn't fucking dare.'

Ray strokes the gun as if it's a pet. 'I hope you don't tell me, to be honest. I hope I get to look you in the eye while I run a straight blade across your darlings' windpipes.'

Beside him, Tanner shifts. This is ugly. This is more than the game he was expecting. There is something about Ray's posture, his stance, that is more terrifying than the weapon in his hand.

'Suppose I'm telling the truth?' says Rourke breathlessly. 'Suppose I know nothing?'

Ray spits. Hawks up something vile from his chest and launches it like a bullet. 'Get the back doors open, Tanner. This selfish prick isn't going to help his doggies.'

Rourke stares into the officer's eyes. Tries defiance. 'You wouldn't do it,' he says. 'Not really.'

Ray takes a step towards him. His eyes are only an inch or two from the traveller's. He says nothing. Just lets Rourke make his own mind up about whether Ray has the balls to make good on his promise.

'You sick fuck. You sick, sick fucker,' says Rourke desperately, looking to Tanner in the hope that the younger man, at least, is bluffing. 'Please, officers. I can't. This isn't right. It's not right . . .'

'Open the van doors, son.'

Ray's voice is cold now. Almost a whisper. He is no longer expecting answers from Rourke. So he is going to kill his dogs.

For a moment Tanner hesitates. The cold night air is cleansing him of the alcohol that has got him this far. He looks at Colin Ray and realises what he is doing. Realises that Ray never expected the man to talk. That he has been brought here to commit murder.

'Just tell him,' says Tanner, suddenly beseeching. 'He'll do it. Look at him. He'll fucking kill them both.'

Rourke's gaze flits between the two of them. For endless hours this man sat in cold cells and colder interview rooms, refusing to give more than a 'no comment' or a 'fuck you'. Here, now, he is crumbling. He seems to be getting smaller under the weight of his indecision. He seems to be trying to decide whether to take a swing or run away. Whether to close his lips or spill his guts.

'Open the fucking doors, Tanner . . .'

'Hamer,' says Rourke, and the name erupts from his lips like air from a popped balloon. 'Giuseppe Hamer. Ronan's godfather.'

Ray nods. Says nothing more. The look on his face is somewhere between fury and disappointment. The gathering wind plays with the tails of his coat. Takes some of the redness out of his face. He wants to shiver suddenly. Wonders if he is ill or in pain. Takes a cigarette from his pocket lights it, and hands another to Rourke, who lights it with an expensive Zippo and inhales deeply.

'Talk, boy. You've got to find a lot of words in the next two minutes or I swear I'm going to—'

'We did time,' says Rourke, gabbling. 'Pepe and me. He's an important man. Not somebody to piss off. A friend.'

Ray takes a drag on his fag. 'I'm not gripped with excitement, lad.'

'Pepe's done a lot of time. Last stretch was a long one. He made some new contacts. Saw a new line of business. Saw an opportunity.'

'Contacts?'

Rourke blows out a cloud of smoke. 'Asians,' he says quietly. 'Vietnamese.'

Ray spits. 'Bollocks. Your lot don't work with that lot. And they don't work with outsiders neither.'

'It's all changed, sir,' says Rourke, staring at the end of his cigarette as if looking for answers in the glowing tip. 'Vietnamese may look after some things, but the people who give them their orders are people Pepe has no problems working with. Never used to, anyways.'

'Spit it out.'

'Pepe's nephew dotes on him. Ronan. Wanted to be like him his whole life. Wanted to impress him . . .'

'And?'

'And Pepe threw some work his way. Asked him to look into this new opportunity for him. He did. Showed a bit of heart. Balls, even. Pepe said he could be the man for these new opportunities.'

'Are we talking in code, Rourke?'

'I'm giving you what I can,' he says, bunching his fists.

'Ronan got in over his head?'

'He doesn't think so. He thinks he's the big man. Ronan's gone off the rails. These new people Pepe set him up with, they're bad news. Filled his head with big ideas.'

'These are the people who run the drugs operation?' asks Ray. 'The cannabis factories?'

Rourke closes his eyes. 'They're big. Bigger than us. Than Pepe. All I know is, Ronan got caught up with people that weren't good for him. And so Pepe asked me to try and get him out of it. Keep him under my wing. Look out for him.'

'And you were willing to do that? Take this nutter in?'

'When Pepe asks, you say yes. You don't upset him.'

'And Ronan didn't want to leave his new mates behind?'

'He wouldn't come. Had to get Pepe to reach out to him direct and tell him that he'd gone too far. That he had to come back with me. Ronan agreed in the end. Did as he was asked. But his new mates didn't give a shit about what Pepe wanted. They said Ronan was part of the operation now. They were going to set fire to the whole bloody halting site. I didn't know which fucking way to turn. It all got out of hand . . .'

Ray pulls a face. Absent-mindedly rubs the stungun over his sore ribs. 'Doesn't sound like it was ever in hand. We got him easy enough . . .'

Rourke grinds out his cigarette with the palm of his hand. 'Copper will pay for that, I promise you. You warn him.'

'Who?'

'Big guy, so Ronan says. Ginger, Scots fella. Fucking giant, according to Ronan.'

Ray looks confused. 'McAvoy?'

'Aye. Hamer's taking it personally. He can't touch the lads who are driving Ronan astray, but he can bloody sort this.'

Ray turns to Tanner. Gives a tiny shake of his head. Screws up his face, trying to make sense of it.

'So Pepe tells this kid to go play with villains, then decides they're too naughty and wants him to come home? Why didn't he sort it himself?'

'He doesn't want the connection ruined,' says Rourke, as if eager to get every last word out of himself while he still can. 'But he wants Ronan out of there.'

'And Ronan's enjoying himself too much?'

Rourke looks down. 'He's running wild. I can't control him. He's giving orders and people are following them. He's just a boy and these fuckers are doing what he says. Had one of his heavies hold some chink woman's hand in hot oil. Melted it down to the bone. Burned down a house on Bransholme where somebody said there was a little cannabis operation. He's living in his head. He's out of it. Threatening us. Threatening fucking coppers. Got his uncle involved now . . .'

'Did you throw the petrol bomb, Rourke?'

Rourke stops talking. Looks away.

'I read his phone when he was having a shower. He'd got a message from his contacts. Told him the warehouse was being watched. Said he wanted a message sending to the coppers outside. I took it on. Called some friends. Cleared the warehouse for him.'

'And the petrol bomb?'

Rourke nods. 'Me and a pal.' He looks up, voice quickening. 'You must know we never wanted to cook anybody. We threw it as wide as we could. Just wanted to show it had been done. Then Ronan wasn't in trouble and nobody was hurt. You tell me – what was I supposed to do? Pepe asks me to keep the boy safe and next thing I'm in the middle of all this shit . . .'

Rourke stops. Closes his eyes. Looks tired, and old. Looks like a man who has been pulled in too many directions.

'How did your prints get on the bottle?'

'I wore gloves, but the bottle we used . . .'

'Yeah?'

'One of my own,' he says, shaking his head. 'I'm a thick bastard.'

'The car you drove?'

'Ronan's. Been driving round like a rock star.'

Ray scratches his face thoughtfully. 'Bet Ronan wasn't pleased.'

'Threatened me with his uncle. Threatened me with his new pals.'

Ray gives a tiny nod. 'And Hamer?'

'He knows I've done what I can.'

'The drug contacts?'

Rourke shrugs. 'Who fucking knows?'

They stand and consider one another for a time.

Broken, humbled, Rourke cannot even raise his head as he asks whether he can have his dogs.

Ray looks at him hard. Turns to Tanner. 'Give him the fucking things.'

He leans back against the side of the van. Listens as the barking increases in volume, and has to suppress a smile when he sees the swarthy, unbreakable traveller down on his knees, weeping into the necks of two excitable, slobbering dogs.

Rourke catches his eye.

'Would you have done it? Pulled the trigger?'

Ray gives his first real smile.

'I still might.'

CHAPTER 29

Suzie wishes she had an addiction.

Wishes that drink or cigarettes or sticking a fucking needle in her veins brought her some vestige of comfort and relief. She has nothing. No chemical crutch. Doesn't know how to soothe herself.

'Breathe, Suzie, breathe . . .'

She half-heartedly punches the passenger seat – a backhand slap that would have made Simon giggle were he there to receive it.

'It's all bollocks.'

She sneers as she says it. Drops her head. Realises that her images of peace are all clichés. Knows that were she to shut her eyes and take deep, cleansing breaths, she would feel no more at ease than she does now: wide-eyed, teary, staring into the gathering darkness with her fingers wrapped around the steering wheel like ivy around a tree trunk.

It is pushing ten p.m. She does not know why she has driven here, to Coniston lay-by. Doesn't know what she hopes to achieve. To see. To feel. It brings her no comfort, but nor did she expect any.

Her day has been a haze. She drove home after fleeing Big Dunc's house, but found her flat as cold and distant as an unloved partner. Wraith-like, she drifted from room to room, looking for familiarity. For warmth. For something that would trigger happier memories or more encouraging thoughts. She found nothing. Took her laptop to the pub and spent money she does not have ordering clothes she does not need. Drank two vodka and cokes then threw up in the toilets and headed to the park. Sat reading a book and picking at a shop-bought sandwich: absorbing nothing and tasting less.

It is only here, now, that she is finding herself again able to connect with her own thoughts. Here, now, she thinks in her own voice.

She fiddles with the radio. Something poppy has been playing and it seems inappropriate. She plays with the dial and finds a classical station. Gives herself over to a melancholy cello concerto that seems a more fitting accompaniment to the gloomy, cloud-shrouded sunset she watches through the dirty glass.

'Miss you, Si,' she says again. She has been saying it a lot. Not chatting to him. That would be odd. Just acknowledging his memory, his presence. The fact that she failed him. Let him be murdered and did not care enough to make a fuss.

Later, should she be given the chance, she will find a place for her guilt. She will never excuse herself, but she will accept that she went mad for a time when her friend died. Became a half-thing. Existed emptily. Closed herself off to thoughts she could not stomach and to fears she dared not acknowledge. She will tell herself that she was young, naive, and that the notion of murder, or deliberate death, had never filtered into her bouncy, silly life. But here, now, she hates herself for not demanding answers when Simon died. For letting it seem she did not care.

'See you soon, Si,' she says softly.

She senses there is a certain truth in the statement. She is not entertaining thoughts of self-harm, but twice this week somebody has tried to kill her. She cannot swallow without pain. Cannot close her eyes without seeing the man crushed against his own car. Keeps remembering the sound of crunching bone and squelching blood, the snippets of vile audio collected as she tumbled down the grass verge, knickers trailing from one leg, dirt and grit on her face.

She looks at her phone. Wishes she had somebody to counsel her. Somebody she could ask whether they think it is a good idea to text the man who tried to kill her, and ask him whether he murdered Simon too.

She is parked away from the main shadow of the lay-by. The car's lights are off, but there is enough daylight remaining for her not to worry, or care, about another vehicle slamming into her. She has been passed by two vehicles already. Saw another half-dozen when she drove through half an hour back.

'What are you going to do?'

She asks the question of herself. Pulls down the sun visor and looks at herself in the vanity mirror. Asks it again and looks at the shape her mouth makes. Looks into her own eyes. Takes off her glasses and wipes away the steam that her hot, wet eyes have created on the lenses. Wipes her eyes with the heels of her hands. Sniffs noisily, and pulls a face at the rather revolting sound.

Suzie has never felt so alone. So lost. She cannot help but consider the shabbiness of her life. To think of her debts. Her tiny flat with its charity-shop and hand-me-down furniture. Her stalling career. Poor CV. Her one, failed, relationship.

'You're not even pretty,' she says out loud, and suddenly feels angry about it. 'Ugly bitch,' she snaps venomously at herself. 'Fuck you!'

She slams the visor back against the car roof. Takes a breath, but as she blows it out her throat hurts and she starts coughing. She begins to cry again, then loses her temper with her frailty and locks her teeth. Angrily, she turns the car key. Stamps down on the accelerator as she wrestles the old Peugeot into gear. Throws the car forward, disappearing into the darkness behind the mound of grass and trees that shields the lay-by from the road, and makes the whole area so appealing.

Four cars are parked up, two on either side of the road. A mass of figures congregates around the windows of a large family saloon. As Suzie approaches, heads turn. She pulls into the kerb close by. Feels perhaps, a frisson of terror. Remembers, fleetingly, the first time she came here. Remembers watching from the safe remove of her car as a husband made love to his wife in the back of a hatchback and a man stood at the window, touching himself, as the pair put on their show. It had all been a novelty then. She had been fresh out of love, eager to live, to experience. To be bad. It had struck her as odd at first. Unusual that men and women should cluster around a cheap car and watch other people fuck. She has seen so much since that she finds it unusual some people don't.

Impulsively, recklessly, she steps out of the car. She is wearing flip-flops and a long dress under a baggy jumper. She has on a scarf to hide the ligature marks. Looks ok. Would be considered a prize were she to let anybody touch her this evening. She wonders whether she will. Whether she'll watch and smile or let somebody enjoy her.

There are three men standing at the driver's side of the saloon. A couple, wrapped up in one another, are on the far side, watching through the passenger window. With the car doors open, the interior light is switched on, and gives off enough light for Suzie to understand the nature of the scene taking place within.

Heads turn her way as she gets closer to the car. She smiles instinctively. Closes her eyes tightly as she passes the spot where, just a few days ago, a man was nearly killed in her stead.

'Evening.'

A male voice. Local. Friendly. Middle-aged.

Suzie nods a hello to the nearest of the group. Feels eyes upon her. Fixes her gaze on the shapes moving in the car. Stops. Looks inside. Locks eyes with the man in the passenger seat. He's young. Maybe eighteen or nineteen. He's wearing a knock-off designer T-shirt and his tracksuit bottoms are pooled around his ankles, sitting atop his dirty white trainers. He is not unattractive. A little ratty and dishevelled perhaps, but he is well muscled and his features handsome.

The shock of hair bobbing up and down in his lap belongs to a large, bulky woman whose clothes suggest middle-age. She has taken her seatbelt off to better go about her work, but Suzie knows from experience that the gear stick will be hurting her breastbone. Squinting, she notes that there is a label sticking out the back of the woman's jumper. It declares her a size 16 and discount shopper.

'You on your own?' asks the same voice.

Suzie looks at its owner. Mid to late forties. Quite tall. Decent-sized gut pushing at cord trousers. Turtle-neck and check suit jacket. Greying hair and two days' beard on his oval, fleshy face. He has nice eyes.

'You think I need a bodyguard?' she asks.

The man smiles. 'Been at it for a while,' he whispers, nodding at the car. 'Thought they'd be done by now. When I was his age I was a two-minute man. Opposite problem now.' He looks her up and down. 'You wanting to play or just watch. My car's nice and warm . . .'

'We'll see,' says Suzie, and realises she has no clue why she is here or what she wants. The knowledge is almost freeing.

Suzie cannot help but want to see more. She gently pushes past the man with the nice eyes and bends down to better see what is happening. She is not aroused. Just curious. Eager to witness something that is worth opening her eyes for.

'You!'

Suzie's head whips left. Searches the source of the enraged exclamation.

The back of the car. Broad back and shoulders against the glass. Skin-tight leggings and a floaty silky top. Multi-coloured bob and rage in her eyes. Melissa. Jarrod's friend. The lady from the swingers' party who didn't smile, and who ended the evening with her partner being rushed to hospital.

Suzie's mouth falls open. She starts to say hello but a sudden fear has taken hold of her. She backs away from the window but pushes against the firm, unyielding bulk of the man with nice eyes.

She sees the woman in the front seat stop her work. Turn her head. She looks familiar. She, too, was at the party. She is in her late thirties. Plain. Pinch-faced. Spent some time in the swing being pleasured by Big Dunc and a vending-machine stockist from Selby.

The back door of the car is swinging open. Melissa levers herself out. Angrily pushes aside the young couple in her way and comes round the back of the vehicle.

'Little slag,' she's saying, face contorted. 'Jarod's going to be a vegetable cos of you. One night was all I wanted. One night with him. And you make eyes and he's off and then he's getting a brick around his fucking skull and you're playing the victim and it's all "poor me, poor me".'

Her words come out in an angry spit. Her lips froth. Teeth are bared. Suzie doesn't know whether to turn and run or stand her ground and defend herself from the woman's lies.

'I'm sorry, nothing happened with us, we were just having a moment . . .'

'You're a little tease,' says Melissa, her face in Suzie's. 'You wave your bits in people's faces then leave them begging.'

'That's not true . . .'

'Little teases, all of you. I've met people like you. The ones on the Internet who say they'll turn up. The ones who go to parties and don't join in . . .'

'I do join in . . .'

The blow comes from nowhere. It is not a slap. It is a right hand delivered with a closed fist, and it knocks Suzie backwards and to her knees. She is dizzy. Sick. The same dirt and gravel in her mouth she has tasted for days.

A boot now. A foot to her ribs, tipping her to her side. Pain explodes inside her. She begins to vomit, but is still gasping for breath and begins to choke, her swollen throat closing.

Now there are fingers in her hair. She is being dragged upright. She hears voices. Protestations. Sees the shape of men moving away. Hurried footsteps, running for cars. Lights, engines.

Her face slams against metal. The cold of the car bonnet. Spit and blood pooling in the corner of her mouth as her face is pushed painfully down . . .

'I'll show you little bitches . . .'

Spit on her face. Another punch to the back of her head.

And now she can feel the cold wind on the back of her thighs. Can feel her dress being pushed upwards and hands clawing at her skin.

She knows, now. Knows what she came for and what she will get.

Then there is a new voice. Loud. Firm. Clear.

She hears Melissa spit and swear. The throaty laugh that follows her suggestion the speaker should wait their turn.

And then the pressure is released. There are no hands upon her. There is no pressure on her face or breeze upon her thighs.

There is a shrieking. More angry threats, growing more frenzied and yet more distant.

Suzie slides down the bonnet of the car. Collapses on the gravel, a mess of twisted limbs and pain.

Her eyes close. None of it seems to matter any more. All the noise. The pain. The threats. She feels somehow free of it. Light. Feels a warmth and closeness around her that she has not felt in an age.

Soft, rough hands upon her face. A giant, tender palm upon her cheek.

She opens her eyes. Lets the features swim into place.

Lets the background roar of her ears tune to the frequency of the gentle, probing voice.

Catches, among the other words, a name.

McAvoy. Detective Sergeant Aector McAvoy. Don't worry, I'm here, you're safe . . .

The coffee is bitter and tastes faintly of soup and orange squash. More than anything it tastes of the flask it has been carried in. Suzie drinks it gratefully. It warms her. Fills her with a flavour that is blessedly removed from the blood and spit of her mouth.

'Better?'

Suzie nods, cupping both hands around the metal mug. She lets the steam rise beneath her nostrils. Inhales deeply.

'Cute,' she says and forces a smile.

McAvoy is holding Lilah against his hip. The baby is wide awake. Trying to reach her daddy's ear with one tiny, grasping fist.

'Thanks,' says McAvoy, kissing his daughter on the head and shushing her softly. 'All babies are cute though, aren't they?'

Suzie appears to think about it. 'I prefer bunnies.'

'Yes? You must be a city girl. Grow up in the country you don't feel the same. Bloody pests.'

'Wouldn't trust anybody who didn't like bunnies.'

McAvoy smiles. 'Didn't say I didn't like them. Said they were a pest.'

Suzie sips her coffee again. 'You don't seem like a policeman,' she says quietly.

'It's the outfit, isn't it?' he says acceptingly. 'I know, I know.'

He is dressed in pyjama trousers and a rugby shirt underneath a waterproof jacket he managed to find in the back of the car. When he took Lilah for a drive to settle her before bed, he had not admitted his intentions to himself. Even went to the trouble of feigning surprise when the car took him to Suzie's flat. Told himself, then, it would be dereliction of duty not to follow when he saw her climbing into the Peugeot and slamming the door.

He has not yet phoned Roisin to tell her why he has been out so long. Will tell her tomorrow that he did not want to wake her. That he and Lilah fell asleep somewhere pretty and had a pleasant night.

Suzie pulls a face as she looks up at the hulking form of McAvoy, and then at his car. She is sitting in the passenger seat, legs outside, door open. She cannot imagine him squeezing himself into the tiny vehicle.

'This really your car? Bet you don't need roll bars.'

McAvoy laughs. Takes the cup from her and sips

from it thoughtfully. 'Used to have a people-carrier. It blew up.'

'You have all the luck.'

'Luck of the Irish, my friend says.'

'But you're Scottish. You sound it, anyway.'

'That's the joke.'

'Oh.'

In silence they pass the drink between them. It feels strangely intimate. They feel oddly comfortable in one another's nearness.

'You were following me?' asks Suzie, struggling to digest the information McAvoy had first imparted as he scooped her from the ground in arms that could have lifted the car too.

McAvoy nods. 'You know what I want to ask you about . . .'

Suzie nods. Bites her lip. She looks up at the sky, where the moon is partially obscured by clouds that put her in mind of burnt popcorn.

'It was me,' she says acceptingly. 'The other night. Here. The man.'

McAvoy pauses. 'I know that. We have your prints.'

She frowns. 'I wiped the receiver.'

McAvoy looks away. 'We got them from the bonnet of the car.'

Suzie pulls a face, embarrassed. 'Oh.'

'What happened?'

'Don't know.'

'Suzie . . .'

'Car came from nowhere,' she says, flatly,

finishing the coffee. 'We were playing. Then the car hit him. I got out of the way just in time.'

'And you left him there.'

'I phoned for an ambulance.'

'But you didn't call the police?'

'No.'

Suzie has tried to hold McAvoy's gaze, but gives up now. Looks at the moon.

McAvoy considers her for a moment. There is dried blood on her chin. One arm is protectively tucked against her bruised ribs. She had refused to go to hospital in the police car or the ambulance that both arrived within minutes of McAvoy's call. A unit from the Holderness Policing Team has taken Melissa to Priory Road Police Station, where tomorrow she will most likely be charged with anything from sexual assault to attempted murder. The young man who had been receiving the passenger-seat BJ needed the ambulance. He had attacked McAvoy while he was trying to restrain Melissa. McAvoy had shrugged him off. The shrug had been enough to cut him down and snap a tendon in his ankle. McAvoy has not yet had time to worry about the repercussions, nor to hate himself properly for how much he longed to slam Melissa's head on the bonnet of his car as she struggled in his grasp and he fumbled for his radio.

'You're not what I was expecting,' he says at length.

Suzie looks up at him and there is a flicker of

warmth in her eyes. 'Did you think I'd be in a basque and clear heels?'

'I should be so lucky,' he says and, unable to help himself, wipes the dried blood from her chin.

'Thank you,' she says, and then impulsively, desperately, grabs his hand with hers. She holds it against her cheek. Closes her eyes. Allows herself to feel a moment of safety. Of solace. Builds comfort and secure into the sensation of this touch.

'Simon Appleyard,' McAvoy says as he slowly withdraws his hand. 'Your friend. He was murdered.'

Suzie nods.

'You knew?' he asks.

'I think I always knew.' She seems to consider it. Shivers and moves back a little into the car. 'Maybe I didn't.'

'But you're convinced now?'

She pulls down her scarf. Shows him the ligature mark. 'I'm next,' she says.

McAvoy crouches down. Examines the marks. When he looks at her again, his face is only inches from hers. Her reflection swims in his eyes, and in this mirror the girl who looks back is lovably pretty.

'Last night,' she says. 'Party. Somebody tried to strangle me. Hurt somebody else.'

McAvoy's face changes. He begins rooting in pockets for bits of paper. Pencil. 'I'll need the details.'

She shrugs it all away. 'I'm tired,' she says and the statement is completely accurate.

McAvoy seems to realise that he is missing an opportunity to crowbar some proper police procedure into his investigation. The notion is tantalising. He feels like a maverick, a private investigator hiding in the police force who is very much at odds with the man he has always been.

'I can take you to the hospital now. We can talk on the way.'

'No, not yet. Let me enjoy the breeze.'

McAvoy narrows his eyes. Tries to understand this girl. To better appreciate her reluctance to go to hospital. To talk to the uniformed officers. To leave his side. It occurs to him what may be going through her mind. 'Suzie, you're not going to get arrested. You're not going to prison.'

'I have a record. Simon and me. We had this idea. Watched a film where this girl tattooed a man who was mean to her. We decided to do it. He was still texting me, my ex. Treated me like shit, but still thought I'd come running for sex. I don't know whose idea it was to persuade him to be tied up. But he liked it. And then when he was under me, I don't know. I had the blade. He was crying. Squealing. I felt sick. Made a couple of scratches and then ran. I was frightened to untie him. I went and got Simon. He came back with me and untied him. He went for Simon and Simon fought back. We ran. It was a mess. It wasn't like we planned.'

'He called the police?'

She nods. 'They took his side.'

McAvoy looks again at this plumpish, bizarrely dressed girl, and finds it hard to reconcile the details on the charge sheet with the person in front of him.

'He must have really hurt you,' he says, at last. 'Your ex. For you to get into all . . . this.'

'I needed to be something more than I was. Needed to be more than this timid, downtrodden little girl.'

'There are other ways. You know, you would both still be in prison if the victim had given evidence, don't you?'

'And maybe Simon would be alive.'

McAvoy nods. Sighs. Lowers himself and sits, cross-legged on the ground: Lilah across his knees.

'You look like one of those Scottish kings,' says Suzie, sniffing. 'Like you should have one of those big swords and be on a throne of skulls.'

'Did Scottish kings have thrones of skulls?'

'I would.'

McAvoy laughs. Shakes his head.

'Who do you think killed him? Who is trying to kill you?'

'I just know he can spell.'

McAvoy stiffens. 'Pardon?'

Suzie hands over her mobile phone. Shows him how to navigate to the string of messages. Tells him how her admirer came into her life and what he has cost her.

'You did this? That's why you were here?'

McAvoy is reading the man's instructions. Trying

455

to work out why she would debase herself to please a stranger.

'It's a game.'

He looks her in the eye and tries to let concern instead of contempt fill his face. 'It's not.'

'No,' she says, holding his gaze. 'I know.'

For a time he thinks about lecturing her. Telling her that her lifestyle killed her friend. But he is not convinced of the truth of the accusation, and already likes her too much to hurt her this way.

'He knew you would be at the party?'

'Yes.'

'And you've had no more messages? Just his temper tantrum?'

'I've been thinking about texting him . . .'

McAvoy clamps his lips together. Considers. 'Not yet,' he says. 'We need to know more.'

'What do you actually know?' asks Suzie, and though there is no accusation in her voice, McAvoy implants his own.

'I think Simon might have been killed because he saw someone, or met someone, who does not want it known how they spend their spare time.'

Suzie nods. 'Some people are like that. They're ashamed.'

'Are you?'

She considers it. 'I didn't think I was. I thought I was empowered. I'm not sure.'

'Simon was your protector, yes? He kept you safe while you played?'

'He was my everything.'

McAvoy nods. Readjusts Lilah and puts his smallest finger in her mouth as he thinks. 'The parties you attend. The people you met. Do you have any kind of record? Any diary. Any way of identifying people?'

Suzie shakes her head. 'People take care. It's all false names and personal email addressed and pay-as-you-go mobiles. People go to the other side of the country to shag a stranger so the wife doesn't find out. It's not like dating.'

McAvoy stands. The movement seems to pain him. He hands Lilah to Suzie, who takes her without thinking, and passes her back without comment.

'If I showed you some photographs, would you be able to remember whether they are people you may have come across in your private life? Whether they are people Simon knew?'

Suzie nods. 'Tonight?'

McAvoy shakes his head. 'Tomorrow. I have to go home. Put the little one to bed. Explain to the wife why I've been up at a dogging spot . . .'

He colours as he says it, afraid he has offended her. Suzie merely smiles.

'Not a nice word, is it? I don't even like dogs. Puppies, yes. But puppying sounds wrong.'

McAvoy realises that when he gets in the car and starts the engine, he will be taking this young, confused girl to hospital and pretty much dumping her. Knows she will be getting a taxi back to her cold and lonely flat. Is not sure he can allow that.

'How are your ribs?'

'Sore.'

'My wife's a healer.'

'A doctor.'

'No. She's just good at making people feel better.'

Suzie grins. Realises she does not want to leave this man's side. 'You're a good pair.'

CHAPTER 30

Monday, mid-morning.

A grassy area set back from a quiet country road, shielded by high hedges and cherry blossoms.

They sit side by side. Arms resting on the damp, bowed wood of the sagging picnic table.

A storm in the air.

Pharaoh sucks an inch off her black cigarette. Sips at her takeaway coffee and is angered to discover the polystyrene cup is empty. She reaches across for McAvoy's bottle of lemonade. Takes a swig and grimaces.

'Did you get crisps and candy too? Packet of cola cubes and a caramel shortbread? It's amazing you've got teeth.'

McAvoy takes back the lemonade. Puts it back down on the bench beside him, away from her reach. Tries one more time to get an answer he can work with.

'Guv, do you think he could have killed Simon?'

Pharaoh throws her cigarette butt onto the ground, then stares at its glowing tip. 'Why did I do that? There were three drags left.'

'Guv . . .'

'Oh, for God's sake, Hector, yes. OK? Yes, he could have killed him. Happy? Anybody could have killed anyone. People act oddly. For instance, I've got this giant fucking idiot of a detective sergeant who works for me. He let a suspect in a murder case sleep at his house last night. Then he invited me for a picnic.'

McAvoy allows himself the tiniest of glances at her chest. It is not the shade of crimson that it goes when she is truly cross, nor is there a sheen of perspiration at her temples or on her upper lip, so he knows her temper is not as intense as she is making out.

'She had nowhere to go. She was hurt. She's got nothing . . .'

Pharaoh looks at him so intensely that he has to turn away. For a moment it feels as though she is reading the back of his skull.

Finally she rubs her hands through her hair and gives a stretch that comes with no accompanying yawn. 'You know the reason we don't carry guns in this country, Hector? It's because, if we did, I'd shoot you.'

'Dead?' he asks, as though this will make a difference.

'No,' she says, thinking about it. 'Just sore. I'd maybe just hit you with it.'

He smiles. 'Thanks, Guv.'

She smiles at him, maternal again. Seems about to beckon him close for a cuddle.

'How is she?'

'Sore. Achy ribs. Nasty bruise.'

'Not her. Roisin.'

McAvoy pulls a face. 'OK, I think. Says she's ok. Was making her breakfast when I left.'

'Anything nice?'

'Scrambled eggs with smoked salmon. Fresh chives.'

'What kind of toast?'

'Not sure. I can ring if you like . . .'

Pharaoh gives in to laughter. 'Fucking hell.'

McAvoy cannot work out which of his indiscretions he should feel most ashamed of. For a long time he wondered whether other people were given a handbook in childhood outlining what is acceptable and what is not. He is never truly sure.

'She likes helping people.'

She looks at him. Pulls a face. 'Yeah, I'd imagine she's big on lost causes.'

Pharaoh wishes she hadn't said it as soon as the words are out of her mouth. Curses when she sees the impact on his face. Pain and uncertainty pass across his face like a ripple on a still pond. He absorbs it and then it is gone.

'He was ok with you?' McAvoy asks, his voice catching. 'Tressider.'

'Professional. Decent guy, really. Inasmuch.'

'Yeah. Inasmuch.'

McAvoy is staring at the damp grass. Watching a cherry blossom that has become trapped in the wooden supports of the picnic table. Wants to free it so it can join its friends and dance on the breeze, but fears more contempt.

'This is something now, isn't it?' he asks quietly. 'It really is a murder.'

Pharaoh seems about to argue, but loses enthusiasm. She nods.

'Are we going to take it to the top brass? Start the investigation? Do things properly?'

Pharaoh shrugs. Sips again at her empty coffee. Reaches into her handbag and retrieves another black cigarette, which she holds but does not light.

'It's my first day back, Hector,' she says to the side of his face. 'As far as the brass know, my team is looking into the drugs. The petrol-bombing. Alan Rourke and the ginger runt. That's what we're doing. And we're not doing it particularly well. Simon Appleyard doesn't figure on anybody's radar.'

'One phone call,' he says, looking at her. 'We make it happen.'

Pharaoh looks up at the sky. There is still some blue up there but the dark, rain-swollen clouds are rolling back. Their undersides hang low, as if waiting to be sliced open with a blade. They seem oppressive. Ominous. They could just as well be as full of black eels as rain.

'It's not me you have to convince,' she says. 'I can't say I'm relishing telling people that Peter Tressider needs to be formally interviewed in connection with a murder enquiry, but I'm willing to do it. What I need before we do is something more than a few concidences, some intuition and a big leap of faith.'

'Suzie,' says McAvoy, reaching down and freeing the cherry blossom, then letting it go on the next gust of wind. 'She'll tell them what has been happening to her.'

'And she's a reliable witness, is she? A swinger with a record.'

'She was attacked.'

'She was at a dogging pit and a sex party.'

'She's a victim.'

'She's a tart.'

'That's not fair. All she's been through . . .'

Pharaoh throws the cup down on the wooden table. It bounces and rolls onto the grass. 'These aren't my words, Hector. They're what I'll be hearing.'

They sit in silence for a time. McAvoy has much to say but cannot find the right order for his words. Sits wondering, instead, whether Roisin is angry with him. Pharaoh, in her turn, lets her mind drift to less confusing thoughts. Looks at her black patterned tights and wonders whether she should have shaved her legs before putting them on. Whether she will have a bruise in her armpits from the underwire of her ill-fitting bra. Whether she should have eaten the brownie McAvoy bought her, or gone for a piece of fruit instead . . .

'Ray didn't seem pleased to see me,' she says resignedly. 'Didn't get much from the interviews, did he? But there was a look in his eye.'

'If he's got something, he has to tell you. That's the chain of command.'

'Oh aye,' she says, sarcastically. 'We're all about procedure.'

The blue sky darkens a shade. The bellies of the clouds sag further. They watch a sparrow flutter down to a neighbouring picnic table and peck at a discarded bottle top, before flying away.

'Pretty here,' says Pharaoh. 'Suzie would like it.'

'I'm sorry?'

'Secluded,' she says, by way of explanation. 'You can get up to all sorts.'

McAvoy half turns to her, but realises he is already mid-blush, so stops and continues staring ahead.

'You know what we should do,' he says quietly. He takes a breath. Lets the colour bleed from his face. Turns, at last, to meet her gaze. 'You know it will work.'

Pharaoh places the cigarette in her mouth, and flicks the filter with her tongue. It waggles in her mouth as she thinks.

'She'd be putting herself in harm's way.'

'I'd be there.'

'Would she do it?'

'I think so.'

Their nods are imperceptible, their acquiescence unspoken. They simply accept the truth of what must happen.

'We need more,' says Pharaoh at last. 'If it comes

to trial, we'll need to demonstrate we had just cause . . .'

McAvoy reaches into his pocket. Pulls out his phone. 'If it's not him . . .'

'I'll be delighted,' says Pharaoh. 'That's the worst bit of all of this. If we've just been off the reservation but come back with a killer, we're on easy street. If we come back with the chairman of the Police Authority in handcuffs, we're making the wrong kind of headlines.'

In the open air, better able to pick up the signal, McAvoy's phone rings. He mouths, 'Excuse me,' and takes the call.

Quietly, discreetly, one of the civilian support workers has been jockeying the database. At McAvoy's request, she has been working through the log, putting together a list of all cars reported lost, stolen or abandoned within a five-mile radius of Simon Appleyard's flat between September of last year and March of this. Pharaoh called McAvoy's suggestion an 'informed hunch' but greenlit his use of resources.

He has been awake most of the night, Lilah dozing contentedly on his chest and Roisin's warm back and buttocks against his side. He listened for a while to Suzie's soft crying, and wondered whether he should take her a blanket or a glass of warm milk before tiredness robbed him of enthusiasm for the trip downstairs. Instead, he thought about the taxi ride. About why a killer would take a cab from a murder. Why they would order one to pick them up from a brightly lit, bustling super-market. He tried to put himself in the killer's shoes. Manipulative. Intelligent. Cunning. He would have driven to the scene, no question. Perhaps parked a couple of streets away from Simon's home, just to be safe. But why the taxi? Why not drive away? The answer hit him as he considered his current car. Its tendency to stall in second gear. Its leaking radiator and shot air-con system. Suzie's car, too, had groaned painfully as it took the sharp left at the entrance to his estate.

Cars, he thought.

Bloody unreliable things.

He utters some platitudes and thanks into the phone. Holds up a finger to delay Pharaoh. Offers heartfelt gratitude. Hangs up and then looks at his screen as the report comes through.

'A blue Honda CRV. Left on Mortimer Close, two minutes from Simon's place. Was blocking the entrance to somebody's driveway. Looked like it had been abandoned. Community Support Officer attended. Vehicle was registered to a timber company at South Cave.'

'Owned by?'

'Registered in the name of Paula Tressider. Executive shareholder for her husband's firm.'

There is little celebration in his voice.

'Tressider was told?'

'Company was. Tow truck came the next day.'

'Any follow-up?'

'No need. Job done.'

They look at one another.

'His car broke down,' says Pharaoh. 'He went to kill Simon and his car broke down. Walked himself to the nearest busy place and called a cab on Simon's phone.'

'Why his own address? Why home?'

'Why not? He planned on dumping the phone. Simon was always going to be a suicide.'

McAvoy flares his nostrils in temper. 'He barely considered us,' he snaps. 'Didn't even try. Chairman of the bloody Police Authority and he knew we were too crap and lazy to give a damn.'

Pharaoh finds herself nodding. 'You care,' she says quietly. 'Me too, though don't tell anyone.'

'We've got enough now, surely,' says McAvoy. 'I'll do all the spade and leg work, you know that. We can fill in the gaps once we've got the cuffs on.'

Pharaoh is about to speak when the sound of an approaching car silences her. She hears the tick-tock of an indicator, and then an old-school Volvo pulls into the picnic area. It is dirty and mud-splattered, and its driver takes little care as he pulls in, deliberately, between Pharaoh's sports car and McAvoy's little hatchback.

'Looker, isn't he?' says Pharaoh, sniffily, as Ed Cocker climbs out of the car.

The political fixer is tieless, in a grey suit with a dark blue shirt. He smiles broadly as he approaches, notebook sticking out of the pocket of his suit jacket.

'Very cloak and dagger, Sergeant McAvoy,' he says, smiling. 'You couldn't have just asked me to meet you in a pub?'

'We like the fresh air,' says Pharaoh, making no move to stand up, and surreptitiously tugging McAvoy back to a seating position as he begins to stand. 'Like to be able to see who's lurking in the bushes.'

'And you must be Trish Pharaoh,' he says, extending his hand.

'I'm Detective Superintendent Trish Pharaoh, yes,' she says, and steeples her fingers under her chin.

'Heard about the petrol bomb. And the dog bites.'

'Been a rough week,' she says.

'Sounds it. You could go for compensation, you know. You would have a lot of public sympathy. Senior female officer? Could be a mint. Cracking story . . .'

'I'm fine.'

'Well, if you decide you want to tell your side,' he says, and puts a business card on the table in front of her. 'I have a lot of friends in the media. People who owe me favours. Take the card . . .'

'I've got one,' she says, flicking it onto the grass. 'You gave one to Peter Tressider. And Stephen Hepburn. Mark Cabourne. My colleague here, too, but for different reasons. You're very open about what you're doing here. Won't be long until somebody on one of the local papers hears about you snooping. Or is that what you want now? Are you trying to discredit him? Do you want Tressider or don't you?'

Cocker looks from one to the other. Spreads his hands in surrender.

'We're keeping our options open,' he says smoothly. 'He could be a find for us or an embarrassment. We all have the capacity to be both.'

'This is what politics comes down to, is it?' Pharaoh looks like she'd like to spit.

Cocker makes no attempt to charm either of them. He has clearly been here before. 'Is this the bit where you suggest I fuck off before I make things difficult for powerful people?'

Pharaoh snorts. 'Which powerful people? A bunch of councillors? People don't care. People don't give a damn. For God's sake, our MPs can do what they like and we at least know what some of them look like. You think people will be shocked that a councillor has a bit of a dodgy past? Seriously? Smells like bullshit to me.'

Cocker opens his mouth, then closes it again. Unasked, he slides onto the opposite bench, then gives an accepting nod.

'Hepburn's not the story,' he says. 'Not really. There is a story there, though. Some way down the line. He's a liar. Bloody fraud, I can tell you that. Got himself into a powerful position playing the gay card and, I can tell you, that particular card isn't all pink. I haven't always done this, you know. I was a lobbyist, for a while. I've just got a

469

knack for sniffing out trouble. And there's trouble here that could embarrass the people who pay my wages . . .'

'You thought Tressider and Hepburn might be having a fling?'

Cocker shrugs. 'It happens. More than you might think.'

'And what did you find out?'

Cocker looks skyward, almost reluctant to admit his hunches have failed to play out. 'Hepburn's a bit of a lad. Some dodgy connections, but nothing that powerful people the world over haven't got in their backgrounds. I know he had a fling with another city councillor. Cabourne, or someone. I know he likes a bit of variety in his life.'

'Variety?'

'I got hold of a police report. From a while back. He got a bit of a telling off from a patrol unit who caught him nuts deep in trouble in the public toilets at Fraisthorpe. You know the caravan park on the road to Bridlington? Arse-end of nowhere? Police caught him in there getting up to no good.'

'Was he arrested?'

'Got a telling off, but no official caution.'

Pharaoh and McAvoy look at one another. 'Do you know who the other person was?'

Cocker smiles, broadly. 'Officers were sympathetic. All boys together. Didn't make her give her name.'

McAvoy's eyes narrow. 'Her?'

'Told you,' says Cocker. 'That pink card he plays is raspberry ripple. He likes a bit of both.'

McAvoy begins to speak, but a sudden pressure on his wrist indicates Pharaoh wants him to be quiet.

'Did you confront Hepburn with this knowledge?'

Cocker nods. 'He's not who we're interested in. But I thought he might be honest with me. Tell me if there really was anything to worry about. He didn't like being asked. Said he didn't think anybody would give a damn. Said he is a single man who enjoys himself.'

Pharaoh smiles. 'So it was just a fishing trip when you visited Tressider?'

'Wanted to see if I could shake something loose. He lost his temper with me. Went crackers about me approaching his wife. She wasn't happy neither.'

'So what will you be writing?' asks McAvoy. 'Your report. Will you recommend him?'

Cocker pulls a face. 'Probably. There's nothing we couldn't manage. I think he'll be a decent MP,' he says grudgingly. 'I'm sure the decision will come down from on high not to mention the money he put Hepburn's way. Doesn't look great and if that's his only indiscretion, would be a shame to lose him for the Party. He's our sort of person. No kids, but they're a strong couple. Respectable. Bit panicky but they'll get used to that.'

'Panicky?'

Cocker waves it away as if it doesn't matter. 'You

can't go ranting and roaring at the people you need on your side. You need some dignity. Screaming, he was. We like them best in photo-shoot mode. Like in that mag you lot have got up here. There was a piece in it about them. "At Home with the Tressiders" sort of thing.'

'*The Journal*?'

'Yeah, our sort of people.' Cocker stops. Rummages in his suit pocket, and frowning, runs back to the car. He comes back with a copy of the mag. Hands it to McAvoy.

'You may as well keep it,' he says. 'Angle's all changed.'

Pharaoh curls her lip. 'We're done,' she says.

'Yeah? That was it? Thought I was going to get a pummelling.'

'Don't count it out,' she says, then waves sweetly to tell him to be on his way. Moments later the Volvo is pulling out and roaring off.

'Weasel,' says Pharaoh and turns to McAvoy, who is opening the mag and leafing through. The weak sunlight bounces off the glossy pages, and he has to hold it straight out in front of him before the images come into focus. He looks at Peter and Paula Tressider. Blinks. Looks again. He swallows hard.

'She was at Hepburn's house,' he says quietly, and scratches his eyelid. 'Offered me a towel.'

Pharaoh takes the mag. 'Perhaps they're friends,' she begins cautiously.

'Perhaps.'

They look at the pictures for another full minute. McAvoy lets his eyes scan the text.

'Paula, 49, runs two boutique shops in Beverley, but is also a director of two of her husband's companies,' he reads. 'She admits to finding the idea of being a politician's wife very daunting, but says she will be at her husband's side throughout his journey to Westminster if he is selected, as many predict, next year.'

Pharaoh takes over. Reads Paula's quotes out loud. 'That's a wife's role – to support her husband. We have always been a strong unit. We have not been blessed with children but we don't feel our lives are incomplete. We've always had this feeling that it's us against the world. It will be hard to let people in.'

She and McAvoy realise their legs are jiggling. Their breathing has slowed. They inhale and exhale almost as one.

'It's a lovely house inside,' says Pharaoh, to break the silence.

He flicks through the mag again. Skims a feature on an up-and-coming polo player, and a six-page spread about an organic deli opening in North Ferriby. Scans the adverts. Butchers. Bakers. Bloody ornamental candlestick-makers.

Turns to the back page. An advert for a jewellers. A posh hairdresser's, at Kirk Ella. A tattoo and henna parlour on Newland Avenue . . .

Squints his eyes against the glare on the glossy page. Knows, even before the image swims into focus, that the picture will be of a skinny young man with peacock feathers on his back, and a fleshy girl with blossoms and lilies upon her shoulder.

Closes his eyes as he passes the magazine across to Pharaoh.

'Same edition,' he says, under his breath. 'Same edition outlining their future, they got a glimpse of their past.'

CHAPTER 31

Half an hour later. Newland Avenue, Hull. Bakers, butchers, charity shops and a couple of decent restaurants and wine bars.

A busy street, where asylum seekers, students and daytime drinkers sit elbow to elbow with besuited businessmen and schmoozing city councillors, smoking everything from roll-ups to fat cigars at metal tables and chairs.

It's the city's melting pot: a beacon of multi-culturalism and a place where most things can be acquired, be it a second-hand Kappa tracksuit, a bag of weed or a tenner's worth of rotisserie chickens.

McAvoy parks down the side street by Planet Coffee. The place is doing a brisk trade. Young office workers reading the papers over soup bowls of latte. Students sharing a muffin at low tables and sifting through purses full of bus tickets to find enough change for the jukebox.

'That one,' says Pharaoh needlessly, as she lets herself out of the car.

Hull Ink occupies a corner plot on the opposite

side of the road. The sign declares it to be an award-winner, though it is clearly not for interior design. The large glass window is papered to halfway up with black-and-white designs, while the glass door is covered in a double-page spread from the *Hull Daily Mail*, showing one of the tattoo artists hard at work scrawling something indistinct into the back of one of the paper's less dull feature writers.

'Me?' asks Pharaoh, as they cross the road.

'Guv?'

'The talking. Me?'

McAvoy isn't sure what to say. Doesn't know whether he should tell his senior officer to leave it to him. 'We'll just play it by ear.'

McAvoy pushes open the door into a large, cream-painted room. The floor is a chessboard of tiles and the walls are a collage of different designs. Behind the till sits a large, heavily inked woman aged around thirty. There are piercings in her eyebrows and through her septum. She is dressed in black and though her arms are uncovered they could not be called bare. No flesh tones can be seen. She is patterned magnificently, a tapestry of intermingled designs and glorious colour.

She smiles brightly. For a Goth, she seems a happy soul.

'Nice,' says Pharaoh enthusiastically. She crosses straight to the girl by the till and begins cooing over her arms.

'You like?' asks the girl, her Hull accent strong.

'Love it! Was it all one design or has it just evolved?'

'Bit of both,' says the girl. 'Got a treble clef and then some stars. Then a band around my bicep. Was becoming a bit chaotic, so we started joining them up. Took a while . . .'

'I bet! Gorgeous. Would love more myself but work would frown. Would love something pretty, though. A bird, maybe. Something free.'

McAvoy turns. Tries not to wonder where she hides her ink. Forces himself back to flicking through the different designs that hang in plastic folders from a newspaper rack.

'That what you're after, is it?' asks the girl. 'We've only got Devon in today. Stefan has weekends off. We've got an appointment in about an hour.'

'Sorry, love, it's actually more business than pleasure,' says Pharaoh, still in the same bright tone. 'I'm Trish Pharaoh. Detective Superintendent, if you're asking. That big lump is Detective Sergeant McAvoy. I know. To tattoo him you'd need a javelin and a pot of emulsion, wouldn't you?'

'I'm just the receptionist,' says the girl, though she doesn't seem worried. 'Devon's upstairs with a client . . .'

'Sounds dubious, when you say it like that,' laughs Trish, who has turned her attention to the magazines on the counter. 'That's nice,' she says, pointing at a little pixie wrapped around a bluebell which snakes down the back of a pale-skinned model. 'It's lilies I'm interested in. Peacocks too. I saw your advert . . .'

McAvoy crosses to the counter. 'In the back of *The Journal*, he says. A boy with peacock feathers and a girl with lilies and blossoms.'

The girl nods enthusiastically. 'Got a good response from that. Stefan's work, though it was their own designs. That's caused a few problems, actually. People who liked the advert can't have the same design. Copyright laws, you see. I mean, it's not like the courts can repossess it if we do breach copyright, but it's not really the done thing.'

'Do you know the couple? The boy and girl?'

'I remember them. He was quite flamboyant. She was fun.'

'What records do you keep? If somebody got in touch with you and wanted to know about the models . . .?'

The receptionist pulls a face. 'We wouldn't tell. We take a phone number and a name to reserve the appointment but that's it, really. Of course, if you go online, you can see who our regulars are, and our best work goes on there . . .'

McAvoy stops her by holding up a hand. 'Has anybody else shown an interest in these particular images?'

The girl looks up, as if trying to see into her own mind. 'Young girl brought in a copy of the mag. Wanted the same as the model. We told her about copyright but she made a few tweaks and that was OK. Wasn't that long since. Go on Facebook – I think it's on there . . .'

McAvoy and Pharaoh exchange a glance. He turns away from the desk, reaching into his pocket for his phone.

'Can you show me?' asks Pharaoh.

The girl, eager to please, retrieves a laptop from under the desk. Opens it up and flicks over to the shop's page.

'There's no real order to it,' she says, flicking through a collage of beautifully inked skin. 'Black and white stuff. Flowers. The rest is all just crammed in.'

'Would the peacocks and lilies be on here?'

'I don't think so. Stefan wouldn't use somebody else's designs on here, I don't think.'

'But the advert was ok? In the magazine?'

'Who reads magazines? It was just nice work. There was no strategy . . . aah, there we go. Georgie-Lee. Beautiful, isn't it?'

She turns the screen so Pharaoh can see. McAvoy views it over her shoulder. Bare skin patterned with branches and blossoms, lily pads and petals.

'Click on the girl.'

The receptionist does as asked.

A moment later, all three are reading page after page of messages, all posted on the wall of a nineteen-year-old girl who, according to friends, is in their prayers.

'Can't believe it,' reads Pharaoh slowly. 'You don't deserve this.'

'Hope they kill whoever did this to you,' reads McAvoy.

'Is that what this is all about?' asks the receptionist. 'What happened? Is she ok?'

Pharaoh scribbles down a name on the front cover of one of the tattoo mags. Rips it haphazardly. Stuffs it in her bag.

'Take the whole thing if you like,' says the girl, but Pharaoh has already turned her back. She is muttering in the big man's ear.

'Do you need to see Stefan?' asks the girl, as the detectives walk quickly across the tiles.

The door bangs behind them.

Pharaoh is sitting in the passenger seat, phone to her face, finger in her other ear, frustration in her eyes as she tells McAvoy to shut up and let her listen.

'And she's home already, yeah? Morpeth Street? That's two minutes, isn't it?'

McAvoy fidgets. Debates turning on the ignition. Decides not to.

Pharaoh hangs up. Raises a hand, then looks at her phone.

'Coming through now,' she mutters.

McAvoy looks at her expectantly.

'DC Jensen took the statement,' she says. 'Queen's Gardens CID. Would have come to us, in time.'

'Guv?'

'Serious and Organised. That's what it smelled

like. That or just some nutter on his way home. Was on its way to our in-box anyway.'

Her eyes narrow as she reads the statement Georgie-Lee gave yesterday morning from her hospital bed, as she waited for a nurse to remove the cannula from her wrist and to check that the stitches in her forehead weren't likely to burst open before she made it to the taxi.

'Friend's birthday party . . . outside for a smoke and a breath of fresh air . . . saw a vehicle, big thing, four-by-four, damage to front end . . . heard a door slam.'

Pharaoh stops.

'The attacker said, "Suzie".'

McAvoy closes his eyes. Turns his head away. Looks out of the window, where a man in running gear is sipping a hot chocolate and smoking a cigarette while chatting up two students. He finds himself shaking his head. Wonders if there will be exhilaration later. He feels none now.

'Pushed to the ground . . . choked her . . . hands in her hair . . . turned her over . . . thought she was going to be raped . . .'

'Jesus,' says McAvoy softly.

'Ripped her dress. Tore it nearly to shreds.'

'Looking for her ink,' says McAvoy needlessly.

'Smashed her head into the ground, after . . .'

Pharaoh pauses.

'Guv?'

'They said sorry.'

McAvoy licks his teeth. Turns the key in the

ignition only to have something to do with his hands.

'Description?'

'Yes. Sketchy, but yes.'

'And she's home?'

'Yes. Two minutes.'

McAvoy pulls out. Makes the brief drive through a network of back roads and one-way streets.

'That one,' says Pharaoh, and he pulls to a stop.

'You have it?' he asks, and Pharaoh pulls the magazine from her bag.

They look at each other. They are suddenly bone-tired. Cold. Drained by the endlessness of what they do.

The front door is answered by an attractive young girl in jogging bottoms and a skimpy top. She announces herself as Jen and tells them excitedly she is Georgie-Lee's best friend. Tells them, too, that she has been looking after her. Keeping her comfortable. Keeping her spirits up, because that is what she always does for everybody else. Tells them, a manic note in her voice, that Georgie-Lee had just organised the 'best birthday party ever' when the attack happened, and that she doubts she will ever get over the shock of finding her there, bleeding and unconscious on the front step.

'Georgie-Lee! Visitors!'

She opens a white-painted bedroom door. A young girl, childlike in pyjamas and bandages, is sitting up in bed reading a magazine and sipping hot blackcurrant. The room is decorated with band posters and dream-catchers, tattooed rockers, and colourful unicorns. She smiles as her friend enters the room, then freezes as McAvoy and Pharaoh enter behind her.

'Are you police?' she asks, instinctively pulling up the quilt. 'Have you got them?'

Pharaoh sits down on her bed.

Does not speak. Just holds the young girl's gaze, and tries to tell her that everything will be ok.

After a moment she pulls the magazine from her pocket. Leafs through. Flinches at the sound of glossy papers catching on the quilt and the tearing of quality paper.

Lays the mag down on the bed, open at the picture of politician and bride.

She does not have to ask Georgie-Lee the question. The shiver of fear and vile memory that ripples across her face is enough.

Suzie is upside down. The blood is pooling in her head and there is a thunderous rushing sound in her ears, broken only by the ceaseless shrieking that fills the living room.

'Give it up. You won't last . . .'

She does as she is bid. Tumbles right way up and gives in to fits of breathless noise.

She and Roisin are having a headstand competition on the sofa, and Lilah is laughing so hard, there is a risk of losing at least one eye.

'You sure this isn't hurting?' asks Roisin, as they

right themselves and pull faces at the giggling baby.

'Hurts anyway,' shrugs Suzie. 'May as well be upside down.'

Roisin nods, and seems to think about the sentence. 'I like that. We should have that on a T-shirt.'

'Or a pair of knickers.'

They giggle like two old friends.

Roisin and Suzie have shared little in the way of their stories. They have not probed one another's secrets. Roisin knows only that the kooky young woman in her house is somebody her husband wants to keep safe. She does not doubt him. Suzie strikes her as somebody the world requires.

Suzie, meanwhile, thinks Roisin may be the best person ever. She wants to tell her. Blurts it out, as the petite, dark-haired gypsy girl straightens her hair in the big mirror above the fire.

'You're so lovely,' she says. 'I can't believe I'm giggling. Being silly.'

'We're a silly family,' says Roisin, blowing a raspberry on Lilah's tummy.

'I'm not sure your husband is silly,' says Suzie, carefully. 'He seems quite serious.'

Roisin smiles warmly, as if looking at a picture nobody else can see. 'He's serious about some things. He's a big eejit a lot of the time.'

'And this is ok?' Suzie asks.

'Nice to have company. Nice to be silly.'

Suzie looks at herself in the mirror. She is

wearing one of McAvoy's shirts, and a pair of Roisin's leggings. She has no make-up on, though Roisin has promised to remedy this after lunch. She feels odd, looking at this unfamiliar reflection. This plain face and unremarkable hair. Comfy clothes and covered-up tattoos.

'Do you think I'd look good with my hair black, like yours?' she asks.

Roisin considers it. 'Might be a bit severe for you. You've got a warm face. Need a warm colour. Your hair suits you.'

Suzie smiles. 'Thanks.'

Roisin picks Lilah out of her playpen. Pretends to bite her tummy. 'Want a hold?'

Suzie shakes her head. 'I'll just stick to performing. I'm clumsy.'

'Aector is too. Should see him trying to get his change ready to pay the toll at the bridge. He can't manage 5p pieces. Hands are too big. Gets in a right state.'

The way she says it is not critical. Roisin seems to think her husband's clumsiness is every bit as laudable as his strength.

'He must make you feel very safe,' says Suzie, and instantly wonders if she has overstepped an invisible boundary.

Roisin looks at her quizzically. Grins. 'There's no world without him.'

They enjoy a moment, two new friends together. As they stand here in front of the mirror, fixing their hair and praising one another, the first fresh handfuls of rain start to beat against the glass. They cross to the window, amazed by the thunderous onslaught.

'It's gone so dark,' says Suzie, marvelling at the sudden gloom beyond the glass. 'Could be night-time.'

'Going to be a good summer,' predicts Roisin. 'Crappy spring means warm summer.'

'That true?'

Roisin shrugs. 'No. If we say it enough, though, it will be eventually.'

As they talk, there is a screech of tyres and a fountain of spray as a car, travelling too fast, is flung around the turn-in to the little close. It is followed by another, uncomfortably close, and both scream to a halt on the kerb opposite.

'Aector?'

Both women watch as the doors are flung open. McAvoy clambers from the driving seat of the hatchback in the lead. A middle-aged, busty woman in leather boots and a too-tight V-neck jumper wrenches open the driver's door of the little two-seater sports car. From this remove, Suzie thinks her bra looks painfully tight.

'His boss,' says Roisin, by way of explanation. 'Likes lamb.'

'Yeah?' asks Suzie confused. 'Bunnies, personally.'

The door swings open and McAvoy, red-faced, bursts into the living room, knocking a picture off the wall. Pharaoh is just behind him.

'These two,' says McAvoy, pulling out a mag and

throwing it open at a picture of a smiling, fifty-something couple in a posh, expensive-looking house.

Suzie looks to Roisin. Glances at Pharaoh, whose eyes are wide and face unreadable.

'Look,' says McAvoy. 'Do you know these two?'

Suzie takes the mag. Looks up into McAvoy's face and gives a nod.

The big detective spins away from her, hands in his hair. Throws a look at his boss. Goes and stands in front of the window with his hands on the sill, collecting himself. Roisin, wordlessly, slips to his side.

'You're sure,' asks Pharaoh.

'It was a place over in west Yorkshire,' says Suzie, and when she hears Lilah's little squeal, drops her voice, as if embarrassed. 'Private members' club.'

'A sex club?'

'Yes.'

'And?'

'Simon had made friends with somebody online. Said we should try it out.'

'When was this?'

Suzie sucks her lip. 'Not even a year, I don't think. I'd only had the tattoos done a wee while. Simon too.' She stops, nods excitedly, as she remembers. 'Yeah, that was his grand unveiling. Couldn't wait to show them off. The tattooist was really pleased. Said he was going to use them in his adverts, Was going upmarket . . .'

Pharaoh moves them both to the sofa. Sits them down. 'Were there many couples there? Would there be more witnesses?'

She frowns. 'People don't like to talk. They give false names. You're pretty safe there.'

'What happened?' asks McAvoy, crossing from the window. 'What did you do?'

Suzie looks at each of their intense faces. 'We played. Him with me. Then him with Simon. Then all four of us. He was nice. Simon said he was amazing. She was a bit of a cold fish. Liked my tattoos, though . . .'

'This couple,' says McAvoy, pointing at the page. 'You're sure.'

Suzie's mouth drops open, horrified she may have misled them. 'Not him,' she says hurriedly. 'I don't know him. Just her. She had this mask. She was a big woman. Like a man, with boobs. She was wearing this silly mask when we went in. I think she'd been to posher parties than ours. We were a bit of a comedown, but she liked roughing it. She took the mask off soon after. Was really into it. Into me. There was another guy too. Just joined in. It's a bit embarrassing talking about all this . . .'

Pharaoh spins in her seat. Locks eyes with McAvoy. He pulls out his phone and quickly finds his way to the Hull Council website. Finds the right picture. Crouches down and shows it to Suzie.

'Him, yes? He was the other man? Stephen Hepburn.'

She nods. 'Yeah. Friendly guy. Funny. Simon liked him. Are they not a couple then? Who's the guy with the beard in the mag? That her husband?'

Pharaoh gives a laugh. 'That's Peter Tressider. Chairman of the Police Authority. Future MP.'

Suzie looks at him, not understanding.

'And he killed Simon?'

McAvoy shakes his head.

'No,' he says, rubbing his head with a large, clumsy hand. 'She did.'

CHAPTER 32

The mask sits on the dressing table in the master bedroom, propped against the gilt-edged frame of the expensive oval mirror and surrounded by vintage perfume bottles, which flicker in the soft light of the large church candles that burn behind the four-poster bed.

Paula remembers the mask's purchase. A little shop filled with grinning faces, laughing gargoyles, down a Venetian side street near the grand hotel where she and her new husband were honeymooning.

'Do you like it?' he'd asked, already reaching for his wallet.

She hadn't needed to answer. She was mesmerised. Lost in the sightless eyes of the gold and crimson face she yearned to pull over her own.

A *bautta* mask, the seller had said. Worn in the eighteenth century by men and women keen to disguise their identities at the gaming tables.

She reaches for it now. Strokes the glossy paint. Touches its nose and its detailed jaw with the back of her knuckles.

Paula has never felt more alive than when looking out through its eyes.

This is the face she wears when she lets herself play. At parties. In hotel rooms. Letting herself be free.

It was only naughtiness at first. Just a chance to feel sexy with a man or two. It became an addiction. And then more than that.

She stares at the mask again.

The colours are entrancing. Traditionally, it should be painted in plain black or white, but the harlequin pattern of luxurious red and gold catches the light better. It is an exquisite work, a gorgeous example of its type. Tied with ribbon at the back, it covers the whole face, but the square jawline points upwards, allowing the wearer to eat and drink without its removal.

From behind this magnificent veil, Paula has experienced pleasure and pain in equal and exquisite measure. She has tongued and tasted, felt and fucked. She has given in to every instinct and desire. And she has never had to look at her face in the mirror.

Of course, her identity had not mattered at the start. She had been a successful man's wife, but the risk of having sex with strangers was no greater for her than for anybody else.

Then his political career took off.

She began having her photo taken. She began to become recognisable.

And they started to talk about Peter becoming an MP.

She had trusted to good fortune at first. Told

herself that anybody who recognised her from her tawdry couplings would have a vested interest in keeping it to themselves. But she could not stop herself from remembering. Could not help but think back to all the nights she had risked everything in the pursuit of faceless sex.

Alone in troubling her among her many indiscretions was the night they slummed it. When she and Hepburn found a couple of playmates online and decided to take a risk.

During their Internet chats, the couple mentioned the private members' place in Huddersfield. Told her and Hepburn all about the love swing. The chains. It had sounded deliciously seedy. Wonderfully downmarket. Instantly arousing in its griminess.

They had decided to take the risk. Convinced themselves eighty miles was far enough from home.

They had let their fantasies take shape and worked themselves up. Given false names and paid their membership. Had a drink with the foul-mouthed old bastard who ran the place and then headed upstairs to one of the private rooms.

Paula had worn the mask. Been waiting in a private room, spreadeagled on the bed, when Simon and Suzie walked in.

Suzie had laughed. Taken a look at the tall, broad-shouldered, middle-aged woman on the bed in her hook-nosed Venetian mask, and she had giggled.

So Paula had taken it off. She wanted the girl as soon as she saw her. Wanted to touch her warm, young skin. Wanted to trace her tongue against the blossoms on her back. She hadn't wanted the evening to dissolve into silliness. She'd taken off the mask and pulled Suzie between her thighs. And the party had begun.

After a time, when her need for pleasure had outweighed all else, she had instructed Hepburn to open the door. To let in the first man he saw. She opened her legs, and allowed herself to be entered by a stranger. His name was Connor Brannick, and the few seconds he spent inside her would eventually cost him his life.

Here, now, Paula drops her head to her hands. She can hear her husband mowing the lawn in the back garden. Wishes she was out there too. Perhaps sitting on a blanket. Drinking wine. She can't go out there, now. Can't even look at the fish pond.

She knows that this cannot go on. That soon her husband will find the time to investigate properly the continued death of his expensive carp. Will drain the pond. Will find Connor's body, stones wedged into his motorbike leathers, decomposing on the plastic bottom of the deep pool . . .

Her husband does not know she has killed. But he knows something has changed. Knows that she is lying. Has asked, more than he should have done, when the motorcycle in his garage will be going back to the 'friend' for whom she claims to be looking after it.

She knows, too, that the big Scottish sergeant is getting closer. That Hepburn's phonecall to his superiors has done nothing but convince him there is something to investigate.

Knows that, far more than her husband, it is her lover, Stephen Hepburn, who is closest to making the accusation. To asking her whether she has killed three people, and is trying, so damn hard, to do it again.

She holds the mask to her face. Stares out through its eyes. Smells the stale sweat and shivers as she remembers the moment she first closed it over her countenance.

Her phone bleeps.

Behind the mask, she gives the faintest of smiles.

They didn't think she was going to reply at first. Sat for hours watching Suzie's phone and waiting for a message back. It came around six p.m., as Pharaoh and McAvoy were sitting at the laptop in his kitchen, eating ham and mustard sandwiches and filling in the gaps in their murderer's life.

Paula Tressider was born in 1959. Nice, middle-class Manchester family. Two sisters. Arty mum and businessman dad. Started university and met the man who would be her first husband. Played at being a political activist but seems to have been more about the outfits than the cause. Married the history student at twenty-two and divorced him a year later. Took a job in a boutique in Leeds. Became the manager. Met Peter Tressider. Married in 1989. Became the good wife. Started appearing on the boards of his various businesses. Turning up on his arm at political functions. Moved to East Yorkshire and opened two fashion houses. Gave talks to the Women's Institute about the importance of a stable family unit. Started wearing twinsets and pearls. Joined the board of governors at a local school. Joined the Conservative Party. Became a pillar of the community and the cardboard cut-out of a politician's wife.

'She must have been terrified,' says McAvoy softly.

'Don't start that,' says Pharaoh between mouthfuls. 'You go soft on me I'll kick your teeth in.'

'Sorry, Guv. Just, I thought we were after somebody who was doing this for kicks. She just wanted her secrets to stay hidden.'

Pharaoh shrugs. 'She got her kicks a different way. Killed to cover it up.'

'You think he knows?'

'Her husband? No. If he does, he turned a blind eye.'

McAvoy looks again at the website. Paula Tressider, pictured in hundreds of pounds worth of designer gear, wearing a forced smile for the camera, shaking hands with the Prime Minister at a Conservative fundraiser a year before.

'When she saw their tattoos in the magazine . . .'

'Yeah.'

The phone buzzes. They each take a breath, before McAvoy reads the text aloud.

'Think it's time we finished our game. You're on.'

His smile contains no mirth. Just a relief that his own message, carefully constructed with Suzie's help, has been received and accepted.

Roisin gives Suzie a cuddle as they head out of the door. She does not know what is happening, but her new friend seems trembly and scared.

'He'll take care of you,' she says, gesturing at her husband.

'I know.'

McAvoy bends down and gives Lilah a tickle. Bumps fists with Fin, who is sitting in front of the TV eating pasta and pesto with sliced-up hot dogs.

'They called,' whispers Roisin in his ear, as he stands.

He turns to her. Looks quizzical.

'Hamer,' she says. 'The new halting site. Anlaby. He wants you there.'

McAvoy's face contorts. He wonders if any more burdens will be laid upon his broad shoulders tonight.

'I'm a policeman.'

She makes sure he is looking straight at her as she replies, 'You're a man.'

He does not speak again. Just quietly closes the door as he leaves. Does not turn up his collar or lower his head as he walks through the pounding rain. Opens the car door and climbs inside. Starts the engine and finds something soothing on a classical station.

Watches the lights come on.

Checks his radio and gives a nod.

Suzie leads the way, her tiny Peugeot at the head of this three-car convoy. She squints through the rain and the gathering gloom, wincing at the distorted headlights of the cars in front and behind, aware that the only reason she is not shaking her legs is because she does not want to stall the car.

On the passenger seat, the phone Pharaoh gave her bleeps. She reads the message. It has been forwarded from her own phone.

Need to Taste Your Skin. Don't be Late.

She closes her eyes for as long as she dares while driving. Instinctively looks across to the passenger seat. Wonders if she can really feel Simon's presence or just wants to.

The journey takes more than an hour in the slow-moving traffic. Twice she fears she has lost McAvoy and Pharaoh, but whenever she prepares to park up and wait for them, her phone flashes to tell her they can see her. That she is not alone.

It is easier when she hits the motorway. She sticks at a steady seventy in the inside lane. Tries to find comfort in the sound of the wet tyres on the road. Concentrates on her breathing. Half wishes she had let Roisin petition her husband into being allowed to come too.

She has been to this hotel before. It sits off the motorway, three miles from Goole. She sat in the car park for two hours while Simon entertained a man he'd met on the website. She had done some drawing and eaten a McChicken Sandwich. Simon had enjoyed his afternoon. Said the man was grateful and kind.

Suzie parks. She wants to look at the other cars in the dark, wet car park. Wants to see if her murderer is already there. Does not let herself. Climbs out of the vehicle and straight-backed, face upturned, walks through the puddles and into the hotel.

'Can I help you?'

The man on reception is younger than she is. He looks bored, and his shirt is too big for his skinny frame.

'I have a room booked.'

She gives her name. Tries to keep calm as he fiddles with the machine and then finally hands her a key. He looks her over, as if appraising live-stock. Even has the temerity to nod.

'Second floor,' he says.

She takes the stairs. Cannot bear the thought that the lift may be mirrored. Does not want to see herself.

Balling her fists, clenching her jaw, she finds the room. Slides the passcard into the lock and pushes open the door. Switches on the light and looks round the dark, characterless, room, her heart thudding painfully against her broken ribs.

Another message on her phone, this time from McAvoy.

Be strong. I'm here.

She undresses. Peels off her borrowed shirt and leggings. Tries to rub the creases out of her imperfect skin. Takes the length of cord from her handbag and wedges the door open with a flip-flop.

Slowly, as if every moment pains her, and each breath is a countdown, she moves to the bed. Lies facedown and naked. Feels the cool blankets against her warm skin. Grips the phone tight. Texts her killer.

I'm ready.

Time slows. Suzie does not know how long she has been here. Her mind drifts. She could not say, with any certainty, that she has not fallen asleep in the time she has been lying here, in this beige room, with its white sheets and thin mattress.

Just knows that this was how Simon died. And that by lying here, like this, she is helping to catch a killer.

There is no prelude to the attack. She hears nothing. No creak of floorboard or clever threat.

One moment she is lying face down on the hotel bed. The next there is a pressure upon her back, and the cord she has draped so invitingly across her buttocks is tight around her neck.

She gasps. Fights. Thrashes like an animal. But the weight upon her shoulders is too great. The hands too rough. It is the same weight that pinned her to the grass two nights ago and which was the last thing her friend felt as he died. It hurts.

Her mouth opens. The tendons in her neck feel, for a moment, to be snapping like a fistful of twigs.

And then it is gone. She is face down on the bed. Her face is on the pillow. The tears upon her cheeks are soaking into the mattress. Warm, tender hands are upon her.

She turns. Manages to wriggle onto her back. Whips her head this way and that. Looks at the devastation of the room. The smashed TV. The spilled kettle and cups. The door that hangs from only one hinge.

'Suzie.'

Shirt torn, bleeding from the nose, McAvoy is standing in the doorway. He gives her a bone-weary smile.

'You ok?'

'Did you get her?'

'Are you ok, Suzie?'

She nods. Breathes, deep and slow.

'Please . . .'

'We've got them both, Suzie. It's a mess . . .'

CHAPTER 33

July, it was. Evening. A Sunday. Halfway through some costume drama on BBC One. A bottle of wine already drained and gravy-streaked dinner plates daringly abandoned on the coffee table.

That was when Paula Tressider took the call that made her a killer.

Four-and-a-half rings, then a weary hello: warm plastic receiver against fleshy cheek.

TV on pause and a shared look of exasperation . . .

Five whole seconds of silence, then a male voice. She didn't recognise it at first. Had not heard it say very much the only time they met. Just a few grunts and a thank you.

Clipped West Yorkshire tones . . .

'You might not remember me. I remember you. Huddersfield, it was. Some enchanted evening. Does your sweetheart know how you spend your free time?'

Thirty seconds more.

No words, just save his breathing.

'I think you have the wrong number . . .'

The laugh. The snuffled, nasal sniggering.

'No, I've got you. Was a surprise, like. Didn't think somebody in your position would be in the phone book. Then again, I didn't think somebody in your position would do the things I saw you do . . .'

Cold fear in a churning belly.

White roses blossoming on red flesh.

'I'm sorry, would there be a better time for you to ring to discuss this more fully? Perhaps if you left me your number I could contact you at a more convenient time . . .?'

No laughter, this time. Just ice in his voice.

'I'll call you. I'll call again, and again, and then I'll call somebody else. I'll tell. I'm sorry to be doing this. I really am.'

A moment's consideration. Eyes closed; hiding from it all. Memories folding inwards over everything else, like petals at dusk.

'Tomorrow. Call me tomorrow.'

A wordless nod.

Click.

A week without food. Of hands trembling and broken sleep. Needing a piss every thirty bloody seconds. Throwing up the wine that brought such feeble relief. Snapping at every gentle enquiry. Swearing at every question over health and happiness . . .

He called back, of course. The other man.

Midday, it was. Friday. Sweetheart at the shops.

Alone in the house. Glass knocking against the receiver; clutched in shaking hands.

'You ready to talk now?'

A nod. Then a deeper, more assertive reply.

'I've done nothing to be ashamed of.'

His smile.

'No? That's fine, then. I'd probably get plenty of money from the papers. I'm only calling you out of courtesy.'

'That's what you want, is it? Money? What makes you think I'd pay? Or that I could?'

Scorn, then. A note of uncertainty? A diversion from the script . . .

'You've got more than me. Everybody's got more than me.'

Resisting feebly. Trying to talk him round.

'How do you know it's a secret? People who know me already know what I like . . .'

'Bollocks. I remember. You told me a dozen bloody times what a risk you were taking. You were slumming it. Roughing it. Playing away, too close to home. You don't want this coming out. I read the papers. I know what they're saying about your future. You're a big deal. And I saw you on top of that pretty little girl with the blossoms, loving every minute of it. Even me, when you let me join in . . .'

Tears. A coughing fit that became puke.

'How much do you want . . .?'

Click.

Life became timeless. Hours became a shapeless, colourless mass.

Days, nights, all spreading out from that one

moment, in the early hours, when her mind was made up.

Broken by tiredness, racked by fear.

Acquiescing to will.

Weighing payment with risk.

Nodding in the dark. Eyes fixed on the ceiling. Tears on cheeks.

Paula Tressider acknowledged what must be done. Decided they all had to die.

Here, now, in the interview room at Courtland Road Police Station, with the rain thundering down outside and their breaths forming into ragged strips on the cold, damp air, Paula Tressider sobs and snuffles into her lap.

McAvoy prompts gently. Nudges along her confession. Tries to pretend they already know what she is giving up so freely . . .

'I said I would pay,' she says, her voice muffled as she drops her face into her fleshy palms. 'Told him to come.'

McAvoy leans forward. 'You need to say his name for the tape.'

'Connor,' she says, choking on the word. 'Connor Brannick.'

It means nothing to him. He tries not to show it. Feels the breeze as Pharaoh leaves the room, name scrawled on her palm in biro.

Paula is too caught up to notice the sudden absence. Just keeps talking. Sniffing. Wiping away tears with the heel of her hand.

'He came on his motorbike. End of summer. Hot day, I remember that. I could barely keep my hands still. It was real then. Him on the front drive, in his helmet and leathers, asking me if he could put the bike in the garage so the sap from the trees didn't drip on the paintwork . . .'

'Go on.'

'He was different from how he'd been on the phone. Embarrassed, even. When he took his helmet off he looked like he was about to cry. Was talking and talking. Said the house was lovely – that his wife would like it. He seemed sorry to be asking me for money. Tried to justify himself by telling me he was struggling. Said he would never do this if he could just get work.'

'Go on, Mrs Tressider.'

'He was talking so fast. Just gabbling on. He was as nervous as I was. I told him to come through to the back garden, be a bit more discreet. He followed. Saw the pond. Started saying how he could fit lights in it. Saying what a good electrician he was. Would look lovely lit from underneath. I was hardly listening. Managed to tell him the money was in the gazebo. I went to get it.'

'And then what, Paula?'

'I came back with the hammer.'

Pharaoh re-enters the room. Slides a warm piece of paper in front of McAvoy.

PARTNER OF MISSING MAN SAYS SHE HAS NOT GIVEN UP HOPE

The common-law wife of a Morley electrician missing for almost eight months has made a renewed appeal for him to come home.

43-year-old Connor Brannick vanished last September. He told his partner, 39-year-old Gwen Simmons, that he was going to price up a new job of work, but never returned home.

Ms Simmons, the mother of his four-year-old son, Andrew, waited several days before contacting police as she said it was not unlike him to go away for several days at a time for work.

But as time went on she began to worry, and calls to his mobile phone went unanswered.

Today she told the *Huddersfield Examiner* that, after he vanished, she discovered that he had been hiding major financial problems.

She said, 'I just wish he'd spoken to me about it. I know everybody's saying that he's done himself in, or just run off and left me to it, but I have to cling to the hope that he's ok and will come home.

'Our son keeps asking where Daddy is. I need him here. It was never about the money. I wish he'd told me how deep a mess we were in. I don't know what to do next or where to turn. I just want him home.'

Mr Brannick's motorcycle, which he was riding when he left the family home, is also missing.

Anybody with information should call West Yorkshire Police . . .

McAvoy looks up. 'His body?'

Paula raises her head long enough to glare at him, then the flicker of defiance is gone. She looks away. 'In the pond.'

'You smashed his skull in?'

Paula nods.

'For the tape, please?'

'Yes.'

For a moment there is silence in the room. Then McAvoy says the name that has brought them here.

'Simon Appleyard.'

Paula turns to the grey-suited solicitor who sits to her left, and who has done nothing but polish his glasses on his tie since she told him to shut up and let her speak.

'The magazine.'

McAvoy nods. '*The Journal*. The advert.'

'They were both there. Him and her. The boy Stephen found for us and the girl he brought. Their tattoos, mocking me, like she did that night. The night she made me take the mask off . . .'

McAvoy licks his teeth. 'Mrs Tressider, do you really believe that either Simon Appleyard or Suzie would ever have tried to blackmail you? Do you think that even if you became the Prime Minister's wife, they would have any notion of who you were, or try and use that to their advantage? Not everybody is like that.'

For the first time, Paula meets his gaze. 'Don't tell me about people. I know what people are. I know what's under the skin. It's not pretty. It's base and it's desperate, and it takes what it wants . . .'

It is Trish Pharaoh who stops her short, slamming her palm down on the desk.

'Did you kill Simon Appleyard?'

She holds Pharaoh's gaze. 'Yes.'

'And you are responsible for the attack on Georgie-Lee Suthers? On the boy at the swingers party? Repeated attacks on Suzie Devlin.'

'Yes.'

Pharaoh breathes out. Looks the burly, dishevelled politician's wife up and down. 'It's always the quiet ones.'

CHAPTER 34

As he walks across the car park in the teeming rain, tired to his bones, aching to his soul, McAvoy considers desire. Wonders at the nature of lust. Pictures Simon Appleyard, naked and holding his own noose, waiting for the stranger who would kill him where he lay. Considers Suzie: still visiting darkened lay-bys and opening herself for strangers, even as the bruises burned on her skin.

Thinks of Paula Tressider.

They'd always gone further afield, she'd told them in her interview. Her and Stephen. Had crossed the country to find playmates. She thought Huddersfield was too close to home. Only eighty miles away. Too risky. But she'd been excited. Liberated. Daring. Had thrown herself into the evening and had fun with the young couple with the tattoos. And then the magazine had arrived. The one she'd been so proud of. The photoshoot of her beautiful home. The picture of her and Peter. Her fingers locked around her husband's. Every inch the politician's wife. And there, mocking her, in the adverts at the back: skin she had tasted and which had touched her own. She didn't know when she'd decided to commit murder. Just knew that she had to make sure they could never talk. Knew only that the boy was into being dominated and liked certain websites. Knew, more than anything, he liked to please. Liked words. Liked peacocks. Could be found, and could be persuaded, to contribute to his own death.

'Hector.'

He turns, one hand on the door handle, rain slicking his hair to his face, soaking his already sodden clothes.

Pharaoh runs across the puddle-filled car park. She has her jacket over her head.

'Suzie,' she says, and it is a question.

'She's ok,' he says. 'Roisin's making a fuss of her. Sounds like they're having a sleepover.'

'She's at your house?'

'No. Roisin's at hers.'

'The kids.'

'There too.'

'And where are you going?'

McAvoy looks at her for a while. Watches the rain run down her face. Sees the black mascara pool in her eyes. Sees himself on her pupils.

'What was all this for?' he asks, raising his voice above the noise of the rain.

Pharaoh gives him an encouraging smile. 'We've got a confession. We've solved a murder.'

'Nobody knew it was a murder.'

'Does that matter? You knew.'

'Why did I do this?' he asks, and she cannot tell if it is rain or tears that spills down his face.

'Cause you're one of the good ones.'

He shakes his head. 'I don't feel any better for it.'

'Is that what you thought would happen?'

'I don't know. I feel worse.'

'Oh Hector, it's not your fault. You're the one that did things right. She'd have killed Suzie, you know that. Tressider had a weak heart. He kept it secret. Thought it would ruin his political chances. You heard her. That's why she turned to Hepburn.'

The affair had started a little over a year ago. Her husband had introduced them at a civic function. Mentioned they had done a little business together, and then left them to share a quiet corner and glasses of tasteless white wine. Hepburn had been vibrant, larger-than-life. Exciting. Flirty. She had thought he was gay until he asked to smell her perfume and then licked her jaw line all the way to her mouth. Had found herself a secret life she did not know that she wanted, and to which she became addicted.

For a moment McAvoy and Pharaoh do nothing but look at one another, trying to see a better kind of sense in the other's approach to crime. They turn as they hear a car door slam, a soft, mechanical sound barely audible over the rain.

They look over at the side street that leads to the front entrance of the police station. Dressed in a T-shirt that clings to his skin and a pair of nondescript trousers, they almost do not recognise Stephen Hepburn. His shoulders are slumped. He is looking back over his shoulder at the car he has parked haphazardly on a kerb.

He pauses now. Standing by the barrier that blocks the entrance to the staff car park.

'News travels fast,' says Pharaoh.

McAvoy is already moving towards the distant figure. He does not bow his head in the face of the gale. Takes the cold and the rain upon his face without complaint or evasion.

Hepburn sees him coming. Straightens himself. Pulls the damp material from his skin. Pushes a hand through his hair and then drops his arms to his side. They hang there, awkward and limp.

'Is it true?'

Hepburn's voice is a tremble.

McAvoy stands in front of him, saying nothing. Looks the smaller man up and down. Tries to place this ragged, unremarkable man at the scene of so many stories. Imagines him, for the briefest of moments, rutting with Paula Tressider on the Welton hillside. Imagines him at his keyboard, persuading sexed-up strangers to meet them in hotel rooms and car parks. Remembers the arrogant, cocksure man who curled his lip in half-hearted contempt when McAvoy told him he was investigating a murder.

'Please,' says Hepburn. 'Paula. Did she kill the boy. The one from the party?'

McAvoy looks him up and down. Stares into eyes filled with bewilderment and tears.

'You really didn't know,' he says, and it is not a question. 'You just didn't give a damn, did you?'

Hepburn opens his mouth to speak.

McAvoy silences him with a shake of his head.

'She didn't just kill him, Councillor. The man who joined you that night in Huddersfield. She did him in too. She killed anybody who might tell about the time she took her mask off.'

A stream of water falls from the end of Hepburn's nose.

'I didn't know,' he begins, before protestation gives way to self-preservation. 'I had nothing to do with it . . .'

McAvoy works his jaw in a slow circle, then clenches his teeth. 'You won't be charged,' he says quietly. 'I don't know what we could make stick. I don't know if there's even a charge for what you've done. I don't even know how I feel about you. I don't know if you've done anything wrong. I just know you've got away with something and I hope you never forget that.'

Hepburn looks up into McAvoy's brown eyes. Sees himself mirrored, fuzzy and indistinct. A dark, shadowy thing, blurred by the storm.

'I just wanted to play.'

McAvoy walks away. Is grateful that the rain running into his mouth tastes so foul. It gives him a legitimate reason to spit.

'All of it,' says McAvoy quietly, as he returns to

his car to find Pharaoh waiting, soaked to the skin. 'Trying to run Suzie over. Attacking her at the party. Smashing the lad over the head and trying to throttle her. She did all of it just to make sure nobody told.'

'I think she got a taste for it,' says Pharaoh, choosing not to ask him what he said to Hepburn. 'I think she started pushing the boundaries. Maybe this became another game. I don't believe that shit about burying the past.'

'What's going to happen, d'you think?' He asks the question cautiously, as if walking on breaking ice. 'Politically, I mean.'

Pharaoh purses her lips. The bandage on her neck is sodden with rain and she reaches up to smooth it back down. 'I think we'll be ok. We did it with kid gloves, didn't we? Kept it off the books. Had a look and then got a result.'

'We should go and see him,' says McAvoy. 'Now. He'll want to talk.'

Pharaoh holds his gaze. 'You think he knew?'

McAvoy nods. 'I think he threw the phone where I would bloody find it. I think I was cheaper than hiring a private detective.'

CHAPTER 35

1 1.14 p.m. Hull Royal Infirmary.
Peter Tressider is sitting up, limply, in his hospital bed, wearing borrowed surgical scrubs. He appears shrunken. Diminished. Small. There is a clump of hair missing from the side of his head, and red skin glares from beneath the coarse hair at his throat.

As he enters the private room, McAvoy is put in mind of a skinned bear. The image flashes through his mind unbidden. His thoughts are filled with raw, pink flesh and bloodied fur. He sees the man in the hospital bed as a beast, hunted, wounded, mutilated inside and out.

'Councillor.'

Tressider opens his eyes. Looks at his visitors. At Aector McAvoy, soaked to the skin and expressionless in his gaze. At Trish Pharaoh behind him, make-up on her cheeks, rain on her chest.

'I won't be hearing that again,' he says softly.

Pharaoh closes the door behind them. Sits down on a hardbacked plastic chair. McAvoy doesn't move. Just holds Tressider's stare.

'You followed her,' Pharaoh says at length. 'Tonight.'

Tressider swallows. Looks away.

McAvoy steps to the side, putting himself back in Tressider's eye-line.

'How long have you known?'

Tressider lifts himself up a little. Rubs his hands in his beard. Lets his fingers fall to his throat.

'You nearly broke my windpipe,' he says, and coughs as he does so. 'When you dragged me off. You're stronger than you look. And you look bloody strong. Scalped me too. Pulled half my bloody hair out by the roots.'

McAvoy doesn't speak. There is silence in the room, save for the rustle of Pharaoh pushing her hair back from her face, and recrossing her legs.

'How long have you known, Councillor? We can do this properly, if you'd prefer. Take you to the station. You can call your brief. There may be photographers at the station though . . .'

Weakly, as if he is past caring about such things, Tressider waves his hand. 'You think I care about all that? You think I ever cared?'

McAvoy says nothing. Waits for the other man to fill the silence.

Tressider screws up his eyes. Talks to the image that is playing in his imagination.

'You're asking if I knew,' he says, licking his lips. 'I'm asking myself too.'

McAvoy leans forward. Peers into the councillor's face like a pathologist examining a corpse.

'Speak to me, sir.' He says it softly. 'So we

understand her. So we understand Paula. So we understand the woman you loved.'

Tressider's eyes lock on McAvoy's. Both see the other, reflected in their pupils.

He breathes out, and there is a sickliness to the sound. A weariness. An approach of the grave.

At length he reaches to his bedside and takes a sip of water. Savours it.

'I knew when we got married that she was full of life,' he says, staring up at the ceiling with its grey tiles and garish lights. 'I knew she had fire in her. Did I know she was playing around? Not at first, no. I didn't think that way. We were happy. Whatever we had, it worked. She seemed to love me, I know that much. Seemed to enjoy our lives . . .'

'But you began to suspect?'

Eyes still closed, Tressider nods. 'She got a second mobile phone. The first one we got through the business. Claimed the tax back on her business calls, you see. All above board. But when you live with somebody, you can't hide everything, can you? I saw it in her handbag. Knew she had hidden it from me. You can't help but think the worst, can you?'

'Did you confront her?'

Tressider swallows painfully. Shakes his head. 'I don't know if I wanted the truth. Not really. Not then.'

'What happened, Councillor?'

Tressider opens his eyes. There are no tears, but

his face is pale and drawn, his lips grey. He is a pencil sketch of himself.

'I tried to stop thinking about it,' he said. 'Told myself that whatever we had, it worked. Tried to be a modern man, I guess. When she got pally with Steve Hepburn, I told her to go for it. To enjoy herself. I thought having a flamboyant, gay friend like that would appeal to whatever part of her I wasn't satisfying. They hit it off. She even suggested we put some money into one of his businesses . . .'

'The phone, Councillor. Simon Appleyard.'

Tressider smoothes down the front of his pyjamas. Presses his lips tight together.

'She got a phone call. A few months ago. We were sitting at home and she answered a call on our home phone. Came back white as a sheet. Wouldn't speak. Wouldn't tell me anything. I tried to cheer her up, but I knew something was wrong.'

'The blackmailer,' says McAvoy, turning to Pharaoh. 'Brannick.'

'She was weird for days. Told me she was just feeling under the weather. Told me to leave it to her and to concentrate on work. On council work. The Authority. Getting into the good books with the Party . . .'

Tressider's bottom lip shakes. He bites it, willing himself to be strong.

'What is going to happen to her?' he asks.

McAvoy rubs his hands through his hair. Picks the damp material of his trousers from his legs.

'She's going to be charged with murder, Councillor Tressider.'

Tressider swallows again. Says nothing for a full ten seconds.

'The pond,' he says at last. 'Brannick's in the pond.'

McAvoy turns to Pharaoh. Back to the man in the bed.

'You put him there?'

He gives a shake of his head. 'I found him there. Staring up at me. Eyes like headlights . . .'

McAvoy needs to move. Has held himself still too long. He crosses to the window and stares, through his own reflection, at the lights of the city. At the yellows and blues that flicker and glare in the darkness and the rain.

'You were a member of the Police Authority and didn't think to call the police?'

He feels Tressider's eyes upon him. Refuses to turn.

'I knew,' he says flatly. 'Knew what she had done.'

Pharaoh clears her throat. 'You didn't confront her?'

'I wanted to,' says Tressider, and his voice is almost a wail. 'But she seemed so happy suddenly. Gleeful. Bouncing, almost. I kept telling myself we'd just have a few days like that, and then we would talk. But days became weeks. We were happy.'

McAvoy turns from the window, face red. 'There was a dead man in your pool, Councillor! You must have needed to know.'

Tressider wipes his nose with the back of his hand. 'I tried to forget . . .'

'And then the happiness stopped,' says McAvoy. 'She started behaving strangely again.'

'It was that damn magazine,' he spits. 'She was so bloody proud of us. Kept flicking through it. Loved the thought of what we were going to become. And then she changed. Became cold. Stopped talking . . .'

'The phone,' says Pharaoh. 'Where did you find it?'

Tressider turns to her. Tries to scowl, but lacks the strength. 'I followed her,' he says, breaking eye contact. 'One Sunday, a month before Christmas. She'd come home in a taxi. Said the car had broken down and needed towing near Anlaby. She had no reason to be there. What was she doing? I couldn't stand it. She said she needed to clear her head and went out again almost as soon as she got in.'

'Where did she go?'

'The dale,' says Tressider, lost in memory. 'Top of Welton. Pretty place.'

McAvoy nods. He knows the area. Steepsided and tree-lined, and scented with bluebells and cow parsley, fresh air and dirt.

'I saw her bury something,' Tressider says. 'Pulling up clumps of dirt with her bare hands. She was crying. I wanted to hold her . . .'

'But you wanted to know what she was doing.'

Tressider falls silent.

'You dug it up,' says Pharaoh.

'Not at first,' says Tressider, as if that's important. 'I tried to stop myself. Tried to tell myself that it was all over. Waited for her to get happy again, like before. But she didn't. She was colder than ever. Always on the computer, out at all hours.'

'You went back.'

Tressider nods. 'I dug up what she had buried. Dug up the phone.'

'It was broken,' says McAvoy. 'You couldn't make it work. You couldn't get answers.'

'I tried,' says Tressider, and his hands make fists around the bedclothes. 'But I didn't know what to do . . .'

'You asked Hepburn,' says McAvoy. 'That day. The first meeting of the Police Authority. You tried to get answers. Wanted to know what he knew . . .'

'He told me they had been having an affair,' he says, and snatches away a tear. 'He didn't hide it. Said he wasn't as gay as people thought. Said he was sorry. Said he hoped we could all move on.'

Pharaoh pulls herself out of the chair. Crosses to his bedside.

'And you decided that you could,' she says icily. 'You decided you could live with the body in the pool. You could forgive her whatever she had done. And you threw the thing in the river.'

Tressider turns away from her. Stares at McAvoy.

'I saw you,' he says softly. 'Had this glimpse of what I thought the police should be. I suppose I trusted in fate . . .'

McAvoy scoffs openly. Sneers with contempt. 'Did you want me to find it?' he asks, making fists. 'Did you leave it for me. Was I your fucking errand boy?'

Tressider looks down at himself. Gives a half-laugh as he takes in the sight he presents.

'I don't know.'

McAvoy spins back to the window. Presses his head against the cool glass.

'Tonight,' he says, and his breath fogs the pane. 'You followed her to the hotel.'

In the reflection he sees Tressider nod.

'You read her phone.'

Another nod.

'You thought she was meeting another man.'

Softly: 'Yes.'

McAvoy licks his lips, Lets his eyelids close. He is suddenly bone weary.

'You're done,' says Pharaoh behind him, and though she addresses her comments to the councillor, it is McAvoy who feels the sting of her words.

His thoughts turn to love. To utter, blinding devotion. To Roisin. He asks himself how much he could forgive. How much he could tolerate. How much pain he would endure to make her love him, and never leave.

He turns away from the window. Stares into Tressider's eyes.

'She loved you best,' he says softly. 'All the things she did were to protect you from people finding out that she had strayed. She wanted you to get all you ever wanted.'

Pharaoh looks at him quizzically, taken aback by the sudden gesture of compassion.

'Yeah,' she says scornfully. 'She was all fucking heart.'

McAvoy holds Tressider's gaze. Breathes out slowly and pulls open the door. Gives a nod to the uniformed constable in the corridor, and stomps, damply, down the hall. He takes the stairs, two at a time. Crashes across the reception area and bursts into the storm beyond the glass.

'McAvoy!'

He doesn't turn, but the sound of Pharaoh's boots on the linoleum is unmistakable, and she pulls him back by the arm.

'You don't want the arrest?'

McAvoy twitches his mouth into a ghost of a smile.

'I don't know what I want.'

Pharaoh opens her mouth. Her tongue flicks out and glosses her full, red lips. She puts a hand on his arm and squeezes, never taking her eyes from his.

'You did good, Hector.'

McAvoy looks away. Shrugs. Begins to walk away.

'Where are you going?'

He answers with one word.

'Roisin.'

He doesn't hear her move. Can picture her standing there, watching him get smaller.

Wonders what she will read into his answer.

Whether she knows he is on his way to a fist fight with a gangster.

CHAPTER 36

1.18 p.m. Anlaby playing field.

Colin Ray is pressed against the damp brick of the changing rooms, tucked into the blackest pocket of shadow that he can find. He is soaked to the bone. His suit is clinging to his gangly frame and every few seconds he shivers, sending a fresh mist of rain from the brim of his borrowed black baseball cap.

'Anything?'

Shaz Archer's voice comes from between locked teeth. She is behind him, better concealed in the doorway of the outbuilding.

'Still just talking.'

The travellers are gone. The mobile homes and the horses, the furniture and four-by-fours, disappeared some time this afternoon. Anybody who saw them go is keeping quiet about it.

They are not why the two police officers are here. They are after the men who sit in the nearby Lexus, parked up on a patch of rutted, rain-lashed gravel a hundred yards away from where they shiver in the sodden clothes, and wait.

Ray is in a foul mood. Already news has filtered

through that McAvoy and Pharaoh have brought in a murderer he did not even know they were seeking. Already there is a chance that the collar he makes tonight will not be the most eye-catching of the day.

'Col, are we sure . . .?'

Ray holds up a hand to shush her. A car is pulling up, nosing in past the wooden fence and coming to a halt around thirty yards from the Lexus.

'Bloody gangsters are on hard times these days,' muses Ray, squinting through the rain, trying to focus on the figure climbing out of the little hatchback.

He feels Archer beside him, unable to keep herself quiet.

'Is that . . .?'

Ray nods. 'McAvoy.'

They watch, silently as the bulky Scotsman walks sure-footedly across the car park to the Lexus. See him tap on the blackened glass.

'Col, what's he doing?'

McAvoy is stepping back. Taking off his coat. Folding it up and laying it on the roof of the big posh car.

'Oh Christ, that's what he meant . . .'

Suddenly Ray remembers Alan Rourke's words. What he said about Hamer's need for respect. His intention to do harm to the copper who hurt his godson.

'Is he on his own?'

Ray doesn't answer. Just watches, as the doors open on the Lexus. Watches four men climb out.

'Your eyes are better than mine,' he whispers, and grabs Archer by the pocket of her soaking denim jacket. Pulls her close. 'Tell me.'

'Ronan,' she says softly. 'Hamer.'

'Fucking hell.'

Wordlessly, they watch McAvoy back up. Watch one figure break off from the advancing quartet. Take the lead.

Ray raises the radio. 'Are you getting this?'

'Sir.'

'Hold positions.'

Through the veil of rain, the lead figure becomes Giuseppe Hamer. Becomes a thickset, burly, middle-aged man in jacket and jeans.

He is talking to McAvoy. Leaning in. Face to face. Pressing a finger in the bigger man's chest.

'Col, he's going to get himself killed . . .'

Ray is not being malicious in his stalling. It is pragmatism that keeps him here in the dark. He sees an opportunity for an arrest. Sees a distraction better than any he could have planned.

'Sir.'

He looks down in irritation as the radio crackles in the dark. He raises his head again.

'Let them play . . .'

'This isn't your fight, Hamer. He's lying to you.'

McAvoy says it again. Shouts it loud enough for

Ronan to hear. Sees the ginger teen flick a V-sign, book-ended by two leather-jacketed thugs.

'You're going to get broken, copper. Broken.'

McAvoy tries to keep his feet as the smaller man comes forward, swinging brisk, powerful blows at his head. He absorbs them with his forearms, jabs and moves away, fending off this bare-knuckle fighter with speed and agility. He tries to make this a boxing match. Something vaguely noble. Remembers his bouts at university; all head guards, mouth guards, vests and padded shorts. The experience helps him little now, on this patch of rutted concrete, lit by strips of moon, and fighting a man whose hand wraps are stained almost black from the blood he has spilled in countless similar bouts.

'Close in now, lads, close in.'

McAvoy doesn't know the referee. He's a short, slightly built man in his middle years, who is exposing little of his face between the collar of his sheepskin coat and the peak of his flat cap. He had given them a brief rundown of what passed for the rules, and told Hamer he wanted none of his usual bollocks. Had asked McAvoy whether he had anybody to stand beside him, and given a shake of his head in response to McAvoy's.

'I'll leave you bleeding, boy,' says Hamer. 'I'll leave you crying for your ma.'

Hamer's words are whispered promises, softly snarled as McAvoy tries to gather him in and hold him, to test his strength and sap his energy

'He's lying to you,' says McAvoy in Hamer's ear,

as a short left-handed blow thuds into his ribs. 'Your godson. He's a liar. He's turned his back on all of you. And now you're fighting his battles . . .'

Another blow connects with his body and this one hurts him. He winces and Hamer scents victory. He swings a hard right hand and catches McAvoy behind the ear. Follows up with a blow to his chin, thumped home with the heel of his hand.

McAvoy's vision blurs. He hears high-pitched song, then static.

He is down to one knee. Raising a hand. Trying to block the blows that rain down upon him.

The referee pulls Hamer back before he can deliver a boot to his fallen opponent. There are rules, here. A code. No kicking. No punching when on the ground. No biting, unless the opponent is trying to rip your tonsils out. Everything else is fair game.

McAvoy pulls himself up, groggy, disorientated. Strong arms push him forward into another flurry of punches. He brings his hands up. Takes the impact on his forearms. Tries to grab the smaller man as if they are on the ropes of a boxing ring.

Hard, thudding right hands pound into his ribs. The air leaves his body. The fight leaves his legs . . .

Colin Ray lifts the radio. Prepares to give the order to move in.

McAvoy is still upright. Refusing to go down.

Refusing to do much more than make himself a target.

'Fight, you Jock bastard,' says Ray, under his breath. 'Take his fucking head off.'

Hamer backs away, looking at the other men, as if unable to understand. The orders he receives in their glances and nods are unmistakable. *Finish it.*

He moves back in, arms by his sides, preparing to swing upwards from the floor at McAvoy's exposed jaw.

McAvoy sees it coming. Sees the scarred, cracked knuckles coming straight up to smash beneath his chin.

He lashes out. A straight right. His fist crunches into Hamer's jaw.

It is the gypsy who yelps, a high, effeminate squeal, like a pained cat.

And now McAvoy is moving forward. He is moving as a boxer, feet balanced, hands raised.

He throws a left that snaps Hamer's head backward. Another that staggers him. Hurls a right that would have taken his head off had he not pulled it at the very last instant . . .

'Go on, son . . .'

Ray watches, open-mouthed, as McAvoy hurls himself forward and bodily picks up Hamer by the waist. Charges across the car park with the other man in his embrace and slams him into the side of the Lexus with enough force to buckle the doors.

'Go, go, go . . .'

Ray has seen enough. Enjoyed every fucking second of it

As Ray and Archer run across the car park, they see the three other figures fall upon McAvoy. Begin thumping elbows, fists, knees into his big broad back as the unconscious Hamer slithers to the ground.

Sirens, now. Flashing blue lights and Colin Ray's shouts.

McAvoy, swinging widly, taking hold of the nearest head and slamming it into the car. Planting a meaty right on the side of a slick, shaved, skull.

Chaos.

The two figures that remain upright seem to freeze.

Then McAvoy drops to one knee. And Ronan runs.

'You all right, son?' bellows Ray, above the rain, as he approaches his fallen colleague. Around him, uniformed officers are jumping out of police cars. To his right, Shaz Archer is slipping cuffs on a black-jacketed, shaven-headed man who is lying groggily in a puddle.

McAvoy looks up at him from under a swelling eye. 'Sir?'

Ray gives a relieved little burst of laughter. Turns from him and takes over from a uniformed officer who is cuffing the other larger, leather-jacketed man. Giuseppe Hamer is being tended to by two officers. In the distance, two constables in fluorescent waterproofs are disappearing into the darkness, sprinting after Ronan's vanishing form.

McAvoy takes an offered hand. Hauls himself upright.

Looks around dazedly. At the reassuring sight of men in uniform and villains in cuffs.

'Sir, I'm not sure . . .'

Colin Ray returns to his side. 'Hamer,' he says, nodding at the man on the floor, groaning and clutching his ribs. 'You were right, son. Alan Rourke gave him up. Tipped us the wink that he was coming up here on business tonight. We figured it was the Vietnamese . . .'

'Sir?'

'His godson, Ronan. He's working for the new outfit that's outmuscled the Chinks. He's got his own little crew. He's the one who's been giving our crime statistics the battering.'

McAvoy presses a hand to his head, trying to take it all in. 'Those two?' he asks, gesturing at the other two men who are being manhandled into the back of squad cars.

'Muscle for the new outfit. Ronan's thugs. Nice little sideline in stolen cars before they started putting ladies' hands in pans of boiling oil.'

'That was these two?'

'According to Rourke.'

'And he'll give evidence?'

'Nope. But Hamer will.'

McAvoy screws up his eyes. 'What?'

'His godson. Ronan. Little shit's gone off the rails. Hamer will see the benefits of getting him away from his new friends.'

McAvoy seems about to fall to his knees. He steadies himself. Rubs the rainwater from his face and winces as he touches his bruised face.

'He won't give evidence, sir.'

Ray smiles and puts a hand on his back. 'I've got ways and means, son. Hamer's a proud man. He won't like finding out what these two bruisers have been doing to his godson.'

'What?'

'He's got quite the temper, has Pepe. And when he finds out his new business partners have been abusing his blue-eyed boy . . .'

McAvoy looks into the long, ratty face of the older man. 'Have they, sir?'

'We're not dealing with a genius here, son. We're dealing with a very bad man.'

They regard one another for a time. Standing in the rain. Soaked to the bone. McAvoy's blood on both their hands.

'Heard you caught a killer,' says Ray eventually.

'She's confessed, yes.'

For a time it is just them and the rain. The sound of three men coming around from painful injuries to find themselves in cuffs.

'You really came here to fight?' asks Ray softly.

McAvoy allows himself the ghost of a smile. 'I hoped I could talk him out of it.'

'Didn't work?'

'Apparently I'm not all that persuasive.'

Ray shakes his head. Grins. Looks around him and gives a grudging nod at a fine night's work. Runs, painfully, across to Shaz Archer, and pretends he is McAvoy. They giggle as he pretends to pick her up and slam her into the Lexus.

McAvoy stands alone. Closes his eyes and waits for the thumping dizziness to cease.

Lifts his face and lets the rain wash him clean. Sniffs hard, but the only blood he can smell is his own.

Finally, he crosses to the Lexus, and retrieves his coat. It is soaked through, but he pulls it on anyway. Removes his phone from the pocket and looks at the message on the screen.

We love you so much. xx

He holds the phone in his hand for a time. Caresses it, as if it is all that keeps him upright. Smiles to himself, as he realises that it is.